New York Times **bestselling author**
STUART WOODS

"always delivers a good story, nail-biting action and a mystery that needs to be unraveled."

—*San Antonio Express–News*

NEW YORK DEAD

"A fast-paced page-turner . . . Suspenseful and surprising . . . His gift for dialogue and description keeps the reader wondering what the next turn will bring."

—*Atlanta Journal Constitution*

"The pace is terrific without being breathless. His prose style is fluid, his dialogue plentiful and excellent."

—*Houston Chronicle*

"*New York Dead* will keep you riveted."

—*USA Today*

DEAD IN THE WATER

"A tale of intrigue, double- and triple-cross . . . spellbinding . . . [with] a bang-up ending that will leave you reeling."

—*St. Petersburg Times*

"Stone Barrington is in a class with classmates like Sam Spade and Travis Magee . . . Suspenseful and surprising . . . This is a superbly crafted yarn."

—*Florida Times-Union*

"A clever, engaging mystery that keeps the reader off-balance . . . You can always count on a solid effort from Stuart Woods, and this is one of his best."

—*Detroit Free Press*

Books by
Stuart Woods

GRASS ROOTS
WHITE CARGO
THE RUN
WORST FEARS REALIZED
ORCHID BEACH
UNDER THE LAKE
RUN BEFORE THE WIND
CHIEFS
SWIMMING TO CATALINA
DEEP LIE
DEAD IN THE WATER
DIRT
CHOKE
IMPERFECT STRANGERS
HEAT
DEAD EYES
L.A. TIMES
SANTA FE RULES
NEW YORK DEAD
PALINDROME

NEW YORK DEAD

STUART WOODS

DEAD IN THE WATER

HARPER

An Imprint of HarperCollinsPublishers

New York Dead was originally published in hardcover by HarperCollins in October 1991 and in paperback by HarperPaperbacks in September 1992.

Dead in the Water was originally published in hardcover by HarperCollins in August 1997 and in paperback by HarperPaperbacks in May 1998 and by HarperTorch in August 2001.

FIRST EDITION

ISBN: 978-0-06-125368-3
ISBN-10: 0-06-125368-5

07 08 09 10 RRD 10 9 8 7 6 5 4 3 2 1

NEW YORK DEAD

This book is for
Nick Taylor and Barbara Nevins,
who are New York Alive

1

*E*laine's, late. The place had exhausted its second wind, and half the customers had gone; otherwise she would not have given Stone Barrington quite so good a table—number 4, along the wall to your right as you enter. Stone knew Elaine, had known her for years, but he was not what you would call a regular—not what Elaine would call a regular, anyway.

He rested his left leg on a chair and unconsciously massaged the knee. Elaine got down from her stool at the cash register, walked over, and pulled up a chair.

"So?"

"Not bad," he said.

"How about the knee?" Anybody who knew him knew about the knee; it had received a .22-caliber bullet eleven weeks before.

"A lot better. I walked up here from Turtle Bay."

"When's the physical?"

"Next week. I'll tap-dance through it."

"So what if you fall on your ass, tap dancing?" Elaine knew how to get to the point.

"So, then I'm a retiree."

"Best thing could happen to you."

"I can think of better things."

"Come on, Stone, you're too good looking to be a cop. Too smart, too. You went to law school, didn't you?"

"I never took the bar."

"So take the bar. Make a buck."

"It's fifteen years since I graduated."

"So? Take one of those cram courses."

"Maybe. You're coming on kind of motherly, aren't you?"

"Somebody's gotta tell you this stuff."

"I appreciate the thought. Who's the guy at the bar?" To a cop's eye the man didn't fit in somehow. He probably wouldn't fit anywhere. Male Caucasian, five-six, a hundred and seventy, thinning brown hair, thick, black-rimmed glasses adhesive-taped in the middle.

"In the white coat? Doc."

"That his name or his game?"

"Both. He's at Lenox Hill, I think. He's in here a lot, late, trying to pick up girls."

"In a hospital jacket?"

"His technique is to diagnose them. Weird, isn't it?"

Doc reached over to the girl next to him and peeled back her eyelid. The girl recoiled.

Stone laughed out loud and finished the Wild Turkey. "Bet it works. What girl could resist a *doctah?*"

"Just about all of them is my guess. I've never seen him leave with anybody."

Stone signaled a waiter for the check and put some cash on the table.

"Have one on me," Elaine said.

"Rain check. I've had one too many already." He stood up and pecked her on the cheek.

"Don't be such a stranger."

"If I don't pass the physical, I'll be in here all the time. You'll have to throw me out."

"My pleasure. Take care."

Stone glanced at Doc on the way out. He was taking the girl's pulse. She was looking at him as if he were nuts.

Stone was a little drunk—too drunk to drive, he reckoned, if he had owned a car. The night air was pleasant, still warm for September. He looked up Second Avenue to see a dozen cabs bearing down on him from uptown. Elaine's was the best cab spot in town; he could never figure out where they were all coming from. Harlem? Cabdrivers wouldn't take anybody to Harlem, not if they could help it. He turned away from them; he'd walk, give the knee another workout. The bourbon had loosened it up.

He crossed Eighty-eighth and started downtown, sticking to the west side of the street. He lengthened his stride, made a conscious effort not to limp. He remembered walking this beat, right out of the academy; that was when he had started drinking at Elaine's, when he was a rookie in the 19th Precinct, on his way home after walking his tour. He walked it now.

A cop doesn't walk down the street like anybody else, he reflected. Automatically, he checked every doorway as he swung down Second Avenue, ignoring the pain, leaning on the bourbon. He had to prevent himself from trying the locks. Across the street, half a dozen guys spilled out of a yuppie bar, two of them mouthing off at each other, the others watching. Ten years ago, he'd have broken it up. He would have now, but it didn't look like it would last long.

The two guys turned away from each other, hurling insults. Neither was willing to throw the first punch.

At Eighty-sixth Street, two hookers were working the traffic. He'd have ignored them on his beat; he ignored them now. He remembered when Eighty-sixth was Germantown, when the smell of sauerbraten wafted from every third doorway. Somewhere along here there had been a place called the Gay Vienna that served kalbshaxe—a veal shank that looked like a gigantic drumstick. The place had had a zither player, the only one he'd ever heard. He'd liked it. He'd lived over on Eighty-third, between York and East End, had had a Hungarian landlady who made him goulash. She'd put weight on him, too much weight, and it had stuck. He'd lost it now, five weeks on hospital food. He was down to a hundred and eighty, and, at six-two, he looked slender. He vowed not to gain it back. He couldn't afford the alterations.

Stone rubbed his neck. An hour in one of Elaine's hard, armless chairs, leaning on the table, always made his neck and shoulders tight. About Seventieth Street, he started to limp a little, in spite of himself. In the mid-Sixties, he forgot all about the knee.

It was just luck. He was rolling his head around, trying to loosen the neck muscles, and he happened to be looking up when he saw her. She was free-falling, spread-eagled, like a sky diver. Only she didn't have a parachute.

Con Edison was digging a big hole twenty yards ahead, and they had a generator going, so he could barely hear the scream.

Time slowed down; he considered whether it was some sort of stunt and rejected the notion. He thought she would go into the Con Ed hole, but she didn't; instead, she met the earth, literally, on the big pile of dirt the workmen had thrown up. She didn't bounce. She stuck to the ground as if she had fallen into glue. Stone started to run.

A Con Ed man in a yellow hard hat jumped backward as

if he'd been shotgunned. Stone could see the terrified expression on his face as he approached. The man recovered before Stone got there, reached down, and gingerly turned the woman onto her back. Her eyes were open.

Stone knew her. There was black dirt on her face, and her red hair was wild, but he knew her. Shit, the whole city knew her. More than half the population—all the men and some of the women—wanted to fuck her. He slowed just long enough to glance at her and shout at the Con Ed man. "Call an ambulance! Do what you can for her!" He glanced up at the building. Flush windows, none open; a terrace up top.

He sprinted past the scene, turned the corner of the white-brick, 1960s apartment building, and ran into the lobby. An elderly, uniformed doorman was sound asleep in a chair, tilted back against the wall.

"Hey!" Stone shouted, and the man was wide awake and on his feet. The move looked practiced. Stone shoved his badge in the old man's face. "Police! What apartment has a terrace on the Second Avenue side?"

"12-A, the penthouse," the doorman said. "Miss Nijinsky."

"You got a key?"

"Yeah."

"Let's go!"

The doorman retrieved a key from a drawer, and Stone hustled him toward the elevators. One stood open and waiting; the doorman pushed twelve.

"What's the matter?" the man asked.

"Miss Nijinsky just took a dive. She's lying in a pile of dirt on Second Avenue."

"Jesus God."

"She's being introduced to him right now."

It was a short building, and the elevator was slow. Stone watched the floor numbers light up and tried to control his breathing. When they hit eleven, he pulled out his gun. As the elevator slowed to a stop on twelve, he heard something, and he knew what it was. The fire door on twelve had been yanked open so hard it had struck the wall. This noise was followed by the sound of somebody taking the steel steps of the fire stairs in a hurry. The elevator door started to open, and Stone helped it.

"Stay here, and don't open the apartment door!" he said to the doorman.

The fire door was opposite the elevator; he yanked it open. From a floor below, the ring of shoe leather on steel drifted upward. Stone flung himself down the stairs.

The guy only had a floor's start on him; Stone had a chance. He started taking the steps two at a time. "Stop! Police!" he shouted. That was procedure, and, if anybody was listening, he wanted it heard. He shouted it again.

As he descended, Stone got into a rhythm—bump de bump, bump de bump. He concentrated on keeping his footing. He left the eighth floor behind, then the sixth.

From the sound of it, he was gaining. Aiming carefully, he started taking the steps three at a time. Whoever was below him was hitting every one. Now Stone was barely a flight of stairs behind him. At the third-floor level he caught sight of a shadow. The ringing of the steel steps built to a crescendo, echoing off the cinder-block walls of the staircase, sounding much like a modern composition a girl had once dragged him to hear.

The knee was hurting badly now, and Stone tried to think ahead. If the man got out of the stairwell before he could be caught, then he'd have the advantage on level ground, because Stone wouldn't be able to run him down before the knee went. Stone made a decision; he'd go for a flight at a time.

On the next landing, he took a deep breath and leaped. He landed right, pushed off the wall, and prepared to jump again. One more leap down the stairs, and he'd have his quarry in sight. This time, as he jumped, something went wrong. His toe caught the stamped tread of the steel step— not much, just enough to turn him in midair—and he knew he would land wrong. When he did, his weight was on the bad knee, and he screamed. Completely out of control now, he struck the wall hard, bounced, and fell backward down the next flight of stairs.

As he came to rest hard against the wall, he struggled to get a look down the stairs, but he heard the ground-floor door open, and, a moment later, he heard it slam. He hunched up in the fetal position, holding the knee with both hands, waiting for the pain to subside just enough to allow him to get to his feet. Half a minute passed before he could let go of the knee, grab the railing, and hoist himself up. He recovered his pistol, and, barely letting his left foot touch the floor, lurched into the lobby. The guy was gone, and there was no hope of catching him now. Swearing, he hammered the elevator button with his fist.

He pressed his cheek against the cool stainless steel of the elevator door, whimpering with pain and anger and sucking in deep breaths.

The bust of the century, and he had blown it.

2

*T*here were only two apartments on the twelfth floor, and the doorman was standing obediently in front of 12-A. The door was open.

"I told you not to open it," Stone said irritably.

"I didn't," the old man said indignantly. "It was wide open. I didn't go in there, either."

"Okay, okay. You go on back downstairs. There'll be a lot of cops here in a few minutes; you tell them where I am."

"Yessir," the doorman said and headed for the elevator.

"Wait a minute," Stone said, still catching his breath. "Did anybody come into the building the last half hour? Anybody at all?"

"Nope. I wake up when people come in. I always do," the old man said defensively.

Sure. "What time did Miss Nijinsky come home tonight?"

"About nine o'clock. She asked for her mail, but there wasn't any. It had already been forwarded to the new address."

"She was moving?"

"Tomorrow."

"What sort of mood was she in?" Stone asked.

"Tired, I'd say. Maybe depressed. She was usually pretty cheerful, had a few words to say to me, but not tonight. She just asked for her mail, and, when I told her there wasn't any, she just sighed like this." He sighed heavily. "And she went straight into the elevator."

"Does she normally get many visitors in the building?"

"Hardly any. As a matter of fact, in the two years she's been here, I don't remember a single one, except deliverymen—you know, from the department stores and UPS and all."

"Thanks," Stone said. "You go on back to your post, and we'll probably have more to ask you later."

Stone stepped into the apartment. He reached high to avoid messing up any prints on the door and pushed it nearly shut. A single lamp on a mahogany drum table illuminated the living room. The place was not arranged for living. The cheap parquet floor was bare of carpets; there were no curtains or pictures; at least two dozen cardboard cartons were scattered or stacked around the room. A phone was on the table with the lamp. Stone picked it up with two fingers, dialed a number, waited for a beep, then, reading off the phone, punched in Nijinsky's number and hung up. He picked his way among the boxes and entered the kitchen. More packed boxes. He found the small bedroom; the bed was still made.

Some penthouse. It was a mean, cramped, three-and-a-half-room apartment, and she was probably paying twenty-five hundred a month. These buildings had been thrown up in a hurry during the sixties, to beat a zoning restriction that would require builders to offset apartment houses, using less of the land. If they got the buildings up in time, they could build right to the sidewalk. There were dozens of them up and down the East Side.

The phone rang. He got it before it rang a second time. "Yes?"

"This is Bacchetti."

"Dino, it's Stone. Where are you?"

"A joint called Columbus, on the West Side. What's up?"

"Hot stuff." Stone gave him the address. "Ditch the girl and get over here fast. Apartment 12-A. I'll wait five minutes before I call the precinct."

"I'm already there." Bacchetti hung up.

Stone hung up and looked around. The sliding doors to the terrace were open, and he could hear the whoop-whoop of an ambulance growing nearer. There was an armchair next to the table with the lamp and the phone, and next to it a packed carton with a dozen sealed envelopes on top. Stone picked up a printed card from a stack next to the envelopes.

> Effective immediately,
> Sasha Nijinsky is at
> 1011 Fifth Ave.
> New York 10021.
> Burn this.

The lady was moving up in the world. But, then, everybody knew that. Stone put the card in his pocket. The ambulance pulled to a halt downstairs, and, immediately, a siren could be heard. Not big enough for a fire truck, Stone thought, more like an old-fashioned police siren, the kind they used before the electronic noisemaker was invented.

He walked out onto the terrace, which was long but narrow, and looked over the chest-high wall. Sasha Nijinsky had not fallen—she had either jumped or been muscled over. Down below, two vehicles with flashing lights had pulled up to the scene—an ambulance and a van with SCOOP VIDEO painted on the top. As he watched, another vehicle pulled up, and a man in a white coat got out.

Stone went back into the apartment, found a switch, and flooded the room with overhead light. He looked at his watch. Two more minutes before this got official. Two objects were on the drum table besides the lamp and the phone. He unzipped her purse and emptied it onto the table. The usual female rubbish—makeup of all sorts, keys, a small address book, safety pins, pencils, credit cards held together with a rubber band, and a thick wad of money, held with a large gold paper clip. He counted it: twelve hundred and eleven dollars, including half a dozen hundreds. The lady didn't travel light. He looked closely at the gold paper clip. Cartier.

Stone turned to the other object: a red-leather book with the word DIARY stamped in gold. He went straight to the last page, today's date.

Hassle, hassle, hassle. The moving men are giving me a hard time. The paparazzi have been on my ass all day. The painters haven't finished in the new apartment. My limo caught on fire on East 52nd Street this afternoon, and I had to hoof it to the network through hordes of autograph-seekers. And the goddamned fucking contracts are still not ready. For this I have a business manager, a lawyer, and an agent? Also, I haven't got the change-of-address cards done, and the ace researchers don't have notes for me yet on the Bush interview, and What's-his-name just called and wants to come over here right now! I am coming apart at the seams, I swear I am. As soon as he leaves, I'm going to get into a hot tub with a gigantic brandy and open a vein. I swear to God it's just not worth it, any of it. On Monday, I have to smile into a camera and be serious, knowledgeable, and authoritative, when all I want to do with my life is to go skydiving without a parachute. Fuck the job, fuck the fame, fuck the money! Fuck everybody!!!

Skydiving without a parachute: his very thought, what, ten minutes ago? He gingerly picked up the phone again and dialed.

"Homicide," a bored voice said.

"It's Barrington. Who's the senior man?"

"Leary. How's the soft life, Barrington?"

"Let me speak to him."

"He's in the can. I just saw him go in there with a *Hustler*, so he'll be awhile."

"Tell him I've stumbled onto a possible homicide. Lady took a twelve-story dive. I'm in her apartment now." He gave the address. "An ambulance is already here, but we'll need a team to work the scene. Rumble whoever's on call. Bacchetti and I will take the case."

"But you're on limited duty."

"Not anymore. Tell Leary to get moving."

"I'll tell him when he comes out."

"I wouldn't wait." He hung up. He had not mentioned the victim's name; that would get them here in too much of a hurry. He heard the elevator doors open.

"Stone?" Bacchetti called from outside the door.

"It's open. Careful about prints."

Dino Bacchetti entered the room as he might a fashionable restaurant. He was dressed to kill, in a silk Italian suit with what Stone liked to think of as melting lapels. "So?" he asked, looking around, trying to sound bored.

"Sasha Nijinsky went thataway," Stone said, pointing to the terrace.

"No shit?" Dino said, no longer bored. "That explains the crowd on the sidewalk."

"Yeah. I was passing, on my way home."

Dino walked over and clapped his hands onto Stone's cheeks. "I got the luckiest partner on the force," he said, beaming.

Stone ducked before Dino could kiss him. "Not so lucky. I chased the probable perp down the stairs and blew it on the last landing. He walked."

"A right-away bust would have been too good to be true," Dino said. "Now we get to track the fucker down. Much, much better." He rubbed his hands together. "Whatta we got here?"

"She was moving to a new apartment tomorrow," Stone said. He beckoned Dino to the table and opened the diary with the pen.

"Not in the best of moods, was she?" Dino said, reading. "Skydiving without a parachute. The papers are going to love that."

"Yeah, they're going to love the whole thing."

Dino looked up. "Maybe she jumped," he said. "Who's to say she was pushed?"

"Then who went pounding down the stairs at the moment I arrived on the scene?" Stone asked. "The moving men?"

"No sign of a struggle," Dino observed.

"In a room full of cardboard boxes, who can say?"

"No glasses out for a guest, if What's-his-name did show."

"The liquor's packed, like everything else. I've had a look around, I didn't see any. She didn't sound in any mood to offer him a drink, anyway." Stone sighed. "Come on, let's go over the place before the Keystone Kops get here."

"Yeah, Leary's got the watch," Dino said.

The two men combed the apartment from one end to the

other. Stone used a penlight to search the corners of the terrace.

"Nothing," Dino said, when they were through.

"Maybe everything," Stone said. "We've got the diary, her address book, and a stack of change-of-address cards, already addressed. Those are the important people, I reckon. I'll bet the perp is in that stack." He took out his notebook and began jotting down names and addresses. Apart from the department stores and credit card companies, there were fewer than a dozen. Had she had so few friends, or had she just not gotten through the list before she died? He looked over the names: alphabetical. She had made it through the *W*'s.

They heard the elevator doors open, and two detectives walked in, followed by a one-man video crew. He was small, skinny, and he looked overburdened by the camera, battery belt, sound pack, and glaring lights.

"You, out," Dino said. "This is a crime scene."

"Why do you think I'm here?" the cameraman said. He produced a press card. "Scoop Berman," he said. "Scoop Video."

"The man said this is a crime scene, Scoop," Stone said, propelling the little man toward the door.

"Hey, what crime?" Scoop said, digging in his heels.

"Possible homicide," Stone replied, still pushing.

"There's no homicide," Scoop said.

"Yeah? How do *you* know?"

"Because she ain't dead," Scoop said.

Stone stopped pushing. "What are you talking about? She fell twelve stories."

"Hang on a minute, guys," Scoop said. He rewound the tape in his camera and flipped down a tiny viewing screen. "Watch this," he said.

Stone and Dino elbowed the other two cops out of the way and focused on the screen. An image came up; the camera was running toward the Con Ed site downstairs. It pushed past an ambulance man and zoomed in on the form of Sasha Nijinsky. She was wearing a nightgown under a green silk robe.

"Easy, now, lady," someone was saying on the soundtrack. "Don't try to move; let us do the moving."

A white-clad back filled the screen, and the camera moved to one side, then zoomed in tight on her face. She blinked twice, and her lips moved.

"Okay, here we go," the voice said, and the ambulance men lifted her onto a stretcher. The camera followed as they loaded the stretcher into the back of the ambulance. One man got in with her and pulled the door shut. The ambulance drove away, its lights flashing and its whooper sounding.

"I had to make a choice then," Scoop said. "I called in the incident, and then I went for the apartment."

"It's impossible," Dino said.

"You saw her move, saw her blink," Scoop said.

"Holy shit," Dino said.

"Okay," Stone said to the two cops. "You work the scene with the technical guys, and then knock on every door in the building. I want to know if anybody saw anybody come into the building after nine o'clock tonight." He grabbed Dino's elbow. "Let's get out of here."

3

Stone hung up the car phone. "The company dispatcher says the wagon is going to Lenox Hill Hospital, but the driver hasn't radioed in to confirm the delivery yet."

"Seventy-seventh and Park," Dino said, hanging a right.

Dino always drove as if he'd just stolen the car. Being Italian didn't hurt either.

The two had been partners for nearly four years when Stone had got his knee shot up. It hadn't even been their business, that call, but everybody responded to "officer needs assistance." The officer had needed assistance half a minute before Stone and Dino arrived on the scene; the officer was dead, and the man who had shot him was trying to start his patrol car. He'd fired one wild shot before Dino killed him, and it had found its way unerringly to Stone's knee. It had been nothing but a run-of-the-mill domestic disturbance, until the moment the officer had died and the bullet had changed Stone's life.

Dino had won an automatic commendation for killing a perp who had killed a cop. Stone had won four hours in surgery and an extremely boring amount of physical therapy. He rubbed the knee. It didn't feel so terrible now; maybe he hadn't screwed it up as badly as he had thought.

They screeched to a halt at the emergency entrance to Lenox Hill, and Stone limped into the building after Dino.

"You've got a woman named Nijinsky here," Dino said to the woman behind the desk, flashing his badge. "We need to see her now."

"I didn't get her name, but she's in room number one, first door on your right. Dr. Holmes is with her."

Dino led the way.

"I'd never have guessed her name was Nijinsky," the woman said after them.

They found the room and a resident taping a bandage to a woman's forehead. The woman was black.

"Dr. Holmes?" Stone said.

The young man turned.

"Yes?"

Stone limped into the room. "You've got another patient, a woman, here."

"Nope, this is it," Holmes said. "An uncommonly slow night."

"You're sure?" Stone asked, puzzled.

The doctor nodded at the black woman. "The only customer we've had for two hours," he replied. He watched Stone shift his weight and wince. "What's wrong with you?"

"I just banged my knee; no problem."

"Let's have a look."

"Yeah," said Dino, "let's have a look."

Stone pulled up his trouser leg.

Dino whistled. "Oh, that looks great, Stone."

"Tell me about it," the doctor said.

Stone gave him an abbreviated history.

The doctor went to a refrigerator, came back with a flat ice pack, and fastened it to Stone's knee with an Ace bandage. Then he retrieved a small box of pills from a shelf. "Keep the ice on until you can't stand it anymore, and take one of these pills now and every four hours after that. See your doctor in the morning."

"What are the pills?" Stone asked.

"A nonsteroid, antiinflammatory agent. If you haven't completely undone your surgery, the knee will feel better in the morning."

Stone thanked him, and they left.

"What now?" Dino asked as they turned onto Lexington Avenue.

Stone was about to answer when they saw the flashing lights. At Seventy-fifth and Lexington there was a god-awful mess, lit by half a dozen flashing lights. "Pull over, Dino," he said.

Dino pulled over. Stone got out and approached a uniformed officer. He pointed at a mass of twisted metal. "Was that smoking ruin once an ambulance?" he asked the cop.

"Yeah, and what used to be a fire truck hit it broadside." He pointed at the truck, which was only moderately bent.

"What about the occupants?"

"On their way to Bellevue," the cop said. "Seven from the fire truck, two or three from the ambulance."

"Anybody left alive?"

"I just got here; you'll have to check Bellevue."

Stone thanked him and got back into the car.

"Is that the same ambulance?" Dino asked.

"It's the same service." Stone stuck a flashing light on the dashboard. "Stand on it, Fittipaldi."

Fangio stood on it.

* * *

The emergency room at Bellevue was usually a zoo, but this was incredible. People were lying on carts everywhere, overflowing into the hallways, screaming, crying, while harried medical personnel moved among them, expediting the more serious cases.

"What the hell happened?" Dino asked a sweating nurse.

"Subway fire in the Twenty-third Street Station," she replied, "not to mention half a dozen firemen and a couple of ambulance drivers. We caught it all."

"There's nobody at the desk," Stone said. "How can we find out if somebody's been admitted?"

"Your guess is as good as mine," she said, wheeling a cart containing a screaming woman down the hallway. "Paperwork's out the window."

"Come on," Stone said, "let's start looking."

Fifteen minutes later, they hadn't found her. Dino was looking unwell.

"I gotta get outta here, Stone," he said, mopping his brow. "I'm not cut out for this blood-and-guts stuff."

"Wait a minute," Stone said, pointing across the room at a man on a stretcher. "A white coat."

They made their way across the room to the stretcher. The man's eyes were closed, but he was conscious; he was holding a bloody handful of gauze to an ear.

"Are you an ambulance driver?" Stone asked. "The one the fire truck hit?"

The man nodded, then grimaced at the pain the motion brought.

"What happened to your patient?" Stone asked.

"I don't know," the man whimpered. "My partner's dead; I don't know what happened to her."

Stone straightened up. "Then she's got to be here," he said.

"But she's not," Dino replied. "We've looked at every

human being, alive or dead, in this place. She is definitely not here."

They looked again, anyway, even though Dino wasn't very happy about it. Dino was right. Sasha Nijinsky wasn't there.

"Downstairs," Stone said.

"Do we have to?"

"You sit this one out."

Stone walked down to the basement and checked with the Bellevue morgue. There had been two admissions that evening, both of them from the subway fire, both men. Stone looked at them to be sure.

He trudged back up the stairs and went to the main admissions desk. "Have you admitted an emergency patient, a woman, named Nijinsky?" he asked. "Probably a private room."

"We don't have a private room available tonight," the nurse said. "In fact, we don't have a bed. If she came into the emergency room, she's on a gurney in a hallway somewhere."

Stone walked the halls on the way back to the ER, where he found Dino in conversation with a pretty nurse. "Say good night, Dino," Stone said.

"Good night, Dino," Dino replied, doing a perfect Dick Martin.

The nurse laughed.

"She's not here," Stone said.

"So, now what?"

"The city morgue," Stone said.

Compared with Bellevue, the city morgue, just up the street, was an island of serenity.

"Female Caucasian, name of Nijinsky," Dino told the night man. "You got one of those?"

The man consulted a logbook. "Nope."

"You got a Caucasian Jane Doe?"

"I got three of them," the man replied. He pointed. "They're still on tables."

Stone walked into the large autopsy room, the sound of his heels echoing off the tile walls. "Let's look," he said.

The first was at least seventy and very dirty.

"Bag lady," the attendant said.

The second was no older than fifteen, wearing a black leather microskirt.

"Times Square hooker, picked up the wrong trick."

"Let's see the third," Stone said.

The third fit Sasha Nijinsky's general description, down to the hair color, but she had taken a shotgun in the chest.

"Domestic violence," the attendant said smugly.

Stone couldn't tell if the man was for it or against it. "It's not she," he said.

"Don't talk like that," Dino whispered. "It's not her."

"It is not she," Stone said again. He produced a card and wrote his home number on the back, then handed it to the attendant. "This is extremely important," he said. "If you get a Nijinsky in here, or a white Jane Doe in her thirties, call me. And please pass that on to whoever relieves you. If someone overlooks her, heads will ricochet off these walls for days to come."

"I got ya," the man said, and he stapled Stone's card to his logbook. "They won't miss it here."

In the car, Dino, who was usually the most cheerful of souls, sighed deeply. "I got a feeling," he said.

"Oh, God, don't get a feeling," Stone whimpered. "Don't get Italian on me."

"I got a very serious feeling that this one is going to be a fucking nightmare," Dino said.

"Thanks, Dino. I needed that."

"And, Stone," Dino added, "never say, 'It's not she' to some guy at the morgue. He'll think you're a jerk."

4

When Stone and Dino got
to the precinct, the two detectives who had been at the Nijinsky
apartment were sitting at their desks, cataloging evidence.

"So?" one of them asked. "Is she alive, or what?"

"Or what," Dino said.

"So she croaked, then, or what?"

"Or what."

Stone tugged at his partner's sleeve. "Let's see Leary."

Lieutenant Leary, the squad's commanding officer, was
in his tiny, glassed-in cubicle, reading Sasha Nijinsky's diary.
He looked up and waved the two detectives in. "Well, it took
a fuckin' celebrity swan dive to get you back on the street,
didn't it, Barrington?"

"I saw it happen," Stone said. "From the street." He took
Leary through everything that had happened at the apartment.

"So, where's Nijinsky now?" he asked.

"It's like this, I think," Stone said. "The ambulance was taking her to Lenox Hill when it got broadsided by a fire truck. Another ambulance was called and took the driver and his partner to Bellevue. The driver's alive, but doesn't know what happened to Nijinsky. The partner's dead."

"So, to ask my question again, where's Nijinsky?"

"We don't know. She wasn't at Bellevue. We looked at everybody there."

"Not in the Bellevue emergency room," Leary said.

"No. Not anywhere at Bellevue. We checked it out thoroughly. Not at the city morgue either. They'll call me if she shows up."

Leary looked bemused. "What the fuck is goin' on here?"

"Probably homicide—attempted homicide, if she's still alive."

"Because of the guy you chased down the stairs?"

"Yes."

"Maybe he was the pizza deliveryman, got there in time to see her take the dive, then ran."

"Maybe. It feels like a homicide."

"And maybe a kidnapping, too. If the lady fell twelve stories and then her ambulance got whopped by a fire truck, she ain't walking around out there somewhere, right?"

Dino piped up. "If she's dead, is it a corpsenapping? And is that a crime?"

Leary tapped the diary with a stubby finger. "You read this?"

"Only the last page," Stone said.

"The last page was one of her better days. This was a very unhappy lady."

"She was about to become the only female news anchor on a major network. I would have thought she had it all."

"Anybody would think so. But she sounds scared to me. Maybe afraid she couldn't cut it."

"Maybe. It's a natural enough reaction."

"The diary makes her sound like a suicide."

"Maybe," Stone said. "I don't think so."

"Okay, here's what happened, maybe," Leary said. "You get this big pileup on Lex, and *two* ambulances respond. You know how competitive they are. One goes to Bellevue with the driver and the other guy, and the other ambulance goes to some other hospital."

"That's what I figured," Dino said.

"Run it down," Leary replied. He handed the diary to Stone. "Read that and tell me she didn't try to knock herself off."

Stone and Dino spent the rest of the night calling every hospital in Manhattan and reading Sasha Nijinsky's diary.

When the day shift came on, Lieutenant Leary called a meeting and brought the new group up to date.

"Okay, now you know everything we know," he said to the four assembled teams. "The press knows about the dive, because this guy Scoop What's-his-name?—"

"Berman," Stone said.

"—Berman shows up and gets his tape. They don't seem to know that the lady hasn't been seen since, and I want to keep it that way as long as possible. This is Barrington and Bacchetti's case, reporting directly to me. Barrington, Bacchetti, go sleep. I don't want you back here before noon. The rest of you, check on every private clinic, every doctor's office in the five boroughs, if you have to. Check Jersey and Westchester, too. On Long Island, just check the fancy private clinics. I want this woman found this morning, dead or alive. When you find her, Stone and Bacchetti get the interview, unless it's deathbed stuff. Nobody, but nobody says a word to the press except me, for the moment. I don't have to tell you what this celebrity shit is like. The mayor'll be on the phone as soon as he wakes up, and he'll want to know. I'll ask him to buy us a few hours to find the woman."

As the detectives shuffled out, Leary called Stone and Dino back. "Barrington, I'm assuming you're up to this. You're still on limited duty, officially."

"I'm up to it, Lieutenant."

"I mean it about the sleep," Leary said. "You grab four or five hours. This one ain't likely to be over today, and I want you in shape to fuckin' handle it."

"Yessir," they replied in unison.

Stone limped up the steps of the Turtle Bay brownstone, retrieved the *Times* from the stoop, and let himself in. He was met by the combined scent of decay and fresh wood shavings. No messages on the answering machine in the downstairs hallway. Too tired and sore to take the stairs, he took the elevator to the third floor. It creaked a lot, but it made it.

His bedroom looked ridiculous. An ordinary double bed stood against a wall, with only a television set, an exercise machine, an old chest of drawers, and a chair to help fill the enormous room. He switched on the television and started to undress.

"Television journalist Sasha Nijinsky last night fell from the terrace of her twelfth-floor East Side penthouse. An off-duty police detective who was at the scene gave chase to someone who had apparently been in Ms. Nijinsky's apartment, but was, himself, injured and lost the possible perpetrator. Astonishingly, Ms. Nijinsky may have survived the fall. She was taken to a Manhattan hospital, and we have had no further word on her condition. We'll keep you posted as news comes in."

"You're guessing about the Manhattan hospital, sport," Stone said to the newscaster. "That was my guess, too."

He stripped off his clothes and stretched out on the bed,

switching the channel to *The Morning Show.*

"Sasha Nijinsky has done just about everything in broadcast journalism, and she's done it fast," a pleasant young man was saying. They cut to a montage of shots from Nijinsky's career, and he continued, voice-over.

"Daughter of the Russian novelist Georgi Nijinsky, who was expelled from the Soviet Union more than twenty-five years ago, Sasha was six years old when she came to this country with her parents. She already spoke fluent English." There were shots of a bearded man descending from an airplane, a surprised-looking little girl in his arms.

"Sasha distinguished herself as an actress at Yale, but not as a student. Then, on graduation, instead of pursuing a career in the theater, as expected, she took a job as a reporter on a New Haven station. Four years later, she came to New York and earned a reputation as an ace reporter on the Continental Network affiliate. She spent another three years here, on *The Morning Show,* where she honed her interviewing skills, then she was sent to Moscow as the network's correspondent in the Soviet Union for a year, before being expelled in the midst of spy charges that she has always maintained were fabricated.

"On returning to this country, she further enhanced her growing reputation, covering both national political conventions before the last election. Then her Sunday morning interview show, *Newsmakers,* pitted her against the nation's top political figures. She proved to be as tough as ever in those interviews, and it was said in Washington that nobody wanted to go on her show, but everyone was afraid not to.

"Earlier this month, the industry was not surprised when it was announced that Sasha Nijinsky would join anchorman Barron Harkness as co-anchor on the network's evening news, which, although still the leading network newscast, had recently slipped in the ratings. Harkness, an old colleague of Sasha's on *The Morning Show,* could not be reached for comment, as he is not due back until today from assignment in the Middle East."

Stone switched off the set. Make a note to talk to Harkness, he told himself, then he put the case from his mind. He thought, as he always did when he wanted to clear his head, about the house and his plans for it. It was in terrible condition.

He turned his thoughts to plumbing fixtures. In minutes, he was asleep.

5

Stone arrived at the station house at one o'clock sharp. The squad room was abuzz with detectives on the phone. He raised his eyebrows at one, and the man gave a huge shrug. A moment later, he hung up.

"Gather round," Stone said to the group. "Any luck?" he asked when they had assembled.

"Zilch. She's nowhere," a detective said.

"How many more places to check?" Stone asked.

"Not many."

"Add all the funeral parlors in the city to your list," Stone said. "Start with the ones in Manhattan. What else we got?"

"We got a suspect," Detective Gonzales said. He referred to a sheet of paper. "One Marvin Herbert Van Fleet, male Caucasian, forty-one, of a SoHo address."

"What makes him a suspect?" Stone asked.

"He's written Sasha Nijinsky over a thousand letters the past two years." Gonzales held up a stack of paper.

Stone took the letters and began to go through them. "I want you all to myself," he quoted. "Come and live with me. I've got a nice place. . . . You and my mother will get along great." He looked up. "This is pretty bland stuff. Not even anything obscene. He doesn't so much as want to sniff her underwear."

"Nijinsky wanted him arrested, but apparently he didn't do anything illegal. She finally got a civil court order, preventing him from contacting her."

"What else have we got on him?"

"Interesting background," Gonzales said. "He went to Cornell Medical School, graduated and all, but never completed his internship."

"Where?"

"At Physicians and Surgeons Hospital."

"Pretty ritzy. Why didn't he finish?"

"File says he was dropped from the program as 'unsuited for a medical career.' There have been some complaints about him posing as a doctor, but since he apparently never actually treated anybody, there was nothing we could do. He worked at the Museum of Natural History for a while."

"What's he do now?"

"He's an embalmer at Van Fleet Funeral Parlor."

Stone felt a little chill. "Pick him up for questioning."

"Here's a photograph."

Stone looked at the picture of Marvin Herbert Van Fleet. "Hang on, this guy's got an alibi."

"How do you know that? We haven't asked him yet."

"Because I saw him at the bar at Elaine's twenty minutes before Nijinsky fell."

There was a brief silence. "Twenty minutes is a long time," Gonzales said.

"You're right," Stone agreed. "I left and walked

down Second Avenue. He could have taken a cab and gotten there before I did. Pick him up. No, give me that address. Dino and I will talk to him."

Dino arrived, waving a magazine. He tossed it onto Stone's desk. "I had to wrestle two women for this," he said. "It just hit the newsstands this morning, and this must be the last copy in the city."

Stone picked it up. The new issue of *Vanity Fair*, and Sasha Nijinsky was on the cover. SASHA! BY HIRAM BARKER, WITH PHOTOGRAPHS BY ANNIE LEIBOVITZ, a headline read. Stone laughed. "Now, *that's* timing. You read it yet?"

"Not yet," Dino said. "Be my guest."

The tone of the piece reeled back and forth between sycophancy and bitchiness. Nijinsky's career was recapped briefly, but a lot of space was devoted to her social and sex lives. All the unflattering stuff came from unnamed sources, including a report of a secret affair between Nijinsky and her old colleague on *The Morning Show*, and new co-anchor on the evening news, Barron Harkness. "They were never seen together in public," the source said, "and a lot of the staff thought they were screwing in her dressing room. She would never go into his."

Stone finished the piece and added Hiram Barker to his list of interviewees. He picked up the phone, dialed the Continental Network, and asked for Barron Harkness.

"Mr. Harkness's office," an interesting female voice said.

"This is Detective Stone Barrington of the Homicide Division, New York City Police Department," he said. "I'd like to speak with Mr. Harkness."

"I'm afraid Mr. Harkness is on an airplane somewhere over the Atlantic," the woman said. "This is Cary Hilliard, his assistant. May I help you?"

Stone remembered the television report that the anchorman had been on assignment in the Middle East. "I want to speak to Mr. Harkness regarding the ... " (What was it? Not a homicide—not yet, anyway.) " . . . about Sasha Nijinsky. Can you tell me what time his plane is due in?"

"He won't be in the office before about five thirty," the woman said. "And he'll be going on the air at seven o'clock, on the evening news."

Stone liked the woman's voice. "I'd like to know the airline and flight number, please. It's important."

The woman hesitated. "What was your name again, please?"

"Detective Stone Barrington. I'm in charge of the Nijinsky case."

"Of course. He's due in on an Alitalia flight from Rome at four twenty, but he'll be met and helicoptered in. You'd do better to see him here. I know he'll want to talk to you. He's very fond of Sasha."

"At what time?"

"It'll be hell from the moment he arrives until the newscast is over. Come at a quarter to seven, and ask for me. I'll take you up to the control room, and you can talk to Barron as soon as he's off the air."

"Six forty-five. I'll see you then."

"Oh, we're not in the Continental Network building. We're at the Broadcast Center, at Pier Nineteen, at the west end of Houston Street."

"I'll see you at six forty-five." Stone hung up. He really liked her voice. She was probably a dog, though. He'd made the voice mistake before.

Dino had turned on the television, and a doctor was being interviewed on CNN about Nijinsky.

"Doctor, is it possible that Sasha Nijinsky could have survived her fall from twelve stories?"

"Well," the doctor replied, "as we've just seen on the videotape, she obviously survived, at least for a few moments, but it is unlikely in the extreme that she could recover from the sort of injuries she must have sustained in the fall. I'd say it was virtually impossible that she lived more than a minute or two after striking the earth."

"That still don't make it a homicide," Dino said.

"It's a homicide," Stone said. "If she's dead."

"Whaddaya mean 'if she's dead'?" Dino asked. "Didn't you hear the doctor, there? She's a fuckin' pancake."

"Look," Stone said, "do you know what terminal velocity is?"

"Nope," Dino replied. Nobody else did either.

"An object in a vacuum, when dropped from a height, will accelerate at the rate of thirty-two feet per second, and continue accelerating—in a vacuum. But in an atmosphere, like the earth's, there will come a point when air resistance becomes equal to acceleration, and, at that point, the object will fall at a steady rate."

"But it'll keep falling," Dino said, puzzled.

"Sure, but it'll stop accelerating." Stone had everyone's undivided attention now. "I read a piece in the *Times* a few weeks ago about cats, and how cats have been known to fall from a great height and survive. There was one documented case where a cat fell twenty-six stories, landed on concrete, and survived with only a couple of broken bones."

"How the fuck could it survive a fall like that?" a detective asked.

"Like this," Stone said. He held out his hand, palm down. "When a cat starts to fall, he immediately orients himself feet first—you know that cats will always land on their feet, right?"

"Right," the detective said.

"Not only does he get into a feet-first position, but he spread-eagles into what's called the flying-squirrel position, like this." He spread his fingers. "Flying squirrels don't fly, like birds, they glide, because they have a membrane connecting their front and back legs, and, when they spread out, they're sort of like a furry Frisbee."

"But a cat ain't a flying squirrel," another detective said.

"No," Stone agreed, "and he can't glide like one. But by presenting the greatest possible area to the air resistance, a cat slows down his rate of acceleration and, consequently, his terminal velocity."

"You mean he falls slow," Dino said.

"Compared to a human being, anyway. A cat's terminal velocity is about sixty miles an hour. But a human being's terminal velocity is a hundred and twenty miles an hour. That's why a cat could survive a fall from twenty-six stories, when no human could."

The group digested this for a moment.

"But Sasha Nijinsky ain't no cat," Dino said.

"No," Stone said, "she's not." He looked up to see that Lieutenant Leary had joined the group. "But," he continued, "she fell from twelve stories, not twenty-six. And not onto concrete, but into a large pile of freshly dug earth. And look at this." He opened the *Vanity Fair* to its center spread and showed a photograph to the assembled detectives.

The shot was of Sasha Nijinsky, and she seemed to be flying. The earth was thousands of feet below her, and she was wearing a jumpsuit and a helmet and had an unopened parachute strapped to her back. She was grinning at the camera, exposing rows of large, white teeth; her eyes were wide behind goggles.

"Sasha Nijinsky was a sky diver," Stone said. "An experienced one, too, with more than a hundred jumps. And that"—he thumped the photograph with his forefinger—"was the position she was in when I saw her falling. Also, she was wearing a full-length nightgown and a bathrobe when she fell, and she might have gotten some extra air resistance by the ballooning out of those garments. When she fell, she automatically assumed the position she'd been trained to assume when free-falling. And, by doing that, she slowed down her rate of acceleration and, most important, her terminal velocity."

No one spoke for a long time. Finally, Dino broke the rapt silence. "Horseshit," he said.

"Maybe not," Stone said.

"Let me tell you something, Stone—I read that lady's diary, and I say she was suffering from too much fucking, too much fuckin' ambition, and too much fuckin' fame, all of it too fuckin' soon." Dino closed the magazine and, with his finger, drew an X over her face. "That girl *jumped* off that terrace. She ain't no cat, and she ain't no flying squirrel."

"I think somebody helped her," Stone said. "And she may still be alive."

Dino shook his head slowly. "I'll tell you what she is. She's New York Dead."

CHAPTER

6

The Van Fleet Funeral Parlor had a Gramercy Park address, but it was around the corner, off the square.

"Italians know all about death," Stone said to Dino. "What do you know about this place?"

Dino shrugged. "It's not Italian, so what could I know? The location tells us, don't it? Good address, not so good location. If you don't want to pay for a first-class funeral at Frank Campbell's, where the elite meet to grieve, then you go to, like, Van Fleet's. It's cheaper, but it's got all the fuckin' pretensions, you know?"

Dino parked in a loading zone and flipped down the sun visor to display the car's ID. They walked back half a block and entered the front door, following a well-dressed couple. They stopped in a vestibule while the couple signed a visitors' book, presided over by a man in a tailcoat.

"The Wilson party?" the man asked Dino, in unctuous tones.

"The NYPD party," Dino said, flashing his shield. "Who runs the place?"

The man flinched at the sight of the badge. "That would be Mrs. Van Fleet," he said. "Please stay here, and I'll get her. Please remember there are bereaved here."

"Yeah, yeah," Dino said.

"You don't like the fellow?" Stone said when the man had gone.

"I don't like the business," Dino said. "It's a creepy business, and people who do it are creepy."

"Somebody's got to do it," Stone said. "We'll do better if you don't give them a hard time."

Dino nodded. "You talk to the creeps, then."

As they waited, Stone looked around. In a large, somewhat overdecorated sitting room to their left, two dozen people talked quietly, while some gathered around an elderly woman who seemed to be receiving the condolences. He looked right and was surprised to see a bedroom. On the four-poster bed, under a lace coverlet, lay a pretty woman in her late thirties. Several people stood around the bed, and one knelt at some sort of altar set at the foot. It took Stone a moment to realize that the woman on the bed was the guest of honor. She appeared to be sleeping.

A door opened at the end of the hallway ahead of them, and a short, thin, severely dressed woman of about sixty approached them. She walked with her hands folded in front of her; it would have been an odd posture anywhere but here.

"Yes?" the woman said, her face expressionless.

"Good afternoon," Stone said. "I am Detective Barrington, and this is Detective Bacchetti, New York City Police. I believe you have an employee here named Marvin Herbert Van Fleet."

"He's not an employee," the woman said. "He's a part-ner in the firm, he's our chief . . . technical person, and he's my son."

Stone nodded. "May we see him, please?"

"Now?"

"Please."

"I'm afraid he's busy at the moment."

"We're busy, too," Dino said, apparently unable to contain himself.

Stone shot him a sharp glance. "I'm afraid we can't wait for a more convenient time," he said to the woman.

"One moment, please," Mrs. Van Fleet said, not happy. She walked down the hallway a few paces, picked up a phone, dialed two digits, and spoke quietly for a moment. She hung up and motioned to the detectives.

They followed her down the hallway. She turned right through a door and walked rapidly down another hall. The decor changed to utilitarian. A vaguely chemical scent hung in the air. She stopped before a large, metal swinging door and indicated with a nod that they were to enter. Then she brushed past them and left.

Stone pushed the door open and, followed by Dino, entered a large room with a tile floor. Before them were six autopsy tables, two of them occupied by bodies covered with sheets. At the far end of the room, the body of a middle-aged woman lay naked on another table. A man stood with his back to her, facing a counter built along the wall. Memories of dissecting frogs in high school biology swept over Stone; the smell of formaldehyde was distinct.

"Marvin Van Fleet?" Stone said.

A sharp, metallic sound was followed by a hollow rat-tling noise. The man turned around, and Stone saw a soft drink can on the tabletop.

"Herbert Van Fleet," the man said. "Please call me Doc. Everybody does."

The man was not handsome, Stone thought, but his voice was—a rich baritone, expressive, without any discernible accent. A good bedside voice. The detectives walked briskly to the end of the room, their heels echoing off the tile floor. They stopped at the head of the autopsy table. Stone introduced himself and Dino.

"I've been expecting you," Van Fleet said. He stepped over to the naked body on the table and picked up the forceps that rested beside the head.

"Oh? Why is that?" Stone replied.

"Well, of course I heard about Miss Nijinsky on television this morning. Given the nature of our relationship, I thought perhaps someone would come to see me." He produced a curved suturing needle and clamped it in the jaws of the forceps.

"Did you and Sasha Nijinsky have a relationship?" Stone asked.

Van Fleet looked thoughtful for a moment. "Why, yes, we did. I was her correspondent, although she seemed to think of me as an antagonist, which I never intended myself to be. She was my . . . " He paused. "She was an object of interest to me, I suppose. I greatly admired her talents. Do you know how she's doing?" he asked, concernedly. "She's in the hospital, they said on television."

"We don't have any information on her condition," Stone said. God knew that was true.

Van Fleet nodded sadly. He bent over the corpse, peeled back the lips with rubber-gloved fingers, and inserted the needle in the inside of the upper lip, passing it through the inside of the lower lip, then pulled it tight.

Stone stopped asking questions and watched with a horrible fascination. So did Dino. Van Fleet continued to skillfully manipulate the forceps and the needle, until the web of thread reached across the width of the mouth. Then he pulled the thread tight, and the mouth closed, concealing the stitching on the inside of the lips. Van Fleet made a quick surgical knot, snipped off the thread, and tucked the end out of sight at the corner of the mouth.

"Shit," Dino said.

"Mr. Van Fleet, could you leave that until we're finished, please?" Stone said.

"Of course."

"Can you account for your whereabouts between two and three A.M. this morning?"

"*You* can account for my whereabouts at two," Van Fleet said, smiling. "I was where you were."

"I remember," Stone said. "At what time, exactly, did you leave Elaine's?"

"A few minutes after you did," Van Fleet said. "About two twenty, I'd say. Maybe the bartender would remember."

"Where did you go then?"

"I drove down Second Avenue, and in the sixties I saw a sort of commotion. It seemed that someone had been hurt. I have some medical skills, so I stopped to see if I could help. They were loading a stretcher into an ambulance. I didn't know it was Sasha until this morning, when I turned on *The Morning Show*."

"Who else was at the scene when you stopped?" Stone asked.

"Two ambulance men, two or three Con Ed men, and a man with a television camera."

"What did you do then?"

"I went home."

"What route did you take?"

"I continued down Second Avenue all the way to Houston, then turned right, then left on Garamond Street. That's where I live."

"Did you see anyone you knew?"

"At two thirty in the morning?"

"Anyone at all. Someone else in your building?"

"There is no one else in my building. I live over a former glove factory."

"We'd like to see your apartment. May we go there now?"

"Why?"

"It would help us in our investigation. If you had nothing to do with what happened to Miss Nijinsky, then we'd like to be able to cross you off our list of suspects."

"I'm a suspect?" Van Fleet asked, surprised. "What do you suspect me of?"

"Well, we haven't established the cause of . . . what happened, yet."

"Was there a crime?"

"We haven't determined that yet."

"My impression from the news was that Sasha's fall was a suicide attempt."

"That's certainly a possibility. We treat any unknown cause of death as homicide, until we know otherwise."

"Then you suspect me of a homicide you're not sure was committed?"

"As I said, Mr. Van Fleet, everyone who had anything to do with her is a suspect, until we know for sure what happened. Do you object to our seeing where you live?"

Van Fleet shrugged. "Not really, but I think I should ask my lawyer how he feels about it."

"That's your right."

"Unless you have a search warrant."

"We can get one if we feel it's necessary."

"If a judge feels it's necessary, you mean."

"We can get a search warrant."

"I watch a lot of police shows on television, you see. I understand these things."

"You object to our seeing your apartment, then?"

"No, I don't, not really. However, I don't think you have a good enough reason to ask. If you do have a good enough reason, then you can get a search warrant, can't you?"

"It would certainly make us feel better about you if we had your cooperation, Mr. Van Fleet."

"Please don't misunderstand me, Detective Barrington, I'm most anxious to help. I greatly admire Sasha, and I would do anything I could to help you resolve what happened to her. But I don't really see how visiting my home would help you, and I think such a visit would be an unwarranted invasion of my privacy. Of course, a judge may feel differently, and, if so, I'll be happy to cooperate."

"I see," Stone said. He was getting nowhere.

"Is there anything else I can do to help you?"

"Not at the moment, Mr. Van Fleet. I expect we'll talk again."

Van Fleet nodded. "Any time. My pleasure. But there's something I think you should consider."

"What's that?"

"It's quite true that I have a history of what some people would call annoying Sasha Nijinsky. But I'm sure you can tell from the letters I wrote her that I had only admiration for her, that, certainly, I had no reason to cause her harm."

"We'll take that into consideration in our inquiry," Stone said.

"I hope you will, Detective Barrington, because, while I will help in any way I feel I reasonably can, I do not intend to have my privacy unduly disturbed, nor do I wish to have my name splashed about in the tabloids, nor my professional reputation besmirched."

"Well, we'll leave you to your work, Mr. Van Fleet."

"Call, if you think of anything else."

"We will."

The front of the funeral parlor was deserted when they passed back through.

"He's dirty," Dino said, when they were on the street again.

"I don't know," Stone replied. "He said pretty much what I'd have said in the circumstances, if I were innocent."

"Maybe he's not dirty on Nijinsky, but he's dirty on something," Dino said emphatically. "He's a gold miner, for a start."

"A what?"

"A gold miner. You're so fucking naive, Stone, you really are. When we got there, he had just finished pulling that corpse's gold teeth. He put 'em in the Coke can. Didn't you hear it rattle? Why do you think he was sewing her mouth shut? Doesn't want anybody poking around in there, that's why."

"Jesus Christ, Dino, how do you think of this stuff?"

"I got a suspicious nature, didn't you know that?"

"I knew that."

"I think when this Nijinsky thing is over, we want to take a closer look at fuckin' Doc Van Fleet."

"Let's not wait until then," Stone said.

They reached the car, and Dino looked at his watch. "You still want me to meet Barron Harkness's plane?"

"Yeah. I wanted us to see Hiram Barker this afternoon, but seeing if Harkness is on that airplane is more important."

"You go on and see Barker, and I'll meet the plane."

"It would be better if we both were there."

"Fuck procedure. We got a lot to do, right? I'll meet you at the TV studio at six forty-five, and we'll do Harkness together."

"Okay, you take the car, and I'll get a cab."

As Dino drove away and Stone looked for a cab, he drew deep breaths of fresh, polluted New York City air into his lungs. From now on he'd have different memories when he caught the scent of formaldehyde.

CHAPTER

7

Stone went to the *Vanity Fair* offices in midtown and, after a phone call was made, he was given Hiram Barker's address. As he entered the lobby of United Nations Plaza, he remembered a line about the apartment house from an old movie: "If there is a god," a character had said, "he probably lives in this building." After another phone call, the deskman sent him up to a high floor.

"I can just imagine why you're here," Barker said as he opened the door.

He was larger than Stone had expected, in both height and weight, a little over six feet tall and broad at the middle. The face was not heavy but handsome, the hair sleek and gray, slicked straight back.

"I'm Hi Barker," he said, extending a fleshy hand. He waved Stone into a spacious, beautifully furnished living room with a view looking south toward the United Nations.

Stone introduced himself. He heard the tinkling of silver in the background; he saw a woman enter the dining room and begin to set the table.

"Can I get you something to drink?" Barker asked solicitously.

Stone was thirsty. "Perhaps some water."

"Jeanine, get the gentleman some Perrier," Barker said to the woman.

She left and returned with a heavy crystal glass, decorated with a slice of lime.

"Sit you down," Barker said, waving at one end of a large sofa, while flopping down at the other end, "and tell me what I can do for you." He cocked his head expectantly.

"You can tell me where you were between two and three this morning," Stone said.

Barker clapped his hands together and threw his head back. "I've been waiting all my life for a cop to ask me that question!" he crowed.

Stone smiled. "I hope I won't have to wait that long for an answer."

"Dear me, no." Barker chuckled. "I got home about one thirty from a dinner at the de la Rentas', then went straight to bed. The night man downstairs can confirm that—ah, the time, not the bed part. Security is ironclad here, you know. We've got Arabs, Israelis, *and* Irish in the building, and nobody, but *nobody*, gets in or out without being seen."

Stone didn't doubt it.

"Am I a suspect, then?"

"A suspect in what?" Stone asked.

"Oh, God, now I've done it! I'm not even supposed to know there's a crime!"

"Is there?"

"Well, didn't somebody help poor Sasha out into the night?"

"I'd very much like to know that," Stone said, "and I'd like to know why you think so."

"She wasn't the sort to take a flying leap," Barker said more seriously.

"That's why I've come to see you, Mr. Barker."

"Hi, please call me Hi. I'll be uncomfortable if you don't."

"Hi it is then."

"And why is it you've come to see me?"

"Because of your *Vanity Fair* piece. I've read it, and it seemed extremely well researched."

"That's a very astute observation," Barker said. "Most people would have thought it produced from gossip. No, I spent a good six months on that. I was researching it even before Tina at the magazine knew I wanted to do it."

"And you talked with Miss Nijinsky at some length?"

"I did, a good six hours over three meetings."

"Did you make any tape recordings?"

"I did, but when I finished the piece I returned the tapes to her, as agreed."

"You didn't, perhaps, make a copy?"

Barker's eyes turned momentarily hard. "No. That's not the way it's done."

"How well did you know her before you began research for the article?"

"We had a cordial acquaintance. We'd been to a few of the same dinner parties. That was before the piece. By the time I finished it, I think I knew her as well as anybody alive."

"You can do that in six hours of conversation?"

"If you've done six months of research beforehand, and if nobody else knows the person at all."

"She had no close friends?"

"None in the sense that any normal person would call close."

•
45

"Family?"

"She hardly ever saw them after she left home to go to college. I think she was close to her father as a young girl, but she didn't speak of him as a confidant, not in the least."

"Did she have any confidants?"

"Not one, as far as I could tell. I think by the time we had finished, she thought of me as one." Barker shook his head. "But no, as well as I got to know her, she never opened up to me. I took my cues as much from what she didn't say as what she said. There was a sort of invisible, one-way barrier between that young woman and the rest of the world; everything passed through it to her, but very little passed out."

"Do you think she was a possible suicide?"

"Not for a moment. Sasha was one tough cookie; she had goals, and she was achieving them. Christ, I mean, she was on the verge of the biggest career any woman ever had in television news. Bigger than Barbara Walters. That sort of person commits suicide only in trashy novels."

"All right," Stone said, "let's assume murder."

Barker grinned. "Let's."

"Who?"

Barker crossed his legs, clasped his hands behind his neck, and stared out at the sweep of the East River. "Two kinds of people might have murdered Sasha Nijinsky," he said. "First, people she hurt on the way up—you know, the secretary she tyrannized, the people she displaced when she got promotions—there was no shortage of those. But you'd have to be a raving lunatic to kill such a famous woman just for revenge. The chances are too good of getting caught and sent away."

"What's the other kind of person?" Stone asked.

Barker grinned again, still looking at the river. "Whoever had the most to lose from Sasha's future success," he said.

"That's an interesting notion," Stone said, and he meant it. "Who did you have in mind?"

"I'll tell you," Barker said, turning to face him, "but if you ever quote me, I'll call you a liar."

Stone nodded. "It'll be just between us."

"Well," Barker said, drawing it out. "There's only one person in the world I can think of who would suffer from Sasha Nijinsky's future success."

"Go on," Stone said.

"Her new co-anchor, who else? The estimable Mr. Barron Harkness, prizewinning television journalist, square-jawed, credible, *terribly vulnerable* Barron Harkness."

"I take it you don't like Mr. Harkness."

"Who does, dear boy? He lacks charm." Barker said this as if it were the ultimate crime. "Sasha would have blown him out of the water in less than a year. His ratings had slipped badly, you know—after a winning streak last year, he has slipped to a point or two behind Brokaw, Jennings, and Rather, and he's still sinking. He's already worked at ABC and NBC, and neither would have him back; and I know for a fact that Larry Tisch despises him, so that shuts him out of CBS. Then here comes Sasha, hipping him over at the anchor desk, loaded for bear. A power struggle began the day the first rumor hit the street about Sasha's new job, and, if Harkness lost, where would he go? He'd be making solemn pronouncements on Public Radio, like Dan Schorr, and his ego would never accept that. No, sir, Barron Harkness is a man with a motive."

"I think I should tell you," Stone said, looking at his watch, "that Barron Harkness got off an airplane from Rome just about an hour ago."

Barker's face fell. "I'm extremely sorry to hear it," he said. "But," he said, brightening, "if I were you I'd make awfully sure he was really on that plane."

"Don't worry," Stone said, "that's been done. Tell me,

would it violate some journalistic ethic if you gave me a list of the people you interviewed about Miss Nijinsky?"

Barker shook his head. "No. I'll do even better than that; I'll give you a paragraph on each of them and my view as to the value of each as a suspect."

"I'd be very grateful for that."

The writer turned sly. "It'll have to be a trade, though."

"What do you want?"

"When you find out what's happened to Sasha and who is responsible, I want a phone call before the press conference is held."

Stone thought for a moment. It wasn't a bad trade, and he needed that list. "All right, you're on."

"It'll take me a couple of hours."

"You have a fax machine?"

Barker looked hurt. "Of course."

Stone gave him a card. "Shoot it to me there when you're done." He got up.

Barker rose with him. "I'm having a few friends in for dinner this evening, as you can see," he said, waving a hand at the dining room. "Would you like to join us?"

"Thanks," Stone said, "but until I've solved the Nijinsky problem, there are no dinner parties in the picture."

"I understand," Barker said, seeing him out. "Perhaps another time?"

"Thank you," Stone said. While he waited for the elevator, he wondered why Hi Barker would ask a policeman to dinner. Well, he thought, as he stepped from the elevator into the lobby, if he solved this one, he would become a very famous policeman.

As it turned out, he didn't have to wait that long. A skinny young man with half a dozen cameras draped about him was arguing with the doorman when he turned and saw Stone. "Right here, Detective Barrington," he called, raising a camera.

The flash made Stone blink. As he made his way from the building, pursued by the snapping paparazzo, he felt a moment of sympathy for someone like Sasha Nijinsky, who spent her life dodging such trash.

CHAPTER

8

Stone had almost an hour and a half to kill before his appointment with Barron Harkness at the network. Rush hour was running at full tilt, and all vacant cabs were off duty, so he set off walking crosstown. He reckoned his knee could use the exercise anyway. He was wrong. By the time he got to Fifth Avenue, he was limping. He thought of going home for an hour, but he was restless, and, even though he had another interview to conduct, he wanted a drink. He walked a couple of blocks north to the Seagram Building and entered a basement door.

The Four Seasons was a favorite of Stone's; he couldn't afford the dining rooms, but he could manage the prices at the bar. He climbed the stairs, chose a stool at a corner of the big, square bar, and nodded at the bartender. He came in often enough to know the man and to be known, but not by name.

"Evening, Detective," the bartender said, sliding a coaster in front of him. "What'll it be?"

"Wild Turkey on the rocks, and how'd you know that?"

The man reached under the bar and shoved a *New York Post* in front of Stone.

The photograph was an old one, taken at a press conference a couple of years before. They had cropped out Stone's face and blown it up. DETECTIVE SEES SASHA'S FALL, the headline said. Stone scanned the article; somebody at the precinct was talking to a reporter.

"So, what's the story?" the bartender asked, pouring bourbon over ice. He made it a double without being asked.

"What's your name?"

"Tom."

"When I find out, Tom, you'll be among the first to know. I'll be here celebrating."

The bartender nodded and moved down the bar to help a new customer, a small, very pretty blonde girl in a business suit.

The bar wasn't the only reason Stone liked the Four Seasons. He looked at the woman and felt suddenly, ravenously hungry for her. Since his hospital time and the course of libido-dampening painkillers, he had given little thought to women. Now a rush of hormones had him breathing rapidly. He fought an urge to get up, walk down the bar, and stick his tongue in her ear. COP IN SEX CHARGE AT FOUR SEASONS, tomorrow's *Post* would say.

The bartender put a copy of the paper in front of her. She glanced at it, looked up at Stone, surprised, and smiled.

Here was his opening. Stone picked up his drink and shifted off the stool. As he took a step, an acre of black raincoat blocked his view of the girl. A man built like a pro linebacker had stepped between them, leaned over some distance, and pecked the girl on the cheek. He settled on a barstool between her and Stone. The girl leaned back and cast a regretful grimace Stone's way.

Stone settled back onto his stool and pulled at the bourbon. His fantasy raged on, out of control. A five-minute walk to his house and they were in bed, doing unspeakable things to each other. He shook his head to clear it and opened the paper, looking for something to divert him. His view of the girl was now completely obliterated by the hulk in the black raincoat. Stone suppressed a whimper.

The *Post* was the first paper to get the Nijinsky story in time for a regular edition, and they had made the most of it. There was a retrospective of photographs of Sasha, from tothood to *The Morning Show.* There were shots of her as a schoolgirl, as a teenager in a beauty contest, performing as an actress at Yale, on camera as a cub reporter—even shots of her at the beach in a bikini, obviously taken without her knowledge.

Sasha looked damn good in a bikini, Stone thought. He wondered where that very fine body was resting at the moment.

He read the article slowly, trolling for some new fact about her that might help. When the bourbon was finished, he looked at his watch, left a ten-dollar bill on the bar, in spite of the bartender's wave-off, and walked down to the street. The worst of rush hour was past, but rain was threatening, and half a dozen people were looking for cabs at the corner. The light turned red, and an off-duty cab stopped. Stone flipped open his wallet and held his badge up to the window. The driver sighed and pushed the button that unlocked the doors.

"Houston Street and the river," Stone said, and leaned his head back against the seat. Heavy raindrops began pounding against the windows. If he had been off women for a while, Stone reflected, he had been off booze, too, and the double shot of 101-proof bourbon had made itself felt. He dozed.

9

Stone was jerked awake by the short stop of the cab. He fumbled for some money, gave the cabbie five dollars, and struggled out of the cab. It was pouring rain now, and he got across the street as quickly as he could with his sore knee. A uniformed security guard sat at a desk, and Stone gave him Cary Hilliard's name. Before the man could dial the number, an elevator door opened, and a young woman walked out.

"Detective Barrington?" she asked, offering a hand.

"That's right," Stone replied, thinking how long and cool her fingers were. All of her, in fact, was long and cool. She was nearly six feet tall, he reckoned, slim but not thin, dressed in a black cashmere sweater that did not conceal full breasts and a houndstooth skirt that ended below the knee.

"I'm Cary Hilliard," she said. "Come on, let's go up to the studio. Barron will be on the air in a few minutes, and we

53

can watch from the control room." They turned toward the elevator. "By the way, a Detective Bacchetti called and left a message for you. He said, and I quote, 'Your man was where he was supposed to be' and 'Tell Detective Barrington that I've been detained, and I'll see him tomorrow.'"

"Thank you." Detained, my ass, Stone thought. Detained by some stewardess, maybe.

She led him upstairs and through a heavy door. A dozen people worked in a room that held at least twenty-five television monitors and thousands of knobs and switches. "We can sit here," she said, showing him to a comfortable chair on a tier above the control console.

The whole of the top row of monitors displayed the face, in close-up, of Barron Harkness, "the idol of the airlanes," someone had called him, stealing Jan Garber's sobriquet. Tissue paper was tucked into his collar, and a woman's hand entered the frame, patting his nose with a sponge. "You've got a good tan, Barron," a voice said. "We won't need much of this."

Harkness nodded, as if saving his voice.

"One minute," somebody at the console said.

"I've got a thirty-second statement before the music," Harkness said into the camera.

"Barron," a man at the console said, "it's too late to fit it in; we're long as it is."

"Cut the kid with the transplant before the last commercial," Harkness said.

"Barron...," the man nearly wailed.

"Do it."

Someone counted down from ten, and stirring music filled the control room. Barron Harkness arranged his face into a serious frown and looked up from his desk into the camera. "Good evening," he said, and his voice let the viewer know that something important was to follow. "Last night, a good friend of this newscast and of many of us personally was gravely injured in a terrible accident. Sasha Nijinsky was to have joined me at this desk tonight, and she is badly missed. All of us here pray for her recovery. All of us wish her well. All of us look forward to her taking her place beside me. We know you do, too."

Music swelled, and an announcer's voice heralded the evening news. Stone watched as Harkness skillfully led half a dozen correspondents through the newscast, reading effortlessly from the TelePrompTer and asking an occasional informed question of someone in Tehran, Berlin, or London, while the control room crew scrambled to squeeze his opening statement into their allotted time.

During a commercial break, Cary turned to Stone. "What do you think?" she asked.

"Very impressive," he said, looking directly at her.

She laughed. "I meant about the newscast."

"Not nearly as impressive."

"Well, Barron's a little self-important," she said, "but nobody does this better."

"Read the news?"

She laughed again. "Oh, come on, now, he's reported from all over the world; he doesn't just read."

"I'll take your word for it."

The newscast ended, and she led Stone out another door and down a spiral staircase to the newsroom set. A dozen people were working at computer terminals.

"They're already getting the eleven o'clock news together," Cary said.

Barron Harkness was having the last of his makeup removed. He stood up and shook Stone's hand firmly. "Detective," he said.

To Stone's surprise, Harkness was at least six four, two twenty, and flat bellied. He looked shorter and fleshier on camera.

"Come on, let's go up to my office," Harkness said.

They climbed another spiral staircase, entered a hallway, and turned into Harkness's office, a large, comfortably furnished room with a big picture window looking down into the newsroom. Harkness waved Stone to a leather sofa. "Coffee? I'm having some."

"Thank you, yes," Stone said. He could use it; he fought off the lassitude caused by the bourbon and the newscast.

Cary Hilliard disappeared without being told, then came back with a Thermos and two cups. Both men watched her pour, then she took a seat in a chair to one side of Harkness's desk and opened a steno pad. "You don't mind if I take notes?" she asked Stone.

"Not at all," he replied. "Forgive me if I don't take any; I remember better if I do it later." He turned to Harkness. "Mr. Harkness—"

"Please call me Barron; I'd be more comfortable. And your first name?"

"Stone."

"A hard name," he said, smiling slightly.

"I'll try not to be too hard on you."

"Where is Sasha Nijinsky? What hospital?"

"I'm afraid I don't have any information on that."

Harkness's eyebrows went up. "I understood you were in charge of this investigation."

"That's nominally so, but I'm not the only investigator on the case, and I don't have all the information." That wasn't strictly true; he did have all the information there was; there just wasn't much.

"I trust *somebody* knows what hospital she's in. Certainly nobody at the network does."

"I expect somebody knows where she is," Stone said. "I understand you were traveling last night?"

"Yes, from Rome. I expect you've already checked that out."

"What time did you arrive at Kennedy?"

"Four thirty or five."

Stone nodded. "Mr. Harkness, did Sasha Nijinsky have any enemies?"

Unexpectedly, Harkness broke into laughter. "Are you kidding? Sasha climbed over half the people at the network to get where she is, and the other half are scared shitless of her."

"I see. Did any of them hate her enough to try to kill her?"

"Probably. In my experience, lots of people kill who have less cause than Sasha's victims."

That was Stone's experience too, but he didn't say so. "Who among her enemies do you think I should talk to?"

"Christ, where to begin!" Harkness said. "Oh, look, I'm overstating the case. I don't think anybody around here would try to kill Sasha. Do you think somebody kicked her off that terrace?"

"We have to investigate all the possibilities," Stone said.

"Well, I can't imagine that, not really. Maybe she caught a burglar in the act? Something like that?"

"It's possible," Stone said. It was, too, given that the doorman spent his evenings sound asleep. "We're looking at known operators in her neighborhood."

"On the other hand," Harkness said, "Sasha was one tough lady; I don't think a burglar could get the best of her. I'll tell you a story, in confidence. After the last elections, Sasha and I left this building very late, and, before we could get to the car that was waiting for us, a good-sized black guy stepped out of the shadows. He had a knife, and he said whatever the ghetto version of 'your money or your life' is these days. Before I even had time to think, Sasha stuck out her left arm, straight, and drove her fist into the guy's throat. He made this gurgling noise, dropped the knife, and hit the pavement like a sack of potatoes. Sasha stepped over, kicked the knife into the river, and said, 'Let's go.' We got into the car and left. Now *that* is what Sasha can be like. She'd been studying one of those martial arts things, and, when most people would have turned to jelly in the circumstances, she used what she knew. Me, I'd have given the guy anything he wanted." Harkness put his feet on his desk. "Now, do you think a burglar—or anybody else, for that matter—could heave somebody like that over a balcony railing?"

"You could be right," Stone said. You could be the guy who heaved her over the edge too, he thought. You're big enough and in good enough shape to handle a woman— even one who had martial arts training. "That brings us to another possibility. Did Sasha strike you as the sort of person who might take her own life?"

Harkness looked down at the carpet for a moment, drumming his fingers on the desk noisily. "In a word, yes," he said. "I think there was something of the manic-depressive in Sasha. She was high at a lot of times, but she was down at times, too. She could turn it off, if she was working; she could look into that camera and smile and bring it off. But there must have been times, when she was all alone, when it got to her."

"Did you ever see it get to her?"

"Once or twice, when we were doing *The Morning Show* together. I remember going into her dressing room once, five minutes before airtime, and she was in tears over something. But when we went on the air, she was as cheerful as a chipmunk."

"Do you know if she ever saw a psychiatrist?"

"Nope, but I'd bet that, if she did, she didn't tell him much. Sasha plays her cards very close to that beautiful chest."

Stone nodded, then stood up. "Well, thank you, Mr.— ah, Barron. If anything else comes up, I hope I can call you."

"Absolutely," Harkness said, rising and extending his hand. "Just call Cary; she always knows where to find me."

"Come on, I'll walk you down," Cary said, leading the way. Passing through the outer office, she tossed her steno pad on a desk and grabbed a raincoat from a rack. On the elevator, she turned to Stone. "Well, now you've had the Harkness treatment," she said. "What did you think?"

Stone shrugged. "Forthright, frank, helpful."

She smiled. "You got Barron's message."

The elevator reached the lobby, and, when the doors opened, they could see the rain beating against the windows.

"Can I give you a lift?" she asked. "I've got a car waiting, and you'll never get a cab down here at this time of the evening."

"Sure, I'd appreciate that." He took a deep breath. "If you're all through with work, how about some dinner?"

"You're off duty now?"

"The moment you say yes."

She looked at him frankly. "I'd like that."

They ran across the pavement to the waiting Lincoln Town Car, one of hundreds that answer the calls of people with charge accounts.

"Where to?" Cary said, as they settled into the back seat.

"How about Elaine's?" Stone said.

"Can you get a table without a reservation?"

"Let's find out."

"Eighty-eighth and Second Avenue," she said to the driver.

Stone turned to her. "I got the impression from what you said in the elevator that I shouldn't necessarily believe everything Barron Harkness tells me."

"Why, Detective," Cary said, her eyes wide and innocent. "I never said that." She scrunched down in the seat and laid her head back. "And, anyway, you're off duty, remember?"

10

*E*laine accepted a peck on the cheek, shook Cary's hand, and gave them Woody Allen's regular table. Stone heaved a secret sigh of relief. This was no night for Siberia.

"I'm impressed," Cary said when they had ordered a drink. "Whenever I've been in here before, we always got sent to Siberia."

"You've clearly been coming here with the wrong men," Stone replied, raising his glass to her.

"You could be right," she said, looking at him appraisingly. "You're bad casting for a cop, you know."

"Am I?"

"Don't be coy. It's not the first time you've been told that."

Pepe, the headwaiter, appeared with menus. Stone waved them away and asked for the specials.

"No, it's not the first time I've been told that," Stone said, when they had chosen their food. "I'm told that every time a cop I don't know looks at me."

"All right," she said, leaning forward, "I want the whole biography, and don't leave anything out, especially the part about why you're a cop and not a stockbroker, or something."

Stone sighed. "It goes back a generation. My family, on my father's side, was from western Massachusetts, real Yankees, mill owners."

"Barrington, as in Great Barrington, Massachusetts?"

"I don't know; I didn't have a lot of contact with the Massachusetts Barringtons. My father was at Harvard—rather unhappily, I might add—when the stock market crash of 'twenty-nine came. His father and grandfather were hit hard, and Dad had to drop out of school. This troubled him not in the least, because it freed him to do what he really wanted to do."

"Which was?"

"He wanted to be a carpenter."

"A *carpenter?* You mean with saws and hammers?"

"Exactly. He took it up when he was a schoolboy at Exeter, and he showed great talent. My grandfather was horrified, of course. Carpentry wasn't the sort of thing a Barrington did. But when he could no longer afford to keep his son in Harvard, well ..."

"What does this have to do with your being a cop?"

"I'm coming to that, eventually. Dad got to be something of a radical, politically, as a result of the depression. He gravitated to Greenwich Village, where he fell in with a crowd of leftists, and he earned a living knocking on people's doors and asking if they wanted anything fixed. He lived in the garage of a town house on West Twelfth Street and didn't own anything much but his tools.

"He met my mother in the late thirties. She was a painter

and a pianist and from a background much like Dad's—well-off Connecticut people, the Stones—who'd been wiped out in the crash. She was younger than Dad and very taken with the contrast between his upper-class education and his working-class job."

Cary wrinkled her brow. "Not Matilda Stone."

"Yes."

"Her work brings good prices these days at the auctions. I hope you have a lot of it."

"Only three pictures; her favorites, though."

"Go on with the autobiography."

"They lived together through the war years—the army wouldn't take Dad because he was branded as a Communist, even though he never joined the party. They had a tough time. Then, after the war, Dad rented a property on Hudson Street, where he finally was able to have a proper workshop. Some of Mother's friends, who had done well as artists, began to hire him for cabinetwork in their homes, and, by the time I was born, in 'fifty-two, he was doing pretty well. Mother's work was selling, too, though she never got anything like the prices it's bringing now, and, by the time I was old enough to notice, they were living stable, middle-class lives.

"When I was in my teens, Dad had quite a reputation as an artist-craftsman; he was building libraries in Fifth Avenue apartments and even designing and making one-of-a-kind pieces of furniture. The Barringtons and the Stones were very far away, and I didn't hear much about my forebears. Somehow, though, my parents' backgrounds filtered down into my life. There were always books and pictures and music in the house, and I suppose I had a sort of Yankee upbringing, once removed."

"Did you go to Harvard, like your father?"

"No; that would have infuriated him. I went to NYU and walked to class every day. By about my junior year, I had decided to go to law school. I didn't have any real clear idea about what lawyers actually did—neither did a lot of my classmates in law school, for that matter—but, somehow, it sounded good. I did all right, I guess, had a decent academic record, and, in my senior year, the New York City Police Department had a program to familiarize law students with police work. I worked part-time in a station house, I rode around in a blue-and-white, and I just loved it. The cops treated me like the whitebread college kid I was, but it didn't matter, the bug had bit. I took the police exam, and, almost immediately after I got my law degree, I enrolled in the Police Academy. In a way, I think I was imitating my father's choice of a working-class life."

"You never took the bar?"

"I couldn't be bothered with that. I was hot to be a cop."

"Are you still?"

"Yes, sort of. I love investigative work, and I'm good at it. I had a couple of good collars that got me a detective's shield; I had a good rabbi—a senior cop who helped me with promotion; he's dead now, though, and I seem to have slowed down a bit."

"But you're different from other cops."

Stone sighed again. "Yes, I guess I am. I've been an outsider since the day I started at the academy."

"So you're not going to be the next chief of police?"

Stone laughed. "Hardly. You could get good odds at the 19th Precinct that I'll never make detective first grade."

"What are you now?"

"Detective second."

"So, you're thirty-eight years old, and..."

"Essentially without prospects," Stone said, shrugging. "I can look forward to a pension in six years; a better one, if I can last thirty."

"Why are you limping?"

Stone told her about the knee, keeping it as undramatic

as possible. She listened and didn't say anything. "Now it's your turn," he said, "and don't leave out anything."

"My bio is much simpler," she said. "Born and grew up in Atlanta; the old man was a lawyer, now a judge; two years at Bennington, which my father thought was far too radical—I was wearing only black clothes and not washing my hair enough—so I finished at the University of Georgia, in journalism. Summer between my junior and senior years, I got on the interns' program at the network, and, when I graduated, they offered me a job as a production assistant. I'm thirty-two years old, and I'm still a production assistant."

"But at a higher level, surely? After all, you're assisting Barron Harkness."

She laughed. "It's a nice place to work, if your father can afford to send you there. The perks aren't bad." She looked at him sideways. "You skipped something."

"What?"

"Married?"

"Nope."

"Never? Why not?"

"Just lucky, I guess."

"Cynic."

"Probably."

"No girl?"

"Not at the moment. I was seeing somebody for a couple of years. When I was in the hospital, she accepted a transfer to LA."

"Sweet."

Stone shrugged. "I didn't come through with the commitment she wanted; she took a hike." He imitated her sidelong glance. "What about you?"

She sighed. "The usual assortment of yuppies during my twenties. I'm just out of a relationship with a married man."

"Those don't work, I'm told."

"This one sure didn't. He kept me on the hook for four

years, and then he just couldn't bring himself to leave his wife."

"That's the drill. Still hurting?"

"Now and then, if I don't watch myself. I think I'm relieved, more than anything else."

"Was it Harkness?"

"No; he wasn't in the TV business. Advertising."

"For what it's worth, I think the guy's nuts."

She smiled, a wide mouth full of straight, white teeth. She started to speak, but didn't. Instead, she concentrated on her pasta.

Stone watched her, and he felt the possibilities in his gut.

When they left Elaine's, the rain had stopped, and the air was cool. The car still waited for them.

"Can I drop you?" she asked. "It's one of the perks of the job; I think I probably spend more of the network's money on cars than they pay me."

"Sure, thanks. It's early; I'll give you a nightcap at my house."

"Sold."

They got into the car, and Stone gave the driver his address.

She looked at him, eyebrows arched. "That's a pretty expensive neighborhood. You on the take?"

Stone laughed. "Nope. I'll explain later."

They drove straight down Second Avenue, and at Sixty-ninth Street they ran into a wall of flashing lights. A uniformed cop was waving traffic through a single open lane.

"Pull over here," Stone said to the driver. He opened the car door and turned to Cary. "Give me a couple of minutes, will you?" He flashed his badge at a uniform and crossed the yellow tape. A Checker cab was stopped at the intersection, and a small group had gathered around the driver's open door. Stone saw Headly, from the detective squad.

Headly nodded. "Cabdriver caught one in the head," he said to Stone. "Looks like he was stopped for the light, somebody pulled up next to him, and just popped him one."

Stone glanced into the cab at the dead driver, sprawled across the front seat. There was a lot of blood. "You got it covered?" he said to Headly.

"Yeah," the detective replied.

Suddenly the cab was bathed in bright light. Stone turned, shielding his eyes.

"Howdy, Stone," Scoop Berman said, still operating his camera. "You on this one?"

"It's Headly's," Stone said. "You can give him the hard time." He stepped out of Scoop's lights and bumped into Cary Hilliard, who was staring at the dead driver. He took her elbow. "You don't want to see that," he said, turning her toward their car. "How'd you get past the tape?"

"Press card," she said, showing a blue, plastic shield on a string around her neck. She took it off and stuffed it into her handbag.

In the car they were both quiet for a block or two.

"You see a lot of that stuff?" she asked finally.

"Enough. More than I'd like to see. Did it upset you?"

She shook her head. "I didn't get a good enough look, thank God. I faint at the sight of blood."

They turned into Turtle Bay, and the car stopped.

"Wait for me," Cary said to the driver.

They climbed the steps, and Stone opened the front door of the house.

"You've got the duplex?" Cary asked, surprised.

"I've got the house," Stone replied. He flipped on the hall light.

"You *are* on the take," she said, laughing. "No honest cop could ever afford a house in Turtle Bay."

"Would you believe I inherited it?"

"No, I wouldn't."

"I did. My Great-Aunt Elizabeth, my grandfather's sister, married well. She always had a soft spot for my father, and she willed it to him. She outlived him, though, only died early this year at the age of ninety-eight, and so her estate came to me."

Stone led her into the library.

"It's a mess," she said, looking around at the empty shelves, stripped of their varnish, the books stacked on the floor, the rug rolled up, the furniture stacked in a corner, everything under sheets of plastic.

"It is now," Stone said, "but I'm working on it. My father designed and built this room; it was his first important commission, right after World War II. Everything is solid walnut. You could still buy it in those days; now all you can get is veneer, and that's out of sight."

"It's going to be magnificent," she said.

He led her through the other rooms, pointing out a couple of pieces that his father had built. "Most of the upholstered furniture is out being re-covered. My plan is to do the place up right, then sell it and retire on the proceeds, one of these days."

"Why not just sell it now?" she asked.

"I had a real estate lady look at it. She says I can triple the price if I put it in good shape—new heating, plumbing, kitchen—the works."

"How can you afford to do that?"

"There was a little money in Aunt Elizabeth's estate. I'm putting it all into the house and doing most of the work myself, with a couple of helpers and the occasional plumber and electrician."

"Where are your mother's pictures?"

"In my bedroom."

"May I see them?"

Stone took her up in the old elevator. "I keep meaning to get this thing looked at," he said over the creaking of the machinery, "but I'm afraid they'll tell me it needs replacing."

She stood in the bedroom and looked around. "This is going to be wonderful," she said. "I hope to God you've got decent taste."

"I'm not all that sure that I do," he lied. "I could use some advice."

"You may get more of that than you want; doing interiors is almost my favorite thing." She walked across the room and stood before the three Matilda Stones. There were two views of West Ninth and West Tenth streets and an elevated view of Washington Square. "These are superb," she said. "You could get half a million for the three, I'll bet, but don't you dare."

"Don't worry. They're a permanent fixture."

"They belong in a house like this," she said, "and so do you. Can't you think of some way to hang on to it? Go on the take, or something?"

"I have this fantasy," he said. "I'm living in this house; it's in perfect condition; there are servants in the servants' quarters, a cook in the kitchen, and money in the bank. I don't dare let myself dwell on it; it's never going to happen, I know that." He turned from the pictures and looked at her. "You said interior decorating was almost your favorite thing. What's your favorite?"

She stepped out of her heels and turned to face him. "I'm five-eleven in my stocking feet; does that turn you off?"

Stone looked her up and down—the luxuriant, dark hair; the chiseled face; the full breasts under the black cashmere; the long legs finishing in slender feet. He hooked an arm around her narrow waist and pulled her to him.

She smiled and rubbed her belly against his. "Apparently not," she said, then kissed him.

Stone slid down a long, velvet tunnel of desire, made no attempt to slow his fall. Their clothes vanished, and they found the bed. Stone made to move on top of her, then cried out when his swollen knee took his weight.

She pushed him onto his back, kissed the knee, kissed his lips and his nipples, kissed his navel and his penis, took him in her mouth, nearly swallowed him, brought him fully erect, then slid him inside her.

Stone looked up at the long body, the firm breasts, freed from the cashmere, the lips parted in ecstasy, the glazed eyes. She sucked him inside her again and again. When he thought he would come, she stopped and sat still, kissing his ears and his eyes, then she began again. Half an hour seemed to stretch into weeks, until, bathed in sweat, his face buried between her breasts, he came with her, and their cries echoed around the underfurnished room.

They lay in each other's arms, spent, breathing hard, caressing.

"You never told me what your favorite thing was," Stone said.

"That was it," Cary replied, kissing him.

Stone woke to broad daylight, and she was gone. A card was propped on the mantelpiece. There were phone numbers for home and work and an address: 1011 Fifth Avenue.

CHAPTER

11

Stone arrived in the detectives' squad room of the 19th Precinct feeling rested, refreshed, fulfilled, and in an extremely good mood. The good mood was tempered somewhat by the rows of empty desks in the room. Twenty-four hours earlier, they had been filled with detectives doing his bidding, chasing down every lead on the Sasha Nijinsky disappearance, leaving only to interview her co-workers and acquaintances, again at his bidding. He had the sickening feeling that his time at the head of the investigation had come to an end.

Dino was in Lieutenant Leary's glassed-in office at the end of the large room. Stone rapped on the glass and joined them. "Where is everybody?" he asked Dino as he pulled up a chair.

"On the cabdriver thing," Dino said.

Stone turned to Leary. "Lieutenant, you're not going to

pull my guys off this investigation and put them on a cab-driver murder, are you?"

"Yeah," Leary said, "but it's *three* murders."

"The cabdriver and who else?" Stone asked.

"The cabdriver and two other cabdrivers," Leary said. "Don't you watch TV or nothing?"

"I got a late start this morning," Stone said. "You mean three cabdrivers on the same day?"

"On the same night, all within an hour of each other," Leary said. "We got a fucking wildcat cabdrivers' strike going, you know that? Park Avenue is a parking lot. There's two thousand cabs just sitting there. You didn't notice?"

"Park Avenue isn't on my way to work," Stone said.

"You're lucky you and Bacchetti are still on Nijinsky," Leary said. "The mayor wasn't interested personally, you wouldn't be. What've you got on the lady?"

"Zip," Dino said.

"Some ideas," Stone said, shooting Dino a glance.

"What ideas?" Leary asked.

"We want a search warrant on Van Fleet," Stone said.

"Dino's been telling me about him," Leary replied. "I like him for this. You got enough for the warrant?"

"The letters ought to do it. We can demonstrate his undue interest in Nijinsky."

"See Judge O'Neal," Leary said. "She's got a hair up her ass about anything to do with any crime against women. She'll buy the letters."

"Right."

"What else you got?"

"Zip," Dino replied.

Stone shrugged. "It's not as though the effort hasn't been made. Every single co-worker has been interviewed; every hospital, clinic, and funeral parlor in the city, Long Island, and New Jersey has been contacted. I want to go through all her stuff today, just as soon as we've searched Van Fleet's place."

"I buy the effort," Leary said. "It's a bitch, ain't it?"

"It is," Dino agreed. "I never knew of nobody going up the pipe like this broad. It's spooky."

"I'll call the chief this morning; he'll talk to the mayor. I'll tell 'em we need more time."

"We do," Stone said.

"Go to it." Leary put his feet on his desk and picked up the telephone.

Stone followed Dino out of Leary's office. "You call Judge O'Neal's secretary for an appointment. I've got a call to make." He sat down at his desk, dug out Cary's card, and called her direct line. He got her on the first ring.

"Cary Hilliard."

"Morning."

"Well, good morning to you!" She was laughing.

"How are you?"

Her voice moved nearer the phone, and she whispered. "I'm sore as hell, and I feel great!"

"Same here"—Stone laughed—"but I'm not sure great describes it; it's somewhere above that."

"I'm free this evening," she said.

"No you're not; you've got a dinner date."

"I'll be done here by seven forty-five. Have you been to the Tribeca Grill?"

"Is that De Niro's new place?"

"That's it. Shall I book us a table?"

"Come to my house first, for a drink."

"You're on. I'll book for nine o'clock. See you at eight."

"You betcha."

When Stone hung up, Dino was looking at him.

"You got laid, didn't you?"

"What are you talking about?" Stone dissembled.

"I can tell." Dino batted his eyes rapidly. "You're just *glowing* all over."

"Jesus Christ! Do I have to take this shit from my own partner?"

"You betcha," Dino said, imitating Stone.

"What about Judge O'Neal?"

"Half an hour."

"What are we going to do for some help with the search?" Stone asked. "Nobody here."

"Well, shit," Dino replied, "if you and me between us can't find a corpse in a funeral parlor, we ought to turn in our papers."

Stone led the way out. "She's still alive, Dino. I can feel it."

"When I can feel *her*, I'll believe it," Dino called after him, hustling to keep up.

Judge O'Neal was youngish, blonde, and extremely good-looking. She sat in her high-backed, leather chair, her robes thrown open and her legs crossed, and contemplated Stone.

Stone contemplated right back. The woman had been wearing an engagement ring during the year since he had first come across her, or he would have asked her out.

"The letters are enough for me," O'Neal said, "even if he doesn't talk dirty. A thousand letters is weird enough for a warrant. Nobody's going to overrule."

"I shouldn't think so," Stone said. "By the way, we've included his place of work in the warrant."

"Off the record, Detective, for my own curiosity, what do you think happened to this woman?"

"Off the record, Judge, I am completely baffled, but I think she may still be alive."

O'Neal's eyebrows went up. "Get serious."

Stone explained his terminal velocity theory.

O'Neal shook her head vigorously, and the blonde hair

swirled around her shoulders. *"That,"* she said, "is the wildest theory I ever heard."

"It may not be plausible, but it's possible."

Judge O'Neal uncrossed her legs and leaned on her desk, resting her chin in her hand. "I've got a hundred bucks says she's stone dead—you should excuse the expression."

Stone laughed. "I'll take your bet, but the loser buys dinner."

O'Neal pursed her red lips for a moment, then smiled. "You're on," she said, signing the warrant.

In the car, Dino looked sideways at Stone while dodging a bicycle messenger. "Jesus, Stone, why didn't you just fuck her right there on the desk? I'd have been happy to watch."

"Come on, Dino."

"She's got the hots for you, I'm telling you."

"She's wearing an engagement ring."

"So what the fuck? She was wearing a wedding ring, that's maybe cause for pause, maybe. A diamond ring is an open door. Anyway, you got a dinner date, just as soon as we find Sasha, dead or alive."

Stone glanced at his watch. "Van Fleet should be at the funeral parlor by now. We'll serve him there, then do the apartment."

12

*H*erbert Van Fleet's mother didn't like it. Stone and Dino waited quietly while Mrs. Van Fleet called her lawyer.

She returned grim faced. "All right, how do you want to go about this?"

"We'd like to see every room in the building," Stone said.

"What are you looking for?" she demanded.

"Anything that might help us in our investigation," Dino said, none too politely.

Seething, the woman took them through the building. Stone saw nothing out of the ordinary—at least, out of the ordinary for a funeral parlor. They finished up in the embalming room, where Herbert Van Fleet was working on a corpse. A tube ran from the man's stomach to a pump, and the machine whirred quietly. Stone looked away.

Van Fleet looked up without surprise. "Well, well, look who's back. I'm not answering any further questions, gentlemen, except in the presence of my lawyer."

Stone handed him the warrant, and, while Van Fleet read it carefully, he went to a row of large drawers.

"I'll do this," Stone said to Dino. "I wouldn't want you to faint on me."

Two elderly men were the only occupants of the refrigerated storage drawers. Stone and Dino had a look in an adjacent storage room, then returned.

"All right," Van Fleet said, "when do you want to go to my apartment?"

"Immediately," Stone replied.

Van Fleet turned to his mother. "But what about Mr. Edmonson?" he asked plaintively, gesturing toward the corpse on the table.

"Just pop him in the fridge," Dino said. "He'll keep."

"You'd better go with them," Mrs. Van Fleet said to her son. "They'll wreck your place if you're not there."

Van Fleet nodded, went to a sink, washed his hands, removed his rubber apron, revealing that he was dressed in a three-piece suit, and said to the officers, "I'm ready."

Van Fleet didn't speak on the way downtown. His building was in SoHo, near the river, and the street seemed to have been missed in the gentrification of the area. A sign on the dusty windows of the empty ground floor read WEIN-STEIN'S FINE GLOVES. Van Fleet unlocked a steel door and led them into a vestibule and onto a freight elevator.

"Who else lives in the building?" Stone asked.

"Nobody," Van Fleet replied genially. "My mother and I bought it as an investment last year. I had planned to renovate the rest of the building and rent lofts, but I ran out of money. Maybe next year."

"Did the glove factory occupy the whole place?"

"No, there was a kosher meat-processing plant and a piecework sewing business, and offices on the top floor, where I live."

The elevator stopped. Van Fleet pushed back the gate and unlocked another large steel door.

"It's sort of like a fortress, isn't it?" Dino said.

"I shouldn't have to tell *you* what a problem burglary is in this city," Van Fleet said. Inside the door, he tapped a code into a keypad. "I've got a very decent alarm system, too."

Stone watched him.

Van Fleet led them into a large, open space. A kitchen had been built in a corner at the far end and a bedroom in the other corner. These rooms were separated from the rest of the loft by a framework of lumber that had not yet had plasterboard applied to it. "I'm doing most of the work on the place myself," Van Fleet said.

Light flooded the loft from three sides; the other abutted another building.

"Nice place, Herb," Dino said admiringly.

"You may call me Mr. Van Fleet," Van Fleet said, almost sweetly. He turned to Stone. "*You* may call me Herbert, if you wish."

"Thank you, Herbert," Stone said. "I feel for you, doing your own remodeling. I'm doing the same, myself." He said this while walking the length of the highly polished oak floor, the expanse of which was broken only by an occasional Oriental rug. A sofa, two chairs, a lamp, and a television set had been placed on one rug, an island of a living room surrounded by hardwood. The two detectives went methodically through the place, but there was hardly anywhere to hide anything. Van Fleet's desk rested against one wall. Stone opened the drawers and found nothing he wouldn't have seen in his own desk drawers: bills, stationery, office supplies.

"Let's see the rest of the building," Stone said to Van

Fleet. His warrant did not cover the whole building, but he hoped the man wouldn't notice.

Van Fleet didn't. He went to a kitchen drawer and retrieved a large key ring, which jangled as he led them to the elevator. They walked through the building a floor at a time. Van Fleet may not have had the money to complete his development project, but he had cleaned out the building; it was as empty as any place Stone had ever seen.

"Anything else?" Stone said to Dino.

Dino shook his head.

"Can we offer you a lift uptown, Herbert?"

"Thank you, no," Van Fleet replied. "As long as I'm here, I'll have my lunch and get a cab later. Sorry I couldn't be more helpful," he said sweetly.

"You've been very helpful, Herbert," Stone said, "and we appreciate your cooperation."

"Have you found out anything else about Sasha?" Van Fleet asked.

"I'm afraid we can't discuss an investigation in progress," Stone said.

"The papers said you're making no progress at all," Van Fleet said, walking them to the front door.

"Don't believe everything you read in the papers," Dino said, as Van Fleet closed the door behind them.

Back in the car, Stone sighed. "Clean as a hound's tooth," he said.

"Yeah," Dino agreed, disconsolately.

"Let's go up to Sasha's and go through those boxes."

"Okay."

There was a different doorman on duty when the detectives arrived at the building. Stone flashed his badge and asked for his key to the Nijinsky apartment. The man handed it over silently.

The moment they stepped off the elevator, it was obvious that something was wrong. The police notice fixed to the apartment door had been removed.

"The seal's broken," Dino said. "What the fuck?"

Stone led the way into the apartment. It was completely empty. The two men stood there looking helplessly about them, as if waiting for inspiration. Stone bent over and picked up a card from the floor.

> Effective immediately,
> Sasha Nijinsky is at
> 1011 Fifth Ave.
> New York 10021.
> Burn this.

"The movers," Stone said.

"What?"

"The movers. She was moving the next morning."

"What's the new address?"

"Ten-eleven Fifth." Stone didn't mention that he knew someone else at that address.

"Let's go see the doorman."

Downstairs, Stone braced the doorman. "There was a police seal on the door of the Nijinsky apartment," he said. "Who broke it?"

"Jesus, Officer," the man pled, "I don't know nothing. The moving people showed up and took her stuff; that's all I know."

They drove uptown in silence. The building was across the street from the Metropolitan Museum of Art. The doorman greeted them.

"Can I help you, gentlemen?" he said, blocking the entrance.

Stone showed his ID. "Miss Nijinsky's apartment."

"Yes? What about it?"

"We'd like to see it. This is part of a police investigation. Did some moving people bring some furniture and boxes here yesterday?"

"Yes, but I'm afraid I can't let you into the apartment without permission, unless you've got a search warrant, of course."

Dino sighed loudly. "I guess you know the lady's in no condition to give permission."

The doorman shrugged. "My hands are tied," he said, "unless you get permission from the cooperative's board of directors. If one of them says it's okay, I'll let you in."

"Who's the chairman of the cooperative's board?" Stone asked.

The doorman went to a tin box on his desk and produced an index card. He handed it to Stone.

The name on the card was Barron Harkness.

Stone registered this for a moment, then showed the card to Dino. "May I use your telephone?" he asked the doorman.

"Sure," the man said, placing a phone on the desk.

"An interesting connection, wouldn't you say?" he asked Dino. He checked his notebook and dialed the number of the network.

13

A woman answered Harkness's phone, a voice Stone didn't recognize.

"Barron Harkness, please. My name is Barrington; he knows me."

"I'm sorry, Mr. Barrington, Mr. Harkness is in a meeting. May I have him return the call?"

"Let me speak with Cary Hilliard, please."

"Ms. Hilliard is in the same meeting."

Stone tried not to sound annoyed. "Please take a note to Mr. Harkness. Tell him Detective Stone Barrington would like to speak with him at once, and that it's important."

"I'm sorry, but—"

"Please do it now. This is police business."

The woman hesitated. "All right," she said finally. "What is your number?"

"I'll hold."

An irritating minute passed, then: "Barron Harkness."

"Mr. Harkness, this is Stone Barrington. I'm at your apartment building, and I want your permission to enter Sasha Nijinsky's apartment. The doorman insists on speaking with you before allowing entry."

"But why?" Harkness asked. "Sasha never moved into the apartment; there's nothing there. Legally, she didn't even own the apartment; she was supposed to have closed on it the morning after she ..."

"It appears that a moving company followed instructions she gave before her disappearance and moved her belongings into the apartment. The doorman let them in."

Harkness hesitated, then spoke. "I'll be right over there," he said, and hung up before Stone could speak further.

Stone replaced the receiver and turned to Dino. "Harkness is coming over here."

"Why?" Dino asked.

"Who knows? Maybe he's being protective of his building's reputation."

The doorman spoke up. "That sounds like Mr. Harkness," he said. "He and the board are very picky about what goes on here. That's why I wouldn't let you in. It woudda been my job, y'know."

Stone nodded, then joined Dino on a sofa in the lobby to wait for Harkness.

They didn't have to wait long. A black Lincoln Town Car pulled up at the curb, and Harkness strode into the building. He shook hands with Stone and was introduced to Dino. "All right," he said, "let's get this over with. I've got to get back to the office."

"We don't really need you for this," Stone said, "if you'd like to go back now."

Harkness fished a letter from an inside pocket and handed it to Stone. It was from a midtown law firm.

"You're her executor?" Stone asked. "But we don't even know that she's dead."

"I got the letter this morning; it was the first I'd heard of it." He shrugged. "I guess I'm representing Sasha in this," he said, "so, unless you want to get a search warrant, I'm going to have to go into that apartment with you."

"All right," Stone said.

"Eddie," Harkness said to the doorman, "I'll use my pass-key. We won't need you."

On the elevator, Stone turned to Harkness. "You say you didn't know that Ms. Nijinsky had appointed you executor of her will?"

"Didn't have a clue," Harkness replied. "I was astonished, to tell you the truth."

"Mr. Harkness, did you and Sasha Nijinsky ever have a romantic relationship?"

Harkness looked him in the eye. "Stone, I haven't the slightest intention of answering that."

The elevator door opened, and they stepped into a vestibule; only two apartments opened onto it, 10-J and 10-K. Harkness opened the door to 10-J and led the way in. There was an entrance hall, then a large living room. Furniture had been dumped here and there, as if the moving men had no instructions, and the boxes Stone had seen at Sasha's old apartment were piled in the middle of the floor. Every one of them had been opened, and the woman's belongings were strewn across the floor.

"Now that's interesting," Dino said.

Stone picked up a yellow movers' receipt from the floor and handed it to Dino. "See if there's a working phone; if not, go down and use the doorman's. Get hold of the movers' supervisor and ask him what the hell went on here."

Dino took the receipt and went in search of a phone. "The one in the kitchen is working," he called out.

"Do you have any idea who might have opened these boxes?" Stone asked Harkness.

"Not a clue," Harkness replied. "As I said earlier, she didn't even own the apartment yet. It would have been like Sasha, though, to have her stuff moved at the moment she would have been closing the sale. She wasn't a woman who liked to be kept waiting."

"I want to go through her belongings," Stone said, "and I may want to remove some things for evidence. Have I your permission to do that?"

Harkness hesitated. "I think maybe I should talk to a lawyer, first. I want to do the right thing, here."

"Look, Barron," Stone said, "Sasha trusted you enough to put you in charge of her estate. There may be something here that will help us find out what happened to her, and we're going to need your cooperation."

Dino returned from the kitchen. "The supervisor at the movers' says his guys didn't open any boxes. I called the doorman on the house phone, and he confirms that they were sealed when he signed the receipt and let the movers out."

"So," said Stone, turning to Harkness, "somebody has been in here since the movers left."

"Don't look at me," Harkness said.

"You've got a passkey, right?"

"I'm chairman of the cooperative board. Look, I thought the apartment was empty. Why would I want to come in here?"

"Who else besides the doorman has a key to this apartment?"

"The owners would, the people who were selling to Sasha. They live in Connecticut; I'll get the phone number for you."

"Who lives in the other apartment across the vestibule, number 10-K?"

"My assistant, Cary Hilliard. You met her the other night."

Stone nodded. "And would she have a key?"

"No."

"Did she know that Sasha was moving in here?"

"No. Sasha wanted her change of address kept quiet until she had moved. She liked to control what people knew about her."

"Where do you normally keep your passkey?"

Harkness held up a gold key ring. "Here, with my other keys. They're always in my pocket. Always. I lost some keys once, and it was such a pain in the ass that I've had a thing about it ever since."

"Who else knew that Sasha was buying the apartment?"

"The owners; the board of directors, four other people besides me—they had to approve the buyer—the doorman, and, of course, anybody Sasha might have felt like telling."

Stone remembered Sasha's change-of-address cards, unmailed. "I want to go through this stuff. Are you going to cooperate, or am I going to have to go to the trouble of getting a search warrant?"

"All right"—Harkness sighed—"do what you have to do, but I'm going to be here while you're doing it." He walked across the room and settled his large frame in a chair. "Have at it," he said.

Nearly two hours later, Stone wrote a receipt and handed it to Harkness. "I want her checkbook and her other financial records—these two boxes here."

"When do I get them back?"

"When I've had a chance to go over them thoroughly, or when Sasha turns up alive, whichever comes first."

Harkness stared at the two boxes.

"Is there something you want to tell me?" Stone asked.

"No," Harkness replied. "If it will help to find out what happened to Sasha, you're welcome to the records."

They parted at the front door of the building, and the detectives lifted the two boxes into the trunk of their car. As they got in, Dino spoke up. "If Harkness keeps his keys in his pocket all the time, then his wife might have gotten to them when he was asleep. If he was fucking Sasha, the lady might have taken an interest in her moving into the building."

"I didn't think of that," Stone said. "I don't even know if Harkness has a wife."

"He's a big guy, isn't he? Wouldn't have much trouble tossing a lady off a balcony, he felt like it."

"I thought of that," Stone said.

14

*I*f you're going to start out the evening kissing like that, then we're never going to make it to dinner," Stone said, feeling her breasts against him. The front door was still open, and he kicked it shut.

"Couldn't help myself." She grinned. "Say, all the way over here, I've been wondering where in this house you're going to offer me a drink. I mean, the place is a wreck."

"Follow me," he said, and he led her to the kitchen.

She stood and looked around the room. "It's beautiful," she said. "You didn't do this yourself."

"I did, with a little help. I didn't build it, I just restored it, refinishing all the original cabinetwork and fitting in the new appliances. It's the only room in the house that's done, except for the floors."

"It's like a turn-of-the-century dream," she said, opening a cabinet. "And you've got your aunt's china, too."

"Hers and my mother's. I could feed an army, if I had a working dining room."

"We've got to find a way for you to keep this house, Stone. You deserve to live in it, really you do. I hate to think of your turning it over to some stranger, just for the money."

"I hate the idea, too, but that's the way it has to be. What would you like to drink?"

"Scotch."

They sat at the kitchen table.

"So how's the Sasha investigation going?"

"Stranger and stranger. Did you know she was going to be your next-door neighbor?"

Cary's jaw dropped. "In 10-J? You're kidding!"

"Barron didn't tell you?"

"Jesus, no." She looked thoughtful. "I wonder why not. I know most of what goes on with him, and if he got her into the building, why wouldn't he tell me that?"

"Did he get you into the building?"

"Yeah. Daddy paid, of course. Dammit, I'll bet Sasha paid less. The co-op market is soft right now, and I've been there two years; I bought in at the top."

"Did you know the people who lived there before?"

"The Warrens? Sure. I mean, they had me in for a drink when I moved in, and I had them in for a drink in return, and after that I just saw them in the elevator. The place was just a pied-à-terre for them; they live in Westport. He was in a Wall Street law firm, and he just retired."

"Did you have a key to 10-J?"

"No."

Stone told her about the day's events.

"Spooky!" she said. "And you wondered if *I* went through her stuff?"

"Had to ask."

"Did you talk to the Warrens?"

"I tried. The maid said they're in London. That lets them out, I guess."

"The painters have been in and out of there, but I guess they finished up before Sasha's stuff arrived. Anyway, the doorman would have let them in and locked up after them."

"Well, enough shoptalk. How was your day?"

It was nine before they reached the Tribeca Grill, riding in the inevitable black Lincoln. The headwaiter knew Cary and gave them a good table.

"Neat place," Stone said. "I've read about it. Is De Niro in here much?"

"From time to time. Sometimes I think a third of the people in here came just to catch a glimpse of him."

"Like those two couples," Stone said, nodding at a table in a less desirable part of the restaurant. They watched as one of the men, dressed in a silk suit and a pearl gray tie, offered the headwaiter money and had it refused.

"Tourists," Cary said.

"Not your ordinary tourists," Stone replied. "They're wise guys."

"Mafia? You know them?"

"I know the look. The suits, the women's clothes. Just about everybody else in here is casual, but they're dressed to kill. Here's how it goes: the wise guys like places they're known, where they're known to be connected; they're treated like princes—the best tables, the best wines on the house. Tonight, though, the ladies wanted to break out, wanted to come to De Niro's restaurant and see him up close. The guys went for it, because De Niro is Italian, he's their hero, and they're already regretting it. They got the worst table in the house, and the headwaiter won't be bought. They'll sulk all through dinner, and it'll be the last time for a while the ladies will get to go to a new restaurant."

Cary laughed. A wonderful sound, Stone thought. "Do you deal much with Mafia guys?"

"Not unless there's a homicide. My partner, Dino, grew up with them, though. Dino says that everybody he was in school with is either dead, in prison, or has his phones tapped by the FBI."

"I'd like to meet Dino."

"He'll charm you right out of your pants," Stone said.

She leaned close. "Only you can do that."

"I'm glad to hear it."

They dined well, and Cary pointed out the regulars to him, told him who the producers and directors were. When coffee came, she was quiet for a while.

"That's really strange, Barron not telling me that Sasha and I were going to be next-door neighbors," she said finally.

"It really seems to bother you," Stone said.

"It does. During the time I've been with Barron, he's come to trust me on just about everything, I think, and then, when there's something you'd think he would just naturally tell me about, he clams up. If Sasha's stuff hadn't got moved in there, I'd never have known about her buying the place."

"Is Barron married?"

"Sure. He and Charlotte celebrated their twentieth anniversary last year. Now, *that* could have something to do with it. Maybe he didn't want Dolly to know—but hell, that doesn't make any sense either. How could he move her into the building and expect to keep it from Dolly? And why would he think I would tell her, anyway? I've never told her about anything else he's done. I hardly know her."

"What's Charlotte like?"

"Straight arrow; utterly conventional. They were college sweethearts, and she worships the ground he slithers on."

"Now, *that* is the first hard word I've heard you say about him. He slithers, does he?"

"Oh, I guess I'm just mad because he didn't tell me about Sasha's moving into the building."

"Was Barron fucking Sasha?"

She turned and looked at him. "Are you on the job, Stone, or is this a personal conversation?"

He didn't blink. "Every cop is always on the job. There are times when I can't separate my work from my personal life. This is one of them."

She didn't blink either. "If you want to interrogate me about my boss, see me at my office. And I might lie to you."

"You should never lie to a policeman," he said.

"I will if I feel like it," she replied evenly.

The evening suddenly turned cool.

Later, when her black car stopped in front of the Turtle Bay house, she declined to come in with him.

Before he got out, he turned to face her. "I'm sorry. I apologize. I stepped over the line, and I'll try not to do it again."

She nodded, but didn't say anything.

He kissed her on the cheek, got out of the car, and closed the door.

She rolled down the window. "Stone," she called after him.

He turned and walked back to the car, leaned down close to her.

"Barron was fucking Sasha," she said. "Secretly, regularly, and for a long time. And I think I'm falling in love with you." She rapped on the back of the front seat and the car drove away, leaving Stone standing in the street.

CHAPTER

15

When Stone arrived at
the precinct, a well-dressed, obviously irritated man was sitting next to Dino's desk. Dino, unaccountably in the station
house early, was interviewing him.

"Look, I've already explained," he said, looking uncomfortably around him. A very dirty, handcuffed black man
was sitting at the next desk, admiring the man's clothes.

"Mr. Duncan, this is my partner, Stone Barrington.
Stone, this is Mr. Evan Duncan, who has something interesting to tell us."

"How do you do, Mr. Duncan," Stone said, extending
his hand. He stepped between Duncan and the black man.

"Would you please tell Detective Barrington what you
saw, Mr. Duncan?" Dino asked politely.

Shielded from the black man and seeming to take confidence from the presence of Stone, who probably looked like

most of the people he knew, Duncan nodded. "I'm an investment banker," he said. "My office is in Rockefeller Plaza." Having established that he was a person worthy of belief, he went on. "Last evening, about six thirty, a friend and I were leaving the Harvard Club, on West Forty-fourth Street. We had ordered a car from the club's service, and a black car pulled up and let a man out. I looked at the number on the window and thought it was car number twelve, which was the number on the slip the steward had given me, so I opened the door and started to get into the car." He paused, as if uncertain as to whether he should continue.

"Go on, Mr. Duncan," Stone said, nodding reassuringly.

"Well, there was a woman in the backseat. She turned to me, surprised that someone was getting into her car. I apologized and began backing out, and she said, 'Don't worry about it, all these cars look alike.' I closed the door and checked the number again, and it was number twenty-one, not twelve." He stopped and looked to Stone as if for approval.

Stone wondered if he had missed something. "Mr. Duncan ..."

"You didn't tell him, Mr. Duncan," Dino said to the man.

"Oh, I'm sorry, I quite missed the main point, didn't I?" Duncan chuckled.

"Yes," Dino said.

"What *is* the main point?" Stone asked, baffled.

"Oh, well, the woman was Sasha Nijinsky," Duncan replied, as if Stone should have known it all along.

The hairs stood up on the back of Stone's neck. Here was an obviously solid citizen with a close-up sighting. "Why did you think it was Sasha Nijinsky?" Stone asked, hoping against hope that the man was not simply some upper-class fruitcake.

"Well, I've seen her on television several hundred times."

"Sometimes people on television look different in person," Stone said.

"And I sat across the table from her at a dinner party less than two weeks ago," Duncan said firmly.

Stone looked at Dino. Dino made a how-about-that face.

"Did she recognize you?" Stone asked.

"I don't think so, and I was in and out of the car so fast that I never really engaged her in conversation. But it was Sasha Nijinsky, I'm absolutely certain of it. I wouldn't really have come in here about this, but my wife said it could be important, since Sasha is missing."

"Missing?" Stone asked. Nobody knew she was missing. The press still thought she was in some hospital or other.

Dino held up a fresh copy of the *Daily News*. SASHA VANISHES, a headline screamed.

Stone picked up the paper and opened it. "A source in the New York City Police Department confirmed last night that, since her fall from the terrace of her East Side penthouse apartment, Sasha Nijinsky has been missing, and no one knows if she is alive or dead." He didn't read the rest. Somebody, probably somebody in this room, was talking to a reporter.

"You did the right thing, Mr. Duncan," Stone said. "Now the car number was twenty-one, the time was about six thirty, you said?"

"That's right, just about exactly six thirty. That was the time I had ordered the car for."

"And the name of the car service?"

"Minute Man. I use them all the time."

Stone held out his hand. "Thank you very much for this information, Mr. Duncan," he said. "You may be sure that we'll check this out thoroughly."

Dismissed, Duncan retrieved his trench coat from Dino's desk and made his way out of the room, giving the leering black man a wide berth.

"Cat's out of the bag, huh?" Stone said to Dino.

"I think a more appropriate description of the situation is that the shit has hit the fan," Dino said. "Leary wants to see us."

"At least we've got some sort of lead," Stone said. "Let's call Minute Man first."

After a long wait for the information, Stone was told that a Minute Man car had picked up a Ms. Balfour at the Algonquin Hotel at six thirty and had delivered her to an East Sixty-third Street address. Stone scribbled it down. "The Algonquin is right down the block from the Harvard Club; the car must have been stopped in traffic when Duncan mistook it for his."

"Sounds good to me," Dino said.

Armed with their new information, the two detectives faced Leary, who was an unhappy man. "I hope to God this is no fuckin' wild-goose chase," he said, when he had heard their story. "The chief of detectives has already been on the phone this morning, and I'm expecting a call from the mayor any minute."

As if on cue, the phone rang. Leary put his hand on it. "Get out of here and run down that lead," he said. "I'll buy you as much time as I can."

Stone and Dino sat in their car outside the address, an elegant town house on East Sixty-third Street.

"I'm scared," Dino said.

"I know how you feel," Stone replied.

"You know how much we need this to *be* something, don't you? I'd like to get a shot at the balls of the guy who leaked to the papers. I'd cut 'em off and make him eat 'em."

"I'd hold him down while you did it," Stone said. "All right, let's go."

They trudged up the front steps and rang the bell, then

watched through iron grillwork as a uniformed maid approached the door.

"Yes?" she said, opening the door slightly.

Stone showed his badge. "My name is Detective Barrington. Is there a Ms. Balfour at this address?"

"Just a minute," the maid said, closing the door and shutting them out. She went to a telephone in the entrance hall, spoke a few words into it, then returned and opened the front door wide. "Please come in," she said. "Mrs. Balfour will be right down."

As they entered, Stone saw half a dozen pieces of matched luggage piled to one side of the front door. The detectives were shown to a small sitting room, and, as they sat down, the maid opened the door to another man, who began removing the baggage.

A moment later, there was the click of high heels on the marble floor of the entrance hall, and Sasha Nijinsky walked into the sitting room.

As the detectives got to their feet, Stone was swept with an overwhelming sense of relief that made him light-headed.

"I'm Ellen Balfour," Sasha Nijinsky said. "How may I help you?"

Something is wrong here, Stone thought. Relief began to be replaced by panic.

"Well?" the woman said into the stunned silence.

"Aren't you…" Stone couldn't get the words out.

"Oh, I see," the woman said, nodding her beautiful head gravely. "It's the third time this week I've been mistaken for her."

"Oh, shit," Dino said, involuntarily, then recovered himself.

The woman turned and looked at him.

"Excuse me, please," Dino pled.

"I wonder, Mrs. Balfour, if you have some personal identification?" Stone said, hoping against hope that this

woman was Nijinsky and hiding it. "Something with a photograph?"

The woman opened her handbag and produced a New
York driver's license with a very nice picture.

"I can only apologize for the intrusion," Stone said,
returning the license to her. "A gentleman turned up at the
precinct this morning and reported having seen Sasha
Nijinsky."

"I'll bet it was the man from the Harvard Club last
night," she said.

"It was."

"He looked as if he'd seen a ghost."

"He was very certain. He'd met Miss Nijinsky only a
couple of weeks ago."

"I've been putting up with this for years," Mrs. Balfour
said, "and I've resisted changing my hair, but now I'm just
going to have to go for a new look, I guess. And after the
newspaper stories this morning, I'm getting out of town."

"I don't blame you," Stone said.

"If you get any reports of sightings in the Hamptons,
please ignore them," Ellen Balfour said. "My husband
doesn't think this is funny anymore."

Back in the car, neither detective spoke until they were
nearly back to the precinct.

"I guess we'd better get into Sasha's financial records,"
Stone said finally.

"Yeah," Dino replied disconsolately. Dino's idea of a
financial record was the color of the sock he kept his money
in. "Tell you what, I'll go through the interview reports again
on the people you and I didn't talk to personally; you do the
financial records, okay?"

"Okay," Stone said.

16

Stone was impressed with Sasha's records. She kept the kind of system that he kept meaning to set up for himself.

Her checkbook was the large, desk model, and every stub was fully annotated; she kept a ledger of the bills she received and paid; there was no preparer's signature on her tax returns, so she must have done them herself. It seemed that Sasha Nijinsky had never been late on a payment for anything, and, periodically, there was a large check written—usually between twenty-five and a hundred thousand dollars—to a brokerage account. The lady had been making a lot of money for years, and she knew how to save it.

Stone was surprised, then, when her most recent brokerage statement showed the value of her holdings was only thirty-seven thousand dollars and change. He began backtracking through the brokerage statements, which were bundled by year and secured with strong rubber bands. They made good reading. Figuring roughly, Stone estimated that Sasha had saved just under eight hundred thousand dollars during the past five years and that, through shrewd trading, this had grown to just over two million during that time. Then, eight months back, an even two million had been withdrawn, paid by the broker with a cashier's check made out to Cash.

Having an easily negotiable instrument of that size in her possession seemed at odds with Sasha's character as revealed in her records, Stone thought; the consequences of losing it would have been catastrophic for her, and he could find no record of the sum having been placed in any other of her accounts. Two million dollars was just gone. Furthermore, at the time she had disappeared, Sasha had been about to close a substantial real estate transaction which, according to her records, she had no ready funds to cover. And there was no record of a mortgage application or commitment letter. Strange.

"Dino, you keep at the interview reports," Stone said. "I think I'm going to pay Sasha's lawyer a visit."

"You find something?"

"No, I'm missing something. Or rather, Sasha is."

It was five o'clock when Stone presented himself at the midtown law offices of Woodman & Weld, and the receptionist fled her desk, clutching her coat, as soon as she had announced him.

"I'm Frank Woodman," a tall, athletic man in his fifties said, extending his hand. "Come on back to the conference room; there's a meeting still going on in my office."

"I'm sorry if I've come at a bad time," Stone said, following Woodman down a plushly carpeted hallway.

"Not at all," Woodman said over his shoulder. "I'm happy to do anything I can to help Sasha." He led the way into an elegant conference room, which was furnished in English antiques, and sat down at the head of the table.

Stone took a chair. "Mr. Woodman, to get right to the point, two million dollars seems to be missing from Sasha's brokerage account."

Woodman nodded. "I know about that," he said, "but only because Sasha mentioned it in passing. I should tell you that, even as her sole attorney, I know less about Sasha's affairs than most lawyers in my position would know. She was . . . well, secretive, I guess I'd have to say."

"You say you know where the money is?"

"I said I knew *about* it," Woodman replied. "Sasha told me a few months ago that she had cashed in her chips after having done well in the market for several years. She showed me a cashier's check made out to Cash for two million."

"I thought you said she was secretive."

"She was, but we were having a drink in the Oak Bar of the Plaza one evening, and I guess she'd had a couple, and she showed me the check."

"Did she say what she was going to do with it?"

"Only that she was Federal Expressing it to a bank in the Cayman Islands the following morning. She said she was making an investment with a friend."

"She didn't say who the friend was?"

"No."

"Have you any idea who it might have been?"

"None."

"Is there some way I might trace the money?"

"I shouldn't think so. Cayman Islands banks are a lot like their Swiss counterparts, in that their transactions are held secret. It's said there's a lot of drug money down there. Even if I knew the name of the bank, and I do not, they wouldn't give you the time of day. They won't even give the IRS the time of day."

"It appears from her records that she had paid the taxes on her profits in the market," Stone said.

"I've no doubt of that," Woodman replied. "Sasha was punctilious in her financial dealings. But when people put large sums of money into Swiss or Cayman banks, they're often trying to avoid paying taxes on the income from that investment. That she may very well have been trying to do, although I would have advised her against it, if she had asked me."

"Do you know how Sasha had planned to pay for her new apartment?"

"What new apartment?" Woodman asked, surprised.

"You didn't know that she was moving?"

"She never mentioned it to me," Woodman said. "Oh, a couple of years back she called me about the availability of mortgages on co-ops in the city, and I told her I would be happy to help her with an application, but, as far as I know, she never applied for a mortgage. Certainly, she had the income to raise one, if she had wished."

"Was Sasha the kind of client who might have been lured into a fast-buck investment by a friend?" Stone asked.

Woodman thought about that. "Yes," he said. "Sasha loved money, loved making it. But she would only have taken that sort of plunge if she had checked it out carefully, and if she trusted the friend implicitly." Woodman's eyebrows went up.

"I find myself speaking of her in the past tense," he said. "Of course, I did read the papers this morning."

"Is that why you let Barron Harkness know that Sasha had appointed him executor of her estate?"

"I did that before I saw today's papers. When I heard about her fall and when I was unable to locate her, I wrote to Harkness simply as a precautionary step. It seemed the prudent thing to do."

Stone stood up. "Thank you for your time, Mr. Woodman," he said. "If you think of anything else that might help me, I'd appreciate a call, day or night." He gave Woodman a card.

"Of course," the lawyer said. "Do you think you can find your way back to reception? I'd like to rejoin my meeting."

"Sure, thanks," Stone replied. The two men shook hands, and Stone turned back toward the front of the office.

Halfway there, someone called his name. Stone stopped and backtracked a few steps to an open office door. A grinning man was rising from a desk.

Stone struggled for a name. "Bill Eggers?" he managed finally.

Eggers stuck out a hand. "Haven't seen you since graduation day," he said, "although I've seen your picture in the paper from time to time."

"So what have you been doing with yourself for all these years?" Stone asked. He remembered Eggers as a companionable fellow; they'd had a few beers after class more than once.

Eggers spread his hands. "This," he said. "I joined a downtown firm after law school, but I've been here for the past eight years."

"What sort of law are you practicing?"

"Oh, I'm the general dogsbody around here," Eggers said. "I do whatever needs doing—some personal injury, a little domestic work, the odd criminal case, when one of the firm's clients crosses the line."

"Sounds interesting." Stone looked around the plush office. Looked as though Eggers had done well at it too.

"More interesting than you would believe." Eggers laughed. "You seeing Woodman about Sasha?"

"Yeah."

"I wondered when you'd get around to him."

"It took me a few days; I've been pretty busy."

"Funny you turning up here; I've been thinking about you lately."

"Kind thoughts, I hope."

"The kindest, I assure you." Eggers looked at his watch. "I've got a client coming in any second, but I'd like to buy you a drink sometime, chew over some things."

"Sure," Stone said, fishing out a card. "Give me a week or two, though. The Sasha thing is taking a lot of time."

"Of course," Eggers said, extending his hand again. "We'll make it dinner, when you've got the time."

On his way home, Stone reflected on Bill Eggers's prosperous appearance, the handsome office, the prestigious law firm. Was it possible that Woodman & Weld might need someone with his background?

When he got home, there was a notice from the NYPD: his return-to-duty physical had been scheduled. Stone flexed the knee. Not bad; he'd begun to forget about it. He tried a couple of half knee bends. It was sore, but he could ace the physical.

CHAPTER

17

*C*an I buy you breakfast?"
her low, pleasing voice said on the phone. "It's the first real day
of autumn outside, and we'll have a walk in the park, too."

"Oh, yes." Stone exhaled. He was pitifully glad to hear
from Cary. Their last, uncomfortable evening had been eating at him, and, in spite of her parting words, he had been
unsure of his reception, should he call her.

"There's a little French place called La Goulue, on East
Seventieth, just off Madison. I've got a table booked in half
an hour."

"You're on."

They sat in the warm, paneled restaurant, a pitcher of
mimosas between them, and drank each other in.

"I don't know when I've been so glad to see anybody," Stone said.

"I'm glad it's me you're glad to see," she replied. She slipped off her shoe, and, under the tablecloth, rested her foot in his crotch. "Oh, you *are* glad to see me, aren't you?" She rolled her eyes.

"That's not a pistol in my pocket." He grinned.

Her eyebrows went up. "You're supposed to wear a gun all the time, aren't you?"

"That's right."

"Are you wearing one now?"

He nodded.

"So that *could* be a pistol in your pocket."

He laughed. "It could be, but it isn't."

"Where are you wearing it?"

"Strapped to my ankle." He hated the bulge under his coat, hated being careful about inadvertently revealing the weapon.

"You have a badge, too, I guess."

"That's right. I wouldn't be a policeman without a badge, would I?"

"Let me see it."

Stone produced the little leather wallet and laid it on the table.

She flipped it open and ran a finger around the badge. "It's gold," she said.

"A detective's badge is always gold. It's what every cop wants, a gold badge."

The waiter came and refreshed their mimosas from the pitcher, leaning over, eyeing the badge.

Stone flipped the wallet shut and put it back in his pocket.

"I want it," she said.

"Want what?"

"The badge."

Stone laughed and shook his head. "To get that badge, you'd have to sign up for the Police Academy, walk a beat for a few years, spend a few more in a patrol car, then get lucky on a bust or two, and have a very fine rabbi."

"Rabbi?"

"A senior cop who takes an interest in your career."

"Do you have a rabbi?"

"I did. His name was Ron Rosenfeld."

"And he helped you?"

"He helped me a lot. I would never have made detective if not for him."

"Why did he help you?" she asked.

"That's a funny question. Why do people ever help each other?"

"But there must have been some specific reason, apart from just liking you. Did he help all young policemen?"

"No," Stone admitted. He thought about it for a moment. "I think it may have been because he was a Jew and I was such an obvious WASP."

"That doesn't make any sense. Why didn't he help Jewish cops, instead of you?"

"I think because he had been discriminated against when he was a young patrolman, so he felt some empathy with my situation. He saw me getting passed over for good assignments, and it rankled, I guess. Oh, he helped a lot of young Jewish cops, too. It wasn't just me."

"Did he retire?"

"He died. It was a lot like losing my father."

"So who helps you now?"

Stone shrugged. "Nobody. Well, Dino helps me."

"But he's junior to you, isn't he?"

"Yes, but he's more inside than I am. I think he defends me sometimes; I think it's made a difference, too."

"It's a funny situation, isn't it?"

"I guess. I can live with it, though. At least I get to keep doing what I like; I have enough rank to get good cases, and I have a good reputation as an investigator."

"I don't want to pry, but I worry about you sometimes. How are you doing on Sasha? I read the papers."

"The papers were accurate. It's a brick wall; very frustrating."

"Are you getting a lot of pressure from above? Political pressure, I mean?"

"So far, my commander has been able to keep the heat off Dino and me. The taxi murders diverted some attention from us at a good time, but they also took all the manpower we had on Sasha's case."

"Is that hurting your investigation?"

Stone sighed. "Not really; not much. The greater part of the legwork had already been done when the taxi shootings happened. We'd interviewed everybody who had anything to do with Sasha by that time. Dino's going over the reports now, just to be sure we haven't missed anything."

"What's going to happen on the Sasha investigation? I mean, what's likely to happen?"

"We'll get a tip," Stone said. "Eventually. That's how most cases are solved—never mind all the scientific stuff: fingerprints, DNA matching—most cases are solved because somebody finally tells us something."

Their eggs Benedict came, and they ate hungrily.

When the check came, Stone paid the waiter, then looked Cary in the eye. "Sometimes, in cases like this, the person waits a long time to come forward. Sometimes it's hard to do the right thing."

She kept his gaze for a moment, then looked down at his jacket and frowned. "Where do you buy your clothes?"

She wasn't going to talk to him; not yet, anyway. He glanced at the brown herringbone. "Different places. There are a couple of discount places downtown that have nice stuff, sometimes."

"I said I'd help you furnish the house; I think I'd better start by furnishing you."

"Okay," Stone said, "I guess I could use some furnishing."

"Come with me."

Stone followed her out of the restaurant. She led him briskly around the block to the corner of Seventy-second and Madison and into a handsome stone building. He had seen the place, but he had never been in. It wasn't the sort of place cops bought their clothes.

The store was a wonderland of beautiful things. She led him to the third floor, where she found a rack of tweed jackets. In seconds she had extracted one and helped him into it.

A salesman sidled up. "Our forty-two long fits you perfectly," he said. "That jacket won't require the slightest alteration."

Stone felt for the tag, but Cary ripped it off and handed it to the salesman. "Never look at price tags," she said. "That's not the way to shop. Buy what's right for you, and worry about the money later. That's what credit cards are for."

She found another jacket, then some trousers, then she started on the suits. He managed to hold her to two, but they were beautiful, he had to admit, and they did fit him perfectly. She shook his wallet out of the old jacket and handed the garment to the salesman. "Send this," she said. "He'll wear the plaid one."

"I guess I should get some shirts," Stone said.

"Downstairs," the salesman said, handing him a credit card chit to sign.

Stone followed instructions and didn't look at the amount. He tried to stop in the shirt department, but she pulled him away.

"They're wrong for you," she said. "We'll get those elsewhere." She hailed a cab. Shortly, they were in a Fifth Avenue department store; she guided him to a shop within the store. "These are English," she said, hauling out a stack of shirts from a shelf, "and they suit you." A dozen shirts later, they were in an Italian shoe store, trying on loafers and featherweight lace-ups.

By the time they reached Central Park, Stone felt like a new man. The mimosas still buzzed in his veins, and the clear, autumn air elated him. Autumn always seemed like the beginning of the year to Stone; New Year's was an anticlimax.

"You look wonderful in that jacket," Cary said.

"I feel wonderful in it," he replied. "I feel wonderful with you."

"That's the way you're supposed to feel," she said. They walked north along the Fifth Avenue side, enjoying the color in the trees, and, at Seventy-ninth Street, she led him from the park. "My place," she said.

The doorman didn't seem to recognize him. On her floor, he glanced at Sasha's door.

"Don't think about that," she said, pulling him into her apartment.

The place was a mirror image of Sasha's, and it was

beautifully put together—feminine, without being cloying, beautiful fabrics, good pictures, expensive things. "This is wonderful," Stone said. "You're hired as my decorator."

"You know the best thing about this apartment?" Cary asked.

"What's that?"

"It has a bedroom. And a bed."

"Oh. I'd better have a look at that."

"Yes, I think you'd better," she said, unbuckling his belt.

Later, when they fell asleep, exhausted, it was with his soft penis in her hand. He liked sleeping that way.

When he got home, the following evening, the Saturday mail awaited him. There was a letter from his bank:

Dear Mr. Barrington:

Just a reminder to let you know that your note is due at the end of the month. The note is, of course, adequately collateralized by your house, and I will be happy to renew it, but I must tell you that, with the softening market in large properties, the bank's new lending policy will require a substantial reduction of the principal when renewing. I might be able to persuade the loan committee to accept a reduction of $25,000. And, of course, there will be $4800 interest due."

The letter hit him like a blow to the belly. He'd borrowed the money to renovate the house, but the banker had promised to keep renewing until he had a buyer. Then he had another thought. He dug out the receipts for the clothing he had bought. The total came to nearly four thousand dollars.

Stone went into the bathroom and lost his lunch.

18

Stone was twenty minutes late to work. When he walked into the squad room, the place went quiet. Dino stood up from his desk and waved Stone toward the stairs.

"What's up?" Stone asked as they trotted up the steps together.

"Leary wants us in the conference room. There's brass here."

"Oh, shit," Stone said.

Down one side of the long table were arrayed the detective squad commander, Lieutenant Leary; Chief of Detectives Vincent Delgado, a slim, rather elegant man in his fifties; and an imposing black man Stone recognized from his photographs, who was wearing the well-pressed uniform of a deputy commissioner. Deputy commissioners were mayoral appointees. Stone didn't know the other man, who looked like a banker, in a pin-striped suit, white shirt, and sober necktie.

"Chief, you already know Barrington and Bacchetti," Leary said.

Delgado nodded, managing a tight smile.

"Commissioner Waldron, these are detectives second grade Barrington and Bacchetti," Leary said unnecessarily.

"I'm glad to meet you, men," Waldron said. "I've heard a lot about both of you."

"Oh, shit," Dino said under his breath, not moving his lips.

"Right," Stone whispered back. Waldron had been a hot assistant DA when he had joined the campaign staff of the mayor, and, after the election, he had been the mayor's first appointee to a law enforcement position. It was said Waldron had mayoral ambitions of his own, since the mayor had let it be known that he would not be running for a third term. Waldron had a reputation for meddling in police investigations.

"And, Detectives," Leary continued, "this is John Everett, special agent in charge of the New York office of the FBI."

Everett, expressionless, nodded sleepily.

"If you'll forgive me, gentlemen," Waldron said to Leary and Delgado, "I'll tell the detectives why we're here."

"Of course, sir," Leary said.

Delgado merely nodded.

Waldron turned to the detectives. "I want to forget what I've read in the reports and what I've read in the papers. I want to hear from you every step that has been taken in the Sasha Nijinsky investigation, from day one. From *minute* one. And don't leave anything out."

Goddamn Leary, Stone thought. If he'd given them a few hours' notice he could have put together some kind of presentation. Now he would have to wing it.

"From minute one," Waldron repeated. "Go."

"Sir," Stone began, "I was proceeding on foot down the west side of Second Avenue at approximately two A.M. on the night of the . . . occurrence. I was off duty. I happened to look up, and I witnessed the . . . Ms. Nijinsky's fall." He was still having trouble calling the event a crime and Nijinsky a victim.

"This actually happened?" Waldron interrupted. "The papers got it right?"

"Mostly, sir." He continued to relate the events of that night. When he got to the collision of the ambulance with the fire engine, Waldron started shaking his head.

"Jesus H. Christ," he said, "that's the goddamndest worst piece of luck I ever heard of."

"My sentiments exactly, sir," Dino said.

Leary and Delgado laughed.

"Go on," Waldron said.

Stone took the man through his and Dino's actions for the rest of the night, then asked Dino to describe the subsequent investigation by the detective squad. Neither detective referred to his notebook.

When they had finished, Waldron spoke again. "Detectives, have you left any avenue uninvestigated?"

"Sir," Stone said, "the detective squad of this precinct interviewed sixty-one witnesses, co-workers, and friends of Ms. Nijinsky and made more than eight hundred telephone calls, all within thirty hours of the occurrence. Since that time, Detective Bacchetti has reviewed each of the interview reports, and he and I have conducted a search of the home and business premises of the possible suspect, Van Fleet."

"Is Van Fleet still a suspect?" Waldron asked.

"Officially, of course, sir. But we haven't got a thing on him, except that he wrote Ms. Nijinsky a great many very polite letters."

"Do you have any other suspects?" Waldron asked.

"No, sir," Stone replied.

There was a brief silence in the room. Nobody seemed to have anything else to say.

Except the FBI man, Everett. "Why didn't you call the FBI?" he asked.

Stone turned to face Everett; he had felt this coming. "Because no federal crime has been committed," he replied. "As far as we know."

"How about kidnapping?" Everett asked.

Chief of Detectives Delgado spoke up. "The lady took a twelve-story dive," he said laconically. "What's to kidnap?"

"Good point," Waldron said.

Everett leaned forward. "Perhaps Detective Barrington would tell us about his terminal velocity theory," he said encouragingly.

Stone felt color creeping up his neck into his face.

"His *what* theory?" Delgado asked sharply.

"Terminal velocity," Stone said, clearing his throat. "It's just a theory, sir. There's nothing really to support it."

"I'd like to hear it anyway," Delgado said.

"So would I," echoed Waldron.

Leary rolled his eyes toward the ceiling.

Stone briefly explained what terminal velocity is and

what part it might have played in Sasha Nijinsky's fall.

No one spoke. No one took his eyes off Stone.

"Of course," Dino interjected suddenly, "the lady's gotta be dead. You don't fall twelve stories and write about it in your memoirs."

"We've treated this as a homicide from the beginning," Stone said.

"But you've no evidence of a homicide," Everett said, a little too smoothly. "In fact, the available evidence—the diary—points to a suicide attempt."

"In any case, the lady's dead," Delgado said irritably.

"But Detective Barrington doesn't think so," Everett replied. "Do you, Detective?"

Everybody turned back to Stone.

"I think it's . . . just possible she may be alive," Stone said uncomfortably.

"I think Detective Barrington thinks it's more than just possible," Everett said. "But what counts is, was she alive when she was taken from that ambulance?"

"She may have been," Stone said.

"We know she was alive at the scene of her fall, because of the videotape evidence Detective Barrington has told us about," said Everett, spreading his hands, the picture of reason. "And the ambulance collision occurred only minutes later."

"It's possible," Delgado said, glaring at Stone.

"All that matters to me, gentlemen," Everett said, "is that she may have been alive when she was taken. Kidnapped. Kidnapping, in the United States of America, is a federal crime."

"Granted," Waldron said. "But, surely, you see our position in treating this as a homicide?"

Everett nodded. "I'm not here for a jurisdictional dispute, Commissioner; honestly, I'm not. But your own chief of detectives has just admitted that Nijinsky may have been alive when she was taken, so I'm calling it kidnapping, for the purposes of investigation, and the FBI is, from this moment, on it. Any objections?"

No one said anything.

Everett stood up. "Well, if you'll excuse me, gentlemen, my purpose here is accomplished. I have an investigation to conduct." He shook hands with those on his side of the table, nodded to the two detectives, and left.

When Everett had gone, Delgado turned to Stone. "Nice going," he said. "Now we've got the feds on our backs."

"If you'll excuse me, sir," Stone said, "I'm glad to have them in. Maybe they'll stumble on something we haven't."

"That's all we need."

Waldron spoke up. "I'm inclined to agree with Detective Barrington," he said to Delgado. "If this case isn't solved, we can share the, uh . . . credit." He turned back to Stone and Dino. "Detectives," he said seriously, "I think you've done a first-class job on this, and I want you to know you have my support. Is there anything you need for your investigation? Anything at all? Just name it."

"We need a break," Dino said.

CHAPTER

19

Dino snatched a file off his desk. "Let's get out of here," he said to Stone.

Stone waited until they were in the squad car before speaking. "What do you think?"

"I think we're in the shit," Dino said.

"I don't know; Waldron seemed to be on our side. Said we'd done a first-class job, remember?"

"You trust Waldron?" Dino asked incredulously. "You're so fucking naive sometimes, Stone."

"Look, among the deputy commissioners, Waldron is the best of a bad lot. I mean, we could have drawn that guy who was in advertising before the mayor made him a DC."

"Waldron's a politician, and that makes him dangerous. And I can tell you Delgado is not happy with us for being

117

involved in something that gets Waldron's attention—plus, he blames us for the FBI."

"Come on, Dino, how can he blame us for that? We're lucky we got this far in our investigation without the feds stepping in. Delgado knows that."

"Delgado's Italian, like me," Dino said. "When there's bad news, Italians shoot the messenger, remember? Right now, 'Messenger' is tattooed right across your forehead and mine, buddy."

Stone shook his head. "I think you're overreacting. If we'd made some huge blunder in the investigation, then I think we really would be in trouble, but we haven't done that; we've run it by the book—well, mostly by the book—and we've covered all the bases."

"Well, we haven't covered our asses," Dino said. "The only way we can do that is by making a bust."

"By the way," Stone said, "where are we going?"

"To the network," Dino said, handing him the manila file. "Out of all the interview reports, this is the only one that looked worth doing again."

"Hank Morgan," Stone read from the file. "Makeup artist."

"Look down at the bottom of the sheet."

Stone read the last line. "Subject was nervous, wary, and gave only the briefest answers to questions, without elaboration." Most innocent people, Stone knew, tended to blabber to the cops when questioned, not clam up. There were those who didn't like cops, who were short with them, but this was interesting. "Did you call to say we were coming?" Stone asked.

"Nope," Dino replied.

"Good."

* * *

Hank Morgan was casually but elegantly dressed: Italian loafers, brown tweed trousers, a striped silk dress shirt open at the throat, a green cashmere sweater draped over the shoulders, the arms hanging loose. The hair was carefully barbered, the skin tan, the teeth white and even. A handsome character, Stone thought. And a woman, though just barely.

"I'll be the bad cop," Dino said through his teeth, as Morgan led them down the hall. "I hate dykes."

Morgan led them into a room lit by rows of small bulbs around a large mirror. A barber's chair was the only furniture.

"What can I do for you?" she asked, her eyes blinking rapidly.

"We're investigating the Sasha Nijinsky matter," Stone said. "We'd like to ask you some questions."

"I've already talked to two policemen," Morgan said combatively. "I don't feel much like talking anymore."

Dino was on her like a tiger. "Well, we didn't like your answers, *lady*," he snarled at her, "and I don't much care if you feel like talking or not."

"Dino . . . ," Stone began.

"This is an investigation into the disappearance, maybe the death of a human being that you knew and worked with, and we intend to find out what you knew about it," Dino continued, unabated. "We can do it up at the precinct, if you like."

Morgan appeared to wither under this barrage.

Stone tugged at an earlobe.

Dino caught the signal. "Where's the men's room?" he said to Morgan.

"Down the hall to your left," she replied.

"I thought you'd know," Dino shot back as he left the room.

When he had gone, Stone closed the door. "I'd like to apologize for my partner's conduct," he said to her gently. "He's under a lot of pressure on this case—we both are—and he sometimes gets a little worked up."

Morgan looked relieved. "I understand," she said. "It's been a strain on me, too."

Has it? Stone wondered. "I take it you knew Sasha quite well," he said. He had no reason to suppose that; it was a shot in the dark.

Morgan nodded, but did not speak.

"Did . . . " Stone stopped. Another stab. "Were you in love with her?" he asked softly.

Morgan nodded again, and tears rolled down her cheeks.

"I'm sorry," Stone said. "I know how hard all this must have been for you." Yet another stab. "Was Sasha in love with you?"

Morgan wiped a cheek and looked directly at him. "Yes," she said firmly.

"Did she tell you so?"

"She showed me," Morgan replied.

"How long had the two of you been . . . seeing each other?"

"A couple of months," Morgan said, drying another tear. She was composing herself now.

"And when was the last time you saw Sasha?"

"The night before she . . . disappeared." She was calm now, and ready to talk.

"Where did you see her?"

"At my apartment. We always met there."

"Did she stay the night?"

"Most of it. Sasha always left around four. She couldn't be seen . . . "

"I understand."

"Ms. Morgan, do you think Sasha might have been inclined to try to take her own life?"

"I . . . I don't know. She was up and down a lot. She'd have these highs, when nothing could get her down; then she'd sink into these depressions. They never lasted long, but they were intense. She could be difficult to be with during those times. Maybe, in the depths of one of those, she might have . . . impulsively . . . done something. I just don't know."

"Would you characterize these mood swings as manic-depressive?"

"I'm not sure. From what I know about that condition, people who have it are unable to function when they're depressed. Sasha could *always* function, and function brilliantly, no matter what her mood. She had a will of iron."

Stone looked Hank Morgan up and down. She was five nine or ten, a hundred and forty-five, with an athletic, even muscular build. She looked as though she worked out regularly. "Ms. Morgan," he asked, "where were you after midnight the night Sasha fell?"

"I was at home in bed," she replied firmly.

"Were you alone?"

Now Morgan looked away. "No."

"I think I'd better have the name of that person," Stone said.

"Is it absolutely necessary?"

"I'm sorry, but it is. I want you to know, though, that I'll do what I can to keep this information from becoming public. I understand your position."

"Her name is Chelsea Barton. She's a set designer here."

"I'll have to speak with her."

"Her office is the other side of the reception area, on this floor."

Dino came back into the room.

"I think we're about finished here," Stone said. "Thank you, Ms. Morgan. I very much appreciate your cooperation." Dino stepped back into the hall, and Stone followed, then stopped. He turned back to the woman. "Ms. Morgan, was Sasha seeing anyone else that you know of?"

Morgan flushed. "Yes, she was. A man. She would never tell me who, but I had the feeling it had been going on for a long time."

"Do you think it might have been someone she worked with?"

"I honestly don't know. Sasha didn't give much away."

"Thank you again."

On their way down the hall, Stone filled Dino in on his conversation with Hank Morgan.

Dino whistled. "So Sasha swung both ways, huh? How about that?"

"There was nothing in her diary to indicate it," Stone said.

"She had a lot to lose," Dino replied. "She wouldn't have written that down."

They found the office of Chelsea Barton. A rather dumpy young woman looked up from her desk as they knocked.

Stone started to introduce himself.

"Yes," Barton said, interrupting him. "I was with Hank Morgan. All night. Anything else?"

"Thank you," Stone said, "no."

Back in the car Dino turned to Stone. "So, if Morgan is in love with the gorgeous Sasha, what's she doing in the sack with Miss Beanbag the very next night?"

"That crossed my mind," Stone said.

"I think Morgan looks good for it. Pansies are always bashing each other's heads in with hammers, and all for love."

"Lesbians don't fit that mold."

"Still, you see the build on that bitch? Sasha was little, compared to her. I think Morgan could have tossed her, no problem."

"I think so, too. But how are you going to break that alibi? Miss Beanbag looked pretty tough to me."

"She was on the interview list, so we've got her address. I think I'll do a little checking into her whereabouts that night," Dino said. "Maybe I can place her somewhere else."

"You do that, and we might have something for Deputy Commissioner Waldron."

20

The phone was ringing as Stone reached his desk. He picked it up. "Hello."

"Detective Barrington?" a husky voice said.

"Yes, speaking."

"This is Hank Morgan."

"Yes, Ms. Morgan. Did you think of something else?"

"I . . . I lied to you, I'm afraid."

"How so?"

"I was at home alone the night Sasha fell. Chelsea wasn't with me. She said that to protect me, but I realize this is serious, and I don't want to involve her. I hope you'll forget that I didn't tell you the truth the first time; I'm telling you the truth now."

"All right, we'll forget your first statement and leave Chelsea out of it."

"Thank you."

"What time did you get home that night?"

"I worked on the evening news, so it would have been about eight thirty."

"Did anyone see you? The doorman, maybe?"

"I live in a walk-up in the West Village. There's no doorman."

"Anybody else? A neighbor?"

"No. There are only two apartments in the building, and my downstairs neighbor was on vacation."

"Did you go out again for any reason?"

"No. I read until about eleven, then I went to sleep."

"I see. Ms. Morgan, I'd like you to come up to the Nineteenth Precinct to be fingerprinted. It might help us eliminate you as a suspect."

She paused for a long time. "I don't think I want to do that," she said. "I've already talked to a lawyer, and he advised me not to cooperate any further than this."

"That's your right," Stone said. "But I have to tell you that the Supreme Court doesn't consider being fingerprinted to be self-incriminating. We may have to insist."

"I suppose that's your right," she replied. "But I haven't done anything wrong, and you don't have any real reason to suspect me. So I won't be having anything else to say."

"I'm sorry you've decided to do it this way, Ms. Morgan."

"Good afternoon, Detective Barrington." She hung up.

Stone told Dino about their conversation.

"Bingo!" Dino cried. "Let's go see Leary."

"Wait a minute," Stone said. "I just remembered something." He went to the evidence room, dug out Sasha Nijinsky's financial records, and began leafing through her checkbook.

"What are you looking for?" Dino asked.

"I remember some checks Sasha wrote. Here! One . . . two . . . three of them, all made out to Henrietta Morgan! The name meant nothing to me at the time." He totted up the amounts in his head. "Total of twenty thousand dollars over eight weeks, listed as loans. You know what this smells like, Dino?"

"Blackmail!" Dino yelled. "Miss Hank says, 'Pay me, Sasha, or I'll tell all!' Let's go see Leary!"

Leary beamed at them. "I knew good police work was going to break this case." He chortled. "Pick her up right now." He reached for the phone. "I'll call Delgado; he'll call Waldron."

"I don't think that's a good idea, Lieutenant," Stone said, "not yet, anyway. Let's get her up here and hear her story first."

"Get your asses out of here and bring in the dyke!" Leary said, dialing.

"This is insane!" Hank Morgan said, interrupting Stone in his reading of her rights. "You aren't handcuffing me!"

"If you can't afford an attorney, one will be appointed for you," Stone concluded. "I'm sorry about the cuffs; it's department policy." He took her raincoat from a hook on the wall and placed it over her shoulders. "Don't worry, no one here will see them."

"Let's go, lady," Dino said.

"I want to call my lawyer," she said shakily.

"You can call her from the precinct," Dino said. "Let's go."

Stunned into silence, Hank Morgan accompanied the two detectives out of the building and into their car.

"Is there anything you want to tell us before we get to the station?" Stone asked her.

Morgan shook her head. "I want my lawyer," she said.

"Uh, oh," Dino said as they pulled up to the entrance of the 19th Precinct. "What's this?"

"Leakiest precinct in the city," Stone said, slamming his fist against the dashboard in frustration.

A knot of reporters crowded the sidewalk. Television lights went on. Stone and Dino got Morgan out of the car and hustled her into the building, shoving the shouting reporters out of the way.

"No comment," Dino kept yelling.

"I want to call my lawyer," Morgan said, when they were safe from the howling mob.

"Just as soon as we've fingerprinted and photographed you," Stone said, unlocking her handcuffs.

She gave the fingerprints without further protest, then, while Stone had her photographed, Dino hand-carried the prints upstairs. Stone took Morgan into the squad room and put her in an empty cubicle, away from the stares of the other detectives.

Morgan put her face in her hands. "This is so humiliating," she said.

"I'm sorry it had to be this way," Stone replied, "but you've made it harder on yourself by refusing to cooperate."

"I want my lawyer *now*," she said.

Stone handed her the phone, and, hands shaking, she dialed a number. Stone noted that she didn't have to look it

•

up. He wondered how many innocent people knew their lawyers' phone numbers off the tops of their heads.

Fifteen minutes passed, and Dino came breathlessly into the cubicle and hauled Stone out.

"Listen to this," he said.

"Was one of her prints in Sasha's apartment?" Stone asked. It would be too good to be true.

"Better than that, pal—we've got a *palm* print—and on the *outside* of the sliding glass door to the terrace. We can put her on the terrace!"

A weak, warm feeling flooded through Stone. "Jesus Christ!" He exhaled. All the work, all the sweat had been worth it. He had not realized until that moment how afraid he had been of this case and what it might do to him. "Let's have another shot at her before her lawyer gets here," he said, heading back for the cubicle.

Morgan was sitting rigidly in the steel chair, her hands clenched in her lap.

"Listen to me, Ms. Morgan," Stone said, pulling up a chair. "You've already admitted to me that you and Sasha were having an affair, and that she was also having an affair with a man; that would make you pretty jealous, wouldn't it? We've got canceled checks showing that Sasha paid you twenty thousand dollars in less than two months; your palm print was found on the terrace that Sasha fell from. We've got all that, Ms. Morgan, and we're going to get more. Now, don't you think it's time you told us about it?"

Morgan's shoulders began to shake, and tears rolled down her face.

Stone thought it was the only moment she had looked

•

feminine since he had met her.

"Oh, God!" she moaned, "I want to tell you . . . "

"Excuse me, gentlemen," a rumbling voice said from behind them.

Stone and Dino turned to see a tall man in a beautiful overcoat standing there.

"My name is Carlton Palmer; I'm Henrietta Morgan's attorney; I know you won't mind if I consult with my client. Alone," he added for good measure.

The two detectives reluctantly gave up the field.

"Shit," Dino muttered. "She was going to confess. We had her in the palm of our hands, and that slick bastard had to show up."

"She had a right to see him, Dino," Stone said. "To tell you the truth, I'd have been uncomfortable with a confession made before her lawyer got here."

"She won't say another fucking word now," Dino complained. "We'll just have to work our fucking balls off, making the case. If we'd had that confession, you and I would have made detective first by tomorrow morning."

"Well, you're right about one thing," Stone commiserated. "She'll never say a word to us now."

Ten minutes later, Palmer came out of the cubicle. "Gentlemen," he said, "my client will answer your questions now."

21

They had moved to the conference room. Tape and video equipment was up and running. Leary had joined them for the big moment.

"I'd like to say something for the camera before you begin," the lawyer said.

Stone nodded.

He got up, walked around to where Hank Morgan sat, placed a fatherly hand on her shoulder, and spoke to the camera. "I am Carlton Palmer, the attorney representing Henrietta Morgan, and I would like this record to show that Miss Morgan is giving this statement voluntarily and of her own free will in a spirit of cooperation with the police." He returned to his seat.

Stone's hands were sweating. "State your full name and address and place of employment for the record," he said to Morgan.

"My name is Henrietta Maxine Morgan; I live at Seventy-one West Tenth Street in Manhattan. I am employed as a makeup artist by the news division of the Continental Network." Her voice quavered a bit, but she was calm.

"Ms. Morgan, have you been advised of your rights under the Constitution of the United States?"

"I have been."

"Are you making this statement voluntarily?"

"I am."

"Have you been subjected to any duress with regard to this statement?"

"No."

"Ms. Morgan, how long have you been employed by the Continental Network?"

"Just over three months."

"And when did you first meet Sasha Nijinsky?"

"Shortly after I joined the network. I did her makeup once, substituting for someone who was out sick, and she began asking for me."

"Did you and Ms. Nijinsky become friends?"

"Yes."

"How long ago?"

"We were on friendly terms from the beginning. We began to become . . . close about eight weeks ago."

"Did you, in fact, enter into a romantic relationship with Ms. Nijinsky?"

"Yes."

"A relationship of a sexual nature?"

Morgan gulped. "Yes."

"Were you in love with Ms. Nijinsky?"

"Yes."

"And was she in love with you?"

"Yes."

"Did she tell you she loved you, in so many words?"

"Yes. Many times."

"Were you aware that, during the same period Ms. Nijinsky was seeing you, she was also having an affair with a man?"

Morgan looked away for the first time. "Yes. She told me so."

"Did she tell you who this man was?"

"No."

"Did she give you any indication, any hint at all as to his identity?"

"No. She referred to him as 'What's-his-name.'"

That rang a bell from Sasha's diary. "How often did you see Ms. Nijinsky outside of working hours?"

"Two or three nights a week; sometimes four."

"Where did these meetings take place?"

"Either at my apartment or at hers."

"And when was the last occasion you saw Ms. Nijinsky?"

"The night before she disappeared."

"Where did this meeting take place?"

"At her apartment."

Stone paused. "Did you not tell me on a previous occasion that this meeting took place at *your* apartment?"

"I have no recollection of that," Morgan replied smoothly.

Why was she changing her story? What did it matter where that particular meeting took place? "Did anyone see you in Ms. Nijinsky's building that night?"

"The doorman saw me when we came in together. It must have been around nine o'clock. He was asleep when I left. That was around four in the morning."

"What did you and Ms. Nijinsky do that evening?"

"I helped her pack her things; she was moving to a new apartment in a day or two. We had a late dinner and drank a bottle of wine together." She paused. "We made love. It was a very happy evening."

"And when did you next see Ms. Nijinsky?"

"I never saw her again."

"We'll come back to that. You were taking money from Ms. Nijinsky, weren't you, Ms. Morgan?"

Morgan frowned. "*Taking* money? Certainly not. I borrowed some money from her, and only at her insistence. I was remodeling my apartment, and I ran out of cash. I had some six-month CDs that were not due to mature for another three months, and Sasha said it would be crazy to cash them and lose the interest, and that she wanted to loan me the money to finish the project. It came to twenty thousand dollars out of the eighty that I spent on the project."

This was not going the way Stone had meant it to. "You want us to believe that Ms. Nijinsky just *loaned* you the money— you, a person she had only recently met?"

"I don't much care what you believe," Morgan said coldly. "The money was a loan; I insisted on giving Sasha a promissory note for the amount, although she wouldn't accept interest."

"You're aware that we have Ms. Nijinsky's financial records and that we can search them for this note?" He was faltering now. Why hadn't he gone through those records more carefully?

"That's fine with me. I have a copy, if you need it."

"Ms. Morgan, after the disappearance of Sasha Nijinsky, police experts removed a palm print from the outside of the sliding glass door of her apartment's terrace. That palm print has since been identified as yours. On the *outside* of the door, Ms. Morgan, on the terrace from which Ms. Nijinsky fell. How do you explain that?"

"I told you that I had seen Ms. Nijinsky many times over the past weeks, often at her apartment. In fact, I think I remember when I could have left that palm print. On our last night together, Sasha and I took our wine out onto the terrace. There was no furniture out there, but it was a nice evening, and there was one break in the surrounding buildings where you could see some city skyline. I got something in my shoe, and I leaned against the sliding door while I shook out the shoe. I'm sure that must be the palm print you're referring to."

Leary, sitting next to Stone, was becoming restive.

Stone hurried. "Ms. Morgan, when Sasha told you she was seeing a man—at the same time she was making love to you—how did you feel about that?"

"I didn't like it much, at first, but, as we became closer, I realized that Sasha's sexuality was truly dual—not like mine. When you've gone through what most lesbian women go through to live their lives openly, you become more tolerant of other people's desires. There was a part of Sasha that liked sex with men, and I soon knew I couldn't change that. I told her I understood that, and the subject ceased to be a sore point between us."

This simple, rational explanation stopped Stone. He turned to Leary. "Lieutenant, do you have any questions for Ms. Morgan?"

Leary shook his head slowly. His face was red.

"Detective Bacchetti?"

"Yes, I have a question," Dino replied. His voice was cold and hard.

Stone wanted to stop him, but he knew he could not.

"This is the way it happened, *Miz* Morgan," Dino spat at her. "You fell madly in love with Sasha Nijinsky, and then you found out she was screwing a man, and that drove you crazy, didn't it?" He continued before she could answer. "So then, to get back at Sasha, you started blackmailing her, didn't you? Demanding money not to talk to the tabloids about her swinging both ways. And when she got tired of paying and told you so, there was a fight, and you heaved her off that terrace, didn't you? Isn't that the way it happened, *Miz* Morgan?"

Hank Morgan leaned forward and looked directly at Dino. "You're insane," she said.

Carlton Palmer spoke up, his deep voice resonating around the room. "Gentlemen," he said, "I think that will be all."

22

*L*eary kept Stone and Dino in the conference room. His face was very red now. "I thought you told me we were going to get a confession," he said, glaring at Dino.

Dino spread his hands. "Boss, how could I know for sure? It felt that way when Palmer said she'd talk to us."

"It did feel that way, Lieutenant," Stone interjected.

"That's a completely unusable tape," Leary said. "Palmer might as well have written and directed it himself."

"She's dirty, Lieutenant," Dino said. "She did it. I can feel it."

"I think so too," Leary said, "but you're going to have to fit her up for it."

"What?" Stone said, alarmed.

"I mean, you're going to have to prove it, get some evidence," Leary said, correcting himself.

"We'll get it," Dino said firmly. "I mean, shit, Lieutenant, we just got on this bitch. Give us a little time, okay?"

"Okay," Leary said. "I'll give you twenty-four hours to come up with one piece of evidence that will put her in Nijinsky's apartment on that night."

"Lieutenant," Stone said, worried now, "that's unreasonable. Morgan is a whole new development in this case—a promising one, I'll grant you, but we're going to need some time."

"You got it," Leary said. "Twenty-four hours." He turned and walked from the room.

Dino flopped down in a chair. "What now?"

"We'd better get going, don't you think?"

Dino nodded. "Okay, I'll check Nijinsky's records for the promissory note from Morgan."

"I'll check out Morgan's address, see if anybody saw her that night. What are you going to do after you check the records? It won't take you very long."

Dino thought for a minute. "Shoot myself, if the note is there," he said.

Stone drove downtown faster than he usually drove, resisting the temptation to using the flashing light and siren. He parked in front of a fire hydrant on West Tenth Street and put down the visor to ward off tickets.

Hank Morgan lived in a handsome brownstone that had been divided into two duplexes; he wondered how she could afford it. Well, hell, he was only a cop and he lived in a whole brownstone in Turtle Bay. Must be her daddy's money. He rang the second bell, the one that said VINCENT.

"Yes?" a woman's voice said over the intercom.

"Good morning, I'm Detective Barrington, NYPD. May I speak to you for a moment, Ms. Vincent?"

A pause. "All right, but I want to see a badge through the peephole."

"Of course."

She buzzed him through the outer door, and he held his badge so she could scrutinize it.

She opened the door but kept the chain on. "How about some ID with a photograph?" she said warily.

Stone handed his ID wallet through the opening.

She closed the door, unhooked the chain, and let him in. "Sorry about that, but you can't be too careful," she said.

Ms. Vincent was a pleasingly plump woman in an apron. "I was just about to have some coffee. Can I offer you some?"

"Thanks," Stone said. "I'd like that." He welcomed the opportunity to stretch out his visit.

She led him into the kitchen and gestured for him to take a seat at the breakfast table. When she had poured them both a cup, she joined him.

"What can I do for you?" she said.

"I want to talk with you about your upstairs neighbor," Stone said.

Ms. Vincent's eyebrows went up. "Really? Is Morgan in some kind of trouble?"

"She's helping us with an investigation, and the credibility of witnesses is always important. Also, I wanted to see if there was anything you could add to her information."

"Sure."

He took her back to the night of Sasha Nijinsky's fall. "Did you see Ms. Morgan at all that evening?"

Ms. Vincent thought for a moment. "We were in Bermuda," she said. "My husband's sister lives there, and we go at least once a year."

"Did anyone stay in your apartment while you were gone?"

She shook her head. "Nope."

"How well do you know Hank Morgan?"

"Not very well. We set up this place as condominiums four years ago with some friends. Then the friends got transferred, and they sold the place to Morgan about three months ago."

"Did you know Hank Morgan before that?"

"Nope. Neither did our friends; a real estate agent found her. I was a little worried at first. Shit, I'm still worried."

"Why?"

"Have you met Ms. Morgan?"

"Yes."

"Then I don't have to tell you she's a lesbian."

"No. She was quite frank about it."

"Well, it's not just that she's a lesbian—hell, I don't have anything against gays in general—it's that she's so . . . *involved*."

"Involved in what?"

"Well, she's apparently in two or three organizations about gay rights, and something to do with AIDS—you know those people who did that sit-in in St. Patrick's Cathedral?"

"I know the group."

"Well, she's always doing things like that; she's a real activist, which is, all too often, another way of saying 'pain in the ass.'"

"Why does that bother you?"

"She's always having meetings upstairs, and, believe me, there are some pretty weird people at those meetings. My God, there have been women in this house who should be playing pro football! It gives me the willies. I'm here by myself a lot; my husband travels in his work."

"Have these people behaved oddly toward you?"

"No, it's not that. I'm not really afraid of being raped, I guess. It's just that I'm an Italian girl from Queens, a Catholic, and I'm nervous about things like that. I was brought up to be nervous about things like that."

"Did you ever recognize any of Ms. Morgan's visitors?"

Ms. Vincent grinned. "Yeah, I recognized Sasha Nijinsky, once."

"Was she here for a meeting?"

"Nope, she was alone. I guess that means Sasha was a dyke, too, huh?"

"How often did you see her here?"

"Only once, and then through the peephole. It was her, though. She and Morgan were holding hands." She gave a little shudder.

"Do you remember the date you saw her here?"

Ms. Vincent shook her head. "Not exactly. Must have been a month or so ago."

Stone finished his coffee. "Do you know any of Ms. Morgan's other friends?"

"Nope. We don't socialize. I mean, we're polite to each other, but it's obvious we have absolutely nothing in common, except this house."

"Has Ms. Morgan been doing some work on her place?"

"I'll say she has! She's had builders in the house almost since the day she moved in; she must have done something pretty major to her place. They've stopped coming, though; they must be finished." She paused. "Did I mention that Morgan has a gun?"

"No, you didn't."

"I saw it when she moved in. I ran into her on the front steps—the first time I'd met her—and she was carrying a cardboard box full of stuff, and right on top was this pretty good-sized pistol in a holster. She made some joke about how you can't be too careful in New York."

Stone stood up. "Well, thank you for your help, Ms. Vincent."

"Wouldn't you like another cup?" She seemed anxious for company.

"Thanks, but I have a lot to do today."

Stone left the building and walked up and down both sides of the street. He checked at a bar, a dry cleaner, and a shoe repair shop; all of them were acquainted with Hank Morgan, but nobody had seen her on the night of Sasha's disappearance. He checked his notebook for the home phone number of the doorman at Sasha's old building, called him, and ascertained that Morgan had been there before Sasha's fall. The doorman hadn't seen Morgan that night. Discouraged, he drove back to the precinct.

Dino was at his desk, looking pleased with himself.

"There wasn't any promissory note," he said, grinning. "Morgan lied to us."

"Not necessarily," Stone replied. "Nijinsky might have kept them someplace else."

"Nah," Dino said. "She kept perfect records, and they were perfectly complete. If Morgan had given her a note, that's where it'd be. What did you come up with?"

Stone gave an account of his investigation. "The downstairs neighbor was on vacation, like Morgan said. The lady doesn't like lesbians, but she had nothing to say that would have incriminated Morgan. I had the feeling she wished she'd had something to tell me."

"Morgan's our killer," Dino said. "I can feel it in my bones."

"I can't feel it in mine, Dino. I know how bad we need a bust on this one, but Morgan's just not it. The lady's clean, except maybe on a weapons charge. The neighbor saw a pistol, but Morgan may have a permit."

"I'll check on that, but, take my word for it, the lady's no lady," Dino said. "And she's dirty."

23

On his way home, Stone was stopped in his tracks by a headline in the *Post*: ARREST IN SASHA CASE! He grabbed a copy.

Henrietta "Hank" Morgan, 32, a makeup artist at the Continental Network and a leading activist in lesbian-rights demonstrations, was taken in handcuffs to the 19th Precinct this morning and questioned for more than three hours about the disappearance of TV anchorwoman Sasha Nijinsky. In what a police source described as a "breakthrough" in the investigation, Morgan is reported to have given a detailed statement on videotape, while her lawyer, Carlton Palmer, was present. While the NYPD has not disclosed the contents of the tape, a source has said, "This all but wraps up the investigation." The source would not reveal what the NYPD thinks has become of Sasha.

Ace criminal trial lawyer Palmer said, in a telephone interview at press time, "My client is innocent of any wrongdoing, and the police know that. This entire episode is a perversion of justice."

Morgan, the daughter of a prominent Pennsylvania manufacturer, has been in and out of a dozen makeup jobs in the film and television industry over the past ten years and is known to have been Sasha Nijinsky's personal choice as her makeup artist at the Continental Network.

The story made Stone grind his teeth. The precinct seemed to be leaking from every pore, and whoever had given the *Post* the story had either not known what he was talking about or had deliberately misled the newspaper. There was going to be hell to pay.

The phone was ringing as he entered the house, tripping over a number of boxes in the hallway. The dentist in the professional suite downstairs received packages for him when he was at work and put them inside the front door.

Dino was on the phone. "Leary wants us downtown at the DA's office tomorrow morning at nine."

"What's going on?"

"He didn't say."

A thought struck Stone. "I'm scheduled for a department physical tomorrow morning."

"If you want, I'll do the meeting, you get checked out."

Stone thought for a moment. "I'd better be there, I think. I don't much like the sound of it."

"You seen the *Post?*"

"Yeah. Who do you think is leaking to the press?"

"Could be anybody."

"I guess so."

"I'll see you tomorrow morning." Dino hung up.

Stone turned his attention to the boxes in the front hall. A glance at the labels told him what they were. Shit, he had intended to cancel the clothes orders. How could they have gotten them here so fast? Furious at himself and annoyed by being called to the DA's office for no apparent reason, he ripped through the day's mail and nearly threw away an invitation, thinking it some sort of classy junk mail. It was for dinner on Saturday, at the apartment of Hiram Barker. That should be an interesting evening, he thought. He rang the number, got an answering machine, and accepted, adding that he would bring a date, if that was all right. Well, he thought, sighing, at least he'd be able to dress well for the occasion.

They were at Elaine's, at a small table all the way in the back. It was a crowded night, as usual, and Lauren, the singer–piano player, was straining to be heard above the din.

"Want to go to dinner at Hi Barker's on Saturday night?" he asked Cary.

She nearly choked on her scotch. "No kidding?"

"No kidding. The invitation came in today's mail."

"You're really coming up in the world. Dinner at Barker's is a hot ticket."

"I interviewed him about Sasha, and he said come to dinner sometime. I thought it was just the usual chat."

"I am definitely available," she said. "Now, what am I going to wear?"

"I don't have any problem about what to wear," he said. "All that stuff we ordered came today. You know what you made me spend?"

She waved away his question. "My daddy always said, 'Buy the things you want, and then figure out how to pay for them. Debt is a great motivator.'"

Stone laughed. "Well, I guess I'd better get motivated."

"Come on, sweetheart, that's what credit cards are for. How do you think everybody else in this town dresses?"

"I never did it that way. I never bought anything on a credit card that I couldn't pay for at the end of the month."

"A very stuffy attitude."

"A very necessary one, when you're on a cop's salary."

"I've been meaning to talk to you about that."

"About my salary?"

"About making a lot more money than you are. You've got a law degree, after all; why don't you use it?"

"I never took the bar exam."

"How about a—"

"I know, a cram course. You're as bad as Elaine. She's been at me about that."

"She's right. You're a highly intelligent man, and a highly handsome one, too, I might add. That counts for more than you might think, and not just with women."

"So, I could just quit the force and live on my looks?"

She laughed. "If it were up to me, you could. Does the practice of law repel you so much?"

"Look, I'm thirty-eight years old. I can't just get in line at the big firms with this year's grads and expect to get taken on. 'So, Mr. Barrington, what have you been doing with yourself in the fifteen years between getting your law degree and passing the bar?' 'Oh, I've been arresting drug dealers and investigating murders and other sordid crimes.' 'Wonderful, that experience will stand you in good stead in our estate planning department. Will a hundred thousand a year be enough?'"

She laughed again. "There are other facets of the law besides estate planning, you know."

"Sure there are. You know which ones I'd be qualified for? I'll tell you; I'd be qualified to hang around the criminal courts picking up burglary defenses, drug busts, and drunk driving cases. That's what ex-cops who are lawyers do—they go to night school, get a law degree, and, when they retire, they pick up an extra income by leaning on their old buddies on the force and in the DA's office to go easy on the scum they're defending."

"You underestimate yourself," she said. "Still, that's an endearing quality in a world where overconfidence is a way of life."

"Let's order," Stone said, picking up a menu.

"I think I'd like you for dinner," Cary said.

"Let's start with a Caesar salad, and go on to the osso buco," he said. "Then we can have each other for dessert."

"I always have room for dessert," she said.

And she did. Stone lay panting in the darkness when she had finished—spent, but still full of desire for her. He had never felt anything quite like it. He was in love with her, but he had been in love before. It was obsession, and that was foreign to him.

She wrapped herself around him. "That was delicious," she breathed, kissing him behind the ear. "I'll want more soon."

"You'll kill me," he panted, "but I can deny you nothing."

"Don't even try," she said.

24

*T*he meeting took place in the district attorney's private conference room, but the DA himself didn't attend. Al Hagler, the chief prosecutor, sat at the end of the table.

Stone had the distinct feeling that this room had not been chosen just because it was available; Hagler believed in effect, and the venue added authority to his position. It was just as significant that the DA was not present, though his presence was felt. The proceedings, whatever they were, had his tacit support, but, this way, he could not be personally tainted by the outcome. It was interesting, too, that Deputy Commissioner Waldron was not in attendance, nor was Chief of Detectives Delgado. It was just Hagler, Leary, Dino, and Stone.

"What have you most recently uncovered?" Hagler asked the room at large.

Leary nodded at Dino.

"There is no promissory note in Nijinsky's files, although they seem complete in every other respect," Dino said. "And Morgan has no gun permit, nor has she ever applied for one."

"Good," Hagler said, looking pleased.

"Why good?" Stone asked. "Just because there is no note in Nijinsky's files doesn't mean it never existed, and what does Morgan's owning a pistol have to do with anything? Nijinsky wasn't shot."

"How do you know that?" Leary asked.

"I saw her," Stone replied. "I didn't see a bullet wound."

"She was covered in dirt, wasn't she?"

"Yes."

"And how long did you see her for?"

"A few seconds."

"Hardly time for a postmortem," Hagler chimed in.

"I heard no gunshot either," Stone said.

"Whether Nijinsky was shot is not relevant to this meeting," Hagler said.

"Just what is the purpose of this meeting?" Stone asked.

"I just wanted to hear from you and Detective Bacchetti before proceeding."

"Proceeding with what?"

Hagler reached into an inside pocket and tossed a document onto the table.

Stone picked it up. "A search warrant for Morgan's apartment? What are we supposed to look for?"

"Anything that might relate to the Nijinsky case," Hagler said.

"On what basis did you get the warrant?" Stone persisted.

"The basis don't matter to you," Leary spoke up. "You

just execute the warrant, you and Dino, right?"

Stone shrugged. "Yes, sir."

"Detective Barrington has a physical at ten o'clock," Dino said.

Stone looked at him, surprised. "I can postpone," he said.

"No, no, that's important," Leary said. "You go on and get examined so we can get you restored to full duty." He turned to Dino. "You pick up a uniformed team and conduct the search."

"I'll send an assistant DA with you," Hagler said. "I'd like one of my people on the spot."

"We won't need you further, Barrington," Leary said, looking at his watch. "You go see the doctor."

Stone looked around the table. Everyone seemed to be avoiding his gaze. "All right," he said, standing up. "I'll see you back at the precinct, Dino."

Dino nodded without looking at him.

Stone took his leave feeling shunned, shut out. What was going on?

The doctor took his time getting around to the knee. "Strip down to your shorts," he said. He took Stone's blood pressure, listened to his heart and lungs, looked into his ears, eyes, and mouth, checked his vision and hearing, and a nurse took blood and urine samples. Only then did the doctor turn his attention to the knee. "Swelling seems to be gone," he said, feeling the joint in a gingerly fashion.

"I hardly notice it anymore," Stone replied, not quite truthfully.

"Stand up and give me five half knee bends," the doctor said.

Stone complied, clenching his jaw against possible pain. The exercise went well.

"Now give me five deep knee bends."

This was harder, but Stone managed it. The knee was hurting a little now.

"Now give me five half knee bends on the left leg."

This seemed extreme to Stone, but, again, he managed. Now the knee hurt like hell.

"Get dressed," the doctor said.

"What do you think?" Stone asked, pulling on his trousers.

"You've healed nicely."

"So, I'm restored to duty?"

"Oh, I expect so, but that's not my decision, of course. I'll just make my report; you'll hear from your commander."

"How long?"

"He'll have my report by the first of the week."

"So long?"

"I'll dictate it today; getting it typed is the problem. We've taken some staff cuts this year."

Stone got dressed and called the precinct. Dino wasn't back yet. He went down to the street and hailed a cab. When he arrived at Hank Morgan's building, Dino's unmarked car and a squad car were still outside, and the downstairs door was propped open. Stone ran up the stairs.

The niceties had not been observed. The search warrant was taped to the door, which had been opened with a sledge-hammer; the jamb was splintered, and the apartment was a mess. Stone walked through the disarrayed living room and followed the sound of voices to a beautifully designed kitchen. Dino, the assistant DA, and two uniforms sat at the kitchen table, drinking coffee. Knives, silverware, and kitchen implements were scattered around the floor.

"Hey, Stone!" Dino called. "You want some coffee?"

"No thanks. You really tore up this place, didn't you?"

"And look what we found!" Dino crowed, dangling a pistol from his finger by the trigger guard. "Three fifty-seven Magnum, and loaded, too."

"What else?"

"No copy of a promissory note."

"So?"

"And I'll bet she won't be able to come up with it when it counts."

"You all finished here, then?"

"Just about. We'll finish our coffee."

There was a noise from the living room, and Stone turned to see Hank Morgan standing in the doorway, the search warrant in her hand.

"What the hell is going on here?" she demanded, her voice shaking with anger.

"A legal and proper search," Dino said, standing up. "You got the warrant right there."

Morgan turned to Stone, as if she expected she might be able to reason with him. "Just what are you looking for, for Christ's sake?"

Stone shook his head. "I just got here myself, Ms. Morgan, but, I assure you, the search is legal and proper. I'm sorry about the mess."

"So, Officers," she said with withering contempt, "did you find anything? A joint, maybe? Or did you plant some cocaine?"

"We don't plant stuff in searches," Dino said, "but we did find this." He held up the pistol.

"That's mine," she said.

"And do you have a permit for it?"

She started to speak, then stopped herself. "I want to call my lawyer," she said.

"You can do that at the precinct," Dino said. He walked over and handed her another warrant. "Right now, you are under arrest for the possession of a firearm without a permit." He began to read her her rights.

Morgan turned to Stone again. "This can't be happening," she said, as if she expected him to make everything all right.

"I'm sorry, but it is happening," Stone replied. He lowered his voice. "And I'd advise you not to say anything further until you've seen your lawyer."

Downstairs, Stone watched as the patrolmen bundled Morgan, now handcuffed, into the squad car.

"You coming back to the precinct?" Dino asked, his hand on the car's door handle.

"Not right now," Stone said.

"How'd the physical go?"

"Okay, I think. He said I'm okay."

"Glad to hear it."

"Dino, where'd you get the arrest warrant for the weapons charge?"

"Hagler had that, too. He came up with it right after you left."

Stone nodded.

Dino got into the unmarked car and drove away.

Stone walked briskly down the street to the corner drugstore and found a phone. He got the number from information, and, when he told the secretary who he was, she immediately put him through.

"Hello, Detective Barrington?"

"Mr. Palmer, Hank Morgan has been arrested on a weapons charge. If I were you, I'd get up to the precinct without delay."

There was a stunned silence from Palmer's end of the line.

"Good-bye," Stone said.

"Thank you, Detective," Palmer managed to sputter before Stone hung up.

Stone walked slowly up Sixth Avenue, not looking for a cab yet. He felt something of the traitor, but he had wanted to do something to redress the balance. He was in no hurry to get to the precinct. He didn't want to be involved in what was going to happen there.

CHAPTER

25

In spite of his lengthy walk, Stone got to the precinct before Morgan's lawyer did. Dino's desk was empty.

"Dino's got the dyke in interrogation room three," a detective at a nearby desk told Stone.

Three had a two-way mirror. Stone walked hurriedly down the hall and let himself quietly into the adjacent viewing room, which was empty. He sat down on a folding chair and took in the scene next door. Morgan was seated at the steel table facing the mirror, with Dino and the ADA on either side of her. She sat rigidly in the uncomfortable chair, gripping the arms. Her knuckles were white. Tears streamed down her face. A tape recorder was on the table.

Stone looked at his watch. She would have been in the interrogation room for nearly an hour. Where was Palmer?

"I want my lawyer," Morgan sobbed.

"You already had your lawyer," Dino replied, "and now you're going to talk to me."

"I have nothing to say to you," Morgan said adamantly, her voice quavering.

Stone could tell she was near breaking. Anything could happen now.

"We've got you cold on the weapons possession charge," Dino said. "That's five to ten, and you won't get sent to a country club. You'll be in there with all the other bull dykes—the muscle freaks, the murderers."

"I have nothing to say," Morgan nearly screamed.

"Let's put the weapons thing aside for the moment," Dino said, his voice kinder. "Let's talk about Sasha."

"I don't want to talk about Sasha," Morgan said. Her head sagged forward until her chin touched her chest. "I don't want to talk about anything."

Dino leaned forward and lowered his voice.

Stone strained to hear him over the speaker.

"Look, nobody's saying you murdered Sasha; I know you loved her, and you wouldn't hurt her on purpose. It was an accident, I know that. You just had a little tussle, and Sasha fell, that's all. You must have felt terrible."

To Stone's astonishment, Morgan nodded slowly. Her face was shiny with tears, and she made no effort to wipe them away.

"That's it," Dino said soothingly, "let it all come out; you're going to feel a lot better when you tell me about it."

Morgan continued to nod but said nothing.

"Look, Hank, tell me about it, and I guarantee you won't do any time. You had a tussle, and Sasha fell; no judge is going to send you to prison."

At the word *prison*, Morgan's body jerked convulsively. "I don't want to go to prison," she said.

Stone stared at her. The woman was starting to come apart; in another minute she would plead to the Kennedy assassination, if Dino wanted her to.

"I won't let them send you to prison," Dino said, "if you'll just tell me the truth, tell me what happened. It was Sasha's fault, wasn't it?"

Morgan broke down now. The sobbing shook her body, and she made a terrible keening noise. She grabbed hold of Dino's forearm. "I'll say anything you want," she wailed, "just don't send me to prison."

"All right," Dino said, "I'm going to tell you what it was like, and we're going to write it down." He handed her a pen and shoved a legal pad in front of her.

Stone began to feel ill. He wanted to pick up a chair and throw it through the mirror. Then the door to the interrogation room opened, and Lieutenant Leary walked in, accompanied by Carlton Palmer.

"That will be quite enough of this!" Palmer shouted, going to Morgan's side and putting an arm around her. "You've got a lot of nerve pulling this sort of stunt!" he yelled at Dino. "I'll have your badge before I'm done."

"Aw, go fuck yourself, Counselor," Dino said, and walked out of the room, slamming the door.

Stone found him pacing up and down alongside his desk in the squad room.

"Two more minutes!" Dino said, slamming his fist into his palm. "Two more fucking minutes, and I'd have had her!"

"Come on, Dino," Stone said. "It would never have stood up; you know that. She'd have recanted on the stand, and the jury would have believed her."

"I've still got her for the gun, though," Dino said. "I'll nail her for that. I won't let the DA deal on it either. I'll send her up for it."

"Dino, stop it. You're dreaming. You can't even convince *me* she had anything to do with Nijinsky, so how is the DA going to convince a grand jury, let alone get a conviction? The woman had nothing to do with it." A hard voice behind him caused Stone to spin around.

"Horseshit," Leary said. "You better get with the program, Barrington, or the world's gonna fall on you."

"You mean Deputy Commissioner Waldron?"

"And the chief of detectives, and the district attorney, and *me*, and the whole world. We've got a chance for a good bust on this one, after you've fucked around getting nowhere all this time, and you'd better not get in the way of it."

Stone felt anger rush through him. "That woman had nothing to do with Nijinsky's fall, and you're not going to prove she did. If I thought you could make a jury believe it, I'd testify for the defense myself."

"If you pull something like that," Leary said, his voice low and cold, "I'll take you out in the alley and shoot you myself." The lieutenant turned and walked away.

Stone turned to Dino. "What about you? Is that how you feel?"

"I'll hold you while he pulls the trigger," Dino said, his voice shaking.

CHAPTER

26

As Stone trudged up the front steps of the Turtle Bay house, his downstairs tenant, dressed in a white nylon coat, came out of the professional suite and caught up with him.

"Mr. Barrington?"

"Hello, Dr. Feldstein," Stone said.

Feldstein was a short, stocky, pink-faced man in his late sixties. Stone had always liked him, not least because he had overlooked chronic problems with the downstairs plumbing in return for a reasonable rent. Feldstein thrust an envelope at Stone.

"What's this?"

"It's my notice of leaving, Mr. Barrington. Thirty days, as my lease requires. I'm sorry I couldn't give you more notice, but my wife's recent illness has made me decide to retire. We're moving to Venice, Florida, next month."

The news struck Stone like a spear in the ribs. That was twelve hundred dollars a month of income gone, and he knew he couldn't rent the place again without major improvements, which he could not afford. "I'm sorry to hear you're going, Dr. Feldstein. You've always been a good tenant."

"And you a good landlord, like your great-aunt before you," Feldstein said.

"I wish you and your wife a happy retirement in Florida."

"She'll like the sunshine; she always has."

They both seemed at a loss for words for a moment, then Feldstein shook Stone's hand and walked back down the front steps.

Stone let himself into the house and tossed Feldstein's letter onto the front hall table with the mail. Nothing but bills there, and he didn't bother opening them. He had a nearly overwhelming urge to call Cary; he needed desperately to talk with somebody, but he couldn't forget that technically, at least, Cary was press, and he couldn't let his thoughts escape in that direction. Normally, Dino would be the one to talk to, but he and Dino were on opposite sides this time. He wished his father were still alive.

He changed into jeans and a work shirt and went down to the kitchen. He had hardly cooked anything since the room had been completed, and now all he could manage in his mood was to microwave some frozen lasagna. He had a bourbon while he waited for the oven to do its work. He felt a curious numbness, a distance from reality. Not even the loss of his income-producing tenant, on top of everything else, could penetrate. He simply felt nothing. When the microwave beeped, he took out the lasagna and ate it immediately, in spite of the instructions to let it sit for five minutes. His was a simple, animal hunger, and he didn't care what he was eating or how it tasted. It was like taking aspirin to make a headache go away. You don't enjoy the aspirin.

He finished the meal and put his plate in the dishwasher, then poured himself another bourbon and went into the study. The room was spotlessly clean now, and an air cleaner was running to remove the dust caused by the constant sanding by his helpers for the past week.

The bookshelves stood empty and bare of finish, ready for varnish, the first of ten coats he planned. Tomorrow, the helpers would come back to sand again. He opened a gallon can of varnish, selected a brush, climbed the ladder, and started at the very top, spreading the sealer with long, straight strokes. It was simple, mindless work, the sort that he needed for thinking. He let his mind wander at will over the events of the past days.

Stone knew he was not the first honest policeman to find himself in this position. When a police department had a major crime on its hands, especially one where the victim was a celebrity, what it needed was an arrest—preferably, but not necessarily, of the actual perpetrator. As time passed without a resolution of the crime, pressure increased on the department to produce results, and after a while the pressure could become too much for certain of its members. Assignments were at stake—promotions, careers, pensions—and policemen, just like everybody else, would finally act to protect themselves. Stone reckoned that most of the innocent people in prison had been sent there by police officers and prosecutors who reasoned that these victims were, after all, probably guilty of *something*, and better a conviction of an innocent person than no conviction at all.

He had seen it happen, but always from a distance. Now he was involved, whether he liked it or not, and he had a decision to make: he could keep his mouth shut and let Dino, Leary, and their superiors try to railroad Hank Morgan; or he could speak up—go directly to the mayor or the newspapers and create a stink. The first course would protect his job, his career, and his pension; the second would subject him to the contempt that came to any policeman who went against his partner and his department. He would be transferred to some hellish backwater, shunned, ridiculed, perhaps even set up to be killed—sent first through some door with death waiting on the other side. It had happened before. Most of all, he would be separating himself from the work to which he had devoted his whole adult life. He would be a man alone, with enemies, and with no friends or support. It was the law of the cop jungle, and no man could last long on the force when he was subjected to it. It was time for him to decide if he was, after all these years, a cop.

The doorbell rang, causing him nearly to topple from the high ladder. He climbed down, moving carefully, cautious of the bourbon inside him. He went to the front door.

Dino stood there. He was dressed to kill in a new suit, obviously on his way to some girl. "We got to talk," he said.

"Come on in." Stone led him to the study. "The booze is in the kitchen. I've got wet varnish going here; I can't stop." He climbed back up the ladder and started to paint again.

Dino came back with something in a glass with ice. "What are you going to do?" he asked. He didn't have to explain; he knew Stone understood the situation.

"I don't know," Stone replied, brushing on the varnish.

"You know what's going to happen, you go against the grain on this one."

"I know."

Dino still hadn't drunk from his glass. "Stone, you got a lot of time in. A little more than five years, you can walk away with half pay and go practice law, you know?"

"I know."

"You and I got four years in together. You're my partner. I respect you." Dino shook his head. "Jesus Christ, Stone, I love you like you was my brother."

Stone kept brushing. "Thanks, Dino, I knew that, but I'm glad you told me."

"I don't want nothing to happen to you, Stone. I'll feel responsible."

"Dino, whatever I decide to do, it's on my head, not yours. I know the score; I know what can happen. It wouldn't be your doing."

"Well, thanks for that, anyway."

"You're welcome."

Dino stood looking up at him. "Stone, I gotta know what you're going to do."

Stone stopped painting and looked down at his partner. "Dino, I swear to you, I just don't know."

Dino looked down at the floor and shook his head. He set the untouched drink on the floor and left without another word.

Stone heard the front door close. He kept painting, smooth and even strokes. He kept sipping the bourbon.

27

Stone woke at seven and turned on *The Morning Show*. Nothing on the national news. He waited impatiently for twenty-five minutes past the hour and the New York affiliate's news. Nothing. Surprised, he got out of bed and dressed.

His decision had been made while he slept. Over an English muffin, he reflected that he had always wondered what would happen if he had to choose between the right thing and the department. His choice surprised him.

He picked up a *Daily News* at the corner newsstand, expecting another headline about the arrest of Hank Morgan. Nothing. Suddenly, for some reason, the leaks in the precinct had dried up.

The squad room was filling up with the morning shift of detectives, and Dino was already at his desk.

"Hi," he said. "Leary wants to see you."

"I figured," Stone said.

"You decide?" Dino asked.

"Yeah." He turned away and started for the lieutenant's cubicle; he'd let Dino stew for a while before he told him. He knocked on the glass door, and Leary waved him in.

Stone sat down and waited. He'd make Leary ask him.

Leary looked at him for a long time before he spoke. He reached into a large, yellow envelope and extracted a letter. "Stone," he said finally, "the results of your physical came in."

Stone was surprised. "The doctor said it'd be next week."

"It's today."

"Great. The sooner I'm officially back on full duty, the better."

"You're officially retired, for medical reasons."

Stone stopped breathing, stared at Leary, unable to speak.

Leary handed him the letter.

Stone read it.

Detective Barrington has suffered severe, perhaps irreparable damage to his left knee as a result of a gunshot wound received in the line of duty. In spite of extensive surgery and physiotherapy, the knee has not responded to treatment sufficiently to permit a return to active police duty. The prognosis is unfavorable. It is therefore recommended that Detective Barrington be retired from the force with immediate effect and with full line-of-duty disability benefits.

Stone dropped the letter and stared at Leary's desktop, his eyes unfocused.

"You can ask for a reexamination after a year," Leary said, "and, if the results are favorable, apply for reinstatement. Of course, if you were reinstated, that would mean a transfer to other duty and probably a loss of seniority."

That was clear enough to Stone. Don't come back. In a flash, he saw himself floundering through a series of unsuccessful appeals.

"There's no point in appealing this," Leary said, reading his mind. "You're out, and that's it."

"I see," Stone said, for lack of anything else to say.

"Let me have your ID card," Leary said.

Mechanically, Stone removed it from his wallet and handed it over.

Leary took some sort of stamp from a desk drawer, imprinted the card, and handed it back. The word *retired* had been punched into the card. "You can keep your badge, and you're entitled to carry your gun, like you were off duty." He handed Stone a thick envelope. "Here are your papers. Fill out the insurance forms and send them in; you'll still be covered under the department medical plan for life. Your pension will be three-quarters of your highest grade pay, tax free. That's a good deal. There's a check in the envelope for the first month."

Stone couldn't think of anything to say, and he couldn't seem to move.

Leary leaned forward and rested his elbows on the desk. "Look, Stone," he said, not without sympathy, "you're a good investigator, but you're a lousy cop. What you have never understood is that the NYPD is a fraternal lodge, and you never joined. You always bothered people. Being whitebread didn't make it any better; I mean, just about everybody on the force is micks, guineas, yids, spics, or niggers. They got that in common. But you're fuckin' J. Stone Barrington, for Christ's sake. That sounds like a brokerage house, not a cop, and you never even let anybody call you Stoney. A lot of the men respect you—*I* do; but nobody trusts you, and nobody's ever going to. You were never really a cop; you were always a college boy with a law degree and a badge."

Stone took a deep breath and struggled from the chair.

Leary started shuffling papers. "Good luck," he said.

"Thanks," Stone managed to say as he turned for the door.

"And Stone," Leary said.

Stone turned and looked at him.

"Stay out of the Nijinsky thing, you hear me? I don't want to read any of your theories in the papers."

Stone left, closing the door behind him. Numbly, he walked back to his desk. Dino was gone. On top of Stone's desk was a cardboard box containing his personal effects. He looked around the place; everybody was busy doing something.

Stone picked up the cardboard box and walked out of the squad room. Nobody looked at him.

CHAPTER

28

The phone was ringing as Stone walked into the house. He picked it up. "Hello?"

"Detective Barrington?"

"Yes?"

"This is Jack Marcus at the *Post*. We're doing a follow-up on the Nijinsky story; does your leaving the force have anything to do with your dissatisfaction with the way the investigation is being conducted?"

Stone was taken aback for a moment. The precinct was leaking again. "I'm leaving the force for medical reasons," he said.

"Weren't your superiors happy about the arrest of Henrietta Morgan?"

"You'll have to ask them about that."

"Do you think Hank Morgan pushed Sasha off that terrace?"

"I don't have an opinion about that. I'm a civilian." He hung up the phone. It rang again immediately.

"It's Cary. It just came over the AP wire."

"That's pretty fast reporting. I only heard myself an hour ago." He had walked home from the precinct.

"Are you all right?"

"I'm okay. Let's have dinner tonight."

"I wish I could. Barron's doing a prime-time special on murder in New York for Friday night. He's shooting every day, and we're editing every night."

"Come over here when you finish tonight."

"I wish I could, Stone; God knows, I'd rather be with you, but you have to understand about my job. I'll be working fifteen-hour days all this week."

"I'm sorry I pressed you; I know the job's important."

"It is, but I'll see you Saturday night for dinner at Barker's."

"Sure."

"Why don't you relax for the rest of the week? Do some work on the house."

"I don't have anything else to do."

"We'll talk about that Saturday. I've got to run now."

"See you."

"Take care."

Stone put down the phone. He could hear the noise of sanding coming from the study. The shelves would be ready to varnish again by late afternoon.

He went upstairs to his bedroom and stood looking at himself in the mirror over the chest of drawers. Nothing seemed different. He unstrapped the gun from his ankle, took the badge wallet from his pocket, and put them both in the top drawer, at the back, under his socks and underwear. As always, he felt naked when he wasn't carrying them. He would have to get used to feeling naked.

He was suddenly overcome with fatigue. He stretched

out on the bed, still wearing his trench coat, and closed his eyes for a minute.

When he woke, it was dark outside, and the noise of sanding had stopped. He still felt exhausted, but he struggled out of his trench coat and suit and into work clothes. Downstairs, he repeated his actions of the evening before— ate lasagna, made a drink, varnished. By the time he went to bed, he was drunk.

The next morning, he forced himself, in spite of the hangover, to work out on the exercise equipment; then he took a cab to Central Park and ran twice around the reservoir. It was a clear autumn day, the sort of day he loved in New York, and it lifted his spirits somewhat. He got a sandwich at the zoo and watched the seals cavort in their pool. What would he do tomorrow, he asked himself, and the week and the month after that? He knew how easy it would be to let himself descend into depression.

He finished his sandwich and found a pay phone, which, miraculously, had an intact yellow pages. He found the number and learned that the next bar exam was in three weeks, and the next cram course began the following Monday. He signed up on the spot, giving them a credit card number to hold his place. The thought of sitting in a classroom repelled him, but the thought of doing nothing was worse.

He bought the *Daily News* and the *Times* and looked for news. Hank Morgan had been arraigned the previous afternoon on the weapons charge and had been released on bail, which her father had covered. The *Times* report went no further than that, but a *News* columnist tied her to the Nijinsky case:

There is little doubt that Henrietta "Hank" Morgan is the chief suspect in the fall of Sasha Nijinsky from the terrace of her East Side penthouse. While everyone connected with the case has declined comment, police sources say that it is only a matter of time before enough evidence will be marshaled for the D.A. to seek an indictment. But an indictment for what? At the moment, there seems to be no proof that Sasha Nijinsky is dead, and even the police have not tried to link Morgan to her disappearance. It looks to this observer that the best the cops can hope for is an indictment for attempted murder, and one wonders how they could get a conviction on even that charge without producing either Nijinsky or her dead body.

It was starting now. The groundwork was being laid for a failure to convict Hank Morgan of anything, the implication being that, even though the police couldn't get enough evidence against her, they knew she was the guilty party. They had solved the crime, and that would get the department off the hook; never mind that Morgan, supposedly innocent until proven guilty, would be branded as a murderer and would live the rest of her life under a cloud.

For the first time, he felt glad to be out of the department. He looked at the photograph of Hank Morgan leaving the court with her attorney, mobbed by photographers and reporters, their lips curled back, screaming their questions. The woman looked terrified, even worse than she had looked in the interrogation room. There was the real victim in all this; Sasha herself had become a secondary figure to the newspapers and television news programs.

Stone forced himself to jog home, and he arrived thoroughly winded.

The answering machine was blinking; he pushed the button.

·

"Hello, there Det . . . uh, Mr. Barrington. This is Herbert Van Fleet. I was very sorry to read in the newspapers about your retirement from the police force. I hope my mother's letters to the mayor didn't have anything to do with this. She has been a big contributor to his campaigns, you know, and she's known him for years. I don't guess I'll be seeing you in the line of duty anymore—the FBI seems to have taken over, anyway. Can I buy you lunch sometime? You can always get me at the funeral parlor." He chuckled. "I guess you have the number."

Stone gave a little shudder at the thought of having lunch with Herbert Van Fleet.

There was a message from Cary, too. "Sorry I couldn't get over. We worked past midnight, and I was exhausted. I wouldn't have been any good to you. It's all over on Friday, though, and I promise to be fresh and ready for anything on Saturday night. I'll have a car; pick you up at eight?"

There was one more message. "Stone, it's Bill Eggers, your old law school buddy, of Woodman & Weld? I heard about your departure from the cop shop. I'm in LA right now on a case, but I'll be back in the office on Monday. Let me buy you dinner next week? I want to talk about something that might interest you. I'll call you Monday."

Stone spent the rest of the week working furiously on the house, making remarkable progress, now that he had the time. There were five coats of varnish on the bookshelves by the weekend, and they were looking good. He got all the floors sanded with rented equipment and got the tile floor laid in the kitchen. A few weeks more, and the place would start to look like home. A bill came from the upholsterer that put a serious dent in his bank account, and he remembered the letter from his banker and the note, which would be due soon. He tried to put money out of his mind. It didn't work.

Dino didn't call.

CHAPTER

29

On Saturday night, Cary turned up not in just a black car but in a limousine. Stone was waiting at the curb, and he slid into the backseat laughing.

He gave the driver the address and turned to Cary. "Are you sure the network can afford this?"

She raised the black window that separated them from the driver and slid close to him. "Don't worry about it. I've been putting in so much overtime, they owe me." She pulled his face down to hers and kissed him.

"There goes the lipstick," he said.

"Fuck the lipstick." She kissed him again and ran her hand up his thigh to the crotch. "Fuck me, too."

"In a limousine?"

"Why not? The driver can't see anything."

"We'll be at Barker's building in three minutes."

"That's just time enough," she said, unzipping his fly.

Before Stone could move he was in her mouth.

She was very good, and he was very fast; by the time the chauffeur opened the door, Stone had already adjusted his clothing, and Cary had reapplied her lipstick.

"You're amazing," Stone whispered as they entered the building. He was trying to bring his breathing back to normal.

"It was the least I could do," she said, "after I abandoned you in what must have been a very bad week."

"I think being alone helped me make the adjustment better," he said, "but I like the way you make up for slights." The doorman took their names and directed them to the elevator.

When the door had closed, she moved close to him. "I wonder how long we have before the elevator reaches Barker's floor?" she said.

Stone leaned down and kissed the top of a breast, accessible above the low-cut dress. "Not long enough for what I have in mind," he said. "By the way, you look spectacular. It's a wonderful dress."

She laughed. "You like cleavage, don't you?"

"The sight of breasts is good for morale."

"You look pretty sharp yourself. The suit suits you."

"I had good advice."

The elevator door opened. A uniformed maid answered the door and took their coats.

"Well, good evening," Hi Barker said, sweeping into the hall from the living room.

Stone introduced Cary.

"You're a fine judge of women, Stone," Barker said, kissing Cary's hand.

"Why, thank you, sir," Cary responded. She turned to Stone. "You didn't prepare me for this man."

"How could I?"

Barker ushered them into the living room, where two other couples and a woman waited. "Meet everybody," he said. "This is Frank and Marian Woodman."

Stone shook their hands. "Mr. Woodman and I have met," he said.

"Oh?" Barker said. "You're better acquainted around town than I thought."

"All in the line of duty," Stone said, "just the way I met you."

"That's right," Woodman said. "Sasha Nijinsky was my client, and Detective Barrington came to see me. Or, I should say, Mr. Barrington. My congratulations; I hear that sort of medical retirement is every police officer's dream."

"Most of the cops I know would rather serve the thirty years healthy," Stone said.

"Oh, the penny just dropped," Mrs. Woodman said. She was a small, handsome woman some years her husband's junior. "You're the detective in the papers."

"I'm afraid so," Stone said.

"You'll have to interrogate him later, Marian," Barker said, pulling Stone and Cary away. "He has other guests to meet." He took them to the other couple. "This is Abbott Wheeling and his wife, India. Stone Barrington and Cary Hilliard."

Wheeling was an elderly man, a former editor of the *New York Times*, now a columnist on the Op-Ed page. He shook hands warmly, and, before Stone had a chance to speak to him, the other woman in the room approached.

"I'm Edith Bonner," she said, shaking hands with both of them. She was tall, on the heavy side, but quite pretty and elegantly dressed.

"Edith is my date for the evening," Barker explained.

A waiter approached and took their drink orders. Bonner excused herself, and Cary pulled Stone to the window.

"It's quite a view, isn't it?" she said, pointing at the United Nations building.

•
175

"I hadn't seen it at night," Stone said.

"Do you know who Edith Bonner is?"

"No, the name doesn't ring a bell."

"She's a sort of society psychic," Cary explained. "She's a wealthy widow who does readings of her friends—strictly amateur—but she has quite a reputation."

The Wheelings joined them at the window and admired the view. "Your leaving the force at this particular time has caused quite a bit of speculation," he said to Stone.

"Well, I was scheduled for the physical some time ago," Stone replied. "It was unfortunate that I was in the middle of an investigation at the time."

"I don't mean to interview you, Mr. Barrington . . . "

"Please call me Stone."

"Thank you, and you must call me Ab; everyone does. As I was saying, I don't mean to interview, and this is certainly off the record, but do you think this Morgan woman had anything to do with the Nijinsky business?"

Stone nodded toward Bonner, who was returning to the room. "Maybe we should ask Mrs. Bonner," he said. "I expect she has just as good an idea about it as anyone assigned to the case."

Wheeling smiled. "You should have been a diplomat, Stone, or somebody's press secretary. That was as neat an answer as I've ever heard, and I couldn't quote you if I wanted to."

The maid entered the room. "Dinner is served," she said. People finished their drinks and filed into the dining room.

Stone was seated between India Wheeling and Edith Bonner and across from Frank Woodman.

"Stone, what are you going to do with yourself, now that you're a free man?" Woodman asked in the middle of the main course.

"I'm returning to the law," Stone said. "It seems to be the only thing I know anything about." He didn't mention that he would soon be cramming for the bar exam.

"Your career as a detective makes for an interesting background for a certain kind of lawyer," Woodman said. "I believe Bill Eggers may have an idea for you."

"I had a message from him this week," Stone replied.

"When he's back from Los Angeles, I hope you'll listen to what he has to say."

"Surely. At this point, I'm certainly open to suggestions."

Edith Bonner, who had been quiet up until now, spoke up. "Mr. Barrington ... "

"Stone."

"Stone. Of course I'm aware of what you've been investigating recently. I read the papers like everybody else."

"Why, Edith," Woodman broke in, "I didn't know you had to read the papers; I thought you had a direct line to the central source of all knowledge."

Bonner smiled. "You'll have to excuse Frank; he's a very bright man, but his curiosity extends only to the literal—what he can see and hear and touch."

"That's right, Edith," Woodman said.

"What Frank doesn't understand is that some of us see and hear and touch things that are not quite so literal. Do you see what I mean, Stone?"

"I believe I do, Edith, but I have to tell you that my experience as a police officer has made me not unlike Frank. I tend to put my faith in what I can see and hear, and I don't have your gifts with the less than literal."

"I believe I might be able to tell you something about what happened to Sasha Nijinsky," Bonner said.

All conversation ceased at the table.

"Would this be something material, or would it be more ... ephemeral?" Stone asked, trying to keep the tone light.

Bonner smiled. "I believe you might think it ephemeral," she said, "but I assure you it is material to me. I would not speak if I didn't feel quite certain about what I want to tell you."

"I'm all ears," Stone said.

"I feel strongly that two persons are responsible for what happened to Sasha Nijinsky," Bonner said.

"Well, since two things happened to Sasha—her fall and her disappearance—it seems quite possible that two people could be involved."

"I was referring to Sasha's fall from her terrace," Bonner said, "and only one of these persons was present when she . . . fell."

"That's very interesting," Stone said. It's not very interesting at all, he thought. So much for ESP.

"I warn you, Stone," Barker said, "Edith does not make such statements lightly. You should take her seriously."

"Unfortunately," Stone replied, "I'm no longer in a position to do so, and I have no reason to believe that anyone assigned to the case would be interested in hearing from me about any theory whatsoever. Edith, if you feel strongly about this, perhaps you should contact Lieutenant Leary, who is commander of detectives at the 19th Precinct."

Bonner shook her head. "No," she said, "he wouldn't listen to me. I've done what I can, now; I'll have no more to say on the subject." She returned to her dinner and her silence.

Soon the party moved back to the living room for coffee and brandy. Stone chatted at some length with Frank Woodman and found that he liked the man.

Later, when people made a move to leave, Bonner appeared at Stone's elbow. "There's something I didn't want to mention at the table," she said.

"Yes?"

"Sasha Nijinsky is not finished with you."

"Well, I'm afraid the NYPD has finished with me."

"But not Sasha. There's a connection between the two of you that you don't seem to know about."

"A connection?"

"A . . . well, a spiritual connection."

"But I never knew her."

"Do you think it was a coincidence that you were there when she fell from that balcony?"

"It couldn't be anything else."

"It was no coincidence. You and Sasha are bound together, and you won't be released until she is found and you know what happened to her."

"Edith, I'm going to do everything I can to put Sasha out of my mind permanently."

Bonner smiled. "I'm afraid you won't be able to do that." Then her expression turned serious. "There's something else," she said.

"What's that?"

"I feel that you are, or will be, in some sort of jeopardy, resulting from your connection with Sasha."

"Jeopardy? How?"

"I don't know. I only know that you are at risk, and, if you are not very careful indeed, this thing with Sasha could destroy you."

"Some would say it already has," Stone said. "At least with regard to my career as a police officer." He was near to confiding in her, now, and it surprised him.

"I mean destroy you entirely—mortally. In fact, I have the very strong feeling that your chances of surviving this crisis are poor—certainly, you will not come through without help, and you may not get it."

Stone pushed away the chill that threatened to run through him. "Edith," he managed to say, "I appreciate your concern for me, but please don't worry too much. It's my intention to stay just as far away as I can from the Nijinsky case or anything to do with it."

"You won't be able to do that," Bonner said. She looked away from him. "I'm sorry."

CHAPTER

30

Stone was awakened in the best possible way. "You're going to kill me," he said.

"Mmmmmmm," she replied, concentrating her efforts. "It's only fair; you nearly killed me last night."

"I couldn't think of anything else to do," he gasped.

Sunlight streamed into the room, and his blurring vision made the sparsely furnished chamber seem somehow heavenly. A moment later, everything came into sharp focus, and he closed his eyes and yelled.

"You're noisy," she said.

"It's your fault. You made me."

"I want some breakfast."

"You just had breakfast, and I'm not sure I can walk."

She got up and went into the bathroom. Stone heard the water running, and he had nearly dozed off when she came back. She crawled into bed, and, suddenly, there was something icy on his belly.

He yelled again and leapt out of bed. "Jesus Christ, was that your hands?"

"New York City tap water gets very cold in the wintertime," she said. "As long as you're up, could I have an English muffin, marmalade, orange juice, and coffee?"

"I suppose if I get back into bed you'll just attack me with the iceberg hands again."

"Right. But they'll warm up while you're fixing breakfast."

Defeated, Stone got into a bathrobe and went downstairs to the kitchen. He stuck the muffins into the toaster oven, got coffee started, and went to the front door. He peeked up and down the street, then tiptoed out onto the frosty stoop and retrieved the Sunday *Times*. He was back inside before he registered all that he had taken in. He cracked the door again and looked up the block. A plain green, four-door sedan was parked on the other side of the street, and two men inside it were sipping coffee from paper cups. He didn't know them, but he knew who they were.

He went back to the kitchen, got the breakfast together, loaded it onto a cart, and wheeled it into the old elevator, which made the usual creaking noises on the way up.

Cary was asleep, sprawled across the bed, the sunlight streaming across her naked body. He stopped and looked at her for a moment, that length of delicious woman, the flat belly, the swelling breasts with their small, red nipples, the dark hair strewn across the pillow. Slowly, quietly, he sneaked onto the bed and carefully set a glass of chilled orange juice onto a nipple.

"Oooooo," she said without moving. "What a nice way to wake up. Could I have something on the other one, please?"

"You're unsurprisable," he said, setting the orange juice

on her belly and returning for the rest of the breakfast. He put the tray on the bed between them while she struggled into a sitting position and fluffed up the pillows.

"I like the sun in the morning," she said. "It's better than blankets."

He drank his juice and reached for the *Times*.

"I get the front page," she said, snatching it away.

He settled for the book review and munched on a muffin.

"Oh, shit," she said suddenly.

"What is it?"

She clutched the front page to her breast. "You aren't at fault here," she said. "You have to get that through your head. This is not your fault."

"What the hell are you talking about?" He tugged at the newspaper, and she gave it up reluctantly.

SUSPECT IN NIJINSKY CASE IS APPARENT SUICIDE

Henrietta Morgan, a makeup artist for the Continental Network who police sources say was implicated in the fall of television anchorwoman Sasha Nijinsky from the terrace of her East Side penthouse apartment, last night apparently took her own life in her Greenwich Village apartment.

Ms. Morgan, who was known as "Hank" and who was active in gay and lesbian rights issues in the city, had been questioned about Ms. Nijinsky's fall, then last week was arrested and charged with possession of an unlicensed pistol. She had been released on bail, but sources in the New York Police Department had told the press that Morgan was the chief suspect in the Nijinsky case.

In a late-night statement from City Hall, Deputy Police Commissioner Lawrence Waldron announced

that the death of Ms. Morgan had effectively closed the
investigation into Ms. Nijinsky's fall. Waldron said
that Ms. Nijinsky's disappearance after an ambulance
collided with a fire truck while on her way to a hospital was still being investigated by the F.B.I., who are
treating her incident as a kidnapping, which is a federal crime.

Stone felt ill. He rubbed his face briskly with his hands
and tried to fight back the nausea.

"It's not your fault," Cary said again, rubbing the back
of his neck.

He got out of bed, went into the bathroom, and splashed
cold water onto his face. Then he thought about the
unmarked car downstairs. He went back into the bedroom
and got back into his robe. "I'll be right back," he said.

He trotted downstairs to the main hall, retrieved a flashlight from the utility closet, and unlocked the basement door. It
took him a minute or so to find the main telephone junction
box, and only seconds to find the wires leading from it to a
small FM transmitter a few feet away. Angrily, Stone ripped
out the wires, then smashed the transmitter with the heavy
flashlight. He walked back up to the main floor, then took the
elevator up-stairs.

"What's the flashlight for?" Cary asked. "It's broad daylight."

"I needed it to find the phone tap," Stone said.

"Somebody's tapped your phone?"

"New York's Finest," Stone said. "Two of them are sitting out in the street in an unmarked car, waiting either to
follow me wherever I go or to record my telephone conversations."

"Why?"

"Because they think that when I hear about Hank
Morgan's death, I might start talking to the press."

"Stone, I'm confused. If you want me to understand what you're talking about, then you'd better fill me in."

Stone took a deep breath. "This is not something you can discuss with anybody at work."

"Of course not," she said indignantly.

He went back to his and Dino's initial questioning of Hank Morgan and told her everything that had happened since.

"I see," she said when he had finished. "So you think Hank had nothing to do with Sasha's fall."

"Nothing whatever."

"But the NYPD and the DA's office were going to try and railroad her for it?"

"Not exactly; they knew they would never get a conviction. They just needed a strong suspect to take the heat off the department. Somebody's been telling a reporter or two that Morgan really did it, but they didn't have enough evidence against her for a conviction."

"So everybody would think Hank did it, even though they couldn't prove it?"

"Right. Except it worked out even better than they had planned. They didn't know that she wouldn't be strong enough to handle the suspicion and the publicity; they couldn't predict that she would finally break and kill herself."

"So what happens now?"

"Nothing."

"Nothing?"

"The investigation into Sasha's fall is over. Hank's suicide was as good as a confession."

"But they still don't know what happened to her, do they?"

"No, but the FBI very kindly stepped in and took responsibility for that part of the investigation, so the department is out of it."

"Are you going to do anything about it?"

"What can I do?"

"Go to the press. I can arrange for you to talk with one of our investigative reporters."

"It wouldn't work. There's just enough substance to the evidence against Morgan to justify the department's actions. I mean, I can't prove that she *didn't* do it." He picked up the bedside phone and dialed a number.

"Hello?" Dino said. He had obviously been asleep.

"Dino, it's Stone; I want you to give Leary a message for me."

"What?" He was waking up now.

"Tell him I found the phone tap, and it's now in several pieces, so there's no need to come back for it."

"Stone, what are you talking—"

"Also tell him"—Stone glanced at the bedside clock—"that it's nine forty-five now, and at ten o'clock I'm going to go downstairs and look up and down the street. If the police car is still sitting out there—or if I ever see any cops taking an interest in me again at any time—I'm going to take a full-page ad in the *New York Times* and publish my complete memoirs. Did you get that?"

"Yeah, but—"

Stone hung up the phone and put his face in his hands.

Cary sat up and began massaging his shoulders. "Just take it easy now; you told them off, and that's it. They won't bother you again, and none of this is your fault."

"You don't understand," Stone said.

"Understand what? It's not your fault."

Stone could not look at her, but he told her what he had been telling himself over and over again. "I would have gone along with it," he said. "If they had let me stay on the force, I would have stood by and let them pillory Hank Morgan. I would have done anything to keep my job."

Cary put her cheek against his back. "Oh, baby," she said. "Oh, my poor, sweet baby."

CHAPTER

31

Stone filed into the huge room with at least three hundred other aspirants to the bar of New York State, burdened like the rest with course materials, his bank account lighter by the substantial tuition. For eight hours, with a one-hour break for lunch, the instructor drilled the class, and Stone found the lectures to be well organized, to the point, with the fat trimmed away. The volume of material was daunting; when the day ended, he felt as if he'd been beaten up.

Back at home, he called Cary. "I'm near death," he said, "but my incipient corpse is yours for the evening, if you want it."

"I'd love to have it, but I'm stuck again," she replied. "Friday night's ratings were terrific, for a documentary, and we're brainstorming after hours all week to come up with ideas for six more specials."

"Shit."

"I know, but you should be concentrating on passing the bar instead of lusting after me. You can lust after me on Saturday, though. Around here, not even Barron Harkness works on a Saturday."

"You're on. I wish I didn't have to wait so long."

"The law is a jealous mistress, remember?"

"Thank you, Madame Justice Hilliard."

"Until Saturday."

"You'd better get ready for this," he said. "On Saturday, I'm going to tell you I love you." He could hear the smile in her reply.

"It's beginning to sound like a perfect weekend."

Stone hung up, then checked the messages on his machine.

"It's Dino, Stone. I didn't know anything about that stuff that was going on. It was Leary's doing, maybe at the suggestion of somebody upstairs. I just wanted you to know that. Take care of yourself."

"Stone, this is Bill Eggers. I'm stuck in LA for at least another ten days—unforeseen circumstances, I believe the term is. It means all hell has broken loose on my case, and I'm going to be putting out fires until pretty near the end of next week, so we'll have to postpone dinner. You impressed Woodman at dinner the other night, and he isn't easily impressed. I'll call you in a couple of weeks."

"This is Abbott Wheeling, Stone. I enjoyed our conversation at dinner the other night. It occurred to me that, in light of subsequent events, you might be willing to talk about the Nijinsky case for publication. Should you feel that way, either now or at any time in the future, I'd be grateful if you'd call me at the *Times.* I can promise you that your views on the case will get the sort of serious public attention that only this newspaper can command. I won't pester you about this, but please be assured of my continuing interest."

Stone endured a moment's temptation to call Wheeling and tell him everything, but the moment passed, and he returned to putting as much emotional distance as possible between himself and the Nijinsky case and the suicide of Hank Morgan.

He made himself some supper and resumed his varnishing of the bookshelves, trying to let his mind run over the day's lecture. He was surprised at the familiarity of the material after so many years, and he was encouraged to think he might pass the bar exam after all.

On Saturday night Elaine gave Stone and Cary a table next to the piano. Stone liked piano music, and he was particularly enjoying the way Lauren was playing Rodgers and Hart. When they had finished dinner, Elaine joined them.

"Remember that guy, Doc? At the bar awhile back? The diagnostician?"

"Yeah. In fact, I saw a lot of him during the Nijinsky thing."

"We had a weird thing in here with him last night. He was playing doctor with some little girl at the bar, and they left together, and, a minute later, she's back in here, nearly hysterical. She said Doc had tried to muscle her into a van, and she was scared to death."

"Did you call the precinct?"

"Nah, it didn't seem as serious as that. I gave her a brandy and calmed her down; she didn't want to take it any farther. I'm going to throw the bum out the next time he walks in here, though."

"He wrote Sasha Nijinsky a thousand or so letters over the past couple of years."

"No kidding?"

"It didn't get in the papers, but we had a look at his place and where he works. He's an embalmer for a funeral parlor, you know."

"He's not a doctor?"

"Nope. He did graduate from medical school, but he was never licensed. I thought the guy was harmless, but when he starts trying to drag girls into vans, well ... "

"He's never setting foot in here again," Elaine said emphatically.

In bed, Cary seemed tired and distracted, and their love-making was brief and perfunctory, something that had never happened before. The extra work seemed to be getting her down, and, God knew, Stone was tired himself. Eight hours a day of class and another four of varnishing was wearing him down.

On Sunday morning, Cary ate her breakfast listlessly. "Are you as zonked as I am?" she asked.

"Yeah. It's okay; we're both under the gun at the moment."

"Thanks for understanding. I've been looking forward to seeing you all week, and now I'm a wreck."

"It's okay, really it is."

"If you don't mind, I think I'll go home and try to get some sleep this afternoon."

He did his best to hide his disappointment. "Next Saturday?"

"Absolutely."

The next Saturday was much the same.

Another letter came from the bank, this time a flat-out demand. Stone, his back against the wall now, called a real estate agent.

"I think it's wonderful what you're aiming at for the

place," she said, "but I guess you know what the New York residential property market is like right now. In good times, with the place finished and ready to move into, we might get three, three and a half million for this house. Right now, for an immediate sale, we might be lucky to get three hundred thousand."

Stone was shocked. "Is the market that bad?"

"It is. Listen, you're lucky; at least you'd get something out of a sale. I've got clients with perfectly beautiful town houses who are being forced to sell for far less than they paid, and they're having to pay off the rest of the mortgage out of savings."

Bright and early on a Monday morning, Stone presented himself to be examined for admission to the bar of New York State, along with about fifteen hundred others. Like everyone else, he labored over the questions. There were occasional gaps in his knowledge, but, on the whole, he thought he did well; certainly, he aced the questions on criminal law. Now there was only the waiting.

He got home feeling enormously relieved. He had finished his study for the bar and the varnishing of the library at the same time. Now, if Cary could just get a break in her work schedule, maybe they could . . .

The phone rang.

"Hello?"

"Hi, it's Bill Eggers."

"Hi, Bill."

"How'd you do today?"

"How'd you know?"

"I have spies everywhere."

"Well, I did okay on criminal law, at least."

"Good. How about dinner tomorrow night?"

"Fine."

"The Four Seasons, at eight thirty?"

"Sounds good."

"Don't bring anybody. It's just you and me."

"If you promise not to put your hand on my knee."

"Don't worry, you're not cute enough. By the way, I might have some news for you."

"What sort of news?"

"Let's wait and see."

CHAPTER

32

*T*he Four Seasons was busy, as always. The hum of voices from the Pool Room echoed enjoyment of the surroundings and the food, but Bill Eggers had a table in the Grill, next to the bar.

"It's quieter here," Eggers said. "It's crazy at lunch, but at dinner everybody wants to be in the Pool Room. Here, we can talk."

Stone wondered exactly what they would be talking about. This felt something like a job interview, but he couldn't see Woodman & Weld hiring a thirty-eight-year-old novice as an associate.

They had a drink and dawdled over the menu. Eggers seemed in an expansive mood, relieved over the resolution of his Los Angeles case. "It was a bastard," he said. "A bicoastal divorce case of one of our biggest clients. He was claiming New York residence, and she claimed they lived in

California—she wanted community property."

"Who won?"

"I did. The LA office is mostly into entertainment work, so I did the dog work while they fronted for me in court. Don't worry about the lady; she's doing very well out of this, but she's not getting the thirty million that community property division would have given her. She's pissed off now, but she'll get used to living on the income from six million."

"You do a lot of divorce work?"

"I'm sort of the firm general practitioner. I have a lot of clients whose personal legal work I handle, and that often leads to divorce work. It's nasty sometimes, but, if you can keep a certain detachment, you can live with it."

"Must be lucrative."

"Not all that much. We only do divorce work for the firm's existing clients, and we don't charge them the earth. In the case of the men, when they see what the wife's lawyer is demanding, they're grateful to us for not taking them to the cleaners; in the case of the women, they're grateful to us for not demanding high fees. That builds client loyalty."

"I should think so."

They ordered their food, and Eggers chose what Stone thought must be the most expensive bottle of wine on a very expensive list. If Stone had been interested before in what Bill Eggers had to say, now he was *really* interested.

Eggers tasted the wine and nodded to the sommelier. When the man had gone, he turned to Stone. "What do you know about Woodman & Weld?"

"Not very much," Stone admitted. "I get the impression that it's a prestigious firm, from what I read in the papers, but I'm not very clear on why it might be so."

"Good. That's pretty much the impression we like to convey. We see that the people who might need us know a lot more, but we keep a fairly low public profile."

Stone sipped the wine; he thought he had never

tasted anything so good. "It's a lovely burgundy," he said to Eggers. "Thank you."

Eggers nodded, pleased that his largess had been noted. "Let me give you the scoop on us. We've got eighteen partners at the moment, and thirty-six associates. That's certainly not big by Manhattan standards, but it's big enough for us to be able to cover a lot of bases. There are seven corporate specialists—we tend to attract companies somewhat below the Fortune Five Hundred level, outfits that don't have huge legal departments; we have four estate planners—that's very important to wealthy individuals—and, just as important, four tax specialists, all Jewish. Nobody seems to take a tax lawyer seriously who isn't Jewish. We're something of a polyglot firm—blacks, women, Irish, Jews, Italians—not unlike the New York Police Department, I expect. That's important to us, because the firm is active in liberal Democratic causes—you'd be surprised how much business comes in that way. Finally, there are three generalists—two of them Woodman and me."

"I liked Woodman when I met him."

"Woodman is a genius, as far as I'm concerned. He's a client man, first and last; he inspires trust. Also, he has a facility for going into a meeting—corporate, tax, whatever—and immediately grasping the issues involved. Clients think he knows *everything*, which isn't exactly true, but he can give that impression effortlessly. I'd be willing to bet that he could engage you in conversation about a homicide investigation and make you think he was an ex-cop."

Their first course arrived, and they dug in.

"You didn't mention any criminal lawyers," Stone said between bites.

"We don't have a criminal lawyer as such, although you'd be surprised at how much criminal work comes our way. Nowadays, it's the corporate executive or stockbroker who's stepped over the line; also, our clients' kids get into trouble—drugs, rape, sometimes even murder."

"How do you handle that?"

"In different ways. If it's something big, we refer to a hotshot mouthpiece; more often, we bring in a consultant and handle it internally. A client likes it when his own lawyer seems to be in charge. Of course, there's a fine line there; we have to make the judgment on when an outsider best serves the client's needs. We can't afford to make a mistake and underrepresent a client. We're very, very careful in the matter of malpractice, and we've never had a suit against us."

"That seems a good area to be careful in."

"In short, Stone, we're a class act. Every single partner is as good as any lawyer in town at what he does and better than ninety-nine percent of the field. We're low profile, highly ethical, and extremely profitable. I will tell you, in confidence, that no partner in our firm is taking home less than half a million a year, and that's the low end. I made a million two last year, and it wasn't my best year."

Stone sucked in a breath at the thought of so much money and what he could do with it.

"Now that I've stunned you," Eggers said, noting Stone's expression, "let me tell you why we're interested in you."

Somehow, Stone didn't think that he was here to be offered a partnership and half a million dollars a year.

"As I've said, we're taking on more and more criminal and domestic work, without even trying. We've handled some ourselves, farmed out some, and brought in consultants on others, but we're still spread thin. Sometimes we need investigative work done, and we're troubled by the quality of the people available to do that sort of thing. There are some high-class people around, but they charge more than a good lawyer gets; generally, what we see in the investigative area is sleaze—the worst sort of ex-cop, the ones who got the boot."

"You might say I got the boot," Stone said.

"But for all the right reasons," Eggers replied. "We have a pretty good idea of why you were pensioned off." He took a deep breath. "Another thing about investigators, they have a tendency to look wrong for some of the work we give them. They dress badly, drink too much, and sprinkle a lot of 'dems, deezes, and dozes' around their conversation. You, on the other hand, look right and sound right."

Stone shrugged. Eggers was looking for a private detective, and the thought didn't interest him much.

Eggers must have read his mind. "Don't get me wrong, we're not looking for somebody to just kick down bedroom doors, although I wouldn't rule that out. What's interesting about you is a combination of things: you understand how the police department and the DA's office work; you have a fine grasp of criminal justice procedure; you are a highly experienced investigator; and, unusually with all that, you have the background, education, demeanor, and the language skills that will let you fit easily into any upper-level social situation. In short, a client would be perfectly comfortable explaining his problem to you."

"What exactly do you have in mind, Bill?"

"You could be very useful to us; let me give you some typical examples. One: a client's son and heir, who has a three-hundred-dollar-a-week allowance, is, inexplicably, caught selling an ounce of cocaine on his college campus. We need somebody who can show up at the station house, talk to the cop in charge, deal with the DA, and get the charges dropped or reduced to a misdemeanor that the kid can plead to as a youthful offender and that will, in time, be expunged from his record. Two: the kid does something really bad—rapes his date, batters, maybe even murders her. We'll need our own investigation into the events, and we'll need to know how the cops and the DA are thinking. A third: A client suspects his wife of having an affair; we need to know for sure, before we can proceed for him.

That's not the whole range of problems that might arise, but it's a good sampling."

"I see." This sounded better than hanging around the criminal courts, picking up burglary and drunk-driving cases.

"Let me lay it out for you. We don't want you to join the firm, as such. Not yet, anyway. What we'd like you to do is set up your own practice, a professional corporation, which would be associated with us."

"You realize I haven't even passed the bar yet."

"Oh, I forgot; that was my news. You passed."

"Now how the hell could you know that? I only took the exam yesterday."

"Friend of a friend had access. He pulled your papers, looked them over, and he reckons you'll finish in the top third, and, since the New York State bar is the toughest in the country, that's damn good. It's not official, of course, but you've got nothing to worry about."

"Bill, this friend of a friend didn't . . . improve my score, did he?"

Eggers looked shocked. "Absolutely not. There's been no tampering here, you don't need to worry about that. I told you, we're an ethical firm. Information was all we were after, and that's all we got; no law was broken; we don't do that."

"Well, in that case, thanks. It's a load off my mind."

"Anyway, as I was saying, we want you to be at our disposal. Of course, you can't actually practice law until your admittance to the bar is official, but you can advise and investigate. In a trial, you can sit at the defense table and whisper into our man's ear. Then, when you're admitted, you can accept cases of your own. We just want priority."

"On what basis?"

"When we hire a freshly admitted associate, the current starting salary is fifty-five thousand. We propose to offer you a retainer of seventy-five thousand dollars annually, against an hourly rate of a hundred and twenty-five dollars."

"What's your hourly rate, Bill?"

"Two fifty to three fifty, depending, but I've been with the firm for twelve years and a partner for eight. Don't misunderstand me, Stone, it's not our intention to keep you at arm's length forever. We're feeling our way, here, with a new kind of association for us. If this works out the way I hope it will, then you would eventually join the firm, and, sometime in the future, a partnership might come into the picture."

"Would you care to be a little more specific about 'eventually' and 'sometime in the future'?"

"No. I can't be. This is simply too new a situation for us. But I'll tell you what I tell our new associates: there are no guarantees, but if you work your ass off for the firm, if you show you can bring in business of your own, and if you can make our clients trust you, then a partnership is almost inevitable. That's what they told me when I joined, and it was true. Of course, under the terms we're offering you, any new business you bring in will be yours entirely. Then, if and when you join us, you bring your clients with you."

Stone leaned back in his chair and smiled. "Bill, I accept. I'm delighted to accept. And, I'll tell you the truth, this could not have come along at a better time."

Eggers leaned forward. "A cash pinch?"

Stone told him about the situation with the house and his bankers.

Eggers took out a pad and made some notes. "You're being badly treated, and I think we can correct that. May I represent you in this matter?"

"Of course."

"Good. I'll get you an advance against your first quarter's retainer, too."

"Thank you, Bill; that would certainly take the pressure off."

Eggers stuck out a hand. "Welcome aboard."

Stone shook it. "When do I start to work?"

"Tomorrow. We've got a couple of things in-house you can look at and advise on. And I think I'll have an investigative job for you soon."

Stone walked home, not even noticing the light rain. He was employed. He wouldn't have to sell the house. The thought of marriage—suppressed because of his financial condition—broke through into his frontal lobe. He flashed ahead five years: he was a partner at Woodman & Weld; the house was beautiful, and it was his; he and Cary were throwing elegant dinner parties in his elegant dining room; maybe there was a child. Maybe two. Things were suddenly falling into place.

A miracle had occurred. He didn't pause to wonder what it might cost him.

CHAPTER

33

When Stone got home, Dino was standing on the front stoop, back against the door, trying to stay out of the rain.

"Hi, Dino," Stone said.

"Hi. Can I buy you a drink?"

"Come on in, let me buy you one."

"Nah, I hate the smell of paint and sawdust. Let's go someplace."

"All right."

They walked silently up Third Avenue to P. J. Clarke's and leaned on the corner of the bar.

"The usual?"

"Fine."

"A Wild Turkey and a Stoly, both rocks," Dino said to the barman. "Make 'em doubles."

They both looked idly around until the drinks came.

Dino held up his glass. "Better days."

Stone nodded and drank.

Dino gulped a quarter of the vodka. "I feel bad about what happened," he said.

"It's okay, Dino. Maybe it was all for the best." He told Dino about his dinner with Bill Eggers.

"That's great, Stone, and I'm happy for you, but it's still not okay with me. You were my partner, and I should have at least warned you what was coming. I didn't know myself until that morning."

"You were my partner, too, and I didn't back you up," Stone said.

"Yeah, but you were right, that's the difference. I was wrong, and because of what I did Morgan croaked herself."

Stone said nothing.

"I took the call," Dino said, blinking.

Stone still said nothing.

"She was in the bathtub, and it looked like the tub was full of blood."

"Jesus," Stone allowed himself.

"She had a straight razor. God knows what she was doing with it, even if she was a dyke. You think she was keeping it in case she grew a beard?"

Stone shrugged.

"She stuck it in right under her left ear and pulled it all the way around, deep."

Stone winced.

"She had guts, I'll say that for her. I couldn't never do that, not in a million years. Pills, maybe. Maybe eat your gun, but you don't die right away when you cut your own throat. It must hurt like all hell, and you got time to think about what you done before you go under." Dino shifted his weight and took another deep pull from his glass. "She left a note."

"The papers didn't say anything about that," Stone said, surprised.

Dino took a folded piece of paper from his pocket and handed it to Stone.

Stone read it.

I have never harmed another human being in my life. I did not harm Sasha Nijinsky. I loved her, and she loved me, and I would never have done anything to hurt her.

I want my friends to know that this is not a suicide. This is murder, and the police are the murderers.

"You can see why you didn't read about it in the papers," Dino said, taking the note back. He took a pack of matches from an ashtray on the bar, lit the note, watched it burn. "You know something? I went to confession. I didn't go to confession since I was fourteen, but I went yesterday. As part of my penance, I had to tell you this stuff. I didn't do the rest of the penance; I'm not going to. But I wanted to do this part."

"Thanks, Dino, I know what it cost you."

"Don't be so fucking nice about it, Stone. I wouldn't have said a word to you, but I know you won't say nothing to nobody about this."

Stone nodded.

"I always been good at looking out for my own ass," Dino said. "Sometimes I fall in the shit, but I come up smelling like a rose, you know?"

Stone laughed. "I know."

"Nah, you don't know. I made detective first grade today. Ain't that a kick in the balls? I get a promotion I would have killed for—" He stopped and laughed ironically. "Shit, I guess I did kill for it, didn't I?"

"Congratulations, Dino." Stone raised his glass.

Dino drank with him. "They made me deputy squad commander, too. Leary's retiring the end of the year, and I'm getting the job, Delgado says."

"That's great, Dino," Stone said, but it was a statement of sympathy.

"Yeah, get me off the street some, I guess. Teach me a sense of responsibility."

"You'll be good at it. Look out for the politics, though."

"What politics? I'm not going anywhere after that. I'm never going to be chief of detectives—they know it, and I know it. Shit, I never expected to make detective first, to tell the truth. Nah, there's no politics to worry about. I'm bought and paid for. I'll do what I'm told and like it."

Stone couldn't think of anything to say.

"Sounds like I'm feeling sorry for myself, don't it? Well, I am, I guess. I found out how far I'd go to cover my ass, and I feel terrible about it." He tossed down the rest of his drink and squared his shoulders. "I'll get over it, though. In a week or two, or when I get Leary's little cubicle, I'll look around and say to myself, 'Hey, this ain't half bad, you know? These fuckers have to do what I tell 'em now! I'm the fucking boss!' And I'll start to feel okay about it. And come spring, I'll forget all about Hank Morgan and how she took a bath in her own blood. I'm good at that—forgetting what a shit I was about something. I'll forget that I wasn't the world's greatest detective, too, that I was lazy and shiftless a lot of the time, that I didn't give much of a shit about my job. I'll forget all that, and when the next batch of detective thirds cruises into the precinct, I'll give 'em the pep talk, tell 'em how it was when I was scratching for promotion, how hard I worked on a case, how many righteous busts I had. I'll be a hard ass, just like Leary—shit, worse than Leary."

"Sure, you will."

Dino picked up the heavy doubles glass and heaved it across the bar. The mirror on the other side shattered, and chunks of glass fell among the liquor bottles, breaking some of them.

The dozen people standing at the bar and the two bartenders froze, staring at Dino.

Finally, a bartender, a red-haired, freckle-faced Irishman who looked right off the boat, spoke up. "The last one o' dose got broke cost eight hundred bucks, Dino," he said sadly. "And that was six, seven years ago. They prob'ly went up." He looked at the mess, shaking his head. "And dere's the booze, too."

Dino put a fifty-dollar bill on the bar. "That's for our drinks, Danny," he said calmly, "and the change is for your trouble. Send me a bill for the rest."

The bartender nodded and began picking up glass. The customers went back to their drinking as if nothing had happened.

Outside, the rain had stopped, and the night had turned clear and frosty. Dino hailed a cab. "Stone," he said, while the cab waited, "I owe you. I'm always gonna owe you. You call me any time you need something. Anytime."

Stone nodded. They shook hands. Dino got into the cab and drove off into the night. Stone walked home thinking that both he and Dino had done all right out of Sasha Nijinsky's trouble.

The only loser had been Hank Morgan.

34

Stone sat in Frank Woodman's large office and sipped strong coffee.

"Stone, I'm very pleased that you're going to be . . . associated with us," Woodman was saying. "I think that, with your help, we can take what has been a nongainful irritant and turn it into a profit center for the firm. That's with you fully on board, of course, after our initial feeling-out period."

"Frank, I should tell you that, for the long term, I'm really more interested in a general practice than solely criminal work, and I'd appreciate it if, after I'm admitted to the bar, you'd consider putting me on an occasional noncriminal case."

"I understand your feelings, and I'll keep that in mind."

Warren Weld, the other name on the door, spoke up. "Are you interested in corporate work, Stone?"

"Not really, Warren. I think I'd prefer to represent individuals."

"That puts you right back in Frank's bailiwick, then." Weld stood up. "If you'll excuse me, gentlemen, I've got a meeting. Welcome aboard, Stone."

They shook hands, and Weld left, leaving only Frank Woodman and Bill Eggers in the room with Stone.

"Bill, you take Stone back to your office, will you? I've got a client coming in." Woodman stood and shook Stone's hand. "I think Bill already has a couple of things for you, Stone. He'll brief you."

They returned to Eggers's office and sat down.

"Frank had a word with your banker yesterday—we keep our trust account at your branch, so we have a little pull there. You're off the hook for the principal reduction they were demanding. You'll still have to make the interest payment, though."

"Thank you, Bill, that's good news."

Eggers handed him an envelope. "And here's ten grand against your retainer."

"You're full of good news," Stone said. "Thanks again."

"Not at all." Eggers looked at his watch. "There's somebody I want you to meet, Stone. He's due in here in ten minutes."

"A client?"

"Son of a client. The father is Robert Keene, of Keene, Bailey & Miller advertising."

"I don't know them."

"The three partners left Young & Rubicam fifteen years ago and set up on their own. Now they're a medium-sized agency well known for good creative work. Warren Weld represents the agency, and I represent Bob personally. Bob Keene is as nice a guy as you'd want to meet."

"And the boy?"

"That's why I want you to meet him. I want your opinion. Bobby Junior is a senior at Brown, and there's a date-rape accusation against him by a girl student. She turned him in to the administration, and, when she wasn't happy with the level of support she got, she added his name to a list of alleged date rapists on the ladies' room wall in her dormitory. Bobby denies everything, and he seems credible. No criminal charges have been filed, yet, but if they are, and, if we feel he's innocent, I want to go on the offensive—sue the girl for defamation, sue the university for allowing his name to remain painted on a bathroom wall, really blast them. And we'll call in a top gun to defend him.

"On the other hand, if he's really guilty, I'll insist that he abjectly apologize to the girl and the administration, and try to avoid criminal proceedings and keep him in school. That would certainly be cheaper for his father, but Bob Senior is willing to do what it takes to defend the boy if he's innocent."

"What does the father think about the boy's guilt or innocence?"

"Oddly, he doesn't seem to have an opinion. I think that, what with the work it's taken to build his business, he hasn't spent a hell of a lot of time with the boy, and they've grown apart. We can't solve that problem for them, but I hope we can give Bob Senior good advice on how to proceed."

"I'll be glad to meet the boy."

"As a cop, you must have gained some insight over the years as to whether an accused man is guilty or not—I don't mean reading the evidence, I mean reading the man."

"I think I have. It doesn't always work, of course. I've been fooled before; so has every cop."

"I want you to question the boy, pull out all the stops, see if you can shake his story."

"You want him cross-examined, as if I were representing the girl?"

"I want him questioned, as if he were a suspect."

The phone on Eggers's desk rang. "Yes? Send him in." He hung up and turned to Stone. "Ready?"

"You be the good cop," Stone said.

"Right."

Bobby Keene was a large young man, whose neck was wider than the top of his head. Stone thought there had been a handsome face in that head once, before the boy had discovered weight training.

"Bobby, how are you?" Eggers said, sticking out a hand.

"I'm very well, Mr. Eggers," Bobby said earnestly.

"Bobby, I want you to meet another lawyer who's helping us out with your case. This is Stone Barrington; Stone's had a lot of experience in this sort of thing, and I think he'll be able to help us a lot."

"Gosh, I hope so." Bobby stuck out a ham-sized hand. "How do you do, Mr. Barrington?"

Stone kept a poker face, shook the hand limply, but did not return the greeting. "Sit down," he said, and it was an order.

Bobby sat, looking worried.

"Tell me about it," Stone said, sounding bored.

"Sir?"

Stone turned to Eggers. "Jesus Christ, Bill, is the kid stupid, or what?"

"Bobby," Eggers said gently, "tell Mr. Barrington what happened on the evening you went out with"—he glanced at a pad on his desk—"Janie Byron."

"Oh, of course, sir. I'm sorry, I didn't know what Mr. Barrington meant."

"Just tell me," Stone said.

"Well, there isn't much to tell. We went to a movie—"

"What kind of a movie?"

"An old one; a John Ford western."

"Downtown, shopping mall, drive-in?"

"Oh, a drive-in, right outside town."

"Then what happened?"

"Well, we got some popcorn, we ate it, we watched the movie, we made out a little."

"Define 'made out.' Exactly."

Bobby retained his earnest tone. "We kissed a few times."

"Did you touch her breasts?"

"Well, yeah, she seemed to want that."

"Oh, she said to you, 'Bobby, please, please grab my tits,' is that how it happened?"

"Well, not exactly."

"Just how did she show you that she wanted you to touch her breasts?"

"Well, when I did, she didn't object much."

"But she did object."

"Well, she played hard to get a little, I guess."

"Then what happened?"

"We started to get heated up a little, and I—"

"Go on, boy, be graphic. We're all grown up here."

"Then she said she wanted to leave, she got all huffy and all, and so I took her back to her dorm."

"Immediately?"

"As soon as I was sure she meant it."

"How long did that take?"

"A few minutes, I guess."

"How many minutes? Exactly."

"Five, I guess."

"Did you lie down on the seat of the car?"

"For a minute or two."

"Did you get your hand in her pants?"

"Yes, sir."

"Did you get your finger inside her?"

"Yes, sir, for a minute."

"Did you get her pants off?"

"No, sir. I didn't do that."

"Why not?"

"Sir?"

"Well, it sounds to me like you were doing real well,

there, Bobby; you got at her tits, you got your finger in her crotch, why stop?"

"I guess she didn't want to."

"If she didn't want to, how'd you get your hand in her crotch?"

"Well, I—"

Stone leaned across to Eggers's desk and picked up a legal pad. "It says here you forced her to have sex with you."

"That's a lie!"

"It says here, you ripped off her underwear, pinned her down with your weight, and fucked her against her will."

"It wasn't against her will!"

"So you fucked her, didn't you?"

"No, I . . . you're getting me confused."

"It says here that when she got back to her dorm, her roommate took a cotton swab and collected a semen sample from her pubic hair and saved it on a glass slide. Her roommate is a biology major. That's your misfortune."

Bobby's eyes widened, and his jaw worked, but nothing came out.

"Do you know what a DNA matching is, Bobby?"

"I . . . well, I read something in the paper about it."

"Give me that lab report," Stone said to Eggers.

Eggers promptly found a sheet of paper on his desk and handed it across to Stone.

Stone looked at the paper, an interoffice memo, and shook his head.

"Listen, I can give you the names of three guys who've screwed Janie Byron," Bobby said. His face was red. "I—"

"I see," Stone said. "So the guys at the frat house are going to back you, huh? They're stand-up guys, so they're all going to go into court and perjure themselves for you and risk going to prison."

Bobby put his face in his hands for a moment.

Stone turned to Eggers. "You can't go into court with

this guy, Bill. He can't even convince his own lawyers, how the hell is he going to convince a jury?"

"Bobby," Eggers said gently, "you see what we're up against, don't you? I mean, Mr. Barrington is on *your* side, and he can't bring himself to believe you. Now listen, if you'll just tell us the truth, all of the truth, then we may be able to get you out of this."

"He'll never tell you the truth," Stone said harshly. "He's a lying little piece of shit."

Bobby came half off the sofa, but, when Stone stood up, he sank back. "Can I talk to you alone, Mr. Eggers?" he said plaintively.

"Sure you can, kid," Stone said, heading for the door. "I wouldn't waste any more of my time." At the door, he turned back to Eggers. "I'll tell you one thing, I wish I was prosecuting this one, instead of defending." He walked out, slamming the door behind him.

In the hall, Stone leaned against the door and took a deep breath. Jesus, it had been awhile. Dino usually played the bad cop.

35

Bill Eggers leaned back in his chair and rested his feet on his desk. "That was good work, Stone. The boy has told me everything, I think; I don't believe he actually screwed the girl, though God knows he meant to. He's down the hall in an associate's office right now, writing letters to the girl and the university administration. I think I can negotiate him out of this. The girl wasn't entirely blameless, and she does have a reputation for sleeping around."

"I'm glad it worked out," Stone said.

"Well, you saved his father seventy-five or a hundred thousand in legal fees. Bob Keene will always be grateful to us for that."

"Frank said you had something else for me."

"I do, and this one's sticky. Or, at least, it could be."

"Tell me about it."

"I'm going to have to be a little circumspect in talking even to you about this," Eggers said. "There's a lot at stake, and I'm going to have to proceed strictly on a need-to-know basis, all right?"

"All right."

"I have a client I've known since I was in high school, whose wife is a prominent businesswoman. They've never had much of a marriage, but there were a couple of kids, and they stuck it out. Trouble is, the wife has had a couple of affairs. In fact, there've been other men all along, I think, but he's finally run out of patience, and, even against my best advice, he's determined to proceed his own way on this."

"What does he want to do?"

"He wants custody of one of the two kids, the boy, and that means he has to nail her with the other guy—photographs, the works. Actually, he wants a videotape of her in bed with him."

"Do you often proceed this way in divorce cases?"

"No, and I've advised him against this, but he's absolutely determined. He wants a quick, clean divorce with no haggling about money, and, I have to admit, if he gets his little video, there won't be any haggling. The wife has too much to lose to allow a Rob Lowe–type tape to be circulated. If her board of directors so much as got wind of such a thing, she'd be finished. Nobody would ever take her seriously again."

"Well, even in an era of no-fault divorce, I suppose there are still certain advantages to having that sort of evidence. What exactly is it you want me to do? Kick down the bedroom door and film them in living color?"

"I definitely do *not* want you to do that. The firm can't afford to have anybody as closely associated with us as you are be directly involved in such a distasteful affair."

"You mean you want me to find someone else who'll do it."

Eggers grinned. "Right. Someone who can be trusted to be discreet, even if he's caught in the act of doing it. Do you know somebody like that?"

Stone did. The man's face popped immediately into his mind. "Possibly," he said. "But this could get expensive. He's going to have to stalk the lady until he can catch her in the act, and that may not be easy."

"I think it's going to be easier than you think," Eggers said, smiling.

"Oh?"

"My client has been very helpful. His wife's company maintains two apartments in a rather elegant building that specializes in company flats—you know the sort of thing— the out-of-town executive stays in the company apartment instead of at the Plaza. It's supposed to save money for the company, but, mostly, it's regarded as just a perk for the upper-level executive. Anyway, my client has been tipped that his wife has been using one of the company apartments on a rather regular basis for her assignations with her male bimbo—a soap-opera actor no less, and he has thoughtfully supplied us with a key to the apartment." He held up a key.

"Your client has been very helpful indeed," Stone agreed.

"As I said, there are two apartments. My client, as a spouse, also has access to them, and what he is prepared to do, next time he thinks his wife is dallying, is to book your man into the other flat for the night. That gets him access to the building." He tossed the key to Stone. "And this gets him access to the other apartment."

"That's very neat," Stone admitted. "Your client is a very cunning fellow."

"I hope I never have the misfortune to be married to somebody as smart," Eggers said. "Can you think of any reason why this wouldn't work?"

Stone laughed. "There are only a few dozen things that

could go wrong," he said, "but it'll be up to our man to handle those. Actually, your client has made it look pretty straightforward. When does he want this done?"

"Within the next few days. Next time the lady says she's working late, he'll call, and it's on. Can you find your man in a hurry?"

"I'll make some calls."

"Let me know what he wants for a fee. I'm authorized to go to ten grand." Eggers reached behind his desk and pulled out a fat aluminum briefcase. "My client has even supplied us with some very neat, lightweight video equipment." He began to laugh. "It belongs to the wife."

Stone had to laugh with him.

Teddy O'Bannion was a thick-set, gray-haired man of, maybe, fifty-five, who had been unfortunate enough to be chosen to take the heat for his precinct a few years back, when one of the periodically instituted crime commissions was going about its work of rooting out corruption in the police department. The evidence allowed against him had been slim, and he had simply been dismissed from the force without prejudice, which allowed him to collect a twenty-year pension, in addition to the very nice monthly stipend his old companions on the pad still paid him.

Teddy could easily pass for your typical out-of-town businessman, in the city for meetings. He looked around the house carefully, obviously trying to figure out how Stone could afford it. "Jesus, Stone, the pad must be bigger than ever," he said, wonderingly.

"I inherited it, Teddy, from a great-aunt, and now I have to spend the rest of my life scrambling to keep it."

"Whatever you say, lad."

Stone handed Teddy a stiff scotch. "I've got a night's work for you. There's five grand in it."

"How many children and dogs do I have to murder?"

"It's a straightforward bedroom job, that's all."

Teddy laughed aloud. "Straightforward? Shit, the last bedroom job I did, the woman flew out of the bed and nearly bit my ear off!"

"Those are the risks you take, Teddy."

"That they are, lad. What's the setup?"

Stone explained about the apartment building. "There are only two apartments to a floor; you'll be booked into 9-B. The wife will be across a vestibule in 9-A. You let yourself in—late, I'm advised—find the bedroom, wake the occupants, and take their picture." He opened the aluminum case and showed Teddy how the camera worked. "You switch on the light; the camera is autofocus, so you just point and shoot. Make sure you get good shots of both faces, and show us a little flesh, if you can. The juicier the better."

"I think I understand your needs," Teddy said. "And I've used this camera before. Is there anything else I should know?"

Stone shook his head. "If there's trouble, don't hurt anybody; if you're apprehended, say nothing and call me. My client will cover any costs. If a case against you comes to anything, there'll be another five thousand for you, if you do the right thing."

"Don't worry, I'm not getting myself apprehended, and if I do, I'll take the rap. Nobody'll trace me back to you. Can I get a look at the place ahead of time?"

Stone shook his head. "I don't want the concierge to see you twice. I'll look it over myself."

"That's okay with me."

"Good. When you've done the job, take a cab to P. J. Clarke's and have a drink at the bar. Make sure nobody's after you. I'll be there, and, when I'm sure you're clear, I'll leave an envelope above the urinal in the men's room with the five grand in it. You go in immediately after me, leave the camera case, take the money, and go home. That's it."

Teddy nodded. "Sounds fine."

"I don't want you recognized, Teddy. What can you do about that?"

Teddy put on his hat, took a pair of heavy, black-rimmed glasses from his coat pocket, put them on, then produced a fat cigar and stuck it in his mouth, distorting his face.

Stone laughed. "Good. Simple and good. Oh, and wear your best suit. You want to look prosperous."

Teddy nodded. "When is it?"

"Probably this week. Stay loose, and I'll give you as much notice as I can. You can pick up the camera stuff here, on your way." Stone gave him a hundred-dollar bill. "Here's cab fare."

Teddy shook his hand at the door. "Thanks, Stone. I'll do it right for you."

Stone hadn't the slightest doubt he would.

36

Your name is Willoughby," Eggers said. "Just check in with the concierge, and he'll give you the key to 9-B. I gave you the key to 9-A, but be careful, there may be somebody in residence."

"Okay," Stone replied.

"I take it you found your man."

"I did. He's waiting for my call."

"Looks like Friday night."

Stone breathed a sigh of relief. He hadn't wanted this to interfere with his Saturday night with Cary. "All right. When will we know for sure?"

"Maybe not until that day. You sure you have to go to the building yourself?"

"Yes. I don't want my man seen there more than once, and, anyway, I'm in no way at risk today."

"Okay, it's your call."

* * *

The building was a small postwar apartment building in the East Sixties that had been refurbished for its current purpose. An elderly man in a blue suit was behind the desk.

"Good afternoon," Stone said. "My name is Willoughby; I believe I'm expected."

The man consulted a list. "Yes, Mr. Willoughby, you're in 9-B. You just need it for the afternoon, I believe?"

"Not even that. I just needed a place to do a little work, and they were kind enough to offer me the apartment."

The man produced a key. "To your right as you leave the elevator. Do you have any luggage?"

"Just my briefcase," Stone said, holding it up. "Is there anybody using the apartment next door? I may have to do some shouting on the telephone." He smiled.

"Shout all you like," the man said. "9-A is empty at the moment."

Stone thanked the man and went to the elevator. When he got off, he put an ear to the door of 9-A and listened for a long moment. No sound. He let himself into 9-B and looked around. The place was handsomely, if impersonally furnished, with good upholstered pieces and one or two antiques. There were two bedrooms, a master and a smaller one, and two baths. After a quick look around, he went next door and let himself into 9-A.

The apartment seemed to be a mirror image of the other, but there was a difference. 9-A had been lavishly done to someone's particular taste, and probably by a very expensive designer. The furnishings were richer and more distinctive than those in 9-B, and the art on the walls was probably a part of the company's collection of expensive paintings. He checked both bedrooms and decided that the master was where the assignation would take place. There was a gorgeous, canopied bed, with a matching silk bedcover, and every stick of furniture in the room dated from the eighteenth century, Stone reckoned. He was about to reenter the living room when he heard the front door open and close.

Oh, shit, he thought, trying to think of some plausible reason why he should be in the apartment. There was a rustling of what sounded like paper bags, followed by a feminine cough. He looked around the bedroom for someplace to hide, should the woman come his way. Her footsteps on the carpet told him she was doing just that.

He ran on tiptoe across the room and practically dove behind the bed. She came into the bedroom, then he heard the hollow click of the bathroom light being turned on. Please close the door, he said to himself, be modest. She did not. He peeped above the edge of the bed and saw it standing wide open and her shadow against the door. There was the sound of water running, then the toilet seat being raised. The water continued to run while she peed. Sitting on the toilet, she would be facing the bathroom door, he knew, so he could not make a run for it. He arranged himself more comfortably and waited.

The woman came out of the bathroom, and he could hear her footsteps approaching the bed. Stone pressed himself closer to it. He heard the rustle of the silk bedcover being turned down and the creak of the springs as the woman lay down.

Stone lay motionless for the better part of a half hour, while the woman tossed and turned, then finally settled down for her nap. When her breathing told him she was sound asleep, he stirred from his position as silently as possible, wincing at the cramps that had formed in his legs. He slipped off his shoes and started for the bedroom door. As he approached the door he glanced back at her, just as she stirred, her back to him. He froze until he was certain she had not actually awakened. Then he made his way across the deep Oriental carpet in the living room to the front door, where he spent several seconds turning the knob as silently as possible. As he closed the door, he saw two large shopping bags from Bergdorf Goodman lying next to a living-room chair.

A moment later, he was back in 9-B, running cold water over his face in the master bathroom. He had done some undercover work in his time, but nothing in his police career had ever prepared him for being a second-story man. Now he knew that burglars are just as frightened as their victims.

He let himself out of the flat and left the building before the lady next door finished her nap.

At home, there was only one message on his answering machine: "Hi, it's me. I'm sorry you aren't in; I wanted to hear your voice. And now I have to go to a production meeting, so you can't even call me back. I'm so looking forward to Saturday; I want to hear this important news of yours—and it must be important, if you want a table at Lutèce. I booked that, which was no problem. Barron goes there all the time, and they know me. After dinner, and after hearing your news, I'm going to make you the happiest man in New York City, I promise. I've missed you so. Until Saturday night, my love."

Stone felt the sort of glow that comes with a double brandy. Saturday night was no longer the loneliest night in the week; it was the only night in the week.

The phone rang. "Hi, it's Bill. We're on for Friday. My client reckons they won't be in the apartment until near midnight."

"Right. I'll let my man know."

"Stone, my client says that this is likely to be the only shot we're going to get at this, so tell him not to fuck it up, okay?"

"Don't worry, he's as steady as they come."

He hung up and called Teddy. "It's Friday night," he said. "I've cased the place already, so be at my house at nine, and I'll brief you and give you the camera."

"Looking forward to it, lad," Teddy said.

"And, Teddy, no booze that night, all right?"

"Lad," Teddy replied, sounding hurt, "I only drink *after* work."

Stone hung up the phone feeling a certain order in his life. There was money in the bank, and he had handled his first assignments for Woodman & Weld in a way that was earning their confidence.

He allowed himself to be troubled for a moment about the ethics of what he was doing, but he brushed the thought aside. An errant wife deserved whatever came her way. Stone was on the side of the angels—or, at least, on the side of the wronged party, his client.

He put the last coat of varnish on the library shelves that night, then slept the sleep of the righteous.

CHAPTER

37

*L*ate Friday morning it started to snow. The big flakes floated straight down, with no wind to blow them into drifts, and, gradually, the city grew silent as traffic decreased and the noise of what was left was muffled by the carpet of white.

As delighted as a child, Stone forgot working on the house and trudged up to Central Park, where he watched children sledding and building snowmen. As it started to get dark, he hiked down Park Avenue, watching the lights come on and the taxis and buses struggle through the deepening snow. By the time he got home, twelve inches had fallen on the city, and it seemed to be getting heavier. Then it occurred to him that Teddy O'Bannion lived in Brooklyn. He grabbed the telephone.

"Don't worry, Stone"—Teddy chuckled—"the subway is just down at the corner, and I can get a cab from your place. I'll start early, so I'll be sure to be on time."

Stone hung up relieved. The thought that he might have to replace Teddy on this mission had never occurred to him, and even the possibility made his knees tremble.

In the study, he pulled the drop cloths off the crates holding his books—his and his great-aunt's and his father's and his mother's. He estimated there were more than two thousand of them. He took them from their boxes and began arranging them carefully on the shelves. This was a job he would not want to do again. He arranged them by category—art books, fiction, philosophy, politics, biography—and alphabetically by author. It was slow going, and he often had to shift books to keep them in order.

At eight o'clock, he fixed himself some dinner and ate it at the kitchen table, watching the news on CNN.

When he had finished his dinner, he returned to the arranging of the books and became so absorbed in the job that it was nine forty before he realized that Teddy O'Bannion had not arrived.

Worried, he called Teddy's number. It was busy, and it remained busy during his next ten attempts. He called the operator and had the number checked: out of order, she would report it. What was going on?

At ten thirty, he began to face the reality that he was going to have to walk into Apartment 9-A and take video-tapes of a strange woman and man in bed together. The thought made his bowels weak. He wished he had not eaten such a large dinner. Teddy's phone number still would not ring.

At a quarter to eleven, Stone realized that he would have to shower and change, so that he would be presentable to the doorman at the apartment building. He hoped to God it would be a different doorman; he couldn't afford to be seen twice by the same man.

In the shower he ran over what might go wrong. The

couple wouldn't be there—that was the best thing that could happen. The man would overpower him and call the police—that would end his relationship with Woodman & Weld, and he would end up in court, if not in jail. The man would produce a pistol from a bedside drawer and . . .

The doorbell rang as he stepped out of the shower. He got into a terry-cloth robe and raced down the stairs. Teddy O'Bannion stood, knee deep in snow, on the front stoop.

"Jesus, I'm sorry, Stone," he began. "There was a fire in the subway station at the corner, and it knocked out not only the trains but every phone in the neighborhood, including mine."

"Come on in, Teddy," Stone said, nearly trembling with relief.

"I'm double-parked out there," Teddy said, brushing snow from his coat. "I had to come in the wife's Jeepster. Good thing I had something with four-wheel drive, but it still took me an hour and a half from the Brooklyn Bridge."

Stone pointed him at the camera case. "Look that over while I change."

When he came back down, Teddy was impatient to go. "I'm not going to get a cab in this," he said.

"I'll come along and wait for you in the car," Stone replied.

Five minutes later, they were grinding slowly up Park Avenue. Stone turned into the right street and stopped the Jeepster a few doors down from the apartment building. "You'd better hurry," he said to Teddy. "You don't want to run into these people in the lobby and let them get a look at you."

Teddy reached inside his coat and produced a nine-millimeter automatic pistol. "Don't worry," he said, grinning, "I'm ready for anything."

Stone grabbed at the pistol. "Are you crazy, Teddy?" Then he laughed. The thing was a water pistol, albeit an extremely realistic one. "What the hell are you doing with this?"

Teddy took the water pistol back. "I'll explain later," he said, getting out of the car. "Keep the motor running, no matter how long it takes."

"Don't worry, I don't want to freeze to death." Stone handed him the key to 9-A.

Teddy pointed at the car phone. "I'll call you, if I can, when I have some results." He closed the door and trudged through the snow toward the building, finally disappearing into the entrance.

Stone turned the radio to a jazz station and settled down to wait. Five minutes later the car phone rang.

"Hello?"

"They were in before me, but I think they're still awake. I can hear music and voices, if I put a water glass against the wall."

"Take your time," Stone said. "We've got all night, if necessary."

"It won't take that long," Teddy said. "In my experience, people who are fucking illicitly don't waste much time getting down to it." He hung up.

Stone turned the heater up a notch, pushed the seat back, and made himself comfortable.

A sharp rapping against the window woke him. He was momentarily disoriented, and, by the time he figured out where he was, the rapping came again on the window. The car's windows were blocked by a blanket of white, and, when he rolled down the driver's side window, snow fell into the car.

"Teddy?" Stone said to the figure outside the car.

"What's up, here, mister?" a voice said.

Jesus, a cop. "Oh, Officer, I'm just waiting for a friend,"

Stone said, scrambling around in his sleepy mind for a story.

"You been here half hour, pal," the cop said. "Let's see your license and registration."

"Well, to tell you the truth," Stone said, "there's somebody in there with my wife, and I mean to find out who it is. She thinks I'm in Chicago on business." This was fairly close to the truth.

The cop shook his head. "Listen, pal, let me give you some advice. Go to Chicago, and forget about it, then come back and forgive her. You don't want to know who the guy is."

"I'm not breaking any laws, am I—parked outside my own house?" Stone tried to sound annoyed.

"I guess not," the cop said. "I won't wish you luck, though." He turned and waded away through the snow.

Stone took a few deep breaths of fresh air before he raised the window. He looked at his watch: ten past midnight. Teddy had been in there less than an hour. He arranged himself again and settled down to wait, switching on the windshield wipers to clear the snow. As he did, Teddy walked out of the apartment building and started toward the car. He didn't seem to be in much of a hurry.

"Get in, and let's get out of here," Stone said, opening the door for him.

"No hurry," Teddy said. "Nobody's going to be following me. Not for a while, anyway."

"Tell me what happened," Stone said, guiding the Jeepster up the block through the deep snow.

"You can hear pretty good with a glass against the wall, you know."

"So what did you hear?"

"I heard the music for a while, and their voices, and then I heard the voices move away, so I figure they'd gone to the bedroom." He shifted in his seat to get comfortable. "Now, there are two ways you can do this," he said. "One, you can wait for them to go to sleep and then wake them up. That's good enough, really; I mean, you got them in bed together, right? But the best way is to catch them doing the actual horizontal bunny hop. That way, there's no talking their way out of it."

"So, what happened?"

"You can hear pretty good with a glass against the wall," Teddy said again, maddeningly. "I could hear them talking over the music. I reckoned they were sitting in front of the fireplace. But then I heard them move away, so I figure they're headed for the bedroom, right?"

"And?"

"I was right. That's where they were going. So I wait, maybe three minutes, and I go in."

Stone's heart was in his mouth. "Teddy, for Christ's sake, tell me what happened."

"I'm telling you, Stone; just be patient. Anyway, I leave the camera case and my shoes outside the door, I unscrew the bulb in the vestibule, and I go in real easylike with my key, and, right from the front door, I can hear them going at it, you know?"

"Teddy, spit it out. Did you get the shot we need?"

"So, what I do is, I switch on the camera, but not the light, so I'm recording sound, right?"

"All right, Teddy, go on, give me the gory details."

"Then I tippy-toe to the bedroom door, and there they are in the moonlight. I think it's probably good enough without the light."

Stone was alarmed. "You didn't use the light?"

"So I run a few feet with just the moonlight. The lady's on top, she's really taking a ride on the guy, you know? And they're building up to it. Both of them are sounding like something at the zoo, no kidding. So, I'm grinding away in the moonlight, and they're grinding away in the bed, and I can tell things are coming to a head, so to speak, so I wait until just the right moment, when they're both bellowing like seals, and I hit the light!" Teddy was sounding absolutely delighted with himself.

"Thank God you hit the light." Stone breathed, his heart pounding.

"Now, tell me, Stone, what's your first reaction, somebody suddenly shines a bright light on you?"

"Oh, shit," Stone said. "I'd throw up a hand to shield my eyes. You didn't get their faces?"

"Stone," Teddy said, sounding hurt, "you underestimate me." He held up the water pistol. "That's where this came in."

"You shot them with a water pistol?" Stone asked, baffled.

"Right. I mean, here you got these two naked people, they're on top of the covers, and they're throwing their hands across their faces to shield their eyes or to keep me from photographing their faces, so with one hand, I give 'em a shot or two with the water pistol, aiming at tender spots like the armpit or the ribs, and, what do they do? Why, they grab at the places I squirted them, don't they? And they leave their faces exposed, just long enough for me to record them for posterity."

"Great! Then what happened?"

"Then the guy, who's on the bottom, remember, tosses the lady in the air, and he starts for me. But I'm outta there, filming all the way, of course, and outside the door I got this little hook that goes one end over the doorknob and the other end hooked to the door molding, so the guy can't open the door from the inside, right?"

"Wonderful," Stone said.

"So, I ring for the elevator, and, while it's coming, and while the guy is trying to break down the door, no doubt bruising his shoulder pretty badly, I slip into my shoes, stick the camera back into its case, and then the elevator comes, I ride down and walk right out of the building. To make it even nicer, the doorman is asleep!"

"Perfection," Stone said. "Teddy, you're a wonder."

"Of course, our guy is going to have to call downstairs and get the doorman to open the door for him, and that's going to be just a little embarrassing for him."

Stone pulled up in front of his house. He reached into a pocket and handed Teddy a thick envelope. "Five thousand, as agreed," he said.

"I thank you, sir," Teddy said, glowing. He handed over the case. "Your camera, and your videotape."

Stone got out of the car, and Teddy drove away. He let himself into the house and called Bill Eggers.

"Jesus, Stone, I haven't slept a wink. How'd it go?"

"It went perfectly, absolutely perfectly."

"You've seen the tape, then?"

"Well, no, I haven't; I don't have a VCR. But my man says he got it all, and he's a good man."

"You gave him the five grand without seeing the tape?"

"Take it easy, Bill, it went well, believe me."

"I hope so, for all our sakes. Meet me at the office at nine tomorrow morning, and we'll have a little private screening."

"All right, but don't worry, Bill. It went well."

"If you say so," Eggers said. "I'll see you in the morning."

Stone wearily got undressed and went to bed, but it was his turn not to sleep. If he'd known where to get a VCR in the middle of the night, he'd have gone out and gotten one. He hoped to God that Teddy O'Bannion's confidence in his own work was not in any way misplaced.

CHAPTER

38

Before leaving the house, Stone shoveled the steps and the sidewalk in front. The weatherman had said there had been eighteen inches of snow over-night, and Stone believed it. He could not remember such silence in the city.

There were no cabs to speak of, and, since the sun was shining brightly anyway, Stone hiked the distance to the offices of Woodman & Weld, walking in the paths broken by buses and the odd cab with chains. The only people in sight seemed to be those who had come out to play. He passed more than one group of adults building snowmen or throwing snowballs at each other. That, and the memory of a task well accomplished, made the day seem festive.

He arrived a little early and waited in the lobby for Eggers. When the lawyer arrived, he introduced Stone to the security guard and had him put on the list for after-hours entry to the Woodman & Weld offices.

"Jesus," Eggers said as they rode up in the elevator, "I hope your man did this right. If we don't have what we need on that tape, it's going to put my client in a very awkward position. I mean, his old lady will be on her guard, and she could make it tough for him."

"My man says he got it," Stone said, "and that's good enough for me." At least, until we see the tape, he thought. It was not going to be good for his position with the law firm if the tape was not good.

Eggers unlocked the front door and relocked it behind them. "Take that stuff down to the small conference room," he said to Stone. "That's where our video system is. Third door on your right. I'll be with you in a minute."

Stone went to the conference room, unsnapped the camera case, took out the camera, and pushed the reject button. The cassette fell out into his hand. He turned to the wall of video equipment but wasn't sure which piece of equipment to use.

Eggers came in. "Pretty impressive, isn't it? We tape depositions, and we have other capabilities, too. You'll see in a minute." He took the cassette from Stone, inserted it into a machine, and flipped a number of switches. Snow filled the screen of a large monitor, then the picture snapped on.

"Here we go," Stone said, sitting down and resting his elbows on the conference table. "Hey, your camera worked pretty well in the low light. Listen."

The sound of two people making love came faintly from the bedroom. The camera moved slowly, smoothly across the living room to the bedroom door. The moonlight was as Teddy O'Bannion had described it, bright as day. The figure of a woman was clearly visible, and she was moving rhythmically in sync with the noises heard a moment before. She was sitting on a man, who was also clearly visible, though neither of their faces could be made out.

"This is sensational!" Eggers said wonderingly. "Hang on a second." He picked up a remote control and froze the frame, then he walked to the wall of equipment and turned on another piece of gear. There was a whirring noise, and, a few moments later, a color photograph slid out of the machine. Eggers looked at it approvingly, then handed it to Stone. "Very artful, wouldn't you say?"

"You're right," Stone said. "It's a beautiful shot, but the faces are shadowed."

"He did turn on the goddamned light, didn't he?"

"Yes, but later; hang on."

Eggers started the tape again. The lovemaking was growing in intensity, and the couple's voices rose with it. Then, at the moment when both seemed to be reaching a climax, the floodlight came on. Instinctively, both the man and the woman threw up a hand to shield themselves from the light. Eggers froze the frame again and made another print.

"This is where the water pistol comes in," Stone said.

Eggers stopped what he was doing. "Water pistol?" he asked incredulously.

"That's how my man gets shots of their faces," Stone replied. "Watch."

Eggers started the tape again and pressed the slow motion button. A jet of water could be seen to enter the frame and strike the man in the chest. His hand started down. Another jet struck the woman just below the armpit, and her arm followed, too.

"There! That's it!" Eggers shouted, freezing the frame. "That's our shot!" He ran to the printer and pressed the button again.

Stone froze to his chair, unable to move, unable to speak. The man's face had surprised him, but the woman's rendered him nearly catatonic. The man was Barron Harkness; the woman was Cary Hilliard.

"Perfect, perfect!" Eggers yelled in triumph, shoving the

print in front of Stone. "You can have that for your scrapbook." He pressed the button for another print. "The cat's out of the bag now, though. I'm sorry for my little subterfuge, but I guess you recognize the guy. His wife is my client."

Stone was unable to speak. His eyes ran up and down the two forms frozen on the screen. Harkness was clearly furious, Cary terrified. Her breasts shone with sweat in the bright light, the nipples erect; her lips were swollen and her eyes round with fright.

"Let's see the rest!" Eggers cried. "Here we go!" He started the tape again.

Harkness reared up in the bed, upsetting Cary from her perch atop him.

"Jesus, the guy's hung!" Eggers said admiringly. "And look at the tits on that broad! Shit, I don't blame the guy!"

The camera backed out of the room as Harkness rose from the bed and came after it. In the nick of time, the front door closed, and the camera wobbled out of control. Teddy's hand could be seen applying his latch to the knob and the molding.

"An absolute goddamned Academy Award winner!" Eggers yelled, jumping out of his chair and doing a little dance. "Gotta call my client; she's waiting on tenterhooks." He grabbed a phone and started dialing. "Stone, you win the Oscar for best producer," he was saying.

Stone willed himself to move. He shoved the photograph into his overcoat pocket and got shakily to his feet.

"Hello, Charlotte? This is Bill Eggers. My dear, your settlement is assured!" Eggers crowed into the phone. "I'm going to come over to your house right now and show you the videotape that's going to do it. Hang on a minute . . . " Eggers looked up to see Stone leaving the room. "Stone, where are you going?"

Stone didn't reply. He continued down the hallway to

the reception room and straight to the waiting elevator. Riding down in the car, he tore at his collar; he couldn't seem to get enough air. Ignoring the security guard's pleas to sign out, he rushed into the street, gulping the cold air, trying to keep his breakfast down. He stumbled through the deep snow, gasping for still more air. After a while, he slowed to a walk; a little while later, he found himself inside his house, leaning against the front door, weeping.

When he had calmed himself a little, he noticed the blinking light on the answering machine. There was only one message.

"Stone, darling," she said, "I've had a little family emergency, and I'm going to have to go to Virginia to see the folks for a few days. I'm leaving this morning, so I'm afraid I can't see you tonight. I'll call you when I get back. Take care."

CHAPTER

39

The rest of the weekend
was awful. Stone felt ill and stayed in bed, getting up only to
make soup and bring in the newspapers. He couldn't concentrate on the papers, and, for the first time in months, the
house did not intrude into his thoughts. He thought of nothing but Cary.

He tried to think of something else, but nothing worked.
Sunday sports on television were a blur; the news meant
nothing; he couldn't keep his mind on the book review or
the Sunday magazine. The crossword puzzle worked for a
few minutes, but every time he stopped to think, Cary
popped into his head—Cary and the awful photograph in
his overcoat pocket.

She had lied to him from the beginning; the married
man in her life had always been Harkness; Stone had been
just a diversion. As Sunday wore on, Stone began to find a

way to deal with his thoughts of her; he hardened himself, belittled the weeks they had had together, made her unimportant. By Monday morning a scab was beginning to form on the wound. He would force it to heal.

On Monday morning a gossip columnist in the *News* had the story:

> The Barron Harknesses are calling it a day, after more than twenty years together and two children. We hear the ice age crept up on the marriage long ago, and the split is just a final acknowledgment of reality.
>
> Insiders say that Barron is being uncommonly generous, that Charlotte Harkness is getting both the house in Easthampton *and* the ten-room Fifth Avenue digs, where Barron has long been chairman of the cooperative's board.
>
> We hear, too, that as part of their agreement, a certain other apartment owner has to leave the building immediately, surely a new wrinkle in divorce settlements.
>
> Since Barron has never been seen squiring ladies around town, speculation on his paramour centers on the Continental Network—insiders figure it must be somebody at the office. Watch this space.

Stone threw the newspaper at the wall, then concentrated on forming the scab again. The phone rang.

"Hi, it's Bill. I just wanted to let you know that the outcome of Friday night's little opus has been most satisfactory for my client."

"I read the item in the news," Stone said. "I'm happier than you know that it worked out so well for her." He did his best to mean this.

"Woodman is delighted, too. He was very, very nervous about your being involved in something like this, and it's unlikely he'll want to do it again soon, but he asked me to express his gratitude."

"Tell him I was glad to be of help."

"I've got nothing on my plate at the moment that I might need you for, so take it easy for a while. Why don't you take a vacation? The islands or someplace?"

"Thanks, but I've got a lot more work to do on the house; I'll use any free time for that. I have to get an office together, too."

"Right, whatever you say. I'll let you know when I have something else for you."

Stone hung up and glanced out the window. A moving van had pulled up outside, and furniture was being loaded into it. Feldstein was moving out of the downstairs professional suite. That suited Stone fine; he'd need the space now.

For the rest of the week, Stone turned his attention to the study. When the books had all been unpacked, dusted, and arranged on the shelves, he waxed the floor, then unrolled the beautiful Aubusson carpet that had come back from cleaning. He got the old desk, now refinished, back in its place, then hung two of his mother's paintings, along with some of his great-aunt's pictures. By Saturday, the room gleamed, but it looked as though someone had always lived in it.

Stone spent a month on the professional suite, ripping out the partitions Feldstein had installed for his treatment rooms, hiring a plumber to replace the old pipes, ducting the new central heating into the space, and stripping and refinishing the original oak paneling. He finished up with a reception room and two offices, plus a storeroom for a copying machine and supplies. He had a discreet brass plate made for the front door that read THE BARRINGTON PRACTICE. He would install it when news of his passing the bar exam came.

He began thinking about a secretary, but, before he could place an ad, Bill Eggers came up with someone who wanted to return to Woodman & Weld after raising children. She was a plump, motherly woman named Helen Wooten, very bright and capable, and she suited his needs perfectly. Not having much else for her to do yet, he put her in charge of his personal finances and the construction costs on the house. She began saving him money immediately.

Bill Eggers arranged a three-hundred-thousand-dollar mortgage on the house that let him pay off his old bank loan and gave him the funds to complete work and furnish the house and office.

Three months passed. Cary never called.

Every couple of weeks he had dinner with Dino, usually at Elaine's. Elaine liked Dino; he made her laugh.

"Stone," Dino said one evening, "you're not going to believe this."

"What?"

"I'm thinking of getting married."

"You're right, I don't believe it."

"A girl from the neighborhood. We know each other since grammar school."

"I don't believe it."

"Mary Ann Bianchi, a good Italian girl."

Stone turned to Elaine. "He's hallucinating."

"I think you're right," Elaine said. "It must be the Sambuca; he's had too much."

"I kid you not," Dino said. "Will you stand up for me, be my best man?"

"I know what this is," Stone said to Elaine, "it's an elaborate practical joke. I'll turn up for the wedding, and the whole 19th Precinct will be there, laughing like hell, because I believed this ridiculous story."

"Stone, I swear to God, I'm doing it. We already got the church booked. I bought her a ring, for Christ's sake."

"You stole it from the evidence room."

Dino looked wounded. "I paid cash money. I know a

guy in the Diamond District."

"This means you can't bring any more girls in here, Dino," Elaine said.

"Don't worry, Mary Ann would kill me in my sleep. She's Sicilian."

"You're in a lot of trouble," Stone said, "but sure, I'll stand up for you."

"It's a week from Sunday," Dino said.

"That's moving pretty quick," Elaine said.

Dino shrugged. "So, it'll be a seven-month kid, so what? Happens all the time in my neighborhood."

Elaine waved at a waiter. "Bring a bottle of champagne, the good stuff. Dino's got a lot to celebrate, here."

They celebrated.

Elaine looked at Stone closely. "You're looking almost human these days," she said. "A few weeks ago you looked like death."

"Hard work on the house," Stone said. "I'm getting used to it."

"He's getting over the broad," Dino said.

"Ahhhh," Elaine said.

"You're right," Stone agreed, "I am." And he was, except for an occasional spear through the heart, when he thought about her. He had stopped thinking at all about Sasha Nijinsky and Hank Morgan.

On the Friday morning before Dino's wedding, Stone received a letter. He recognized the handwriting immediately.

Dear Stone,

Please pardon the familiarity, but, although we've never met, our lives have been so intertwined that I feel you are a friend.

I'm sorry that my problems at least indirectly resulted in your leaving the police force, but I understand that you are now doing well. I saw your name in the *Times*, on the list of those who had passed the bar exam.

I think, perhaps, the time is coming when we should meet. Maybe you would come to dinner sometime soon? It would be so nice to meet you, at last.

I'll be in touch.

Best,

S.

CHAPTER

40

They sat at a table in the little room in back of the bar at Clarke's. The mirror behind the bar had been replaced; everybody seemed to want to forget the incident, and Dino was obviously welcome.

"You're looking better," Dino said. "You put the girl behind you for good?"

"What else can I do?"

"We've all been there, Stone, believe me. Thank God that's all over for me."

"I'd like to think so, Dino."

"Believe me, it's over. When you marry a Sicilian, it's for life, and that can be short if you fool around."

"How are things at the office?"

"Looks like we got *two* serial killers on our hands."

"The taxi killings, I guess."

"That's one of them. It's the most trouble, too, because

every time another cabbie gets greased, the rest of them go bananas and block a major artery for the day."

"I read about it. Any suspects?"

"Negative."

"What's the other case?"

"That one's even weirder. We got two men and two women in the past seven weeks who just went *poof*. Right off the street."

"Where?"

"Everywhere. All over Manhattan."

"No bodies?"

"No nothing."

"What do they have in common?"

"Fuckall. The women were twenty-six and thirty-two; the men were thirty-seven and thirty-nine. The guys were a stockbroker and a Porsche salesman; the women were an advertising art director and a VP at a cosmetics company."

"No ransom notes?"

"Nope. They only got one thing in common I can see."

"What's that?"

"They're good looking, all of them. Good dressers, real prime-time yuppies."

"Where were they last seen?"

"Leaving work; restaurant; leaving exercise class; jogging in Battery Park."

Stone shrugged. "Good luck, Dino."

"I'm going to need it. What're you working on at the law firm?"

"A fairly juicy one. A client—chairman of an electronics firm—is accused of beating up a high-class hooker in the Waldorf Towers. Looks like it'll go to trial, and I'll assist in the defense."

"They're not giving you nothing to try yourself, huh?"

"Not yet. I think they expect me to come up with my own. Any ideas?"

"I'll keep it in mind, tell a couple of the guys. You never know."

Stone took the letter, in a plastic envelope, from his pocket. "I've got something to show you." He handed it over.

Dino read it and stopped chewing his salad. Then he started again and swallowed. "So? Who's 'S'?"

Stone stared at him, unbelieving. "Come on, Dino, you read her diary; don't you recognize the handwriting?"

"Can't say that I do," Dino said, concentrating on the salad. "I never had much memory for handwriting."

"I didn't expect this."

"Expect what? You expect me to recommend reopening the investigation based on this?" He tossed the letter back across the table.

"I didn't expect you to stonewall me."

"I ain't stonewalling you, Stone. You come up with something substantial, and I'll go with you on it."

"Substantial? A letter from a dead woman isn't substantial?"

"Where was it mailed?"

"Penn Station."

"Any prints? I know you checked."

Stone held the plastic holder at an angle and pointed. "Three. Will you run them against what we found in her apartment?"

Dino looked skeptical, then shrugged. "Okay, I'll do that. It may take a few days; the records have probably left the precinct."

"As soon as you can. And will you have the handwriting analyzed?"

"Against what?"

"The diary, the other stuff in evidence."

"The case has been cleared. I expect all that stuff has gone back to her estate, to her family, by now."

"Dino, if I can get a good analysis done, and the prints turn out to be hers, will that be enough for you to reopen?"

"Tell you the truth, I don't know. I'd have to go to Delgado; he'd have to go to Waldron; he might even have to go to the mayor. The thing is, even if an analyst says it's her handwriting, even if the prints are hers, what have we got to go on? We can't trace the letter. It looks like pretty ordinary stationery to me; it was mailed in the biggest post office in the city. What could we do?"

"We'd know she's alive." He pushed the letter back across the table. "That's a start."

Dino laughed and shook his head. "You still got a hair up your ass about that, ain't you? All that crap about cats bouncing off concrete and walking away. You know, if *I* had come to *you* with that kind of a theory, you'd have kicked my ass."

Stone laughed. "I don't know, Dino, I think I'd have given your idea a hearing."

"I gave your idea a hearing," Dino said.

"For about fifteen seconds."

"That was all I needed."

"Okay, okay, but will you have the lab look at the paper and anything else they can find?"

"All right, but I'll have to get somebody to do it on his own time. If word got around about this, I'd be pounding a beat, pronto."

"Thanks, Dino."

"I'll owe somebody a favor, too."

"I'll owe you one."

They paused outside the restaurant.

"One forty-five, Sunday, at the church?" Dino said. "You got the address?"

"I've got it."

"Tuxedo. I'll pick up the rental."

"I own one."

"We're coming up in the world, aren't we?"

"I've actually used it a couple of times. A firm party, that sort of thing."

"I'll see if I can have something for you on the letter by then. Otherwise, it'll have to wait till after the honeymoon."

"Where you going?"

"Vegas—where else?"

"Sounds great. I'll see you Sunday."

"You ever been to an Italian wedding?"

"No."

"You got an experience coming."

Dino turned out to be right.

CHAPTER

41

Frank Woodman was at his desk, dictating something into a recorder, but, when he saw Stone at the door, he waved him in. "How are you, Stone?" he said, pointing at a chair.

Stone sat down. "I'm fine, Frank. There's something I want to ask you about."

"First," Woodman said, "there's something I want to say to you, and I'm sorry I didn't seek you out and say it sooner. Stone, only Bill Eggers, Charlotte Harkness, and I have seen that tape, and I'm the only one who knows you knew Cary Hilliard. I want you to know that it won't go any further than that."

Stone nodded. He couldn't think of anything to say.

"You did a fine job for us, and I'm sorry the result had to cause you pain."

"Thank you, Frank."

"Enough said about that. What can I do for you?"

"I was wondering if you have the effects of Sasha Nijinsky that the NYPD took."

"They sent them back to me a couple of weeks ago. After going through them myself, I sent them to Sasha's father."

"I see."

"Why? Did you want to see them again?"

"Yes, I wanted to get a look at her handwriting again."

"Why?"

Stone handed Woodman a copy of the letter.

Woodman read it through twice, and his expression revealed nothing. "What do you make of this?" he asked at last.

"I'm not entirely sure what to make of it. A friend of mine at the 19th Precinct is getting it looked at by the lab, but I wanted to compare the handwriting to something of Sasha's."

"That's no problem," Woodman said, rising and going to a file cabinet. "Sasha didn't type. She told me once that she refused to learn, so that she wouldn't get shunted aside into 'woman's' work." He flipped through a folder, extracted a letter, and handed it to Stone. "She did all her correspondence by hand."

Stone laid the two letters side by side on the desk, and both men bent over them. Woodman produced a magnifying glass, and they examined them closely.

"They're a lot alike, I'd say, but the one sent to you looks a little cramped," Woodman said.

"The lines are not as straight, either," Stone added.

"This is over my head," Woodman said, picking up the phone. "Sophie, please find the name of that handwriting man we used on the mineral rights case last year, then see if you can get him over here right away." He hung up. "When did you get this, Stone? It's not dated."

"Friday. It was posted the day before at Penn Station."

"It must be some kind of crank who read your name in the papers as being associated with the case."

"That seems more than just possible. Still, there's the handwriting."

"I suppose someone who knew Sasha might have had a letter of hers and used that to make a forgery."

"But why?"

"Maybe someone who isn't satisfied with the outcome of the case. A lot of people aren't; I'm one of them. Maybe someone's just trying to get you interested again."

"The letter certainly had that effect," Stone said.

The phone rang, and Woodman picked it up. "Good," he said, then hung up. "Man's name is Weaver. His office is only a couple of blocks away; he's coming over." Woodman looked uncomfortable for a moment. "Stone, I get the impression that you are at least considering the possibility that Sasha might still be alive. Is that right?"

"Yes," Stone replied. "I think it's just possible." He explained the circumstances of Sasha's fall and his terminal velocity theory.

"Jesus Christ," Woodman said.

Weaver was a tall, thin man in his sixties. He looked at both letters carefully. Woodman had folded the letters so that the signatures did not show. "This is a Xerox copy, I presume," he said, holding up Stone's letter.

"Yes, I don't have the original at the moment."

"I'd like to see it, but it probably wouldn't make much difference in my opinion."

"What is your opinion, Mr. Weaver?" Woodman asked.

"I'd say there's about an eighty percent chance that the same person wrote both letters."

"Why can't you be sure?" Stone asked.

"Well, the similarity in the shaping of the letters is profound, but there's anomaly that could mean it's a forgery. You see, here, the spacing in the more recent letter is closer; it has a cramped quality. Its lines aren't as straight, either."

"We noticed that," Woodman said. "Could there be some other reason than forgery for the difference between the two letters?"

"Well, yes. The recent letter doesn't have quite the vitality of style that the earlier one exhibits. That's a common trait of forgeries, but it often turns up, too, when the writer is ill or injured or is convalescing." Weaver held his right elbow close to his side and demonstrated. "A person who is weakened or in pain would characteristically hold his arm in like this, restricting the movement of his hand. This would especially be true in the event of injury—say, a broken arm or ribs. That could quite easily account for the cramped nature of the second letter."

Stone and Woodman exchanged a look. Woodman raised his eyebrows.

Weaver continued. "In my experience, this characteristic of what you might call the 'wounded writer' would be more evident in the writing of a woman, but both these letters were, of course, written by a man."

"By a man?" Stone asked, incredulously.

"In my opinion, yes; definitely," Weaver replied.

"Anything else you can tell us?" Woodman asked.

"That's about it, I think, though I would like to see the original of the second letter."

Woodman escorted the man to the door. "Thank you, Mr. Weaver, and please send me your bill." Woodman came back to his desk and sat down. "This is the goddamndest thing I ever heard," he said.

"Frank, are you certain that Sasha, herself, wrote you this letter?"

Woodman went back to his file and extracted a small sheet of paper. "I watched her write this," he said. "She was sitting where you are now."

Stone picked up the paper. It was the address and phone number of Sasha's new, Fifth Avenue apartment. He compared the note with the first letter, then the second. "The handwriting seems identical to me," he said, handing Woodman the papers.

"Me, too," Woodman said, poring over them.

"Now, why would Weaver think the writer was a man?"

"Well," said Woodman, "for a lady, Sasha always had incredible balls."

At home, Stone built a fire in the study, poured himself a drink, and stretched out on the leather sofa before the fireplace. He sipped the drink and cast his mind back over the events surrounding Sasha Nijinsky's dive from the terrace, letting them run though his mind without hindrance, comparing one event with another, listening to fragments of conversation from people he had interviewed. Something nagged at him, something he should be remembering. The phone rang.

He reached out to the extension on the coffee table. "Hello?" he said.

"Hello."

Stone tightened his grip on the phone. Images flew before his eyes—a breast, a wrist. He felt her body against his, her hair in his face, her legs locked around him, her mouth on his penis.

"I want to see you," she said.

Stone wanted to speak, but his throat tightened.

"I want to see you tonight," she said.

He made a huge effort to control himself, to make his voice work, to tamp down the rage and hurt inside him. It didn't work. He hung up the phone.

He lay on the sofa through what should have been dinner, until past midnight, waiting for a knock on the door or another call. Neither came.

42

Dino Bacchetti and Mary Ann Bianchi were married at San Gennaro's Church in Little Italy on Sunday. Stone had never worn a tuxedo at two o'clock in the afternoon, but he stood as best man for Dino, and he was impressed with the elaborate and somber Roman Catholic ceremony. Dino kissed his bride, and the wedding party began moving back down the aisle, the happy couple leading the bridesmaids and groomsmen.

Near the back of the church, Stone glanced to his right and stopped in his tracks. Cary Hilliard was sitting in the back pew, bundled in a mink coat. Somebody behind Stone stepped on his heels, and he moved on with the wedding party. Stone was trapped on the front steps of the church as the party posed for photographs, then the group was bundled into limousines and driven to a restaurant for the reception, so he did not see what became of Cary.

The restaurant was not large, and two hundred happy people were crammed into it, singing, dancing, and generally raising hell. The only non-Italians, besides Stone, were the Irish, Puerto Rican, and black cops who worked with or for Dino. Stone kissed the bride and was surprised at the enthusiasm with which she responded.

He shook Dino's hand. "Well, you did it," he said, laughing.

Dino looked supremely happy. "You goddamned right I did, *paisan*."

"Speaking of *paisans*," Stone said, nodding at a group of severe-looking people across the room, "who's that?"

"That's Mary Ann's people," Dino replied. "Her old man's a capo in the Bonanno family. Well respected."

"No kidding?"

"No kidding."

"Why do they look so . . . unhappy?"

"Because their most beautiful daughter got knocked up by a cop, that's why. The old man's really pissed off. If I wasn't Italian, I'd be at the bottom of Sheepshead Bay with a concrete block stuck up my ass."

"Dino, you better be very, very good to that girl," Stone said gravely.

"Don't worry." Dino took an envelope from his inside pocket. "Here's your report on the letter," he said. "I don't want to hear about it again, okay?"

Stone put the envelope in his pocket. "Okay."

"Guess who sent us a real nice piece of silver?" Dino said.

"Who?"

Dino nodded. "The very beautiful lady over there," he said.

Stone followed Dino's gaze and found Cary standing on the opposite side of the dance floor.

"See you later, pal," Dino said, and vanished.

Stone stood and watched her make her way across the dance floor toward him. Under the mink coat, she was wearing a very short silk dress that made her legs seem longer than he remembered. Stone's mouth went dry.

She took his hand and led him onto the floor; the band was playing something romantic and Italian; he followed her dumbly. They began to move together; she laid her head on his shoulder and kissed him on the neck.

"God, but I've missed you," she said.

Stone was unable to say anything; he put his hand inside the coat and pulled her to him. The familiarity of those curves pressed against his body made him light-headed, and he lost himself in the music and the feel of her. Her cool hand was on the back of his neck, her fingers in his hair, her tongue played at his ear. The music continued—a medley— and she seemed to become more and more a part of him. Suddenly, she stopped dancing.

"Come with me," she said, tugging at his hand.

He followed her across the dance floor, through the crowd, along a wall to a door. She opened it, looked in, then pulled him inside with her. They were in a small office—only a desk, a chair, and an old sofa. She closed the door and locked it.

"Where have you—"

"Shhhh," she whispered, throwing the mink coat onto the sofa and snaking an arm around his neck. "Don't say anything." She was unzipping his trousers; in a moment, she had him in her hand.

After that, things happened effortlessly. They were on the sofa, on the luxurious coat, his trousers around his knees, her legs around him. She wasn't wearing underwear. They both gave themselves to the moment, made it last, then came with a roar of blood in the ears, her cries mixing with the music, loud through the thin walls.

They lay limp in each other's arms for a few minutes,

then Cary found a toilet off the office, and Stone tried to make himself presentable again. She was a long time in the john, and, when she came out, Stone was reading the lab report.

"What's that?" she asked, putting a hand at the back of his neck and reading over his shoulder.

Stone handed her the letter without comment.

She read it, and her eyes went wide. "Sasha's *alive?*" she asked, stunned.

"It would seem so," Stone said, reading the report. "An expert says it's almost certainly her handwriting, and her fingerprints are on the letter." He read on. "They were very clear, because she had olive oil on her fingers—extra virgin olive oil, according to this."

"It doesn't seem possible," she said, incredulously.

"No, it doesn't," he replied. "Nevertheless ... "

She walked over to the sofa and retrieved her coat, seemingly lost in thought. "That means she's going to be able to identify whoever pushed her off that balcony, doesn't it?"

"I hope so. I wonder why she hasn't done it already."

Cary slipped into her coat and walked to the door, unlocking it.

"You're leaving? When can I see you?"

"I'll call you," she said. "I've left my job, and I'm staying with a friend. Don't worry, we'll see each other. You'll see me sooner than you think. Pay no attention to what you hear."

"What am I going to hear?" he asked.

She ignored his question; her brow was furrowed. "There's something I never told you," she said. "I should have told you a long time ago." She seemed to be wrestling with whether to tell him now.

"What is it?"

She looked at the floor. "Barron wasn't on that airplane from Rome."

Stone stared at her. "But Dino saw him . . ."

She looked up at him, then slipped through the door. "Dino didn't do his job," she said, then closed the door behind her, leaving him alone in the room.

Stone went to the bathroom and splashed some cold water on his face, his mind racing. Then he rejoined the crowd and found Dino, who was making his way out of the party with Mary Ann. He could see the car outside, festooned with tin cans and old shoes.

"Dino, when you went to the airport to meet Barron Hark-ness's plane, did you actually see him get off?"

"Stone, c'mon, okay?" He kissed an old lady on the lips.

Stone managed to stay alongside him. "You didn't actually *see* him, did you?"

"I checked the manifest, all right? Hey, Cheech, how you doin'?"

Stone bodily prevented a fat woman from squeezing between them. "Dino, you didn't *see* him."

"Stone, I'm leaving on my honeymoon; gimme a major fucking break, will you?"

Stone stopped moving, and the crowd surged past him. He watched Dino carried along by the crowd to the car, then he was driving away, waving.

43

*L*ate in the evening, as Stone was drifting off to sleep, the telephone rang. He fumbled for it. "Hello?"

"Mr. Barrington?" The voice was vaguely familiar.

"Yes?"

"This is Herbert Van Fleet."

Stone looked at the clock. "Jesus Christ," he muttered under his breath. "What is it?"

"I know I must have awakened you. I'm very sorry."

"What do you want, Mr. Van Fleet?"

"I want to retain you."

"Retain me?"

"I understand that you are practicing law now."

"Yes, that's right, but why do we need to talk about this at eleven o'clock on a Sunday night? Can you call my office number tomorrow morning?"

"I'm afraid it's more urgent than that. I've been arrested."

Stone sighed and swung his legs over the side of the bed. "What were you arrested for, Mr. Van Fleet?"

"Please call me Herb."

Annoyed. "What were you arrested for, *Herb*?"

"They're calling it attempted rape. They want to arraign me in a couple of hours, in night court."

"Where are you now?"

"I'm in a place called the Tombs. They let me make this one call."

"You're going to need to raise bail, Herb. Can you lay your hands on some money?"

"How much money?"

"I should think that, with no previous arrests, the judge might want as much as twenty-five thousand dollars in cash, or you can put up ten percent and some property to a bail bondsman. You won't get the ten percent back."

"I've got about forty thousand dollars in a money market account," Van Fleet said.

"That should do it," Stone said. "All right, Herb, I'll represent you at the arraignment. My fee for that will be a thousand dollars. If you want me to represent you after that, we can talk about a further retainer."

"All right, that's acceptable."

"I'll meet you at night court." Stone hung up, oddly elated. Herbert Van Fleet was a strange person, but this was the first time somebody had asked Stone to represent him, his first client outside Woodman & Weld. It promised to be a fairly lucrative representation too. He began to get dressed.

Night court was a zoo. Every prostitute, vagrant, and petty criminal arrested during the past few hours would be arraigned there, and the crowd was colorful and noisy. From the back of the huge courtroom, Stone could barely hear the judge, who was shouting.

Stone counted. Standing before the bench, looking at the floor and shifting their weight from one foot to the other, were twenty-four Chinese men, all neatly dressed in business suits. He took a seat down front and listened, curious. The men had been gambling in the basement of a restaurant in Chinatown, only a few blocks away, and an old lady next door had turned them in. Their Anglo lawyer, in unctuous tones, was explaining to the somewhat amused judge that his clients were all respected members of the community, businessmen out for an evening of diversion. They were not criminals, not really, and were very sorry to have disturbed the old woman's sleep. The judge released the men on their own recognizance.

Stone got up, introduced himself to the bailiff at the door to the holding cells, and, shortly, Herbert Van Fleet appeared, in handcuffs. Stone sat him down in one of the little rooms set aside for consultation with attorneys. "All right, Herb, tell me exactly what happened."

Van Fleet sighed. "I was at the Tribeca Grill, having a drink, and I got to talking to this girl. I offered her a ride home—she said she lived in the West Village—and, on the way, we were getting sort of friendly, and—"

"Exactly what do you mean by 'getting sort of friendly'?"

"We were holding hands, and she was sitting close to me. We stopped at a traffic light on Sixth Avenue, and we kissed."

"Did you put your hands between her legs or on her breasts?"

"Yes, on her breasts, and she seemed to like that. It was when I put my hand down the front of her dress that she became difficult."

"Difficult?"

"She started screaming at me. I didn't realize how drunk

she was until that moment. She started to get out of the van, and I tried to persuade her to calm down, and then she started screaming for help."

"Were you fighting?"

"I had hold of her wrists and was talking to her, trying to get her to calm down, when a police car pulled up alongside us at the light, and she jumped out of the van and started screaming hysterically about how I had tried to rape her."

"Did you ever get your hand on her breast—inside her dress, I mean?"

"Yes, but just for a minute."

"Herbert, is that all that happened? Is there any more? I have to know if I'm going to be able to give you a proper defense."

"I swear to you, that was all there was to it. If the police car hadn't just happened to show up, it would have been all over in a minute. She would either have calmed down, or she would have gotten out of the van. This whole thing about attempted rape is completely crazy. Oh, I forgot, the policemen gave me a breath test—made me blow up one of those balloons."

"Did they indicate what the results were?"

"No, I asked them, but they didn't answer."

"Did they give the girl the same test?"

"I don't know, I didn't see them do that. They put me in the back of the police car while they were talking to her and calming her down."

"All right, you go with the officer back to the holding cell, and, when they bring you before the bench, I'll be waiting for you."

Van Fleet stuck out his hand. "Thank you for coming, Stone; I really appreciate this. I didn't want to get my mother involved, you know?"

"I know, Herb. Maybe we can deal with this without her knowing about it; we'll see."

* * *

When the charges were read against Herbert Van Fleet, Stone pointed out to the judge that Van Fleet had no record of arrests or of criminal activity, that he was gainfully employed in a supervisory position, and that he was a responsible member of the community. He mentioned also that the woman making the complaint was unharmed, unless she had a hangover, and that there were no witnesses to support her complaint. He asked that Van Fleet be released on his own recognizance. The judge thought for about three seconds, then set bail at ten thousand dollars and ordered the release of Van Fleet's vehicle. An hour later, Stone and Van Fleet met in front of the courthouse, and Van Fleet thanked him profusely.

"What happens next?" Van Fleet asked.

"If you want me to represent you, what I'll do first is to try to prevent the case going to trial. The district attorney might offer us a deal, but I don't think we'd take it. If what you've told me is the truth, and there were no witnesses to any of this, then it's your word against the girl's. In fact, it sounds to me as though the police officers should have dealt with this on the spot, just put the girl in a cab and sent her home, then lectured you and let you go."

"I'd like you to represent me," Van Fleet said.

"All right; my fee will be ten thousand dollars, including tonight's court appearance—that's if I can negotiate this without a trial. If we have to go to trial, I'll represent you on the basis of two hundred dollars an hour, with a guaranteed minimum of twenty-five thousand dollars, which will include any previous pretrial negotiations. And my fee will be payable in advance, as is customary with criminal cases."

Van Fleet thought for a moment.

"Of course, I'm sure you can find another lawyer who will do it for less, and you're free to retain anyone you wish.

At the moment, all you owe me is a thousand dollars." Stone watched the man think. He didn't mention that he knew of the altercation outside Elaine's some months before, and he thought that Van Fleet might be guiltier than he was admitting.

"All right, that's acceptable," Van Fleet said finally. "I'll give you a check for ten thousand dollars right now."

Stone nodded and watched while Van Fleet wrote the check. They shook hands. "I'll call you as soon as I find out which assistant DA your case has been assigned to, and after I've had a chance to talk to him."

"Good night, then, and thank you again for coming down here and getting me out."

Stone watched the man walk to his van and drive away, then he caught a cab uptown.

Later in the week, Stone visited the offices of the district attorney and found the assistant DA assigned to Van Fleet's case. She was a rather plain young woman named Mendel. She offered him the other chair in her tiny cubicle, then flipped quickly through the file.

"Your client is a potentially dangerous man, Mr. Barrington," she said. "If the police had not arrived on the scene, chances are this young woman would have been raped."

"Come on, at a traffic light?" Stone said derisively. "This was nothing more than a quick grope, and the girl encouraged it."

She glanced at the file again. "Your client had been drinking."

"But he wasn't even over the limit for driving, was he?" Stone asked, taking a stab. "And what was the girl's blood-alcohol content?"

Mendel snapped the file shut. "I can't discuss that."

"Come on, Ms. Mendel, the police didn't even test her, did they? How is that going to look in court?"

"I might be able to reduce to simple battery," she said. "Your client, as a first offender, wouldn't do any time. I'd recommend counseling and community service."

"How long have you been on the job?" Stone asked.

"That's not relevant to this discussion," she replied primly.

"As little time as that, huh?" She had probably been a member of the bar longer than he had, but she didn't know that. "Look, if this went to trial, I'd blow you right out of the water. In fact, I could insist on going down the hall to the chief prosecutor right now and get this one tossed, but that would embarrass you and take up my time. Please don't think I'm patronizing you, but I want to give you some advice. The traffic is too heavy in this office to give your time to anything but cases you have a real chance of winning. This one is a nonstarter, and we both know it. Why don't you just drop charges now—you have that authority— and let's save ourselves for something worth going to trial on?" He smiled.

"Oh, shit, all right," she said, tossing the file on her desk. "But I'm going to take it out of your ass when I do get you into court." She smiled seductively.

Stone thanked her and fled the premises. Back in his new office, with Helen typing in the reception room, he called Van Fleet and gave him the news.

"Oh, thank you so very much," Van Fleet breathed into the phone. "I can't tell you what a load off my mind this is."

"Glad to be of help, Herb," Stone said, "but let me give you some advice. Stop picking up girls in bars. This was a close call, and, if you keep it up, you're going to get in trouble. I don't want to see that happen."

"Don't worry, Stone," Van Fleet said. "You won't have to defend me again."

Stone hung up and reflected on what an easy ten thousand dollars he had made.

Helen came into his office. "A Ms. Hilliard called while you were on the phone. She dictated this message to me."

Stone read the message:

Please meet me in the lobby of the Algonquin Hotel at four o'clock this afternoon. Don't disappoint me.

Stone felt an involuntary stirring in his crotch. The hell with her, he thought; he wouldn't do it.

CHAPTER

44

Stone arrived at the Algon-
quin at four on the dot. The Japanese had bought the hotel,
as they had seemed to buy nearly everything else, and had
restored the lobby. It was beautiful, he thought, gazing at the
polished oak paneling and the new fabrics. He looked
around for Cary; she had not yet arrived. He snagged the
headwaiter and was given a table. He ordered a drink and
waited.

Five minutes later, a bellman walked among the tables
calling, "Mr. Barrington, message for Mr. Barrington!"

Stone accepted an envelope and tipped the man. It was a
hotel envelope, and inside was a plastic card with a lot of holes
punched in it. A number had been written on it with a marking
pen. He paid for his drink and walked to the elevator. Sweat was
beginning to seep from his armpits and crotch, and he was
breathing a little faster than he normally did.

The room was at the end of the hall. He inserted the card in a slot, there was an audible click, and the door opened into a nicely furnished sitting room. The door to the bedroom was closed, and he opened it, letting a shaft of light into the darkened room. He closed the door behind him and took off his overcoat. There was a slit of light from under the bathroom door and the sound of water running. Breathing harder now, Stone began ridding himself of his clothes.

When she opened the door, the bathroom light illuminated her from above for just a moment. She was wearing only a terry-cloth robe, and it fell open. She switched off the light and crossed the room to him. Somewhere along the way, the robe disappeared.

He rolled off her and sprawled on his back, panting and sweating. It had been the third time in two hours; he hadn't known he was capable of that. In the time since he had entered the room, neither of them had spoken a word that had not been connected with what they were doing to each other.

She handed him a glass of water from the bedside. He drank greedily from it, then handed it back.

"Turn on a light," he said. "It's on your side."

"No."

"I want to see you."

"No."

"Why are we doing this in a hotel room? I have a home; you could have come there."

"It would have been an unnecessary risk," she said.

"Risk? What risk?"

"We can't be seen together."

"Cary, for Christ's sake! I think you owe me some sort of explanation for your behavior."

"My father always said to me, 'Never explain, never apologize.'"

He got angrily out of bed and went into the bathroom. He peed, then turned on the light and looked at himself in the mirror, his hair awry, his face streaked with sweat. He found a facecloth and cleaned himself, brushed his hair with his fingers, rinsed his mouth. When he came out of the bathroom, she was dressed and pulling on a coat. A silk scarf was tied around her hair.

"Cary, stay here and talk to me."

"I can't."

The photograph of her and Harkness in bed together was still in his overcoat pocket. He felt an urge to thrust it into her face, but he held back. It disgusted him that he still wanted her, but he did, and he could not afford to push her further away.

"Did you check on the Rome flight?" she asked casually.

"Yes. Dino didn't see Harkness. His name was on the manifest, though; that means someone used his ticket."

"Probably a crew member." She was buckling the belt of her trench coat.

"I can't prove he wasn't on the airplane, and, if he wasn't, then I can't prove where else he was. Not without your help."

"I can't do that."

"Why not? If he murdered her, don't you want him caught?"

She went into the bathroom and began putting on lipstick. "There's something else you could look into, though."

"What's that?"

"Sasha gave him a very large amount of money; I'm not sure how much."

Stone remembered the funds missing from Sasha's accounts. "Could it have been as much as two million dollars?"

"Yes. She wanted it back, and he couldn't come up with it."

●
267

Motive, he thought. Finally, a solid motive. Harkness borrowed the money, then lost it somehow—gambling? Bad investments?

"Why did she give him the money?"

"To invest. Barron thinks of himself as God's gift to Wall Street. Wall Street thinks of him that way, too; he's lost millions in his time." She put her makeup back into her purse and snapped it shut.

"How can I get in touch with you?"

"I told you before, you can't. I'll call you soon." She was in the living room and opening the front door before he could move to stop her. She paused there and looked back. "You were wonderful," she said. "You're always wonderful." She closed the door behind her.

He nearly went after her, then remembered he was naked.

When he got home, there was an invitation in the mail, postmarked Penn Station:

> *The pleasure of your company is requested for dinner, Saturday evening at nine. A car will call for you at eight thirty.*   *Black tie*

A handwritten note was in a corner:

I so look forward to meeting you.
S.

CHAPTER

45

Stone spent a good part of the night restless in his bed, wondering how he could use the new information Cary had given him about Barron Harkness. He found a possible answer in the television column of the following morning's *New York Times:*

BARKER GETS LATE-NIGHT SHOW

Hiram Barker, the writer and social gadfly, has landed his own interview show, Sunday nights at 11:30 P.M., on the Continental Network, beginning this Sunday. Barker, contacted for comment, said that negotiations had been going on for several weeks and that he expected to be able to attract guests who did not ordinarily give interviews.

Stone picked up the phone and called Hi Barker.

"Hello, Stone, how are you? I hear good things about

you from Frank Woodman."

"I'm very well, Hi. I see in this morning's *Times* that you've landed a television show."

"That's right. In fact, I had hoped to interview you about the Sasha business."

"It's a little early for that, I think, but you may remember that when we first met I agreed to tell you what I knew first, in return for your help."

"I remember that very well indeed, dear boy, and that's an IOU I intend to collect."

"Well, I'm not ready for you to publish just yet, but I am ready to start telling you what I know about the case."

"I'm delighted to hear it."

"How about lunch today?"

"You're on. Where?"

"The Four Seasons at twelve thirty?"

"Fine. Use my name; you'll get a better table."

"There's just one thing, Hi."

"What's that?"

"If I'm going to tell you all, you're going to have to do the same."

"But I thought I already had, Stone." Barker sounded wounded.

"You held something back, Hi, something important, and today I want to know all about that."

"Hmmmm," Barker said, "I wonder if you're fishing."

"Today, I'm catching," Stone replied. "See you at lunch."

He was fishing, indeed. He didn't know what Barker was holding back, but he figured there must be something. Most people held back something.

Stone arrived first, and Barker's trip to their table was slowed as he stopped at half a dozen others to greet their occupants.

"I love this place," Barker sighed as he slid his bulk into a seat. "It's just so . . . *perfect.*"

"I'm glad I chose it," Stone said. He ordered a bottle of wine.

"All right," Barker said when their lunch had come, "you first."

Stone began at the beginning and took Barker through his investigation of the Nijinsky case. He glossed over the business with Hank Morgan's suicide to protect Dino, and Barker didn't call him on it. When he had finished, Barker looked skeptical.

"Then you're still nowhere on this?"

"Not quite nowhere," Stone replied. "I have some new information."

"Tell me, dear boy."

"I've learned that Barron Harkness wasn't on the airplane from Rome."

Barker's eyebrows went up in delight. "And how did you learn that?"

"I must protect my source."

"So now you'll have him arrested?" Barker seemed thrilled at the prospect.

"No. I can't prove he wasn't on the airplane. His ticket was used, so his name appears on the manifest."

"How about questioning the flight attendants? Surely, they would remember such a celebrity."

"Not necessarily. Months have passed. The flight attendants might testify that they don't remember seeing him, but they couldn't credibly swear that he was not on the plane."

"Hmmmm. I see your problem."

"There's something else. Sasha gave Harkness two million dollars to invest, and he was having trouble returning it."

"Now *that's* very interesting."

"Yes, but again, I can't prove it. The money seems to

have been laundered through a Cayman Islands bank, so there's no paper trail. The only person who could testify to the transaction is Sasha, and she's not available—at least, not yet."

"Not yet? You sound as if you think she might still be alive."

Stone took Barker through his terminal velocity theory.

Barker looked doubtful. "That's pretty farfetched, Stone. I think you're grasping at straws."

Stone took the note and the invitation from his pocket and put them on the table.

"Jesus H. Christ," Barker said. He took out his glasses and examined the note carefully. "I've had a couple of letters from Sasha in the past, and that certainly looks like her handwriting."

"An expert says it almost certainly is," Stone said. "What's more, her fingerprints were on the note."

Barker forgot about his food. *"Her fingerprints?"*

"I kid you not."

"Well, if Sasha is alive, and if you are having dinner with her on Saturday night, then you'll soon have her testimony about Harkness."

"If she's alive, and *if* the dinner isn't some sort of elaborate hoax perpetrated by some demented Sasha fan. I can't depend on that to nail Harkness. I need your help."

"I would be absolutely delighted," Barker said, grinning. "Barron has never been one of my favorite people. What is it you want me to do?"

"I want you to invite him to be your first guest on your new television show."

"And?"

Stone told him.

Barker chuckled as he listened. "I *love* it," he said.

"That's even better than writing about it in *Vanity Fair,* isn't it?" Stone asked.

"Oh, I could do that, too," Barker said, laughing. "Print *all* the details." He laughed again. "You know, I'm going to see Barron this afternoon at a social event. I'll corner him there and get him to agree to do the show. He's never given personal interviews, you know."

"I'd heard that. Now, Hi, it's your turn. I want to know what you didn't tell me about Sasha."

Barker looked at Stone appraisingly. "I've underestimated you," he said. "I wouldn't have told anybody in a million years, but now you've trapped me."

Stone sat back and waited.

"There is one promise I must extract from you," Barker said.

"What's that?"

"If Sasha is alive, you will never tell a living soul what I am about to tell you. If you find out she's dead, then I'll tell the world."

"All right, I agree." Suddenly, Stone knew what he was about to hear.

"This really has no relevance to your investigation, at least I can't imagine how it could be relevant, but who knows?"

"Come on, Hi, tell me."

"It came out in my research. I do a great deal more research for my profiles than anybody imagines. I use only a fraction of what I learn, but I learn *everything*." Barker leaned forward and wagged a finger. "You must never let me do a profile of you, if you have anything to hide."

Stone sat back and relaxed. Barker was going to stretch it out.

"At the time I was researching the Sasha piece, I knew a fellow in the American embassy in Moscow. I asked him to get me a copy of Sasha's birth announcement and fax it to me, along with a translation. Her father was a member of the academy and a very famous writer in the USSR, so I knew there would be an announcement in *Pravda* or *Izvestia*. And there was." He paused for effect.

"Go on," Stone said.

"And what do you think the baby was named?"

Stone let Barker have his moment. "I can't imagine."

"The baby was named Vladimir Georgivich Nijinsky." Barker rested his chin on his folded hands, looking pleased with himself.

"A boy's name? But when her family came to America six years later, all the pictures showed a little girl. What about the passport?"

"They had no passports. They were thrown out of the Soviet Union and given asylum here. They had no records of any kind, not even birth certificates. The Soviets refused to supply them. The State Department, as was usual at the time, issued them documents based on sworn statements from the parents."

"And Georgi Nijinsky swore that little Vladimir was a girl named Sasha?"

"Precisely. I never got the whole story—God knows, I would never have asked Sasha—but I surmise that, from birth, the little boy exhibited female traits, and the parents accepted that and raised him as a girl. I did find out that they took her to Morocco on a six-week vacation when she was twelve, and I believe she must have had hormone treatments and a sex-change operation at that time. After all, the onset of puberty was at hand, and people would have begun to notice if little Vladimir wasn't developing breasts, et cetera." Barker looked at Stone closely. "You don't seem particularly surprised. I thought I would knock you right out of your chair with this story."

"I figured it out when you began to tell me, but I had the advantage of an important clue."

"What was that?"

"The handwriting expert who compared this note to a

sample of Sasha's writing said that both letters were written by a man."

"Oh, that's a wonderful touch for my *Vanity Fair* piece!" Barker crowed. Then he became serious. "But tell me, Stone, what happens if neither of these things works—if Sasha isn't alive, and if Barron refuses to do my show?"

"Well, I have an ace up my sleeve—my source for the information about the flight and the money. This would be a reluctant witness, but a subpoena can work wonders, especially if the witness may be an accessory to the crime because of withholding information."

Barker looked down at the table. "Stone, I know you were seeing Cary Hilliard—you brought her to my house, remember? Might Cary be your source?"

Stone played cagey. "Why do you ask?"

"I didn't want to bring this up; I got the impression at that time that you and Cary were close."

"You could say that."

Barker's voice was sympathetic. "Stone, I have to tell you that Barron Harkness and Cary Hilliard are being married this afternoon, at three. I was invited to the wedding."

Stone took a quick breath. "I wasn't," he said.

"And, Stone, after they're married, Cary can't be subpoenaed to testify against her husband, can she?"

"No," he said.

CHAPTER

46

*T*he carpet layers took up much of Stone's time on the afternoon of Cary Hilliard's wedding, but his mind was not on the work. He walked through the house looking for the thrill that usually came when he thought about its completion, but it did not come.

He mustered his defenses and thrust the thought of Cary into a corner of his mind from which he was determined not to let it escape. Instead, he thought about Barron Harkness, of his every contact with the man, their every conversation, trying to remember something that would help connect him with Sasha's fall.

He told himself that his desire to nail Harkness had nothing to do with the loss of Cary, but, when he looked at his watch and saw that it was a little after three, he fantasized that he was interrupting the ceremony at the point where the minister asks for reasons why the marriage should not take place. "Reverend," he would say loudly from the back of the congregation, "I am here to arrest the groom for murder. I should think that sufficient cause for the wedding not to take place." For some reason, in his fantasy, he spoke these words with an English accent.

He used an old technique for when he was stumped on a case—go back to the beginning and review possible suspects. But in his attempt to incriminate Barron Harkness, he came up dry. There was only one other conceivable suspect, now that Hank Morgan had removed herself from the scene: Herbert Van Fleet. But, in spite of his obsession with Sasha, Van Fleet had come up clean. Dino didn't think so, he remembered, and Dino's instincts were often good; but, for that matter, so were his own, and he could not bring himself even to dislike Van Fleet, strange as he was.

Then, he remembered something else odd about Van Fleet, though it did not seem connected to Sasha. Van Fleet had finished medical school but had been rejected during his internship as "unsuited for a medical career." That was the statement Dino had read to him, something one of the investigative teams had turned up, a statement from somebody at Physicians & Surgeons Hospital, where Van Fleet had served his abortive internship.

When the carpet layers had finished, Stone retrieved his badge from a dresser drawer and caught a cab uptown. Dino was still on his honeymoon, he reasoned, and there was nobody he could turn to for the original record of the investigation, so he would have to do this himself. Anyway, it kept his mind off Cary.

The hospital was the most prestigious of its kind in the city, having treated the great and near great for more than a century. There was as much cachet attached to checking into Physicians & Surgeons as there was to moving into a Fifth Avenue apartment.

"Can you tell me who is in charge of interns?" he asked at the front desk.

"The chief resident," a young woman replied.

No good. The chief resident would not have been at the hospital long enough. "And who does he report to, ultimately?"

"The chief of medicine," the young woman replied. "His name is Garfield. Did you wish to see an intern, sir?"

"No, I just need some information, and I think the chief of medicine is the person I should see."

"Well, his office is on the fifth floor, but I shouldn't think he'd see you without an appointment."

"Thanks, I'll just have a word with his secretary. By the way, how long has Dr. Garfield been chief of medicine?"

The woman shrugged. "I've been here for twelve years, and he had the job when I arrived. Since Adam, I guess."

Stone took the elevator to the fifth floor and followed the signs. The chief of medicine occupied a spacious corner suite, and two secretaries guarded his door. Stone showed the badge to one of them. "My name is Barrington. I'd like to see Dr. Garfield."

"I'm afraid he's in a staff meeting at the moment, and he has another appointment immediately after that," the woman replied, unimpressed.

"Would you please take him a note saying that I'm here and that I would like to see him? This is a serious matter."

The woman seemed uncertain, but she disappeared through a door for a minute, then returned. "Dr. Garfield will be finished with his staff meeting in just a few minutes. He asked that you wait."

Stone took a seat and picked up a magazine.

Shortly, a tall, elderly man dressed in a long white coat appeared in the reception room. "I'm Garfield. What can I do for you?"

"I wonder if we could talk privately?" Stone asked, glancing at the two secretaries.

"I suppose so," Garfield said, striding toward his office door, "but I haven't got a hell of a lot of time."

"This won't take long," Stone said, following him.

The doctor did not sit, and he did not ask Stone to. "Well?" he said impatiently.

"I'm inquiring about a former intern at this hospital named Herbert Van Fleet," Stone said.

Garfield didn't reply immediately. "There was somebody here about him a few months ago," he said finally.

"Well, somebody's here again, Doctor, and it's important."

"Why is it important?"

"Let's just say that it's in connection with a serious crime."

"What do you want to know?"

"Were you in charge when Van Fleet was interning here?"

"I was."

"Why was he terminated from his internship?"

Garfield stared at him for a moment. "Am I going to end up testifying in a court of law about this?"

"That's unlikely," Stone said. "This is purely for background."

"It's about the Nijinsky woman, isn't it?"

"I can't say, sir."

"Well, Mr. Barrington, you'd better say, if you want to get anything out of me. I read the tabloids, from time to time, and I'm aware that you are retired from the police department."

Stone tried to keep from showing embarrassment. "That's true, sir."

"Then why are you flashing a badge around here?"

"Retired officers are allowed to keep their badges."

"I don't have to talk to a retired detective, you know."

"I know that, sir, but I think the information I'm asking for could be important."

"You don't have the slightest notion of whether it's important, do you? You're just curious."

"To tell you the truth, sir, I am. I couldn't break this one when I was on the force, and it bothers me that it's no longer being investigated."

"The Morgan woman didn't do it, then?"

"No, sir, she didn't."

Garfield sat down behind his desk and waved Stone to a chair. "Let me explain something to you, Mr. Barrington. This is a very highly regarded institution of healing, and we get some very well-known people in here as patients."

"I'm aware of that, Doctor."

"It's conceivable that if the information you're asking for got into the papers, there could be . . . repercussions for this hospital."

"I assure you, Doctor, nothing you tell me will become a part of any public record, and I certainly won't pass it on to the press."

The doctor looked at Stone thoughtfully. "I'd like to know what happened to Sasha Nijinsky myself," he said.

"So would I, Doctor; that's why I'm here."

"All right, but if it ever comes up, I will deny I ever told you any of this."

Stone nodded. "I understand."

Garfield took a deep breath and began. "This happened, what—twelve, thirteen years ago?"

"That sounds about right."

"You have to understand that interns, like everybody else, have their own little . . . eccentricities. I have seen year-end pranks pulled that would stand your hair on end—cadavers in the cafeteria, you know? We try to be a little tolerant of these things—after all, these young people are

under a lot of pressure, and they don't get much time off—
but we keep a close eye on them, all the same. I've had alco-
holics, drug addicts, nymphomaniacs—all sorts of problems
exhibit themselves, and, usually, with a little counseling, we
can keep the offender in the program, maybe make a fine
physician out of him later on. We're not out to wreck careers,
here; these kids come to us with eight years of higher education, and they've worked hard. But we have to draw the line
somewhere."

"Where did you draw it with Herbert Van Fleet?"

"Van Fleet was one of our brighter interns," Garfield
said, placing his feet on his desk, unwilling to be hurried.
"He finished, I don't know, sixth or seventh in his med
school class at Columbia, and he exhibited an inclination
toward pathology. Might have been good at it, too; unfortunately, that was not the only inclination he exhibited." He
paused.

"Go on, Doctor," Stone encouraged.

"Van Fleet appeared to be attracted to sick people."

"That seems like a desirable quality in a physician."

Garfield shook his head. "I'm not making myself clear,"
he said. "I mean he exhibited a sexual attraction for the ill.
Women, that is. He seemed very uncomfortable with male
patients, didn't like to touch them. One of his professors at
Columbia told me that, as a med student, he had refused to
work on a male cadaver, except when forced to study the
genitalia. My guess is that he was suppressing homosexual,
or at least bisexual, tendencies, and that he had difficulty
accepting these tendencies or dealing with them."

"How did this attraction to ill women manifest itself?"

"The chief resident noticed that he was spending a lot of
extra time with young women patients, especially those
recovering from injury or surgery, looking frequently into
the rooms of these patients. If someone else was in attendance, he'd leave; he'd wait until they were alone before he

visited them. The nurses noticed him, and there were jokes about it. The patients always seemed to be those who had IV's running. We started to keep a watch on him, surreptitiously.

"About that time, we had a very well-known actress in here as the result of an automobile accident. She had to have extensive reconstructive surgery done on a hand, and, as you can imagine, the reaction among the interns to the presence of this famous and beautiful woman was startling. A lot of them suddenly exhibited a keen interest in surgery of the hand. Van Fleet, in particular, was attentive.

"Then one night, only a few hours after a surgical procedure, a nursing supervisor walked into the woman's room and found Van Fleet on top of her."

"On top of her?" Stone asked, unbelieving.

"He'd taken a syringe of morphine from a drugs cabinet, injected it into her IV, which immediately put her to sleep; then he had removed his clothes, had removed *her* clothes, and he was . . . copulating with her."

"Jesus Christ."

"Indeed. I was summoned from my bed and told the circumstances. The actress was still sleeping peacefully, and Van Fleet, as you might imagine, was distressed at having been caught in the act. While they were waiting for me to arrive, he threatened the nursing supervisor if she reported him. She did, of course, and I made short work of young Dr. Van Fleet."

"I can imagine."

"The nursing supervisor cleaned up the patient and put her clothing in order, and no more was said about it. I should have called the police, I suppose, and had him charged with rape, but you see the position I was in: the papers would have had an absolute field day, the actress would have sued us—and won—and this hospital would have been done irreparable harm as a result."

"And the actress never knew?"

Garfield shook his head. "I lived in fear for months that she would turn up pregnant—she didn't, thank God. I'm not sure what I would have done if that had happened." Garfield sighed. "You see why I'm concerned that this go no further."

"I do, and I promise you it won't."

Garfield stood up and slipped out of his white coat. "I'm afraid I'm going to have to run now." He got into his suit jacket. "I hope this story might somehow help you."

"It might, Dr. Garfield, and I thank you for confiding in me." He shook the doctor's hand and turned to go.

"Mr. Barrington," Garfield said, "whatever became of Van Fleet? What's he doing now?"

"He's a mortician," Stone said.

Garfield gave a little shudder. "How very appropriate," he said.

CHAPTER

47

When Stone woke on Thursday morning, his first thought was that only three days remained until Sasha's dinner party. His second thought was that there was someone in his bathroom.

It could be only one person, he knew; she had a key, and she knew the code for the security system. He was flabbergasted and revolted that she should be in his house only days after her marriage, but his revulsion vanished when she came out of the bathroom.

She was naked, and the sight of her body had always had a powerful effect on him. It came to him at that moment that he was lost; that she could, if she wished, lead him around by the cock for the rest of his life. So this is obsession, he thought, as she silently slid under the sheets and drew close to him. He gave himself to it.

* * *

"You know this was a completely disgusting and immoral thing to do, don't you?" he asked when they had finished and lay panting in each other's arms. He was not joking.

"Of course, my darling," she replied. "That's why it's so much fun."

"Has anyone ever completely satisfied you?"

"You satisfy me, for a time, but to answer your question honestly, no. At least, no man ever has. I knew a girl in college who could satisfy me longer than anyone. She was only twenty, but she knew everything about pleasing a woman, because she was a woman, I suppose."

"Do you still see her?"

"No. She committed suicide our senior year, shot herself with a pistol borrowed from a boy we knew. She left a note saying she had done it for me, because she knew she could never have me, and she wanted to prove she really loved me. The housemother in the dorm found the note and showed it to me, then destroyed it."

"How did you react to that?"

"I was elated. It did wonders for my self-esteem, that someone could love me so much. I never loved her, of course, I just liked having her make love to me."

"You don't make love, Cary. You merely fuck."

Cary raised herself on an elbow and looked at him. "Do you really think so?" she asked wonderingly.

"Yes."

She nodded. "You're right, I think, but I do fuck surpassingly well, don't I?"

"You do," Stone said; then he fucked her again.

When they had exhausted each other, she lay on her back, her breasts pointing at the ceiling. "You think it's terrible that I'm still fucking you, now that I'm married," she said.

"Yes. And it's just as bad that I'm still fucking you."

"You wait. One of these days, perhaps before very long, you'll get married, but you'll still want to fuck me. And believe me, my darling, you will. Because I'll never let go of you."

"Yes," he said, "I will." Whenever she wanted him, for as long as she wanted him.

On Thursday nights at Elaine's, the big table across from the bar was kept for the guys—the regulars who had been coming for years, whom Elaine had fed when they were broke, the starving writers who might not have made it in New York without the nurturing and bonding that went on in an uptown neighborhood saloon. They wandered in and out during the evening, bitching about their agents and the promotion budgets for their most recent books, moaning about the pitiful advance sales and the huge reserve for returns on their royalty statements.

There were guys who were getting a million dollars a book now—sometimes more—and others who were getting twenty-five thousand and pretending it was two hundred. There were guys who had given up on writing fiction and were churning out screenplays for the movies and television, and there were guys who were doing it all—books, magazines, television series—the works. They were bonded by the common knowledge that nobody—not their wives, sweethearts, or publishers—believed they really worked for a living, and, sometimes, they weren't too sure of that themselves.

Stone often sat with the bunch these days, and he liked them. He wasn't exactly sure he was working for a living either, so they had something in common. Most Thursday nights, somebody would bring a girl, and they were always smart and pretty. Stone envied them their girls.

This Thursday night, drained of desire by Cary, relaxed,

and depressed, Stone got drunk. He had three Wild Turkeys before dinner—which was, in itself, a big mistake—drank most of a bottle of wine with his pasta, and, when Elaine said she was buying, couldn't resist a Sambuca or two. He switched to mineral water for a while, until he felt steadier, then started on cognac. By the time he and a couple of other guys closed the place at 4:00 A.M., he was ambulatory, but only just.

He walked carefully from the place, uncharacteristically gave the bum on duty a buck, and thought for a minute about whether he should walk. He usually walked; it was good for the knee and for the gut, but tonight walking seemed out of the question. He flagged a cab, gave the driver the exact address, explaining that he wished to be driven to the door, not to the corner, then hunkered way down in the backseat and tried to keep from passing out. That was what he was doing when the shooting started.

They had pulled up to the light, and the cabbie had decided he felt like talking. "You follow baseball?" he asked, half-turning toward the backseat.

Stone was trying to answer him when there was a sound like a watermelon being dropped from a great height, and the driver's face exploded, leaving a huge hole spouting blood. As Stone hit the floor of the backseat, the screech of rubber on pavement told him the shooter was on his way.

Stone scrambled out of the cab, and, operating instinctively, yanked the left side door open, shoved the dead driver aside, and got the cab in gear. A block and a half ahead, a van was roaring away. Stone stood on it. He switched the blinking caution lights on, leaned on the horn, and streaked off down Second Avenue after the van.

There was almost no traffic on the avenue at 4:00 A.M. "Where the fuck are the blue-and-whites?" he demanded aloud, suddenly aware that he was now cold sober. "Where are you, you sons of bitches?" The cab was new, and he gained on the van for a minute, until the driver realized he was being pursued. Still, Stone was keeping pace a block behind. He wasn't sure he wanted to get any closer, since he wasn't armed; all he wanted to do was to attract a blue-and-white or two. He tried to make out the license plate on the van and failed.

At Forty-second Street, the van hung a left and nearly turned over. "That would be good," Stone said, "turn the fucking thing over and save me some trouble!" Good luck, too. On Forty-second Street a blue-and-white was parked in front of an all-night joint, the cops drinking coffee from paper cups. Stone glanced in the rearview mirror as he passed and saw the cups go out the windows on both sides and the car start after him.

The van turned left again and started up First Avenue, keeping all four wheels on the ground this time. Stone managed a wide four-wheel drift and made up a few yards on him. The blue-and-white was doing even better; it was faster than both the van and Stone's cab. At Fifty-seventh Street, the blue-and-white overtook Stone, and the cop in the passenger seat was waving him over. Stone shook his head and pointed ahead. "No! Get him! Get him! He's the cab killer!" The cop didn't seem to understand, but the driver floored it and went after the van. Stone followed. At Seventy-second Street, another blue-and-white joined the chase. At Eighty-sixth Street, the van driver made his mistake. He started a turn to the left, then saw a hooker crossing the street. He wavered, missed her, then, too late, tried to get the van around the corner. It teetered on two wheels, then went over and slid twenty feet on its side, coming to rest against a parked car.

"This is one for Scoop Berman," Stone cackled, skidding to a halt behind a blue-and-white. "I wonder where the little guy is tonight."

The little guy came out of the driver's window, holding

an impossibly large pistol equipped with a silencer. He popped off one shot, which shattered the window of a blue-and-white, then a returning fusillade knocked him back inside the van.

Four cops approached the van warily now, three pistols out in front, another with a riot gun. They hesitated, then the bearer of the shotgun crept around the front of the van and peered in through the windshield. The shotgun went off, and Stone made it around the van in time to see the cop reach into the cab through the hole he had blown open and remove Scoop Berman's pistol.

The cop used the butt of the shotgun to clean out a larger area of the windshield, and with help, pulled Scoop out of the van onto the pavement.

"You the cabdriver?" a cop asked Stone as they crowded around Scoop.

"No, the passenger. The driver's in the front seat, there, missing most of his head."

"Well, we finally got the fucker," another cop said. "That's cabbie number six he's offed. We'll get a fucking commendation for this one." He pulled out his notebook. "Let's have your name," he said to Stone, "and we'll want a statement from you."

"My name's Barrington. I was fourteen years on the job, detective second, most recently out of the 19th."

"I know you," another cop said. "You were Dino Bacchetti's partner."

"Right."

"Let him write out his own statement," the cop said to his colleague. "He'll do it better than you."

"I know this guy," Stone said, nodding at Scoop. "His name's Berman; he's a free-lance television cameraman. You want me to talk to him?"

"Yeah," said the cop. "If you know him."

Stone went and knelt over Berman. "Scoop, how are you

feeling? An ambulance is on the way."

Scoop was gutshot, twice, and there was blood around his lips. His eyes focused. "Hey, Stone," he said. "I thought you was out to pasture."

"I was, buddy, but I was in the cab."

Scoop looked worried. "I'm sorry about that," he said. "You okay?"

"I'm okay. Scoop, did you shoot the other cabdrivers?"

"Yeah, the bastards always got in my way when I was on a story. Other cars would get out of the way, you know? But not hacks, the sons of bitches."

Stone turned to a cop, who had a notebook out. "You get that?"

"Yeah," the cop said. "You know, I wanted to shoot a few cabbies myself, at times."

"Stone," Scoop said.

"Yeah, Scoop?"

"There's something I never told you. I shouldda told you, but I didn't. I wanted it for myself."

"What's that, Scoop?" He could hear the ambulance approaching.

"The night Sasha took her dive, remember?"

"You bet I remember."

"I was there, remember?"

"I remember. You got her on tape. It was a good job."

"There was a guy on the scene had these black glasses, with tape on them."

"I remember. His name is Van Fleet."

"That's right. He works on stiffs."

"Right."

"I think he knows something. I think he saw who tossed Sasha, or something. He was acting funny at the scene. I tried to find him after I showed you the tape, but he was gone. I bought him a drink later, tried to get it out of him, but he wouldn't talk to me."

"Okay, Scoop, I'm glad to know that. Thanks."

The ambulance screeched to a halt, and two men came with a stretcher. Stone stood up to let them at Scoop, and, as he did, he saw Scoop's eyes glaze over and his head fall to one side. A paramedic produced a stethoscope and listened to his chest.

"This one's had it," he said to a cop. "No ticker at all, and, with those kind of holes in him, he ain't gonna resuscitate, believe me."

"Ah, shit," the cop said. "I wanted to see him stand trial."

"No, it's better this way," Stone said. "All neat and tidy; you got your confession."

Later that morning, when Stone finally got into bed, he discovered he was drunk again.

CHAPTER

48

On Friday, Stone sat
down and thought about his options. He should have gone
to the FBI, he knew, when he got the first letter. Their kidnapping case was still open and would remain open until
there was some sort of resolution, but they had already conducted their own investigation of Van Fleet and had turned
up nothing. Neither had their search of his loft produced
anything, and they were unlikely to find Stone's new information compelling. Anyway, his years as a police officer had
made him very nearly constitutionally incapable of going to
the FBI for anything.

He could, too, have gone to the police, maybe
approached Delgado directly, but it had already been made
abundantly clear to him that the police hierarchy considered
the case closed and did not want it reopened. If he could
deliver Van Fleet and Sasha, handcuffed together, Delgado

might listen to him, but not otherwise.

His best alternative was Dino. Dino was even less anx-ious than Delgado to reopen, because he didn't want to piss off his superiors, but Dino was his friend, and he still felt guilty about the treatment Stone had received from the department. The trouble was, Dino was in Las Vegas. Stone called Dino's mother and learned that he was due back from his honeymoon sometime the following day. Stone heaved a sigh of relief. Dino wasn't going to be easy, but at least he would be in town.

The phone rang.

"Stone. It's Hi Barker."

"What's happening, Hi?"

"I got him. He's mine for the Sunday-night show. Is there anything else I should know before I interview him?"

"I told you everything at lunch. I'll leave it to you how to handle him."

"Will you be there?"

"I'll be there with a cop," Stone said. "Where do I go?"

"We're broadcasting from what the network calls the 'executive studios,' on the top floor of their headquarters building on Seventh Avenue. You know the building?"

"Yes."

"I'll leave your name with the security guard—and what's the name of your cop?"

"Bacchetti. What time?"

"Be there at a quarter to eleven, sharp, and go straight to the control room and stay there. We go on the air, live, at eleven thirty, and I don't want Barron to see you."

When Stone hung up, he was starting to feel excited.

At noon Saturday, Stone called Dino's new apartment in the West Village. A woman answered.

"Hello?"

"Is Dino back in town yet?"

"No, who is this?"

"This is Stone Barrington."

"Oh, yes, we met at the wedding. This is Mary Ann's mother. I'm just over here tidying up a little so the place will be nice when they get in."

"What time are they due, Mrs. Bianchi?"

"I'm not sure exactly. They were supposed to come home last night, but Dino was on a winning streak, and they missed their plane. He said they'd get whatever flight was available today. Dino wanted Sunday to rest before going back to work."

"I see. Mrs. Bianchi, would you write a note to Dino and ask him to call me the moment he gets in? Say that it's important."

"Okay, I'll tack it to the door, so he'll be sure to see it."

Stone thanked her and hung up.

The day droned on with no word from Dino, and Stone began calling every hour on the hour. There was no answer. At seven thirty, he got out his tuxedo and began to get dressed. At eight, he called Dino again and still got no reply. At eight thirty, the doorbell rang. Stone thought about it for a moment, then he retrieved his badge and gun from the dresser drawer and strapped on the ankle holster.

When Stone opened the front door, a limousine was at curbside and a mustachioed, uniformed chauffeur stood on the stoop. Stone asked the chauffeur to wait. He went to the living-room phone and called Dino's number again.

"Yeah?" Dino—sleepy, exhausted.

"Dino, it's Stone, hang on." He ran back to the front door. "What address are you taking me to?" he asked the chauffeur.

"Sorry, sir," the man said, with what seemed to be an Italian accent, "I can't tell you; it's supposed to be a surprise. I'm not supposed to wait either; I've got a schedule to keep.

If you can't come now, I'll have to leave."

"I'll be right with you," Stone said and ran for the phone again. "Dino."

"Huh?"

"Listen to me now. I need your help."

"You listen to me, Stone. I've hardly had any sleep for the past three nights, you know? Now, I'm going back to bed; you call me tomorrow."

"Tomorrow may be too late, Dino. Sasha has invited me to a dinner party."

"Oh, Jesus," Dino moaned, "will you ever let go of that? I told you I don't want to hear about it again."

"I've got some new stuff on Van Fleet, Dino, and he may be mixed up in this thing tonight."

"I told you, I don't want to hear it."

"Dino, I need some backup. I don't even know where I'm going."

"I suggest you call nine-one-one when you get there, Stone. I'll call you when I'm coherent. In the meantime, fuck off!" He slammed down the telephone.

Stone ran back to the front door to see the chauffeur heading for the car. "Wait!" he called out, locking the door behind him. The chauffeur came wearily around the car and opened a door for him.

The limo was an old one, sixties vintage, but well cared for. The upholstery was well-worn velour, and black velvet curtains were drawn over the side and rear windows. "Come on," he said to the driver, "where are we going?"

"Sorry, sir," the driver said cheerfully and raised the glass partition between his compartment and the rear seat.

Stone found himself looking into a mirror. He picked at the side curtain; it was sewn or glued down. He immediately felt that he had walked into a nineteen-forties B movie. Bela Lugosi would be waiting for him at his destination. He decided to sit back and enjoy the experience. For a few minutes, he tried counting the left and right turns and estimating his position, but he became disoriented. The car seemed not to stay long on any street, not taking any avenue up or downtown, as far as he could tell. He found a light and glanced at his watch from time to time. They had left his house at eight thirty-two.

At exactly nine o'clock, the car stopped, and Stone could hear a garage door being raised. He was being taken indoors without getting out of the car first, and he didn't like it. He tore at the side curtain, but by the time it came loose he could hear the garage door winding down again.

The chauffeur opened the left-hand door for him, and, as he got out of the car, Stone saw another door leading off the garage. The chauffeur opened that one for him too, then quickly closed it behind him.

Stone looked around. He was in a nicely decorated vestibule with one other door, probably leading to the street. He tried that door and the one behind him; he was locked in. There was nowhere to go but up. An open elevator awaited him, and there was only one button. He pressed it, and the elevator rose slowly, creaking, reminding him of the one in his own house. Old. The elevator stopped, and the door opened.

Stone stepped out of the car into another vestibule, much like the one downstairs. There was an elegant, gilded mirror and a vase containing a large flower arrangement resting on an antique table. A hallway led away from the vestibule, and from that direction he could hear a murmur of conversation and the tinkle of silver against china. They had apparently started without him. A woman's laugh rose above the talk, then subsided. Was that voice familiar?

Stone walked slowly down the hallway and emerged into a very large, rectangular room, which had been divided into two areas. Ahead of him was a living area, with two leather sofas facing each other before a fireplace, in which a fire merrily burned. Soft chamber music came from speakers somewhere. There was something familiar about the room. To his left was a dining table set for eight, and, apparently, Stone was not the only one late for dinner, for three places were empty. The conversation was louder now.

A woman in a backless dress sat with her back to him, a man next to her, and a couple faced him from across the table. Both the men were in evening clothes. At the end of the table, to his right, dressed to kill, her elbow resting on the table, her hand holding a glass of wine, her face turned to greet him, smiling invitingly, was Sasha Nijinsky.

Stone took a step forward and opened his mouth to speak. Instead of what he had intended to say, a scream burst from his lips. A searing pain had thudded into his buttocks; his back arched, his knees bent, and he fell heavily onto the polished hardwood floor, his body convulsing.

He had only a moment of consciousness to grasp that Sasha and the other people at the table were immobile; were glassy eyed; were, of course, dead.

CHAPTER

49

Stone came awake slowly. His first sensation was that his ass was on fire; the second was that every joint, every muscle in his body hurt like hell. His vision was cloudy for a moment, and he blinked his eyes rapidly to clear it. He became aware that he could not move.

He was naked. His shoulders lay on a hard table, his hands were bound behind him, and his feet were tied and suspended from a block and tackle above him, which raised him half in the air. Instinctively, he squirmed, tugging at his bonds, but they were too tight. His hands were numb.

He could move only his head, and he craned his neck to see as much as he could. He was in a long, narrow room; the walls and ceiling were covered in white tiles, aged and cracking. Two overhead bulbs were protected with steel screens. The tabletop was made of metal and sloped from head to foot. There was a faint chemical smell, something he couldn't identify.

He craned his neck farther. Near the other end of the room, just at the edge of his vision, was a vertical object, but he could not swivel his head and eyes far enough to make it out. He tried the bonds again, trying at least to stretch them enough to allow the flow of blood to return to his hands. No luck.

Minutes passed, and he wracked his brain for some other means of escape. He found that by manipulating his shoulders he could creep sideways on the table, but it became apparent to him that, since his feet were elevated, if he slipped over the edge, his head would strike the floor very hard. He stopped moving and waited.

Perhaps twenty minutes passed before he heard a scraping noise somewhere behind him, followed by hollow footsteps striking the cement floor. The chauffeur appeared, upside-down, the collar of his uniform hanging open. He reached up and ripped the mustache from his upper lip.

"There, thatsa better," he said in his Italian accent. Then he laughed.

"Herbert?" Stone said.

Van Fleet laughed again. "Didn't recognize me, did you?"

"No, I didn't. Listen, Herb, could you loosen whatever you've got around my wrists? The circulation has stopped."

"Sure," Van Fleet said. He grabbed Stone under the arms, lifted him, and flipped him over on his stomach. He fiddled with the bonds.

Stone's ankles hurt now, but he could feel the blood flowing back into his hands. "Thank you," he said. "Now, could you turn me back over, please?"

Van Fleet turned him over on his back again. "Are you cold?" he asked solicitously.

"No, it's quite warm in here. Where am I, exactly?"

"You are in what used to be part of a kosher meat-processing plant. It runs along one side of my loft, and it is accessed by moving the refrigerator in my kitchen, then removing a panel from the wall." He laughed again. "Neither you nor the FBI were able to figure it out."

"It's very clever, Herb. Now, can we talk about what's going on here?"

Van Fleet stepped forward and began feeling around Stone's neck.

"Don't do that," Stone said, irritably. He didn't like the man's hands on him.

Van Fleet took his time at whatever he was doing. "Sorry to disturb you," he said. "Just to rest your mind, I have no sexual interest in you. I don't like men that way."

Stone was relieved to hear that, but not much.

"How much did you take in before I used the stun gun?" Van Fleet asked.

"So that's what it was."

"That's right. Something like fifty thousand volts, but only for a few milliseconds."

"That was enough."

"It was, wasn't it?"

"To answer your question," Stone said, "I took in a number of corpses sitting at a dining table."

"Let's not refer to them that way, please," Van Fleet said. "They are my friends, and, if they could hear you, they'd be very upset."

"As you wish. How did you get, uh, meet these people?"

"Oh, here and there. You might say I picked them up around town. They're all very interesting people who do interesting work. I find that interesting work makes an interesting person, don't you?"

Stone realized that he had now solved the disappearance of Dino's yuppies, not that it mattered much. "Sure, I think that's true. But, somehow, I don't think they make very interesting conversationalists at the moment."

"You're quite wrong," Van Fleet said. "I know you think of them as dead, but they're not, you know. In fact, I've given them a whole new kind of life. It's a technique I've developed myself, over the years, one I refined both in my work at the funeral parlor and in my previous job, at the Museum of Natural History. They remain as supple as when they were alive, in the usual sense of the word."

Stone could think of nothing to do but keep the conversation going. Besides, there was more he wanted to know. "Tell me about Sasha, Herb."

"Ah, Sasha." Van Fleet sighed. "She is the centerpiece of my little dinner party, of course. Everybody likes a celebrity at the table. Adds spice to the evening."

"Was she alive when you brought her here?"

"I told you, they're all alive," Van Fleet said emphatically. "Please don't make it necessary for me to mention that again, or I will terminate this conversation immediately."

"I'm sorry," Stone said. "I meant alive in the usual sense of the word. What I meant to ask was, after her fall and the ambulance wreck, what sort of condition was she in?"

"Well, when I took her out of the wreck," Van Fleet said, "she was in very poor condition, indeed. The fall had broken some bones, but, oddly, not the skin. The traffic accident had done somewhat more damage. It took me quite a long time to bring her back to her present condition."

"Was she . . . breathing when you took her?"

"Amazingly enough, yes," Van Fleet said. "In fact, I believe that, if not for the traffic accident, she might have continued to breathe. As it was, she lasted only a few days, in spite of the very excellent medical care she received from me."

Stone winced at the thought of Sasha alive for days with this creep. His terminal velocity theory, though, had panned out, sort of. "Who wrote me the letter?" Stone asked.

"Oh, Sasha did—with my help, of course. She wrote me two letters, you know, when I first began writing to her, so we had something to help us with her handwriting."

"Why did she have olive oil on her hands?"

"Oh, you noticed that, did you? Well, I wanted an agent that would make a good fingerprint, and, since I was in the kitchen at the time, the oil was handy."

"Herb, we have to talk seriously now. We have to get you some help."

"Help?" Van Fleet sounded surprised. "I don't need any help. I've done all this work on these people alone, without any help at all. And it was pretty good work, don't you think? Let me explain it to you. I'll skip the technical parts, but have a look." Van Fleet took hold of the table and dragged it until Stone was facing down the room, then he put a hand under Stone's head and raised it, so he could see.

At the other end of the room was the object Stone had not been able to make out before. The body of a young woman hung by its heels, the fingertips just brushing the floor. She had been opened with one long incision from her pubic hair to her sternum, and the abdominal cavity had been emptied. "Oh, God." Stone breathed. He turned his head away.

"Oh, I'm sorry, I didn't mean to upset you," Van Fleet said, turning Stone back to his original position. "I was going to take you through the process, but if you'd rather not . . . "

"I'd rather talk," Stone said. "When I said you needed help, I didn't mean with your work."

"Oh, you mean a psychiatrist. That was suggested to me once, a long time ago."

"By Dr. Garfield?"

Van Fleet walked around Stone so that he could look at him. "What do you know about Garfield?"

"Oh, Dr. Garfield and I had a long chat about you the

other day, Herb. He told me about your internship, about why you didn't complete it."

Van Fleet bristled. "This is not an amusing conversation," he said. "I hope when you're at the table you can find something more interesting to talk about." He turned and walked out of Stone's line of vision, then seemed to leave the room.

At the table? Stone began to sweat, then, almost immediately, to shiver.

Van Fleet returned. "Sorry, I had to get my instruments. Since you're going to be such a boring conversationalist, I may as well start work on you now."

"Wait a minute, Herb," Stone said quickly. "We have more to talk about."

"Do you think you can refrain from referring to past unpleasantness?"

"Oh, yes. I'm terribly sorry about that; it was rude of me."

Van Fleet dragged a stool over and sat down facing Stone. "All right, what would you like to talk about?"

"Tell me about the night Sasha fell from her balcony."

"Oh, that. I've told you about taking her from the wreck of the ambulance. Before that, well, I left Elaine's a bit after you did, I guess, and, on the way home, I thought I'd drop by Sasha's building. I often did that on the way home, just to catch a glimpse of where she lived. When I turned into the block, I could see the doorman through the glass front of the building. He was asleep in a chair, and I saw somebody walk right past him into the building, and he never woke up.

"I found that very interesting, so I parked the van and went into the building. I just walked right past him, and he never turned a hair. I took the elevator up to the twelfth floor—I knew Sasha's apartment number from my research—and, to my surprise, her door was open. I had just planned to leave a little present and go, but there was that open door. I couldn't resist.

"I crept into the apartment, and I could hear these angry voices from out on the terrace. I peeped out there, and she and this other person were having a knock-down, drag-out fight, and, all of a sudden, Sasha was just dumped over the railing.

"I jumped back behind the door, and I could hear this other person rummaging around the room, looking for something, I guess. That went on for a minute, then I heard the elevator start up, and I guess the . . . well, the murderer heard it too, and ran. I heard the fire stairs door open, then the elevator door open, and I heard somebody running down the stairs.

"I peeped out the door, and the doorman was standing at the top of the stairs, looking down, so I just popped into the open elevator and rode down. I got out on the second floor and tiptoed down the stairs. When I saw you get back into the elevator, I left the building, got into the van, and drove around the block to where Sasha was. The ambulance arrived about that time, and I followed it. I wanted to see which hospital Sasha was being taken to, so I could send flowers.

"Then, wham! That fire truck came out of nowhere, and the ambulance got hit. You know the rest."

"Herb, who threw Sasha off the balcony?"

Van Fleet shrugged. "Nobody I knew," he said.

"Can you describe him?" Stone asked.

Van Fleet started to speak, then stopped. "No, I don't think I will," he said petulantly. "You were unkind enough to bring up the past, so I don't think you deserve to know, at least not yet. Later, if you're nice, you can bring it up at dinner, and maybe I'll tell you." Van Fleet stood up, reached down, and picked up his case. He set it on the stool, opened it, and took out a large scalpel. "Don't worry, I'm very good at this; it'll be absolutely painless, I promise."

Stone had thought about dying before, but never in such

close proximity to the event. Would his whole life flash before his eyes? Would it be less painful if he just relaxed and let it happen? He discovered he could not give in to it; he would go down fighting, with what meager resources he had left. "Wait a minute, Herb!" he said. "There's something I have to tell you."

"You can tell me at the dinner table," Van Fleet said, sliding his hand under Stone's chin and pulling it up to extend his neck.

Stone jerked his head free. "It's about Sasha!" he said, and watched Van Fleet's face.

Van Fleet showed interest. "What about Sasha?"

"Something you don't know about her, something important. I wouldn't want to say this in front of her at the table."

"What is it?"

"You like guys, don't you, Herb?"

"What do you mean?" Van Fleet replied indignantly. "I'm no queer. I like women."

"What about your relationship with the men at the table?" Stone asked.

"You have a filthy mind," Van Fleet said. "I have no kind of *relationship* with anybody at the table. Except Sasha, of course. We have a perfectly normal sex life."

Perfectly normal? Stone laughed aloud. "Come on, Herb, you're as queer as a three-dollar bill." Words were all Stone had left to fight with, and he was at least going to get in a few punches before this maniac slaughtered him.

"That's a lie!"

"Then why do you think you like fucking Sasha so much?"

"Sasha's a woman, you idiot," Van Fleet said. "We have a heterosexual relationship!"

"Sasha's not a woman, Herbert. I found out. When she was born in Russia, her parents named her Vladimir, because she was a boy. They raised her as a girl, though, and, when she was twelve, she had a sex-change operation in Morocco!"

"You're insane!" Van Fleet cried.

"You're fucking a guy, Herbert, you goddamned faggot!" Stone screamed. "All this time you've been fucking a guy's corpse, a dead guy, Herbert!"

Van Fleet was making animal noises now, and spittle had formed on his lips. He raised the scalpel over his head, and his voice became a howl.

Stone braced himself, baring his teeth. He'd bite the bastard's arm off, if he could.

Then a huge noise filled the room, echoing off the tile walls, and, simultaneously, a hole appeared in Van Fleet's throat; a moment later, the noise came again, and another hole appeared under his right eye. Van Fleet reeled backward and disappeared from Stone's view.

Stone was nearly deaf from the noise, which was now settling into a constant ringing in his ears.

Then Dino walked into Stone's view and looked down at him. "Jesus, Stone," he said, shaking his head. "How do you get yourself into these situations?"

50

Well, I always told you Van Fleet was dirty, didn't I?" Dino said. He and Stone were sitting facing each other on the sofas in front of Herbert Van Fleet's fireplace.

Stone was dressed again and was rubbing his ankles where they had been bound. "Jesus, Dino, I guess I should have just listened to you all along," he said sourly. He took a large swig of Van Fleet's bourbon.

"I wouldn't have recognized this place," Dino said. "He's sure done a lot to it since we were here before."

"I didn't recognize it either," Stone said. "I didn't remember the garage door in the building. I had no idea where I was. How did you figure it out?"

"You mentioned Van Fleet; that was all I had to go on. I had to take a tire iron to the downstairs door, or I would have been up here sooner."

"How much of my conversation with Van Fleet did you hear?"

"Most of it, I guess. I had to duck out when Van Fleet came back to the kitchen to get his tools."

"Well, why did you wait so fucking long to stop the bastard?"

"I wanted to hear it all. Anyway, you were in no trouble; I wasn't going to let him carve you up."

"I wish I'd known that. He gave me about the worst hour of my life."

Dino picked up the phone on the coffee table. "I guess I'd better call it in."

"No!" Stone said, snatching the phone away from him.

"Look, Stone, I'm beat. Between screwing Mary Ann twice a day and shooting craps all night every night, I'm coming apart. Let's get this over with."

"You can't call it in, yet. We still don't have the guy who tossed Sasha off the balcony, and, if he finds out Sasha's dead, he'll feel safe."

"It's Harkness, then?"

"Damn right, and, if you'd done what I asked you to at the airport, we might have had him long ago."

"Come on, Stone, his name was on the manifest; let's not go over old stuff again, okay?"

"All right, let's not. But tomorrow night, Hi Barker is going to have Harkness on his TV show, and I mean to see him nailed, right there on television. I want you to be there to bust him."

Dino thought for a minute. "I gotta cover my ass some way, here, in this place."

"Do this: seal the place, and put a blue-and-white outside to make sure nobody disturbs the scene."

"Not until I get the medical examiner in here. We can't just let Van Fleet's corpse rot for a couple days, you know."

"Look, we have no solid evidence against Harkness,

and, unless Barker can force some admission out of him on the air, we'll never get him. If somebody in the ME's office leaks this to the press, we're cooked; we'll never get him."

"Too bad you pissed off Van Fleet when you were on the table in there. He might have given us Harkness."

"He might have given us Harkness anyway, if you hadn't blown him away."

"What was I supposed to do? Stand there and watch the ritual slaughter? Shout 'freeze!'? What if he didn't freeze? You're pretty fucking ungrateful."

"Ungrateful? I've dragged you kicking and screaming through this whole thing, and now, when you turn up at the last possible minute, like the cavalry, you want gratitude?"

"That's the second time I've taken out somebody who wanted to kill you, and, come to think of it, you didn't thank me the first time either!" Dino was standing up now.

Stone stood up too. "If you'd been a little quicker the first time, I wouldn't be hobbling around on this knee, and I'd probably still be on the force!"

"Yeah, instead of a tax-free pension and a big-time law practice! I really did you a fucking disservice, didn't I? And, now, you got the cabbie killer, you cleared four murders, and you're going to bring down Barron Harkness—all in one week! It's a rough life you're gonna be living, ain't it, Stone?"

Stone opened his mouth, then shut it. Then he started to laugh. So did Dino. They sat down again and laughed until they were exhausted.

"Okay," Dino said, "you get out of here." He handed Stone his car keys. "I know a guy in the ME's office who can keep his mouth shut. I'll get him to check Van Fleet into the morgue as a John Doe, then I'll seal this place until Monday morning."

"Okay. You meet me tomorrow night at ten forty-five sharp at the Continental Network headquarters building on Seventh Avenue. We'll go up to the studio control room together. And have a blue-and-white waiting downstairs."

They both got up and walked toward the door, passing the dining table where the five mute conversationalists still carried on.

Dino walked over to Sasha's corpse and ran the back of a finger along her cheek. "Soft as a baby's ass," he said. "I wonder how the son of a bitch did it?"

CHAPTER

51

Stone could not concentrate on the Sunday papers. Oddly, he gave little thought to the events of the night before. What he thought about was the evening ahead and what it might mean to him.

From the point of view of solving the case, he was unconcerned about proving the guilt of Barron Harkness, but, he was convinced, his future happiness depended upon that proof.

Throughout his adult life, it had been Stone's habit to go out with one woman at a time. Some of these affairs had been important—marriage had been discussed, although it had never happened. Others were less important, even unsatisfactory, but he had usually stuck with them for a time, because it was easier.

But now he was in love, with all that implied; he had not so much as thought of another woman since the moment he had met Cary. She had consumed his body and his mind from the beginning, and, when she had suddenly disappeared from his life, he had clung to the belief that there was a reasonable explanation for her conduct, if he could only know it. Now, on this late-winter Sunday afternoon, with a high wind howling around his house, he sought that explanation and found it.

From the beginning of their relationship, Cary had urged him to improve his position in life, to leave the police force and practice law. He had steadfastly refused even to consider this. Then, when he had been, in rapid succession, kicked off the force and offered an opportunity by Woodman & Weld, he was suddenly in a position to offer her what she wanted. It was at that moment, before he had had a chance to tell her what the future held, that she had returned to Barron Harkness.

It had always been Harkness, he now believed. When she had told him of her long affair with a married man and had disguised his identity, it was Harkness she was protecting. Then, in despair of Stone's ever getting anywhere, she had returned to Harkness, and Stone had, himself, made it possible for her to marry him, by making Harkness's divorce inevitable. Now she had the position and money she coveted, although she still loved Stone. He was certain of that. Why else would she still be sleeping with him?

All that remained to correct this situation was to put Harkness away for attempted murder. Hounded by publicity, Cary would seek shelter with Stone, who would now have the means to give her the life she wanted. That result was what he wanted of tonight's events. Dino could have the bust—it was his anyway. All he wanted was Cary, in his life and in his bed, all the time. Tonight, he would go as far as necessary to make that happen.

* * *

Dino was late. There was nothing new about this, but Stone waited impatiently in the lobby of the network building, afraid that Harkness would arrive before Dino did. Dino arrived at eleven, and Stone hustled him into an elevator.

"Jesus, Dino," Stone said as the car rose, "I thought that, just this once, you would be on time."

"Stone, I made it, didn't I? Don't I always make it?"

"Is there a car downstairs?"

"They're ready and waiting, don't worry."

"This is your bust, Dino. I don't want any of it."

"Thanks," Dino said. "Maybe it'll help take the curse off the Morgan thing."

"I hope so."

The elevator doors opened, and an anxious Hi Barker awaited them. "You're late," he said, and he was sweating. "Barron just arrived downstairs and is on the way up. Come with me." He led them to the control room door and ushered them in. "Jimmy," he said to a man wearing a headset, "these are police officers. I don't want Harkness to see them."

"Don't worry, Hi," Jimmy replied. "I've got a light on the glass partition that will make a reflection; Harkness won't be able to see into the control room."

"Good," Barker said. "I've got to go and meet him now. Anything else you want to tell me, Stone?"

Stone shook his head. "If you get into trouble, I've got an ace up my sleeve. I'll send you a note."

Barker nodded, then fled.

Stone looked around the control room; it was a smaller, simpler version of the one he had seen months ago at the news division. The executive studios, he had learned, were a couple of sets designed for small-scale interviews, like *The Hi Barker Show*. The backdrop of the set was simply the New York City skyline, looking south, as seen from the sixty-fifth floor, their current level. The exterior windows were of non-reflective glass, and the view was spectacular.

Hi Barker appeared on the set, followed by Barron Harkness and, to Stone's surprise, Cary. He hadn't expected her to be here. Harkness looked flushed, and he tripped on the carpeting and nearly fell as he stepped up to the platform where his seat would be.

"They must have been out somewhere before this," Dino said. "This is going to be even easier, if he's a little drunk."

Stone nodded. He watched as Harkness sat down and had a microphone clipped to his lapel. Hi Barker was flitting about, putting his guests at ease; Cary was given a folding chair just out of camera range. The whole group was no more than twelve feet from where Stone stood. "You're sure they can't see us?" he asked the director.

"Not a chance," Jimmy replied. "I checked it out earlier."

Two other people, a man and a young woman, came into the control room now and took seats on either side of Jimmy, paying no attention to Stone and Dino. "Ten minutes," the woman said, looking up at a clock above the row of monitors.

Stone watched the monitors as cameras were pointed at Barker and Harkness. For a moment, a camera rested on Cary, sending Stone a pang of desire. She looked beautiful and serene in her mink coat.

"One minute," the young woman said, jostling Stone from his reverie. He had been fantasizing about life after Barron Harkness.

"Ten seconds," she said, then counted down from five. Jimmy pushed a button, and lively music filled the control room.

The man next to Jimmy leaned into a microphone. "From the executive studios of the Continental Network, high above Manhattan, we bring you the premiere of *The Hi Barker Show*."

A camera moved in on Hi Barker. "Good evening," he said amiably. "We're off to a flying start with this new series. Our aim is to bring you guests who don't often appear on programs like this one, and our guest tonight is one who, although he appears on television five nights a week, rarely talks about himself. I welcome my old friend, Barron Harkness. Good evening, Barron."

"Good evening, Hi," Harkness said, managing a smile. "I'm glad to be here . . . I think. It's been a long time since I let myself in for the sort of grilling I ordinarily hand out to others, and I'm not sure I'm looking forward to the experience."

Barker laughed. "You're not trying to get my sympathy, are you, Barron? I think you know how to take care of yourself in a clinch."

Smart, Stone thought. Set him up as somebody who can't be sandbagged on television, then sandbag him. He watched as Barker skillfully put Harkness over the jumps, starting with his early career, and occasionally interjecting a sharp, almost rude question about the newsman's behavior on some occasion. Harkness fenced well, and he was beginning to relax. Twenty-five minutes of the program passed in this vein, with Barker increasingly pressing Harkness for his personal views on politicians and events. Then Barker paused and sorted through his notes for a moment.

Now we begin, Stone thought. He leaned forward and grasped the railing in front of him.

"Barron," Barker began, "I know you were as shocked as we all were at the disappearance and probable death of Sasha Nijinsky, who was to have been your co-anchor on the evening news."

"Yes, I certainly was," Harkness said, looking a little uncomfortable. He crossed his legs and tugged at the knot of his necktie. "A horrible and tragic event."

"You were . . . elsewhere at the time all this happened, I believe."

●
315

That's right, Stone thought, let him set his own trap.

"Yes, I was. I had been reporting from the Middle East. Not for the first time, I might add—more like the twentieth—and I was returning to New York on a flight from Rome."

"I see," Barker said, looking regretful. "I'm extremely sorry to hear you say that, Barron; I had hoped for a little more candor on this subject."

Harkness looked alarmed. "I don't know what you mean," he said, as if he couldn't think of anything else to say.

Dino laughed aloud. "Sure, sure, Harkness; go ahead and paint yourself into the corner."

Barker shook his head. "Barron, in light of information that has come into my possession, I should warn you now to abandon this pretense."

"What pretense?" Harkness asked weakly. "What on earth are you talking about?"

"Barron, I have it on the authority of an unimpeachable source that you were not on the flight from Rome that day, that your ticket was used by another person. Tell us, now, Barron, where were you when Sasha Nijinsky was thrown from her balcony?"

Harkness said nothing for a moment, clearly stunned; then his eyes narrowed and he sat up straight.

Stone was reminded of a contentious interview with Richard Nixon many years before, when Harkness had gotten angry with good effect. What was he up to?

"Let me tell you something, Hi," Harkness said, with tightly controlled ire. "I don't know who has misinformed you, but I have made that particular flight from Rome six times in the past twelve months, and I've gotten to know some of the crew. When that airplane landed at Kennedy, I was sitting in the cockpit jump seat, watching the captain execute an instrument approach. His name is Bob Martinez, he's a senior captain with the airline, and he will vouch for my presence in his cockpit during that flight." Harkness took a breath. "What's more, I was traveling on that occasion in the company of Herman Bateman, the president of Continental Network News, and *he* will vouch for my presence on that flight. Now, do you have any other questions?"

Dino leaned forward and looked at Stone. "What the fuck is going on?"

"Shhh," Stone said. He took a folded sheet of paper from his pocket and handed it to the director. "Please get this to Hi at once."

Jimmy nodded and handed it to the young woman. "Just walk out on camera, and hand it to him."

The woman left as Hi Barker continued his questioning.

"Yes, I do have another question, Barron," Barker said, not intimidated. "A police source has informed me that when detectives went through Sasha Nijinsky's financial records, it was discovered that a sum of two million dollars was missing from her funds. Another source has now told me that Sasha had transferred those funds to you for investment, and that they have not been seen since, that you have been unable to return these funds. Would you care to comment on that?"

"I certainly would," Harkness said, not missing a beat. "It is true that Sasha asked me to invest such a sum for her; she had considerable faith in my financial judgment. In January of last year, she gave me a cashier's check for two million dollars made payable to an offshore bank with which I sometimes invest. In the autumn of last year, she asked me to withdraw her cash in the investment, so that she could purchase a cooperative apartment. I did, in fact, receive into my account on the day Sasha disappeared the full amount of her investment, plus a considerable profit. The following day, not knowing of Sasha's whereabouts or condition, I personally delivered a cashier's check in the amount of two million, four hundred and thirty-nine thousand dollars to Mr. Frank Woodman, Sasha's personal attorney."

Before Harkness had finished speaking, Stone was dialing Frank Woodman's home number.

"Hello?"

"Frank, it's Stone; I must be brief—are you watching *The Hi Barker Show*, by any chance?"

"As a matter of fact, I am."

"Is what Harkness just said true? Did he deliver those funds to you?"

"Yes, he did. They were disbursed as a part of Sasha's estate."

"Thanks." He hung up and watched as the young woman walked onto the set and handed Barker the unfolded sheet of paper. Last chance.

Barker read the paper, and his eyebrows shot up. "Barron," he said, "I have just received a news bulletin, and I wonder if you would like to modify any of your statements in the light of this." He read from the paper. "'The New York City Police Department has just announced that Sasha Nijinsky has been found in a downtown Manhattan loft, alive and well.' That's all it says. What is your response?"

Barron Harkness smiled. "Why, that's wonderful news! Is there anything about where she's been?"

"No, but clearly Sasha will now be able to identify the person who threw her from that balcony to the street."

Stone missed Harkness's response to this, because his attention had been caught by a movement near the set. Cary Hilliard had stood up. Her eyes as wide as those of a frightened deer, she stood still for a moment, then walked quickly across the set, directly in front of the cameras. Barker and Harkness, distracted by the movement, both turned and watched her. The director pushed a button, and the show's theme music came up again.

The announcer spoke up. "This has been the first *Hi Barker Show*. Tune in next Sunday night when Hi's guest will be . . . "

Stone burst out of the control room and ran for the elevators. Cary was banging on the button as he approached, and, when she saw him, she bolted.

"Cary!" he shouted down the length of the hallway. "Stop! Wait!"

She ducked down another corridor, out of his sight. He followed and was met with an expanse of closed doors. He began trying them.

A dozen doors down the hall, one was unlocked. He opened it and heard the clang of footsteps on fire stairs. He stopped for a moment and leaned against the wall. The memory of another set of steel stairs in another building flooded back to him. Now he knew whose footsteps those had been.

He started down, only to realize that the sound of footsteps was coming from above. He reversed his direction and followed the sound.

One floor up, the exit door stood open, and he found himself on a gravel roof. A gust of wind nearly knocked him off his feet. He grabbed at a ventilator pipe and held on. The view was all the more spectacular because there was nothing between him and the lights of the city but blustery air. Twenty feet away, only the modern building's low railing separated him from the lights. He looked around and saw a flash of mink coat disappear behind an air-conditioning unit. He followed.

He came around the unit, and she stood perhaps thirty feet from him, her feet spread in something like a fighting stance, leaning against the wind. She was no more than six feet from the low railing. Stone began walking toward her.

"Stop, Stone," she said. "Stop right there, or I'll jump."

He stopped, but he had already covered twenty feet; only ten separated them.

"You made me believe you were protecting him, but all along you were protecting yourself, weren't you? Right from the very beginning," he shouted over the wind.

"No," she said.

"You wanted to be with me so you would know what I knew about Sasha's case, that's all."

"No, Stone," she said. "I loved you from the start. I love you now, believe me. Get me out of this, and I'm yours. Barron can go to hell. Just get me out of this, and I'll make your life wonderful. Really, I will."

"You were sleeping with Sasha, weren't you?"

"Yes, but it meant nothing. It was just another erotic experience, don't you see?"

It was coming together for him now. "You were fucking Sasha, and so was Harkness. Harkness wanted her, not you, didn't he?"

"We were all fucking each other, sometimes all at once," she said. "She wanted him—not because she loved him, but because she could destroy him if she was married to him. She only wanted to cut off his balls, and then the evening news would have been all hers."

"And you, what did you want?" He edged a little closer.

She backed up a couple of steps. The edge was nearer now. The wind was gusting, and she leaned into it for a moment. "Well, you were useless, weren't you?" She spat. "You wouldn't free yourself of that dead-end job, so that you could get ahead. Barron was simply the best alternative. I didn't love him, though; I loved you. Why do you think I kept seeing you?"

"You didn't love me any more than you loved Barron or Sasha, Cary." He stepped closer; he could grab her now. He put a foot forward but kept his weight on the rear one. He reached out and snaked a hand around her waist.

There was a howl from behind him, and the wind struck his back. Involuntarily, his weight shifted onto the forward foot, and then to the toe. He let go of Cary. Slowly waving his arms for balance, he fell toward her, still pushed by the wind. Cary stepped instinctively back from him, and her calf struck the railing. In desperation, she reached out and grabbed at his coat lapel. Then they both toppled over the railing, out into the night. Sixty-five stories of thin air welcomed them.

Stone stopped short; something had his ankle. He ignored it, watched Cary slip from him and fall, facing him, revealed by flashes from lighted windows, all the way down until she struck the top of what looked like a Yellow cab.

Chunks of gravel were spilling from the top of the building now, falling past Stone to the street. Whoever had him was slipping over the side with him. He'll let go, Stone thought, and I'll join her. Then he stopped moving.

There was a chorus of grunts and muffled shouts from above, and, inch by inch, he was hauled back to the top of the building, scraping his shin quite badly. When he was back on top, lying with his cheek pressed gratefully to the gravel, he could see Dino hanging on to his ankle, and Barron Harkness and Hi Barker hanging on to Dino. They let go of each other reluctantly.

Stone crawled over to a ventilator and sat down with his back to it. "Thanks, Dino," he was finally able to say. "You did it again."

"And it's the first time you ever thanked me for it," Dino puffed.

"I don't believe any of this," Hi Barker said to nobody in particular. "But it's going to make one hell of a story."

Only Barron Harkness seemed to give a thought to Cary. "She's gone," he said absently. "My wife is gone."

Dino was the first to answer him. "Get used to it, pal." He snorted. "She's New York Dead."

CHAPTER

52

Stone sat with his client and watched the jury file back into the courtroom. He had a sinking feeling about this. He didn't like his client much, and he wasn't sure the man was innocent. He was afraid the jury didn't share his indecision.

"Has the jury reached a verdict?" Judge O'Neal asked.

Stone thought she was looking particularly attractive today, as much as she could in judicial robes.

The foreman stood. "We have, Your Honor," he replied.

"The foreman will hand the verdict to the clerk."

The clerk received the verdict, read it to himself, then handed it to Judge O'Neal. She read it and handed it back to him.

"The defendant will rise and look upon the jury; the jury will look upon the defendant."

Stone stood with his client.

"The clerk will read the verdict."

The clerk looked at the piece of paper. "We, the jury, unanimously find the defendant guilty as charged."

Stone's client sighed audibly.

Well you might sigh, Stone thought. I tried to get you to plead to the lesser charge, you dumb schmuck. But you thought you could beat it.

"The jury is released with the thanks of the court for a job well done," Judge O'Neal said. "Sentencing is set for the twenty-fifth of this month; bail is continued pending." She struck the bench with her gavel and rose. The courtroom rose with her.

Stone turned to his client. "I'm sorry we couldn't get a better verdict."

"You warned me," the man said. "Can I go home now?"

"Yes. We have to decide whether to appeal; I really think you should consider the expense."

The man sighed again. "Why bother? I'll do the time."

"You're free until sentencing, but you'd better be prepared not to go home after that. Bring a toothbrush."

They shook hands, and the man walked sadly away. Stone began gathering his notes.

"Mr. Barrington?"

Stone looked up. Judge O'Neal was standing to one side of the bench, behind the railing.

"In my office, please," she said primly.

Stone groaned. He had pressed his luck often in cross-examining the prosecution's witnesses, and she had repeatedly called him down for it. Now, the lecture. Hell, he thought, I'm lucky not to have been held in contempt. He trudged into her chambers, ready to take his medicine.

She had perched on an arm of the big leather sofa. She undid her robes, and they fell aside to reveal a bright red dress that went particularly well with her blonde hair. She crossed her legs.

They look awfully good, he thought. Something stirred in him for the first time in a long while.

"I read about the Nijinsky case, of course," she said. "I believe you discovered Ms. Nijinsky in a thoroughly dead condition."

"That's right, Judge. She was what a friend of mine calls 'New York Dead.'"

"In that case, I will remind you of our wager of some time past," O'Neal said, uncrossing her legs and recrossing them in the other direction.

He had forgotten.

"You, sir, owe me a dinner," she said.

Stone smiled. "Yes, Your Honor," he replied.

ACKNOWLEDGEMENTS

The Public Affairs Department of the New York City Police Department was not helpful in the research for this book. Individual officers were, however, and I would particularly like to thank Detective Jerry Giorgio of the 34th Squad Homicide Team for some enlightening conversations.

I thank Elaine Kaufman for keeping the home fires burning on Second Avenue and for running a place where a writer can get a decent table.

I am grateful to my editor, Ed Breslin, my London publisher, Eddie Bell, and all their colleagues at HarperCollins for their appreciation of this book and their hard work on its behalf.

Once again, I want to extend my gratitude to my agent, Morton Janklow, his associate, Anne Sibbald, and all the people at Janklow & Nesbit for their continuing care and concern for my career.

DEAD IN THE WATER

*This book is for the saints
of Washington, Connecticut,
Paul and Joan Marks*

1

Stone Barrington slowly opened his eyes and stared blearily at the pattern of moving light above him. Disoriented, he tried to make sense of the light. Then it came to him: he was aboard a yacht, and the light was reflected off the water.

He sat up and rubbed his eyes. The night before had been the stuff of bad dreams; he never wanted to have another like it. The nightmare had started at Kennedy Airport, when his live-in girlfriend, Arrington Carter, had not shown up for the flight. She was supposed to come directly from the magazine office where she had been meeting with an editor, but she had not arrived.

Stone had found a phone and had tracked down Arrington, still at *The New Yorker*.

"Hello?" she said.

Stone glanced at his watch. "I guess you're not going to make the plane," he said. "It leaves in twenty minutes."

"Stone, I'm so sorry; I've been having you paged at the terminal. Didn't you hear the page?"

He tried to keep his voice calm. "No, I didn't."

"Everything has exploded here. I took the proposal for the profile on Vance Calder to Tina Brown, and she went for it instantly. Turns out she had tried and tried to do a piece with Vance when she was at *Vanity Fair,* and he would never cooperate."

"That's wonderful," he said tonelessly. "I'm happy for you."

"Look, darling, Vance is coming into New York tomorrow, and I've got to introduce him to Tina at lunch, there's just no getting around it."

"I see," he replied.

"Don't worry, I'm already booked on the same flight tomorrow. You go ahead to St. Marks, take delivery of the boat, put in some provisions, and get gloriously drunk. I'll be there by midnight."

"All right," he said.

"Oh," she sighed, "I'm so relieved you're not angry. I know you can see what a break this is for me. Vance hasn't sat still for an in-depth interview for more than twenty years. Tina says she'll bump up the printing for the anticipated increase in newsstand sales."

"That's great," he said, making an effort to sound glad for her. "I'll meet you at the St. Marks airport tomorrow night, then."

"Oh, don't do that; just sit tight, and I'll grab a cab." She lowered her voice. "And when I get there, sweetie, try and be well rested, because I'm going to bounce you off the bedsprings a whole lot; you read me?"

"I read you loud and clear. I'd better run; they've

almost finished boarding. And remember, we've only got the boat for ten days; don't waste any more."

"I really am going to make it up to you in the best possible way, Stone," she said. "Bye-bye."

"Bye." Stone hung up the phone and ran for his plane. Moments later, he had settled into a comfortable leather seat and had in his hand a rum and tonic, in honor of his long-anticipated winter holiday. As the big jet taxied out to the runway he looked out the window and saw that it had started to snow. Good. Why have a tropical holiday if you can't gloat?

Vance Calder was, arguably, Hollywood's premier male star, often called the new Cary Grant, and he had played an important part in Stone's and Arrington's lives already. She had been in Calder's company when they had met at a dinner party at the home of a gossip columnist nearly a year earlier. Although Stone had been struck by her beauty and had found her marvelous company, he had not bothered to call her, because he hadn't believed for a moment that he could take a girl away from Vance Calder. Instead, Arrington had called him. Vance, she had explained, was no more than an acquaintance who, when he was in New York, liked to have a pretty girl to squire around, especially at dinners like the one at Amanda Dart's apartment, which she would feature in her column.

Inside a few weeks they were living together, and Stone had never been happier. At forty-two, he was still a bachelor, and he liked it that way. Living with Arrington, though, had made a lack of freedom seem very attractive, and he was determined to hang on to her, even if it came to marriage. Marriage had been increasingly on his mind of late, especially since Arrington had been showing signs of feeling a lack of commitment on his part. On the plane down to St. Marks he had reached a decision. They would have a wonderful cruise on the chartered boat, and they would come back engaged, unless it turned out to be easy to be wed in St. Marks; in that case, they would come back married. He was looking forward to the prospect.

Then the night began to go wrong. In San Juan, their first stop, he learned that his flight to St. Martin, the next leg, had been delayed by two hours. In St. Martin, the connecting flight to Antigua had also been delayed, and by the time he had arrived there, the light twin that would take him to St. Marks had already left and had to be summoned back at great expense. He had reached St. Marks sometime after 3:00 A.M. Nevertheless, he had been met by the charter agent and taken to the boat, a Beneteau 36, a roomy French design, and had, without unpacking, fallen dead into the double berth in the little owner's cabin.

He got out of bed and stumbled naked into the little galley and found half a jar of instant coffee in a cupboard. Shortly he had found the gas tap in the cockpit, boiled a kettle, and made himself a really terrible cup of coffee. While he drank it he took a stroll around the interior of the little yacht, a very short stroll indeed. He was glad there would be only the two of them aboard.

There was a very nice dining table, some books, no doubt left by previous charterers, and a small television set. He wondered what he might receive on that. He turned it on and, to his surprise, found himself looking at CNN. The marina must have a satellite dish, he thought. He slid into the navigator's seat, the leather cool against his naked buttocks, and looked around the chart table. All the island charts were there, plus a small Global Positioning System (GPS) receiver, a VHF radio, and everything else they needed to navigate in the islands.

He found some stale cereal and ate some, watching CNN. A major snowstorm would reach the New York City area by evening, and travel was expected to be disrupted. *Thank God Arrington is getting out this afternoon,* he thought. He washed his dishes, then unpacked and put away his clothes. A swim might be nice, he thought; he got into some trunks and climbed into the cockpit.

As he did, a yacht of about forty-five feet hove into view, under engine. It had a dark blue hull and teak decks, and her name, *Expansive,* was lettered on her bow in gilt. Two other things about the yacht caught his eye: the mainsail was still up, and in tatters, and it was being steered by a quite beautiful young woman. She was small and blond, wearing a bikini bottom and a chambray shirt knotted under her breasts, leaving a fetching expanse of tanned midriff showing between the two. The yacht passed within twenty yards of Stone's boat, but she never looked at him. Oddly, no one came on deck to help her dock. He started to go and help, but a yellow flag was flying at the crosstrees, signaling that the yacht was arriving from a foreign port, and he saw a uniformed customs officer waiting to take her lines. Stone watched the somewhat clumsy operation and wished he had gone to help. He'd have liked a closer look at the woman.

He put down the boarding ladder, then dove off the

stern into the bright blue water, which turned out to be exactly the right temperature—about eighty degrees, he reckoned. Maybe later today he'd call somebody in New York and gloat. He swam out about fifty yards into the little harbor, then sprinted back to his boat, hauling himself up the boarding ladder. He got a towel from below, made himself another cup of the awful coffee, and settled into the cockpit to get some sun on his all-too-white body. As he did, he saw the customs officer leave the yacht and, at a dead run, head for the little police shack fifty yards away. Odd.

A moment later, the customs officer emerged from the shack in the company of two police officers, one of them of rank, judging from his uniform. The three men marched rapidly back toward the blue yacht and went aboard, disappearing below. Stone watched with interest to see what would happen next. Ten minutes passed before the young woman skipper appeared on deck wearing a cotton dress. Accompanied by the three uniformed officers, one of them carrying a small nylon duffel, she walked toward the police shack and disappeared inside.

What the hell was going on? Stone wondered.

He kept an eye on the police shack all afternoon. Finally, sometime after five o'clock, the woman left the shack in the company of two uniformed policemen, got into a waiting car, and was driven away. Stone didn't know what sort of trouble she was in, but he felt for her, alone in a foreign place, at the mercy of the police. He had seen many people in custody, and he had never envied any of them.

2

*S*tone showered, shaved, and
got into some of his new tropical clothing—a short-
sleeved silk shirt, Italian cotton trousers, and woven
leather loafers, no socks. He found it an unexpected
pleasure to dress so lightly in January; there was much
to be said for winter in the tropics.

As the sun set he wandered across a wide green lawn
toward a wide thatched roof covering a bar and restaurant open to the breezes. It was early, and there were few
customers. A black bartender stood behind an expanse of
varnished mahogany, idly polishing a glass. A television
set over the bar was tuned to CNN, the sound muted.

"Evening to you, boss," he said amiably, with what
sounded to Stone like a Bahamian accent.

"Evening," Stone said.

"And what might be your pleasure this fine
evening?"

"Oh, something tropical, I guess, to celebrate my first evening in warm weather."

"A piña colada, mebbe?"

"Sounds good." Stone looked up at the television and saw a woman in a heavy coat standing on what looked like a New York City street corner. A blizzard was raging about her. "Could you turn the sound up on the TV for a minute?" he asked the bartender.

"Sure thing, boss."

". . . was predicted for later this evening, but it started around noon, and we already have a foot of snow on the streets, with at least twenty inches expected by the wee hours of tomorrow morning. Kennedy, La Guardia, and Newark Airports closed at midafternoon, so nothing is flying into or out of the city until further notice. The Port Authority predicted that no flights would be moving until noon tomorrow."

"Shit," Stone said aloud. "Okay, you can turn the volume down again."

"What you care, boss?" the bartender asked, turning down the TV. "You already here."

"Yeah, but my girl isn't. She was due to leave at four this afternoon."

"Bad luck, boss," the man said.

"Where are you from?" Stone asked.

"Born right here on St. Marks, boss."

"Funny, you sound Bahamian. You shining me on with that accent?"

The man grinned. "You're too good for me, pal." He stuck out his hand. "I'm Thomas Hardy, like the writer." Now the accent was more island British, with an extra, familiar layer.

Stone shook his hand. "Do I hear a little New York in there somewhere?"

"Lived in Brooklyn a long time; worked all over the city."

"I'm Stone Barrington; I'm on a charter yacht over at the marina."

"That's kind of a familiar name," Thomas said.

"Don't know why; it's my first time in St. Marks."

"Were you ever a cop?"

Stone blinked in surprise. "I was, mostly in the Nineteenth Precinct. Have we ever met?"

Thomas shook his head. "No, but I heard about you. I was walking a beat in the Village when you left the force; everybody was talking about you, said you got a bad deal."

"I can't complain," Stone said. "I left with the full pension after fourteen years."

"Yeah, but you took some lead with you, huh?"

"They got it out. What are you doing in St. Marks?"

"I was born here, like I said. My mama moved to New York when I was a kid. I joined the force, did my twenty, and brought my savings and my pension down here and put it to work."

"This your place?"

"Lock, stock, and liquor license."

"How long you been at it?"

"Six and a half years."

"Business good?"

"Not bad; a little better every year. That blizzard in the Northeast is going to cost me, though. A lot of people will be in your girl's shoes."

"I guess so." Stone sighed. "I was looking forward

to a more romantic week than this. Where can I make a phone call?"

Thomas reached under the bar, pulled out a phone, and set it on the bar. "I charge the tourists a buck a minute, but for an old cop, I'll just put what they charge me on your tab. Got a fax machine, too, if you should need one."

"Thanks." Stone called his home number.

"Hello?"

"I guess you're not going to make it tonight, huh?"

"You heard? I tried to call you at the charter office, but I didn't get an answer."

"They get CNN down here."

"I'm sorry, baby. It started to come down around midday, and let me tell you, it's really something. I'm a southern girl; I've never seen snow like this."

"CNN says the airlines will be flying again tomorrow afternoon. See what you can do."

"I'm already rebooked on tomorrow's flight, assuming it goes."

"Good. What are you up to now?"

"I'm having dinner with Vance and some friends of his. He actually found a Range Rover somewhere, and he's picking me up."

"Where are you dining?"

"Wherever's open, I guess."

"I miss you, babe."

"And I miss you, my darling. I was looking forward to that first piña colada."

"I'm drinking it for you right now. Say, let me give you this number."

Thomas shoved a card in front of him.

Stone read off both the phone and fax numbers. "Keep me posted on the flight situation, will you? The boat is moored no more than a hundred yards from this phone."

"I will, baby."

Stone said good-bye and hung up. "Well, Thomas, it looks like you and me." He sipped the piña colada. It was perfect—cold, sweet, and pineapply.

"Let me know when you're ready for dinner," Thomas said. "I'll keep a table for you." Customers were drifting in now, and a waiter was seating them.

Stone watched as a large black man dressed in a white linen suit, and in the company of a beautiful café-au-lait woman, entered and was shown to a prime table overlooking the harbor. "Impressive-looking fellow," he said.

"That's Sir Winston Sutherland, the minister of justice," Thomas said.

"A mover and shaker?"

"He both moves and shakes. And if his own opinion holds, he just might be the next prime minister."

Stone heard a car door slam and turned to look. The blond woman from the blue yacht, *Expansive,* had left a police car and, alone, was making her way across the lawn toward the marina.

"Very nice, huh?" Thomas said.

"Very nice indeed. She spent the afternoon with the local cops, though. I wonder why."

"Word is, the lady left Europe with a husband but arrived in St. Marks without him."

Stone turned and looked at the bartender. "I didn't see anybody else on board when she came into the harbor."

"That's because she was all alone on that big boat."

"You mean she sailed it all the way across the Atlantic?"

"Well, not all the way," Thomas said. "Her husband was along for part of the time."

"Is foul play suspected?"

"On this island, foul play is always suspected," Thomas replied. "That lady is going to have to convince a number of people"—he pointed at Sir Winston Sutherland—"that man first among them, that she is as innocent as a newborn lamb."

"And how difficult is that likely to be?" Stone asked.

"It could be very difficult indeed," Thomas said. "There's going to be a coroner's jury over at the town meeting house tomorrow morning. Word is, Sir Winston is asking the questions."

"Is that unusual?"

"Usually the coroner does it."

Stone looked over at Sir Winston Sutherland, who was digging into a bowl of something. "What's he eating?" he asked.

"Conch chowder."

"Well, I suppose you have to be careful of any man with enough daring to eat conch chowder in a white linen suit."

"Oh," Thomas said, "there's more reason than that to be careful of Sir Winston."

When Stone got back to his boat, late, there were lights on in the big blue yacht. He was tempted to call on the lady to offer his condolences, but he was a little drunker than he liked to be when he introduced himself to a beautiful woman.

CHAPTER

3

*S*tone, a little worse for the wear, entered the Markstown Meeting Hall at ten o'clock the following morning, just as the coroner, a wizened little black man with snow white hair, was about to call the proceedings to order. A jury of five black men and one white sat on folding chairs along one side of the hall; the coroner sat on a folding chair at a card table at the front of the room, and the woman from the blue yacht sat in the front row of chairs, dressed in a trim black dress that set off her tan. The dress was not quite demure enough for mourning, but it bespoke a certain dignity. Stone took a seat in the front row, across the aisle from her, just as Sir Winston Sutherland made his entrance, carrying a large satchel briefcase and dressed in a double-breasted blue suit with chalk stripes. He looked very official.

"These proceedings will come to order," said the

13

coroner. "We meet to hear testimony on the death of Paul Phillips Manning; we are pleased to have Sir Winston with us to conduct questioning."

Stone glanced at the woman, who sat, looking tired but somehow radiant, staring serenely at the coroner. She glanced briefly at Sir Winston. Stone wondered if she knew who he was and what was about to happen.

The coroner spoke again. "Call Mrs. Allison Manning."

The woman rose and walked toward a folding chair set next to the coroner's card table, between him and the jury. The scene resembled a rehearsal of a high school play set in a courtroom.

"Hold the book," the coroner said to her, extending a Bible. "Do you swear by Almighty God that the evidence you are about to give will be the truth?"

"I do," Allison Manning replied.

"State your full name and age for the record."

"Allison Ames Manning; I am twenty-nine years old."

Stone now noticed a stenographer seated near the jury, taking down the proceedings in shorthand.

Allison Manning gazed evenly at Sir Winston as he rose from his seat to his full height, which was a good six-three, and approached her.

"Mrs. Manning," Sir Winston said gently, "may I begin by expressing my condolences on the loss of your husband?"

"Thank you," she replied.

"Mrs. Manning, how long were you married to Paul Phillips Manning?"

"It would have been four years next month."

"And how old was your husband at his death?"

"Forty-two."

"And where did the two of you reside?"

"In Greenwich, Connecticut."

"Would you be kind enough to tell us of your last months with your husband?"

Allison Manning took a deep breath and spoke in a clear, well-modulated voice. "My husband and I left Newport, Rhode Island, last May and crossed the Atlantic to Plymouth, in England, just the two of us. Paul had had the yacht built in Finland and fitted out with some extra equipment after it was delivered to Newport. From Plymouth, we cruised up the English Channel to Cowes, on the Isle of Wight, then crossed the Channel and cruised the coast of Brittany, in France. We made a long passage to Bilbao, in northern Spain, then went on to Lisbon and Gibraltar. In the Mediterranean, we cruised the Greek islands and the Balearics and then sailed out to Madeira and the Canary Islands. We called at Las Palmas and did some refitting there, then at Puerto Rico, a port on the southernmost island of the Canaries, and our last port of call before starting across the Atlantic, bound for Antigua." She took a sip of water from a glass poured by the coroner.

"Please go on," Sir Winston said.

Allison Manning looked a little sadder. "We sailed southwest from the Canaries down to the latitude of Antigua, then turned west. We had picked up the trade winds by then, and we were making good time. We were ten days out of Puerto Rico, over halfway to Antigua, when the incident occurred."

"Tell us about the incident, with as much detail as you can recall."

"It was on the early afternoon of the tenth day," she said. "We had been in and out of squalls, then the wind dropped, and we were very nearly becalmed. The weather had been very changeable. We had been down to short sail in the squalls, using a roller-reefing head-sail, which was like a big window blind, and when Paul began to unroll the sail in the light winds, the top swivel of the roller-reefing gear separated into two parts. The sail fell down with the bottom part, and the top part of the gear remained at the top of the mast, attached to the halyard. I hope I'm making this clear."

Sir Winston turned to the jury. "Gentlemen, do you understand?"

The jury nodded as one man.

"Please go on, Mrs. Manning," Sir Winston said.

"This wasn't the first time this had happened," she said, "and it meant that someone had to go up the mast and pull the top part of the swivel down to deck level so that it could be reattached to the bottom part."

"And who went up the mast?"

"I did."

"Was this usual? Did your husband often send you up the mast at sea?"

"No. I had done that a couple of times before, but when we were tied up alongside in port. It was easier for Paul to hoist me up the mast with a winch than for me to hoist him. He is . . . was a large man. On this occasion he wanted to go himself, but he had woken up not feeling well that morning and was obviously not well. He had a thing about making good time at sea, and he didn't want to wait until he felt better, so I said I would go up the mast."

"And how did you accomplish that?"

"Paul lowered the mainsail; I got into the bosun's chair, which is a canvas sling, and Paul winched me to the top of the mast on the main halyard, then cleated the line while I hauled the genoa halyard down to deck level. There wasn't much wind, but there was a sea running from the last squall, and it was pretty uncomfortable at the top of the mast. I called to Paul to lower me to the deck, and that was when I saw him, sitting on a cockpit seat, holding his arm, near the shoulder." For the first time, her voice quavered. "His left arm."

"What happened then?"

She seemed to struggle to keep control of herself. "I called to him again, and he looked up at me. Then he seemed to be in terrible pain, and he sort of just lay down on his side on the cockpit seat." Tears appeared on her cheeks now. "I was very frightened. The wind began to get up again, and with no sail up, the boat was rolling very badly. I continued to call out to him in panic—panic that I was stuck at the top of the mast, and panic that he seemed to be having a heart attack, and I couldn't help him." Now she began to cry in earnest. Sutherland stood without speaking while she produced a tissue and dabbed at her eyes. Finally in control again, she continued. "A few minutes passed—I don't know how long—then Paul slid off the seat onto the cockpit sole. He just lay there, facedown. It was obvious that he was unconscious; he just sort of flopped about when the boat rolled."

"And then what did you do?"

"I just clung to the mast and cried."

"For how long?"

"A long time. Two hours, maybe three. I wasn't wearing a watch. Finally the sun got low in the sky; I realized that Paul wasn't going to help me, and that I had to do something to help myself."

"And what did you do?"

She took a deep breath and let it out. "I hugged the mast as tightly as I could, then I slipped out of the bosun's chair and began sliding down the mast, except I slid a lot faster than I meant to. I went down very quickly until I came to rest on the crosstrees, in a sitting position. That hurt, and I was sort of stunned for a minute, so I just stopped and collected myself for a few minutes. The rolling wasn't quite as bad, since I was farther down the mast. Finally I got up enough nerve to go the rest of the way down. I still don't know why I didn't fall and hurt myself."

"Then you went to help your husband?"

"No, not immediately. I was so terrified and so exhausted from clinging to the mast that I just lay there in a heap. I think I may have even fainted for a while; I don't know how long. When I could get up again, I made my way back to the cockpit. Paul was dead."

Stone found that he had been holding his breath. He let it out in a rush, and everyone in the room—the coroner, the jury, and Sir Winston—turned and looked at him. "Excuse me," he said sheepishly. He looked up and found Allison Manning staring at him. It seemed to be the first time she had been aware of his presence.

"Please go on," Sir Winston said. "What did you do next?"

"I tried to give him cardiopulmonary resuscitation," she said.

"Had you been trained in this technique?"

"I took a class once, at the yacht club at home."

"Did this have any effect?"

"No. I couldn't get a pulse at all, and Paul . . . I couldn't get him to breathe, and his body was growing quite cold by this time."

Stone marveled at how calmly she related all this.

"And then what did you do?"

"I sat and cried for a while and let the yacht take care of herself. When I finally got a grip, I started thinking about what to do next. It was dark by then, and it seemed so strange that Paul was dead. I kept expecting him to come up from below and adjust the sails or something."

"Did you move the body at all?"

"Not at first. Paul is . . . was a big man, and I'm quite small. I thought about moving him down below, to a berth, but then it occurred to me that if I did, I'd just have to get him up again, sooner or later. So I left him in the cockpit that night. I was exhausted, so I got some sleep. I couldn't eat anything, though. The boat took care of me; the wind dropped, and she lay fairly quietly."

"What did you finally do with the body?"

"When I woke up it was still dark, but there was about three-quarters of a moon, so the night was bright. It was clear to me that in that climate, I was going to have to bury Paul at sea. I went up into the cockpit and tried lifting the body, but I couldn't budge it. Finally I got the main halyard around him and winched him into a sort of standing position. When I let out on the line, he fell to leeward, and I was able to get him onto the side deck and undo the halyard. Then I released the lifelines and got him overboard."

"What did you do next?"

She swallowed hard, then continued calmly. "I said a prayer for Paul's soul, then I began to think about sailing the boat. Dawn came; I got the mainsail up with a winch and got us headed due west, and I repaired the headsail reefing swivel with a little steel clip. We had half a dozen spares, and we had already used half of them. Paul often talked about finding some more permanent solution to the problem, but he never did. Finally I got the headsail up again. I set the self-steering gear, as Paul had taught me, and I got a sleeping bag and slept in the cockpit through the morning. It was easy sailing, and with one or two direction changes as the wind came up, I got through the day. I slept in the cockpit that night, and by the second day, I was getting used to sailing the boat."

"So you just kept heading due west?"

"No, there was a book on board about celestial navigation; I couldn't find the manuals for the GPS or the high-frequency radio. I had never taken any real interest in the subject before—Paul had always done the navigating—but he had shown me how to use the sextant. From the book I learned how to find our latitude, and I just tried to keep us on the right latitude the rest of the way. We finished up a little farther south than I had tried for; our landfall was at St. Marks, instead of Antigua."

Sir Winston reached into his briefcase and brought

out two books. He showed one to Allison Manning. "And you kept this logbook?"

"Yes, after Paul died I kept the log in a sort of abbreviated fashion. Paul was always very meticulous about recording everything, as you can see by reading the earlier entries."

Sir Winston held up the other book, a leather-bound volume. "And do you recognize this book?"

She looked at it. "Yes, he bought that in Las Palmas, and he wrote in it a lot."

"Did you ever read what he wrote in this book, Mrs. Manning?"

"No. He often made notes in such a book."

"Mrs. Manning, are you quite able to continue? Would you like a rest?"

"No, I'm fine; I'd like to go on."

"Good, good. Tell me, Mrs. Manning, how would you describe your relationship with your husband?"

"We had a good marriage; we were very content and happy."

Sir Winston looked surprised. "Really? You didn't have fights, arguments?"

"Rarely. Oh, I suppose anyone who's married has an argument now and then, but we got along well."

"No children?"

"No. Paul didn't want children."

"But you did?"

"Well, yes, but I suppose Paul was more important to me. I didn't want to ruin our marriage by having a child unless Paul wanted one, too."

"So you were deeply in love with your husband?"

She hesitated. "I loved him, yes," she said finally.

"Did you treat him well?"

"Yes, I did."

"You were a good wife at all times?"

"I tried to be," she replied. "Excuse me, sir, but what are you getting at?"

Sir Winston opened the leather-bound book and showed her a page. "Is this your husband's handwriting?"

"Yes, it is." Allison Manning was looking concerned for the first time.

"Let me read you some of what your husband wrote in this book," Sir Winston said, opening the book at a marked page. "I quote: 'They had been on the boat together for months now, and she had been the perfect bitch.'" Sir Winston paused, looked at the jury, then continued. "'She had always had a temper, but now she frightened him with the intensity of her anger.'" He looked at Allison Manning as if to elicit a response, but she said nothing; she looked stunned.

Sir Winston turned to another marked passage. "'They argued one day as she was making lunch. She had a chef's knife in her hand, and for a moment, he thought she might use it on him. He slept badly that night, waking often, expecting to feel the blade in his back.'"

Allison Manning was suddenly on her feet; her face was red and contorted with anger. "That's not about us, dammit! It's written in the third person, don't you see? What are you trying to do, you bastard?"

Sir Winston feigned shock at her outburst, but before he could speak, the coroner broke in. "Please compose yourself, Mrs. Manning; Sir Winston is only doing his duty." He looked at his watch. "I think we will stop now for lunch. We will resume in one hour. Gentlemen of the jury, please do not discuss these proceedings among yourselves during lunch." He stood, and the jurors stood with him.

Sir Winston collected the books and his briefcase and strode quickly from the room, leaving Allison Manning standing, staring after him. Finally she collected her purse and walked slowly toward the door.

Stone, nearly as shocked as she at the turn in Sir Winston's questioning, followed her from the building. "Mrs. Manning?" he called.

She stopped and turned. "Yes?"

"My name is Stone Barrington; I'm an American, too. My chartered boat is moored near yours."

"Oh, yes," she said absently. She turned to go.

"I wonder if I could speak with you for a moment?"

"What about?" she asked, looking puzzled.

"I was present at the inquest this morning, and I heard what took place. I think you may be in over your head."

"How do you mean?"

"Do you know who this Sir Winston is?"

"No."

"Nobody mentioned that, huh?"

"No. Just what is your interest in this, Mr. Barrington?"

"Back in New York, I'm a lawyer, and right now, I think you need a lawyer very much. Can I buy you lunch?"

CHAPTER

4

*T*hey walked quickly across the lawn to her boat and went down below. "Would you like some lunch?" Allison Manning asked. "I'm going to make a sandwich."

"Thank you, yes," Stone replied.

She went to the galley and began putting together some sandwiches. "Please tell me your name again," she said. "It always takes me a couple of times."

"Stone Barrington. If you'll forgive me, we only have an hour before the inquest resumes, and we should talk quickly."

"All right."

"First of all, let me explain the proceedings. A coroner's inquest is . . ."

"To make an official determination of the cause of death," she said.

"The cause and the circumstances. In this case, the

jury could probably return one of three verdicts: death from natural causes, death by homicide, or an open verdict, which means the jury doesn't feel it has enough evidence to decide how your husband died."

"I understand," she said, handing him a sandwich. "Something to drink?"

"Anything diet," Stone said and accepted a soda.

"What are the consequences of these three possible verdicts?" she asked, then took a big bite of her sandwich.

"If the determination is natural causes, the coroner will give you a death certificate, and you can get on with your life. If it's an open verdict, maybe, but not certainly, the same. But if the verdict is death by homicide, then Sir Winston is going to be very nearly obliged to bring a charge of murder against you."

She gulped down the bite of sandwich. "Murder? I didn't murder Paul!"

"I don't believe you did," Stone said, "but Sir Winston may have a very different opinion. If you should be charged with murder, your alternatives would be to stand trial or to plead to a lesser charge for a reduced sentence or a suspended sentence, if the circumstances warranted."

"I have no intention of pleading to any charge," she said.

"I understand," Stone replied. "Now we have to talk about what's going to happen when the inquest resumes. My assumption is that Sir Winston has other kinds of evidence to present which might cast you in a bad light. I think that to adequately present your side of this, you need more time and a good local lawyer, so the best thing to do would be to ask for a recess of the inquest until such time as you are ready to present your case."

She shook her head vigorously. "I'm not going to hang around this godforsaken island for days or weeks. I want to get home, get Paul's estate settled, and get on with my life."

"That's certainly understandable," Stone said. "Alternatively, you can allow the inquest to resume on time and present the best case you can in the circumstances and take a chance on the outcome."

"What's your recommendation?"

"I think it's always a mistake to rush the legal process unless you're in a very strong position, and I'm not at all sure you are."

"If I go back to the hearing, will you represent me?"

"Yes, if the coroner will allow it. I'm not licensed to practice in St. Marks, but an inquest is less formal than a trial, and he might do it. But there's Sir Winston to consider, too."

"You asked me if I knew who he was. I don't."

"He's the minister of justice of this island country, and I'm told he aspires to be the next prime minister. If that's true, and if he sees some political advantage in pursuing this, he could be dangerous to your interests."

"I see," she said. She leaned against a galley counter and looked down at her feet, silent. Finally she spoke again. "I want to get this over with and get out of here. I can't believe he could possibly convince a jury that Paul's death was anything other than natural. After all, there were no witnesses; they'd have to take my word, wouldn't they?"

"No, they wouldn't, not if Sir Winston can present

convincing evidence to the contrary. Your husband's diary, for instance."

She waved a hand. "I can explain that; it's no problem."

"I'm glad to hear it," Stone said. "Did the police remove anything else from the yacht besides the logbook and the diary?"

"Not that I'm aware of," she said.

"All right. First, let's talk about the diary, then let's see what else we can dig up that will react to your benefit." He glanced at his watch. "We have forty-five minutes to build our case."

Stone looked at his watch again. Five minutes to go, and she was in the head. "Better hurry," he called out.

"Won't be a minute," her muffled voice called back.

Stone took the opportunity to look around the interior of the yacht. It was gorgeous. The maker was Nautor of Finland, and the boat was a Swan, widely held to be the best production yacht in the world, and very close to being custom-built. She had obviously been built with little regard to cost; every piece of equipment aboard was the best that money could buy—the electronics, the sails, even the galley equipment. He reckoned the boat had cost between a million and a half and two million dollars.

She popped out of the head, her makeup redone, her long, blond hair combed. "Okay, let's go," she said.

Stone picked up the documents she had given him and followed her up the main companionway ladder.

Five minutes later, they were back in the Markstown meeting hall, and Sir Winston Sutherland was resuming his questioning of Allison Manning.

CHAPTER

5

*S*ir Winston rose to his full height and addressed Allison Manning. This time he was not bothering with charm. "Mrs. Manning," he said, "was your husband a wealthy man?"

"We're well off, I suppose," she replied, looking a bit nonplused. "Paul never really discussed money with me; he took care of that. I mean, on the boat, he tied the knots and spliced the wire and fixed the engine and navigated, and I did what I did at home—I kept house. I'm not a business executive or an entrepreneur or a stockbroker or a lady lawyer or a yachtswoman. I'm a housewife, and that was all I ever did. Paul made the money and invested it and, except for my clothes and the things in the house, he spent it; I hardly gave it a thought. We have a nice house, we drove nice cars, but the only really extravagant thing Paul ever bought was the boat, and I don't even know what it cost."

"I see," Sir Winston said, as if he didn't see at all. "You never give money a thought."

"I think I see what you're getting at," she said. "You're implying that I hit my husband over the head or stabbed him with a kitchen knife and dumped him overboard so I could have his money, right? Well, do you have any idea how big Paul was? He was as big as you!" She seemed to reconsider. "Well, almost as big."

The jury tittered at this. Allison Manning was becoming very assertive now, and it worried Stone a little. He had instructed her not to argue with Sir Winston, not to lose her temper again.

"Well, Mrs. Manning," Sir Winston continued, seeming to regroup, "let me ask you this: what were your husband's toilet arrangements on the yacht?"

She looked at him as if he were a raving lunatic. "What?"

Sir Winston looked flustered for a moment. "Let me rephrase, please. When your husband was on deck, and he felt the need to relieve himself, how did he do it?"

"In the usual way," she replied.

The jury began laughing, but a sharp look from the coroner subdued them.

"I mean, Mrs. Manning, did he go below and use the toilet, or like most men on a boat, did he just pass his water into the sea?"

"He stood on the stern of the boat, held onto the backstay with one hand, unzipped his fly with the other, and peed overboard."

"Ah," said Sir Winston, as if he had caught her in some monumental admission. "This large husband of yours made himself vulnerable for just a moment when he urinated. A small shove, even by a small woman, was all it would take, eh?"

She fixed him with a hard stare. "That speculation, Sir whatever-your-name-is, is not worthy of a reply."

Stone sensed his moment; he rose and addressed the coroner. "Pardon me, Your Honor," he said. "My name is Stone Barrington; I am an American attorney, and Mrs. Manning has asked me to represent her in these proceedings. I wonder if I might put a few questions to her?"

Sir Winston spun and looked at him. "Are you licensed to practice in St. Marks or in Britain?" he demanded.

"No, I am not," Stone said evenly, "but if these proceedings are so informal as to allow the minister of justice to question a witness at an inquest, then perhaps Mrs. Manning might be questioned by someone of her own choosing."

"Well . . ." the coroner began.

"Are you a barrister? A trial lawyer?"

"I wasn't aware that this was a trial," Stone replied.

The coroner asserted himself. "I will permit Mr. Barrington to put questions to Mrs. Manning, if he believes he can shed some light on this matter."

"I believe I can, Your Honor," Stone said. He hadn't the faintest idea how to address a coroner in a former British colony, but "Your Honor" seemed to do the trick. He picked up a manila folder, stepped forward, and addressed his new client. "Mrs. Manning, how did your husband earn his living?"

"He was a writer; he wrote spy and mystery novels, mostly; he had quite a following."

"And when your husband was preparing to write a book, was it his practice to make notes?"

"Yes, he made very extensive notes, sometimes writing almost the whole book in telegraphic form."

Stone picked up the leather-bound book from Sir Winston's table. "In a form like the contents of this diary?" he asked.

"Exactly like that. Paul bought that blank-paged book in Las Palmas specifically for the purpose of outlining a new novel. He mentioned it to me over dinner, and he wrote in it often. He liked to save his notes in a bound form, because the university he attended had asked to be the repository for his personal and professional papers."

"And why, when Sir Winston read you the passages from this outline, did you not mention your husband's usual practice?"

"He didn't give me a chance," she said, casting a withering look at Sir Winston.

"I see," Stone continued. "Mrs. Manning, what was your husband's state of health shortly before his death?"

"Well, Paul had never been seriously ill, but he wasn't in very good shape."

"How do you know this?"

"We both had thorough physical examinations before we set out across the Atlantic."

Stone removed a sheet of paper from the manila folder in his hand and presented it to her. "Is this a copy of your husband's examination results?"

She looked at the paper, then handed it back. "Yes, it is."

Stone looked at the jury and the coroner. "Please

follow as I read from the doctor's report." He held up the paper and began to read. "'Paul Manning is a forty-two-year-old author who has come in for a physical examination prior to an extensive sea voyage. Mr. Manning has no complaints, but he is desirous of being examined and taking a copy of his medical records on his journey.

"'Mr. Manning is six feet, two inches tall and weighs two hundred and sixty-one pounds, rather too much for a man of his frame. The results of blood tests show a serum cholesterol count of 325 and serum triglycerides are 410. These are both dangerously elevated, the high end of normal being 220 for cholesterol and 150 for triglycerides. Because of these numbers, in conjunction with Mr. Manning's lack of regular exercise and a history of heart disease in his family, I have advised Mr. Manning to immediately undertake a program of exercise, a diet low in cholesterol and other fats, and to bring his weight down to a maximum of two hundred pounds.'"

Stone handed the coroner the page and turned to his client. "Mrs. Manning, did your husband take his doctor's advice and go on such a diet?"

"For about a week," she replied. "Paul was incapable of dieting for longer than that."

"Right," Stone said and addressed himself to the coroner and the jury. "Paul Manning was grossly overweight and had been clogging his coronary arteries with cholesterol for many years. He was, in short, a heart attack waiting to happen, and happen it did, in exactly the way Mrs. Manning has described. You have heard how she coped with this disaster at sea, and I put it to you that she could not have invented such a story. It is simply too heartrending not to be true. This brave woman has lost her husband under extraordinary circumstances and then mustered the fortitude to save their yacht and her own life. You cannot believe otherwise. Thank you for your time, Your Honor, gentlemen." Stone sat down.

The coroner turned to Sir Winston. "Do you have any further questions?"

"None," Sir Winston replied almost inaudibly, looking at his knees.

"Gentlemen," the coroner said to the jury, "do any of you have a question?"

The jury was mute.

"Then I will ask you to retire and consider your verdict."

Stone and Allison Manning sat at the bar of the Shipwright's Arms, as Thomas Hardy's restaurant and inn was called, and sipped piña coladas.

"I can't thank you enough," she said. "I'll give you my address in Connecticut, and you can send me your bill."

"For practicing law in a foreign country without a license?" Stone asked. "I'd be disbarred."

"What do you think the verdict will be?"

"You can never tell about a jury, even a coroner's jury, but I believe we answered every point Sir Winston made. I'm optimistic."

"So am I; you did a brilliant job."

"You're too kind. What are your plans now?"

"I suppose I'll go home and settle Paul's affairs. He had a lawyer and an accountant; I'm sure they'll help me. We both made wills before we left on the transatlantic—simple ones, each leaving everything to the other."

"What will you do with the yacht?"

"Sell it, I suppose; I've spent all the time on that boat I ever want to."

"I'd buy it myself—I've always admired Swans—but I think I'm a few years away from being able to afford one. My advice is to get it ferried back to the States—Fort Lauderdale, maybe—where there's a brisk market in expensive yachts."

Thomas tapped lightly on the bar and nodded in the direction of the meeting hall.

Stone turned and saw the coroner approaching, an envelope in his hand. They had not yet been out of the meeting hall for half an hour.

CHAPTER

6

*T*he coroner handed the envelope to Allison Manning. "Here is your husband's death certificate," he said. "Please accept my condolences."

"Thank you," Allison replied.

He turned toward Stone. "For what it's worth, I thought you did a very good job." He turned and walked away.

Allison handed the envelope to Stone. "You open it," she said.

Stone tore open the envelope and read the certificate.

"Well," Allison asked, "what was the verdict?"

"It's an open verdict," Stone said. "The jury felt it had insufficient information to assign a cause of death."

"And what does that mean to me, legally?"

"In my opinion," Stone said, "it means you should get the hell out of St. Marks right now."

"Do you mean you think Sir Winston might still come after me?"

"It's certainly possible," Stone replied.

"If you'll forgive me for butting in," Thomas Hardy said, "I think it's more than just possible."

"Thomas used to be a New York City policeman," Stone said, "and he knows how things work here. Thomas, do you have any idea what the airline schedule is?"

Thomas looked at his watch. "There's a daily flight out of Antigua for San Juan in an hour and a half, and you'll have to get Chester to fly her to Antigua."

"Who's Chester?" Allison asked.

"He flies a Cessna twin to Antigua, by arrangement," Thomas replied. "Would you like me to call him and the airlines?"

"Please," Stone said.

They sipped their drinks nervously while Thomas did his telephoning.

"You're on the flight from Antigua," Thomas said, hanging up. "Now let me see if I can raise Chester." He dialed another number. "Chester? You got room for one lady to Antigua, right smart? Good. She'll be along." He hung up. "You'd better get going," he said to Allison.

"I'll go get my things," she said, hopping off the barstool.

"Forget your things," Stone said. "I'm sure Sir Winston had the verdict before we did. If he wants you, the police could be here any minute."

Thomas put some car keys on the bar. "A cab could take a while to come; my car is out back."

"I've got to get my passport," Allison said. "And a few other things."

"Run," Stone said. "Don't take a second longer than absolutely necessary. I'll get the car."

She jogged off toward the marina.

"Thanks, Thomas," Stone said.

"You take the main road and turn right after about two miles," Thomas said. "There's a sign. Chester's airplane is white with blue stripes."

Stone ran to the rear of the restaurant, found the car, a new Toyota Camry, got it started, and drove around front. He looked toward the marina but saw nothing of Allison. "Jesus H. Christ!" he muttered, getting out of the car. He was halfway across the lawn when he saw Allison hurrying across toward him, carrying a duffel and a man's briefcase. Stone opened the door. "Let's go!"

Allison dived in and slammed the door. "I'm not accustomed to running from the law," she said.

"Don't say things like that," Stone replied, driving off. "As far as we know, the law has no interest in you. You've accomplished all the legal necessities in St. Marks, and you're leaving for home like any other tourist."

"Just in more of a hurry," Allison said. "Do you think they might come after me at home?"

"I think that if you were arrested, then ran, they probably would go for extradition, but since no charge has been made, well, there are no guarantees, but I think it's unlikely they'd come after you. If they do, my advice is to get the best lawyer you can and fight it tooth and nail. Would you like me to recommend a lawyer?"

"Yes, please."

"I'm of counsel to a firm in New York called Woodman and Weld."

"I've heard of it; very prestigious."

"Call Bill Eggers there. The firm probably has someone who specializes in this sort of thing, and if they don't, Bill can recommend the best man in town. If this happens, it's going to cost; how are you fixed for money?"

"I won't know that for sure until I've talked with Paul's lawyer and accountant, but I think I'll be all right. I can always sell the boat."

Stone turned right onto the airport road. "As soon as you get home, find a yacht broker and have him fly a ferry crew down here at the earliest possible moment to get the boat out of here."

"All right." She dug into her handbag and came up with a card. "Here's my number in Greenwich; will you call me when you get back? I'll buy you dinner."

"That might be tough to explain to the lady I live with," Stone said, "but I would like to know how things work out. I'll call you."

"So why isn't this lady with you?"

"She got snowed in. Oh, I hadn't thought of it, but the airports might still be closed up there. When you get to San Juan, check with the airlines. It might be best to spend a night there and wait for the weather in the Northeast to clear up."

"Thanks, I'll do that." She smiled at him. "Sure you don't want to come with me?"

"It's a lovely thought, but I've got a yacht charter here, and I hope Arrington will be here soon."

"My bad luck," she said.

God, Stone thought, *you're supposed to be the grieving widow!* He drove through the airport gates and toward a large hangar. The Cessna was parked in front of it, and the pilot who had flown him to St. Marks from Antigua was waiting. "There's Chester," Stone said.

"Thank God," she said.

Stone pulled up next to the plane, took her duffel and her briefcase, and stowed them in the baggage compartment. He walked back to the wing and held open the door for her. "You're on your way," he said.

An engine coughed to life, followed by another.

She slung an arm around his neck and gave him a much bigger and wetter kiss than he could have expected. "I'll never be able to thank you enough, but I'll try," she shouted over the roar of the engines. "Good-bye."

"Good-bye," Stone said. Then an unexpected sound reached his ears. He looked back toward the airport gate and saw a Jeep driving toward them, making some sort of strange siren noise.

The vehicle skidded to a halt next to the airplane, and two starched and pressed black policemen got out. The officer gave them a casual salute with a swagger stick. "Mrs. Allison Manning, I presume?"

"Yes," she said.

"Good afternoon," he said, smiling, then handed her a document. "You are under arrest for the crime of murder. You will be charged tomorrow morning at ten o'clock at the courthouse in St. Marks City. Do you have any luggage?"

"No," Stone said quickly, "Mrs. Manning does not have any luggage." He took the document and looked at it; it appeared to be a properly drawn warrant. He turned to Allison. "You'll have to go with them. I'll get you a local lawyer and see you at the hearing tomorrow morning. I doubt if I can get anything done until then."

Allison looked stunned. "All right," she said. She put a hand on his arm. "I'm so glad you're here." She got into the Jeep and was driven away.

Chester killed the engines. Stone watched until the Jeep had driven through the airport gates, then went and got her duffel and briefcase from the luggage compartment. He didn't know what was in that briefcase, but he knew that he didn't want Sir Winston Sutherland rooting around in there. *Poor Allison Manning,* he thought. *She's in for a rough time, and I suppose I'm going to have to help her.*

7

Stone drove back to Markstown, mulling over what he might do to help Allison Manning. There wasn't a whole lot, he reckoned. He could find her a local lawyer, and that was about it. Then he recalled that Sir Winston had asked him, during the fateful coroner's jury, if he were licensed to practice in Britain. Maybe, with the help of Woodman and Weld in New York, he could get hold of some high-class British barrister and have him flown in, if Allison Manning could afford it. He parked the car behind Thomas Hardy's restaurant and walked in.

Thomas was alone at the bar, writing on a steno pad. He looked up as Stone came in. "I heard," he said. "Chester called me."

"It looks bad," Stone said, taking a stool and handing Thomas the arrest warrant. "I'm going to have to find her a first-class barrister."

Thomas shoved a pad across the bar. "I thought that might be the case. Here's a list of three who might—I stress, might—take her on."

Stone read four names. "What about the fourth name?"

"First we'd better call the first three. Shall I?"

"Please."

Thomas picked up the phone and dialed a number.

Ten minutes later, after the third call, Thomas hung up the phone.

"Well?" Stone said.

"No hope," Thomas replied. "The word is out that Sir Winston really wants this one—nobody knows exactly why—and nobody is going to go up against him right at this moment in time, with an election coming up soon. The consensus seems to be that a conviction would give him a lot of favorable publicity, and nobody wants to get between Sir Winston and publicity."

"What if Sir Winston should lose the case?"

"As far as I can tell from these phone conversations, nobody in the legal community thinks he's going to."

"How about somebody else?"

"Not a chance," Thomas said. "I eliminated most of them before I made my list. Those three were the only ones who might have opposed Sir Winston."

"What about the fourth name on the list?"

"Sir Leslie Hewitt," Thomas said.

"Yes, what about him?"

"He'll represent her," Thomas said. "He hates Sir Winston's guts, as his father before him did."

"Well, then, give him a call."

Thomas shook his head. "You don't understand."

"Explain it to me."

"Leslie was once a first-rate barrister, one of the best, in fact."

"And now?"

"He's well past eighty; he hasn't tried a case in at least fifteen years; and . . ."

"And?"

"And he's . . . failing, you know? I mean, he's bright as a new penny at times, but at other times . . ."

"I think I get the picture," Stone said. "You're suggesting that an eighty-year-old barrister who's half gaga should defend Allison Manning?"

"No, that's not what I'm suggesting. You've got a hearing tomorrow morning at ten, and somebody besides you has got to be there to go through the motions, to be the barrister of record until you can get somebody in here from out of the country."

"You mean from England?"

"Probably. You could go to Antigua, which is another former British colony and which has a similar legal system, but that's too close to home. Those people are going to have to get along with Sir Winston, too, if his political dreams come true, and they are very likely to."

"I thought about London. I do a lot of work for a firm in New York, and I can ask them to recommend somebody in London. But I don't know whether Allison can meet that kind of expense."

"Then she's between a rock and a hard place," Thomas said. "Right now, I think you and I had better go see Leslie Hewitt."

They drove along the coast road to the western end

of the island and turned off toward the beach onto a rutted dirt road.

"Where are you taking me?" Stone asked.

"Leslie has a cottage down by the beach," Thomas replied. "It's been in his family since the seventeenth century."

"Is he black?"

"Yes."

"I would have thought that in the seventeenth century, any blacks on this island would have been slaves."

"You're not far off the mark there, but an ancestor of Leslie's bought his freedom and started a stevedoring business. They were a very prosperous family indeed until we got our freedom from Britain. Then the new government confiscated nearly everything Leslie had inherited. His wife died, his children fled the country, and he was left here with nothing but this cottage." He pulled up before a whitewashed building.

It was larger than Stone had imagined. He got out and, with Thomas leading the way, approached the Dutch front door, which was open at the top.

"Leslie!" Thomas called out. He beckoned to Stone and entered the cottage. They walked through a small foyer and into a comfortably if somewhat seedily furnished living room. "Leslie!" Thomas called out again, but there was no reply. "Let's take a look out back." They walked through a neat kitchen and through a pretty garden, then down to the beach. A tiny black man in faded shorts and a straw hat was pulling a dinghy up the beach from the water. "There he is," Thomas said, approaching. "Leslie, how you doing?" he asked.

"Thomas? Is that Thomas Hardy?" Leslie Hewitt asked, shielding his eyes from the light.

"Sure is," Thomas said. "Come to see you, and I brought a friend." He introduced the barrister to Stone.

"How do you do, Sir Leslie," Stone said.

"I'm very well, Mr. Barrington; and you?"

"Very well, thank you."

"Leslie, can we go into the house?" Thomas asked. "There's a matter we need to discuss with you."

"Do I owe you money?" Hewitt asked, removing his straw hat and mopping his brow with his forearm. He had short, snow white hair.

"Certainly not, Leslie."

"Then this is very surprising," he said. "It's been a very long time since anyone needed to discuss anything with me except a bill."

Sitting in a small study crowded with dusty books, Thomas Hardy explained the situation to Leslie Hewitt. "What do you think, Leslie?"

"Well, I certainly don't like the sound of it," Hewitt replied, crossing a bare leg over another and dusting off his foot. "All happening very quickly, isn't it?"

"Very quickly indeed," Thomas said.

"I shouldn't be surprised if, in the circumstances, Winston will ask for an early trial date. What is it you want of me? I don't know if I'm up to trying a murder case, not unless you enjoy a hanging."

Thomas and Stone laughed. "We need your help for the hearing, Leslie," Thomas said. "To hold the fort until we can get a barrister in from London."

"Ah, I see," Hewitt said. "Well, I can certainly help you to that extent."

"There's the matter of bail, too, Sir Leslie," Stone said.

"Please call me Leslie," the little man said. "Everyone does."

"Leslie, do you think there's a chance of bail?"

"It's not unheard of in such a case," Hewitt replied. "It's not an easy island to get off of, especially if you're a foreigner, so the judge might smile on such a request. Bail might be steep, though."

"How steep?"

"A hundred thousand dollars, perhaps twice that."

"Cash?"

"Does the lady have any property in St. Marks?"

"An expensive yacht."

"That might do very nicely, if the judge is sure she won't sail away."

"That's good news; I'll pass it on to Mrs. Manning."

"I shall want to meet her before the hearing," Hewitt said. "May we meet at the courthouse at, say, nine in the morning? That should give us time."

"Of course," Stone said. "Ah, you mentioned hanging; I hope that was in jest?"

"Oh, no," Sir Leslie said, shaking his head. "Certainly not in jest."

"St. Marks has capital punishment, then?"

"Oh, yes; it's quite easy to get hanged in St. Marks. You see, Mr. Barrington, there's no prison system to speak of on our lovely island. Crimes tend to get divided into three classes: first, there's anything from petty theft through assault and battery up to, say, multiple burglaries. These crimes are dealt with by fines and short sentences, up to about three months, in our local jail. If there's no room in the jail, then the fine is increased, and the Ministry of Justice is very scrupulous about collecting the fines. Then we have a second category of offenses, starting with armed robbery and running up through assault with intent to kill—virtually any crime involving violence but not death. These are dealt with by exile, permanent exile from our island. For natives of St. Marks, who love their island, this is a crueler punishment than you might imagine. Then, lastly, we have crimes involving death: voluntary manslaughter, any degree of murder, conspiracy to murder—these crimes are capital offenses, and death is by hanging. We have one or two hangings a year."

"You mean, then, that if Allison Manning is found guilty of any degree of homicide, she will be hanged? They would hang a woman?"

"Quite so. Only about one in ten persons hanged is a woman, but it happens."

"What about race? Would the fact that Mrs. Manning is white be a factor in a possible death sentence?"

"I should say that would increase her chances of hanging," Sir Leslie said, "especially since her jury is very likely to be all or nearly all black."

Stone swallowed hard. "I see."

"I should mention, too," Sir Leslie continued, "that in St. Marks, jury verdicts are by majority, not unanimous vote, so a white juror or two would not be able to cause a deadlock, and the judge elects the jury."

"Jesus Christ," Stone said quietly.

Sir Leslie smiled. "I'm glad to see you are taking this seriously."

"What is the appeals procedure?" Stone asked.

"There is only a single appeal," Sir Leslie replied. "All capital convictions are automatically referred to the prime minister, whose word is final. He generally responds the next day, and, should his decision be negative, the hanging takes place on the following day." He smiled. "Since our system is so efficient, we tend to think that capital punishment really is a deterrent to capital crime."

"Yes," Stone replied, "I can see how it might be."

Thomas turned to Stone. "You're going to be doing a lot of telephoning tomorrow, I should think. There's a room with a phone over the bar you can use."

"Thanks, Thomas," Stone said. "Maybe I should just take the room for the duration."

"That will be fine."

"Is there somewhere I can rent a printer for my laptop?"

"My bookkeeper is on vacation; I'll move hers in there for you."

They turned back to Leslie Hewitt, who seemed to have dozed off.

"Leslie?" Thomas said.

The little man opened his eyes. "Thomas? Is that Thomas Hardy?"

"Yes, Leslie."

"How very good of you to come and see me," he said, beaming at them. He turned toward Stone. "And who might this be?"

When they returned to the restaurant, Thomas handed Stone a fax. "This came for you while we were gone."

DEAD IN THE WATER
•

Dear Stone,

> *I cannot find a way to tell you how impor-*
> *tant this assignment has become, but the fact is,*
> *I have to spend as much time as possible with*
> *Vance Calder while he is in New York, which is*
> *for the rest of the week. I know how angry and*
> *disappointed you will be to read this, but there's*
> *simply no way I am going to be able to get to St.*
> *Marks in time to go sailing with you, no matter*
> *how hard I try, so we may as well both face it*
> *now. I ask your forgiveness, and I look forward*
> *to your return.*

> *Love,*
> *Arrington*

Stone wadded up the paper and tossed it into a wastebasket.

"Bad news?" Thomas asked.

"Is there any other kind?" Stone replied.

8

S tone sweated through a nearly sleepless night, tossing in his berth, trying in vain to think of some tactic to abort this whole process. He rose at dawn, had a swim in the harbor and showered off the salt water, then forced down some breakfast. He left his chartered yacht, walked to the berth where *Expansive* lay, and went aboard. Below, he found a makeup kit in the head, and he chose a demure dress and some shoes from a clothing cupboard. In a drawer he found fresh lingerie and, feeling odd, chose some lace bikini panties. There were no bras in the drawer. He stuffed the lot into a small duffel he found in a locker. He was about to go up the companionway stairs when he stopped and looked around.

Allison Manning was an innocent woman, he was sure of that, but if there was anything incriminating on this yacht, he wanted to know about it. He certainly wasn't going to tamper with evidence, but he needed to know what was here. He set down the duffel and went to the galley. He had no idea what sort of criminal investigation skills were available to the St. Marks police force, but he thought it wise not to leave a lot of fingerprints about. He went to the galley and found a pair of rubber kitchen gloves and put them on. Then he went to the bow of the yacht and started working his way toward the stern, looking at everything along the way. He paid particular attention to the chart table and bookcases, then moved on to the master cabin. He found nothing incriminating. Then he found himself staring at Allison Manning's briefcase.

He was torn between his lawyer's respect for his client's privacy and the cop in him who wanted to know everything. If she was guilty, did he want to know? Probably not. Yes. Finally he made his decision; he laid the briefcase on the large bed and pressed the releases on the locks. Nothing happened. Then he saw the combination locks. Frustrated, he tried changing the last digits one, then two notches in each direction, then he turned the combinations to zero on both sides. The case would still not unlock. "Shit!" he said. Well, it was none of his business anyway. He left the briefcase on the bed, returned the rubber gloves to the galley, picked up the duffel, and went on deck.

He trudged up to the Shipwright's Arms and climbed upstairs to the room over the bar. Nobody ever seemed to lock anything in St. Marks; he walked in, tossed Allison's duffel onto the bed, sat down at the desk, picked up the phone, and dialed Bill Eggers's home number.

"Yeah?" Eggers said grumpily.

"It's Stone, Bill. Wake up; I need you to pay attention."

There was a groan as Eggers apparently sat up in bed. "What are you doing back?" he asked, awake now.

"I'm not back; I'm still in St. Marks."

"Then you must be in jail," Eggers chuckled. "I can't think of any other reason you'd call me from there."

"Close. I have a client who's in jail, and it's very, very serious; a murder charge."

"Did she do it?"

"No, but what does that matter?"

"What do you want from me?"

"She needs an English barrister badly; nobody here will defend her, for political reasons, but it's a former English colony with an English-style court system. I don't know any English barristers; you got any ideas?"

"We deal with a firm at Gray's Inn in London. Let's see, it's . . . six forty-five?! Jesus, Stone; you ever hear of office hours?"

"Bill, I've got a preliminary hearing at ten o'clock. It's what, noon in London? You need to catch these people before they go to lunch."

"Yeah, yeah; what's your number there?"

Stone read it off the telephone on the desk.

"I'll call you back in a few minutes."

Thomas knocked and walked into the room. "Everything you need here?"

"Yes, it's fine, Thomas; I'm just waiting for a call back from New York about an English barrister."

"How about some breakfast?"

"I've had something, but I'd love some coffee."

They sat and drank their coffee together.

"Thomas," Stone said, "there's something I need to know."

"What's that?"

"Is Leslie Hewitt going to be able to get through this hearing without . . . you know?"

"I wouldn't worry about it. Leslie is very sharp when his mind is fully engaged. He'll manage."

"God, I hope you're right." The phone rang, and Stone picked it up. "Hello?"

"It's Bill; I've got you a guy, but . . . has this client of yours got any money?"

"Maybe."

"Maybe won't do it. This guy's fee is a retainer of two hundred thousand pounds sterling against an hourly fee of two hundred pounds an hour, and travel time counts; he wants the retainer in his bank account before he even makes an airline reservation."

"That's a fee of more than three hundred fifty thousand dollars plus more than three hundred fifty dollars an hour. He must be an absolutely fucking wonderful lawyer," Stone said.

"That's what he tells me; what do you want me to tell him?"

"If I had my druthers I'd tell him to go fuck himself, but I guess I'd better ask my client first."

"The fee is not out of line, Stone. After all, you're asking a top-flight barrister to fly halfway across the world on short notice and to stay indefinitely. A top New York man would cost at least that. Oh, by the way, he'll want to bring a clerk with him; that's seventy-five pounds an hour."

"And he'll want to fly first class, too, I suppose."

"Of course."

"Tell him you'll get back to him after I've talked to my client."

"Okay. When will you want him?"

"We'll probably get a trial date set today, and it could be soon; things move quickly here."

"I'll tell him. See you." Eggers hung up.

Stone turned to Thomas. "Well, I hope her husband turns out to have had a hell of a lot of money."

Thomas Hardy pulled into the Government House parking lot simultaneously with Sir Leslie Hewitt, who was driving an ancient Morris Minor station wagon festooned with rotting wood paneling.

"Good morning, Leslie," Stone said, getting out of Thomas's car.

"Good morning, Stone, Thomas," Sir Leslie called back. He reached into the rear of the little car and removed a long plastic garment bag and a small suitcase, then led the way into the building.

They signed in to the jail, were searched for weapons, then were led to a small cell that held a table and four chairs.

A moment later Allison Manning was led into the cell by a black matron. She was pale and rumpled and seemed to have had little sleep. She went to Stone and put her head on his shoulder. "I am so glad to see you," she whimpered.

Stone patted her back awkwardly, then introduced her to Sir Leslie. "Sir Leslie is going to represent you at the hearing and apply for bail," he said.

She shook the barrister's hand. "Thank you so much for being here, Sir Leslie," she said.

"I am happy to represent you," the little man replied. "Please sit down, and I'll tell you what is going to happen this morning." Everyone sat down, and Sir Leslie continued. "This will be a short meeting of the court at which the presiding judge will ask the prosecutor if he has sufficient evidence to bring a charge of murder to trial. Then we will ask for bail, and I'm told you have a yacht which might serve as your security."

"Wait a minute," Stone said. "Won't the prosecution have to present evidence of the crime? I was hoping we might get a dismissal."

"Oh, no," Sir Leslie replied. "The judge will simply take Sir Winston's affidavit that he has enough evidence for trial; it's all very gentlemanly."

"It's all very unheard of," Stone said.

"Stone, you must understand that although our court system is based on English law, over the years, in the interest of efficiency, certain procedures that the court thinks superfluous have been pared away from the process."

"Superfluous? This court thinks that the presenting of evidence in a preliminary hearing is superfluous?"

"I'm afraid so," Sir Leslie said. "I assure you that if Sir Winston wants this to go to trial, it will go to trial, no matter what evidence might be presented, and no matter how we might challenge that evidence."

"Leslie," Stone said, "this crime—I mean the alleged

crime—occurred on the high seas, in the middle of the Atlantic Ocean. Can't we ask for a dismissal on jurisdictional grounds?"

"Oh, no," Sir Leslie said. "You see, many of the cases tried in our courts over the past two hundred years were based on crimes that occurred at sea. The local rule is that the defendant will be tried in the jurisdiction of the first port he puts into after the act."

Stone nodded dumbly.

"Now, Mrs. Manning," Sir Leslie continued, "I understand you have a yacht which might be used to secure your bail, is that correct?"

"Yes," she replied.

"What is the value of the yacht?"

"I don't really know," she said. "I'm sure it's expensive."

Stone spoke up. "A minimum of a million and a half dollars American."

"Oh, that should be quite sufficient. And where does the yacht lie?"

"In English Harbour."

"Good, good."

"Leslie," Stone said, "Mrs. Manning will need to live aboard the yacht until this matter is disposed of."

"I'm sure His Lordship would agree to that."

"Who?"

"The judge, Lord Cornwall."

"Oh."

"Stone, did you ever see the film *Witness for the Prosecution*?"

"Yes."

"Well, that is a pretty good model for how court is

conducted. I expect you've seen other such films as well."

"Yes, I suppose so. Oh, Allison, I brought you some things." He shoved the duffel across the table. "I couldn't find a . . . I hope these are all right."

Allison held up the dress and looked at it. "Well, at least you didn't bring the sequined cocktail dress."

Sir Leslie opened his garment bag and removed two black robes, handing one to Stone. "You'd better get into this."

Stone stood up and put on the robe; it was ridiculously small on him.

"And this," Sir Leslie said, opening his small case. He handed Stone a wig.

"You can't be serious," Stone said, regarding the thing at arm's length.

"Oh, yes, quite serious," Sir Leslie said. "On second thought, just carry it; don't put it on."

"Good," Stone said. "I'll carry it."

Thomas put a hand over his face and laughed quietly.

CHAPTER

9

Allison was taken away by the matron, and Stone, Sir Leslie, and Thomas left the jail, walked upstairs, and found the courtroom. Thomas took a front row seat, and Sir Leslie led Stone to the defense table. Sir Winston and another man, probably his supporting attorney, were already seated at the prosecution table. Various people milled around the room until the bailiff stood and shouted for all to stand. A moment later a red-gowned, bewigged black man entered from a side door and took the bench. He was middle-aged, tall and thin, with short, graying hair under his gray wig.

"Be seated," the judge said. "Bring up the prisoner."

Stone turned and watched as Allison came up from a hidden stairway and entered the dock. She had pulled back her hair, and in her fresh dress looked quite normal.

"Madam, would you like a chair?" the judge asked.

"Thank you, yes, Your Lordship," she replied, giving him a grateful smile.

That's it, Stone thought, *pour on the charm for the judge; wouldn't be the first time that had worked.*

"Sir Winston," the judge said, "do you have a request for this court?"

Sir Winston stood and handed a folder to the bailiff. "Thank you, Your Lordship, yes. The government petitions this court for the trial on a charge of murder of one Allison Ames Manning, now present in the dock. We certify that we have sufficient evidence to bring this case to trial and to convict the defendant."

The judge accepted the folder, flipped through it for a moment, and addressed the middle distance. "All is in order; who will appear for the prosecution?"

"I will, Your Lordship," Sir Winston replied, "assisted by Henry Porter."

The judge turned to the court reporter. "Write down that Sir Winston Sutherland and Mr. Henry Porter will appear for the prosecution." He looked over at the defense table. "And who will act for the defense?"

"I will, Your Lordship," Sir Leslie said, standing, "and I request to be assisted by Mr. Stone Barrington." He turned to Stone and whispered, "Stand up."

Stone stood, feeling foolish in the tight robe, the wig in his hand.

"I do not recognize Mr. Barrington," the judge said.

"Your Lordship, Mr. Barrington is an American barrister, a prominent member of the New York bar. I request that he be admitted to the St. Marks bar for the duration of this action, so that I might have his advice."

"Will he question witnesses?" the judge asked.

·
59

Stone spoke up before Sir Leslie could. "Yes, Your Lordship."

"Mr. Barrington, have you had the experience of defending in a murder trial?"

"I have, Your Lordship, on four occasions."

"And how did you do?" the judge asked impishly.

"They were all innocent, Your Lordship," Stone replied with mock seriousness, "but only three were acquitted."

The judge smiled. "Three out of four acquitted, eh? But then, you have such a lenient judicial system, don't you?"

"On the contrary, Your Lordship, in a lenient system all four would have been acquitted."

The judge laughed. "Very well, Mr. Barrington, you are admitted to the St. Marks bar for the duration of this trial." He turned to the reporter. "Write down that the defense will be represented by Sir Leslie Hewitt and Mr. Stone Barrington."

Sir Leslie leaned over and whispered out of the corner of his mouth, "Put on the wig."

"What?" Stone whispered back.

"Put on the bloody wig!"

Stone put the wig on and stood there, feeling extremely foolish.

The judge smiled broadly. "Very becoming, Mr. Barrington. I'm sure you will do the St. Marks bar proud. You may be seated."

Stone sat down, but Sir Leslie remained standing. "Your Lordship," he said, "the defense requests bail for the defendant to extend through the trial."

"Well," the judge replied, "in a capital case, the bail

would have to be substantial. Is the defendant possessed of a substantial sum of cash?"

"Your Lordship, the defendant owns a large yacht moored in English Harbour, which I am assured is valued at in excess of one and one-half million dollars in U.S. currency. I request that the yacht secure her bail, and that she be allowed to live aboard the vessel until these proceedings are concluded."

The judge turned to the prosecution. "Sir Winston?"

"I have no objection, Your Lordship, as long as the defendant has a clear understanding of the terms of her bail."

"Quite right, Sir Winston," the judge replied. He turned to Allison, sitting in the dock. "Mrs. Manning, in St. Marks, bail is more than security, it is a sacred obligation. In order for me to grant bail, you must agree not to leave this island, and you should know that if you should do so, you would not only forfeit bail—in this case, your yacht—but under St. Marks law your departure would be tantamount to a plea of guilty to the charge, and you would stand convicted of murder."

Holy shit, Stone thought.

"Do you understand the terms of your bail?"

Allison stood. "I do, Your Lordship."

"Very well, bail is granted, and the yacht will be secured to the dock." He looked down at his calendar. "Trial is set for Monday next, at 10:00 A.M."

Stone's jaw dropped. "Your Lordship," he managed to say, "that gives us only six days to prepare for trial."

"Quite right, Mr. Barrington," the judge replied. "Any problem with that?"

Sir Leslie spoke up. "The defense is satisfied with the trial date, Your Lordship," he said.

"But we have to get a barrister in here from London to conduct the defense," Stone said. "If it pleases the court."

"Mr. Barrington," the judge said, as if speaking to a backward child, "it is already in the record that the defense will be conducted by Sir Leslie, with your assistance. The record cannot be changed." He stood.

"All rise," the bailiff called out.

The judge turned and left the courtroom.

Stone turned to Sir Leslie. "Leslie, what the hell is he talking about?"

"What?" Sir Leslie replied, packing his wig into his case and removing Stone's.

"I thought you understood that we have a barrister coming from London."

"What?" Sir Leslie asked.

"Leslie, you cannot conduct this trial; you said so yourself."

Sir Leslie turned on him. "To whom do you think you are speaking, sir? I have conducted the defense at five hundred and eighty-three trials in this court! This one will be five hundred and eighty-four! I will discuss my fee with you later." He wheeled and walked out of the courtroom, carrying his robe and his wig.

Stone turned and looked for the first time at Thomas Hardy in the front row.

Thomas sat with his head in his hands, making a moaning sound.

Allison came down from the dock. "All ready to go?" she asked cheerfully.

10

*T*homas drove while Stone sat beside him and Allison took the backseat. For all of Stone's life, extreme worry had caused him to become sleepy, and right now he was having a very hard time staying awake.

"God, but I'm glad to be out of that place," Allison said.

"Were you treated all right?" Thomas asked.

"Well, yes, and contrary to what I've heard about jail, the food was pretty good. I had a cell to myself, and except for the open toilet, it wasn't bad."

"I'm glad to hear it," Thomas replied.

"I had some absolutely fascinating conversations with the woman in the next cell, too; she was in for shoplifting, and it wasn't her first time, so she knew the drill. Stone, I can't thank you enough for getting me out of there."

Stone stirred from his lassitude. "Don't mention it," he said.

They pulled up at the restaurant, and Stone and Allison got out so that Thomas could park the car. An American-looking man was seated at the bar, drinking what looked like a gin and tonic; his suit and briefcase made him look out of place, made him look like an insurance salesman. He seemed to recognize Allison and approached her, handing her a card. "Mrs. Manning, I wonder if I could speak with you for a few minutes."

Stone turned to Allison. "If you don't need me for a moment, I have some phone calls to make."

"Go right ahead," she said to him, then turned to the other man. "Of course," she said, "let's take a table."

Stone went up to his new room over the bar, threw his newly acquired barrister's robe at the wall, and called Bill Eggers.

"Yes, Stone, are we a go for the London man?"

"I'm afraid not, Bill; it seems I've wasted his time and yours."

"Why? What happened?"

"Bill, I hardly know where to begin: I have this perfectly innocent woman for a client who it seems is being railroaded by the judicial system in this godforsaken island country, and unless I can think of something fast they're going to hang her."

"Hang her?"

"I'm afraid so." Stone explained the chain of events thus far.

"That's the craziest thing I've ever heard," Eggers said when Stone had finished.

"I wish I were hearing about it instead of living it," Stone said.

"And your barrister is gaga?"

"At least some of the time; he appeared to be perfectly normal in court, except that he seemed to forget that we were bringing in the London man."

"Well, at least he knows the score down there; that's worth something."

"I hope you're right, but it's Tuesday, and I'm going to have to be prepared to try this case next Monday morning."

"Is there anything else I can do to help?"

"Not right now; believe me, I'll call in a hurry if there is."

"I'm here if you need me," Eggers said, then hung up.

Stone made another call, to Bob Cantor, a retired cop who had been helpful on a previous case.

"Hello?"

"Bob, it's Stone Barrington."

"Hi, Stone; aren't you supposed to be on vacation?"

"I'd rather not talk about that; I'm in big trouble on a case, and I want you to do some things for me. Can you clear the decks for the next week?"

"Sure; I'm not all that busy."

"Good. The first thing I want you to do is to get on a plane for the Canary Islands."

"Where the hell is that?"

"It's a Spanish possession a few hundred miles out in the Atlantic, off North Africa."

"Back up here, Stone; tell me what's going on."

Stone related the events of the past few days.

"That's the craziest thing I ever heard," Cantor said. "They want to hang her?"

"That's right. Now look, their last landfall before St. Marks was the Canaries; they were in Las Palmas, the capital, for some work on the boat, then they stopped on the southernmost island, which is called Puerto Rico, their last night before starting the transatlantic. I want you to go to both places and ask about the yacht, which is called *Expansive.*"

"Got that," Cantor said, obviously scribbling.

"Talk to anybody who saw them, talked to them, had a meal with them, saw how they interacted."

"What exactly are you looking for?"

"Straws to grasp at; God knows I've got nothing else. See if you can find me a witness who can, from personal experience, characterize the relationship between Paul Manning and his wife during the last few days they were in the Canaries—ideally somebody who can say he saw a lot of them and that they obviously adored each other."

"Anything else?"

"Anything else you can possibly think of. You understand the situation now and something of what I need. If I'm going to get this woman off I'm pretty much going to have to prove that she didn't do it."

"That's impossible," Cantor said. "There were no witnesses."

"I'm going to have to do it anyway."

"What airline goes to the Canaries?"

"I haven't the faintest idea; call my secretary and tell her to book it for you, tonight if possible."

"Right. Anything else?"

"Yes, I want you to dig up everything you can on Paul Manning for me—library, Internet, credit report, criminal record, military record, anything you possibly can before you leave for Las Palmas. FedEx it to me here." He gave Cantor the address and phone and fax numbers. "If you can think of any other avenue to pursue, pursue it; if you need outside help, hire it; if you have any ideas for me, fax them, okay?"

"I'm on it," Cantor said, then hung up.

Stone called his secretary. "Hi, Alma."

"Hi, Stone. I saw Arrington this morning; why is she still here?"

"Don't ask; she's not coming. I'm going to be busy down here for at least another week, so scrub anything I've scheduled through the middle of next week—reschedule or tell them I'll call as soon as I'm back."

"Okay."

"Any calls or correspondence worth bothering with?"

"Nothing that won't wait until you're back."

"Oh; call one of the judges' clerks and find out where they buy robes, then get one in my size and FedEx it to me."

"You doing some judging down there?"

"I'll explain later. Is Arrington upstairs?"

"She was on the way out when I saw her; a limo was waiting for her."

"I'll call her later, then." He gave her his address and numbers. "You can always leave a message at the bar if I'm not here. I'm still sleeping on the boat; it's all the use I'm getting out of it."

"Okay; anything else?"

"Oh, I almost forgot: Bob Cantor is going to call you in a minute about some travel arrangements. Get

him on a plane tonight, if possible, and give him a thousand dollars in cash for expenses. Anything else he
needs, get it for him, all right?"

"All right."

Stone hung up. He felt a little better now that he was
actually doing something about the mess he was in. He
went back downstairs just as Allison was saying good-bye
to the businessman.

"Who was that?" he asked.

"An investigator from Paul's insurance company. If
we need any cash for legal expenses, it'll be in my bank
account in Greenwich shortly."

"Good; we ought to give Leslie Hewitt his fee up
front; it's usual in this kind of case."

"He's such a sweet old man," she said. "I just loved
him."

"Yeah," Stone said. "Allison," he said, taking her
arm and leading her to a table, "you and I have to talk,
and right now."

"Sure," she said. "You're looking pretty grim."

"I'm feeling pretty grim, and I'm going to tell you
why." He pulled out a chair for her and sat her down,
then took a deep breath and started in.

11

S tone sat her down and talked to her. "I don't have time to be gentle about this or pull any punches, so here's your position as I see it. This Sir Winston Sutherland has it in for you, apparently because he thinks it will help him politically. He somehow engineered an open verdict in the coroner's jury, which gave him a legal basis for charging you with Paul's murder. Now you're going to be tried, and there's nothing I can do to stop it."

"Surely any reasonable jury will acquit me," Allison said. "I don't really have anything to worry about, do I?"

"Allison, I don't know if we're going to have a reasonable jury. The judge picks the panel, and no objection from me is going to stand; the jury may be all or mostly black, and they may or may not be more likely to convict a white person, I don't know. All I know is that this is a capital offense."

"You mean I could get the death penalty?"

"Yes, and the way things apparently work on this island, if you're convicted there's no other penalty you could expect to get."

Allison stared at him, her mouth open. "Are you serious?" she managed to ask.

"Perfectly serious. What's more, there's no lengthy appeals process available; the only appeal is to the prime minister, and he apparently acts on appeals very quickly."

"How quickly are we talking about?"

"The appeal must be lodged within twenty-four hours after the trial ends, and he normally acts on it within twenty-four hours after that."

"Let's look at the worst case," she said. "I'm tried on Monday—how long is that likely to last?"

"The way things are done here, no more than a day, possibly two."

"Then if I'm convicted on Monday, the appeal has to be filed on Tuesday, and the prime minister would either grant or deny it on Wednesday. If he denies it, then I would be . . . How do they do it?"

"Hanging."

"I could be hanged . . . when?"

"The day after the prime minister acts."

She swallowed hard. "So by a week from Thursday I could be dead?"

"Worst case."

She put her elbows on the table and her face in her hands. "What can we do?"

"Put on the best defense we can, in the circumstances. I had wanted to bring in a top barrister from

London, but the judge has precluded that by making Leslie Hewitt the counsel and me his assistant."

"Isn't there anything else we can do?"

"There are two ways we can go: I've already said that we have to put on the best defense that we can, and I've got somebody in New York working on that now. He's leaving for the Canaries right away to see what he can find to help us there. Did you make any friends while you were there? Someone who might testify as to your relationship with Paul?"

"No, not really; we pretty much stayed to ourselves. What's the other thing we can do."

"Well, we know that Sir Winston somehow finds it politically desirable to try you on this charge; what we might be able to do is make it politically undesirable for him to convict you, or, if he should, to make it desirable for the prime minister to uphold your appeal."

"How do we do that?"

"By letting the press know about your predicament."

"On this island? What press?"

"Not here; in New York, in London; wherever people read newspapers or watch TV."

"You want me to become famous?"

"Yes."

She shook her head. "I just don't see how that's going to help."

Stone spread a hand as though he were tracking a headline. "BEAUTIFUL BLOND AMERICAN GIRL LOSES HUSBAND AT SEA! CONNIVING POLITICIAN CHARGES HER WITH MURDER IN BACKWATER ISLAND NATION!!! It's called marshaling public opinion; it might bring pressure to bear."

"How do we accomplish this?"

"I'll call New York and get a public relations firm involved. Can you afford that?"

"How much?"

"I'm no expert at this, but I should think fifty to a hundred thousand dollars would go a long way toward accomplishing what we want. Woodman and Weld would hire and instruct them, and you'd have to pay their fees, too. Will the insurance money cover it?"

"Yes," she said, but she looked doubtful.

"What's the problem?"

She shrugged. "I just don't know if I want to be that kind of celebrity. I'm really a very private person."

"Allison, let me put this to you as strongly as I can. If we don't do something you're going to be a very dead private person. In St. Marks, Sir Winston holds all the cards; he's in control. But he can't control the rest of the world. This island subsists mostly on tourism; if he wants to become prime minister he's not going to want somebody telling the world's tourists that if they come to St. Marks they're liable to be arrested, tried, and hanged on spurious charges. That translates into a lot of empty hotel rooms and a catastrophic loss of revenue for the government."

She wrinkled her brow. "Why don't I just get the hell off this island? There must be a way."

"Didn't you listen to His Lordship this morning? If you try that and they catch you, it's tantamount to conviction; they could hang you before the week is out. Even if you made it off the island, they could come after you, maybe extradite you; then you'd be worse off than you are right now; you'd be guilty."

She shrugged and said nothing, but she seemed to be imagining something terrible.

"Will you let me get this PR campaign in gear?"

"All right," she sighed.

"Good. I suggest you get a hundred thousand dollars sent to Bill Eggers at Woodman and Weld as soon as possible. Nobody's going to want to extend credit to you in the circumstances."

"All right; I'll call my bank in Greenwich; the insurance money is supposed to be deposited there soon."

"Allison, speaking of insurance, did you mention to the investigator that you had been charged with the murder of the insured? That might make them reluctant to pay."

"It never came up," she said.

"Hello, Bill, it's Stone."

"What's happening?"

"Allison Manning is sending you a hundred thousand dollars from her Greenwich bank tomorrow."

"How nice! Do I have to do anything for it?"

"I want you to get ahold of the hottest PR firm you can find and have them start a campaign in the media to get Allison Manning released."

"I believe I get the picture," Eggers chuckled. "Barbaric islanders persecuting American blonde?"

"You're a quick study, Bill."

"How much does she want to spend?"

"I told her I thought fifty thousand would do the job; spend more if necessary. By this time the day after tomorrow I want this island overrun with wild-eyed reporters, photographers, and television crews. See if you can get *60 Minutes* interested, but tell them they have to move fast; she goes on trial on Monday, and she could be strung up by the middle of next week. It's this Sunday night, or nothing."

"They'll want as much background on her as possible."

"Call Bob Cantor." He gave Eggers the number. "He's researching her husband; tell him to copy you on anything he finds. Paul Manning was a well-known writer, so lots of people should have heard of him. Try to be careful what you release to the PR people; don't let anything unfavorable get into the mix."

"I get the picture."

"The firm has got a lot of Washington connections, right?"

"Right."

"Find out who her congressman is in Greenwich, get ahold of him and both Connecticut senators and tell them they're about to lose a voter. Get them to get on to the State Department and tell them an American abroad is being railroaded. There's no consulate here, but there's bound to be one on a neighboring island. Have them issue the strongest possible protest to the St. Marks government."

Eggers was laughing now. "Why don't we get the president to send a cruiser down there to drop anchor in the harbor, with her guns pointed toward the capitol building?"

"Send a fucking aircraft carrier, if you can."

"Are there any communists in the St. Marks government? That always helps, especially in the Caribbean."

"Let's assume there are, for the moment; we can always apologize later."

"Call me tomorrow."

"Right." Stone hung up and walked downstairs, where Thomas was getting the bar ready for lunch. "Thomas," he said, "you'd better prepare for some business. Maybe we can even make up for the New York blizzard."

"Sounds good to me," Thomas said, laughing.

12

*S*tone dialed the number and waited. "This is Stone Barrington," his own voice said. "Please leave your name and number and I'll get back to you." "Arrington?" he said into the phone. "Pick up, Arrington." Nothing. He hung up.

He felt he had done all he could for the moment, so he left the room above the restaurant and walked down to his chartered yacht; he was weary and aching, as if he had run several miles. He fell onto his bunk and slept.

A rapping on the hull woke him; a glance through the hatch showed him dusk outside. He poked his head up.

Allison was standing on the pontoon between their boats. "How you doing?" she asked.

"How you doing is a better question."

"I had a little cry; now I feel better. Come over and have some dinner with me?"

"Sure, I'd like that."

She held up a finger. "One condition: no talking about my problems; I've put them out of my mind until tomorrow."

"Agreed. Give me time for a shower? I've been asleep, and I'm a little groggy."

"I hate a groggy date," she replied. "See you in half an hour."

Stone hunted down his razor, then squeezed himself into the tiny head and turned on the cold-water shower. In St. Marks, it wasn't all that cold.

He rapped on the deck of the big blue yacht and stepped aboard.

"Come on down," she called out from below.

Stone walked down the companionway ladder, which, on a yacht this size, was more a stairway. Allison was at work in the galley, and the saloon table had been set for two, side by side. Whatever she was wearing was mostly concealed by a large apron.

"Can you make a decent martini?" she asked.

"I believe I can handle that."

"The bar's over there." She pointed. "Just open those cabinet doors."

Stone followed her instructions and found a handsome bar setup, nicely concealed. He found a cocktail shaker, two glasses, and ice cubes, then the gin and vermouth. "You sound awfully cheerful," he said as he mixed the drinks. "I don't know how you do it."

"It's a gift," she said. "For my whole life, when faced with something awful, I do as much as I can, then I put it out of my mind. I mean really right out of my mind. Then I find that the next day, things seem clearer."

"That's a great gift," he said.

"You can cultivate it if you work at it."

He handed her a martini. "I'll start right now."

She was sautéing chicken breasts in a skillet on the four-burner gas range, which was large for a yacht.

"When did you find time to get to the grocery store?" he asked.

"I didn't. I provisioned in the Canaries, and I've got lots of cold storage here, plus a large freezer. There won't be a salad, though; sorry about that."

They clinked glasses. "Better times," Stone said.

"I'll drink to that." She took a swig of her martini. "Expert," she said.

"A misspent youth. I tended bar in a Greenwich Village joint one summer, during law school." He leaned against a galley cabinet and sipped his drink. "Tell me about you," he said.

"That's easy," she replied. "Born in a colonial village in Litchfield County, Connecticut, father a country lawyer, mother a volunteer for this and that; went to local private schools, then Mount Holyoke, in Massachusetts; did a graphics course at Pratt, in Brooklyn, worked as an assistant art director for an ad agency in Manhattan, met Paul, married Paul; lived . . . well, lived. What about you?"

"Born and raised in the Village, father a cabinet-maker, mother a painter; NYU undergrad and law school. NYPD for fourteen years, eleven of them as a detective."

"Why'd you quit?"

"A very bad boy put a twenty-two slug in my knee, and the force quit me, gave me their very best pension.

That's the short version; I won't bore you with the long one, which involves a lot of department politics and a very strange case I worked on. Anyway, once off the force, I crammed for the bar, and an old law school buddy hooked me up with Woodman and Weld."

"How much money do you make?"

The bald question stopped him for a moment, then he recovered. "I made about six hundred thousand last year," he said. "My best year so far."

"You're doing well, then."

"By New York law firm standards that's only middling, but I have a lot more freedom than I would as a partner in a firm. I'm lucky that I can pick and choose my cases. If I want to bugger off to St. Marks for a week's sailing, I can manage it."

She put an oily hand against his cheek. "But you got stood up, didn't you? Poor baby."

"That's me."

"Who is she?"

"Name's Arrington Carter; she's a freelance writer."

"And when the blizzard was over, what kept her in New York?"

"She's writing a *New Yorker* profile of Vance Calder."

"Ooooh, lucky girl."

"I guess. She's known him for a while; matter of fact, she was his date the first time I met her."

"And you won out over Vance Calder? You must be sensational in bed."

He laughed. "You think that was it? I always thought it was my boyish charm."

She gave him a bright smile. "That, too." She

opened a sealed packet of smoked salmon and arranged the slices on two plates. "First course is almost ready," she said. "There's a bottle of white on the table; will you open it?"

Stone went to the table, found a corkscrew, and opened a bottle of Beringer Private Reserve '94, then tasted it. "Excellent," he said. "Was Paul a connoisseur of wines?"

"Paul was more of a wino; I'm the authority." She handed him a bottle of red. "For the main course; might as well open it and let it breathe."

"Dominus '87. Very nice."

"You know wines?"

"Enough to stay out of trouble." He opened both bottles.

She set the two plates of smoked salmon on the table and untied her apron. Underneath it she was dressed in a very short skirt and a white cotton blouse, unbuttoned and tied under her breasts.

Stone remembered that the first time he had seen her she'd been wearing that sort of blouse, tied that way.

They finished their smoked salmon, then she whipped up a chicken dish over rice, with a lovely sauce. They were both warm with the wine and laughing easily. Allison cleared the table, then pressed a button and it folded away electrically.

"Very slick."

"Glad you like it." She caught him looking at her breasts. "Any yachtsman should be able to deal with a simple square knot," she said, knocking back the last of her wine.

•

Uh-oh, Stone said to himself. But he had had nearly a bottle of wine on top of the martini, and he was feeling hurt by Arrington, feeling incautious, and feeling extremely attracted to Allison Manning.

She went to a switch panel and lowered the lights; when she came back the knot in her shirt had been untied. She bent to kiss Stone, and her breasts fell free. "Let's forget about the attorney–client relationship for the night," she said.

Stone had a decision to make, and it didn't take long. "It's forgotten," he said.

She straddled his bare legs, and he found that there was nothing under the short skirt. He shucked off his shorts, and she pulled his polo shirt over his head. A tug at a zipper and a shrug of her shoulders, and they were both naked.

"I don't think I can wait," Stone said.

"I can't wait, either," she said, reaching down and slipping him into her. "We'll wait longer next time."

They were both very quick and very together; they finished, clutching each other and smothering their cries in each other's flesh. When they had both stopped trembling, she stood up, took his hand, and led him toward the aft cabin.

"Now we can start working on the next time," she said, "and we can practice waiting."

CHAPTER

13

S tone woke not long after dawn as a shaft of new sunlight fell across his face; it had been a warm night, and they were both lying on top of the bedcovers. She lay on her stomach with her head turned toward him, a strand of blond hair falling to a corner of her mouth and a tiny frown on her face, as if she were trying to figure out something about a dream. The frown lent her the innocence of a little girl.

Stone didn't know what had motivated her to make love to him—maybe the realization that she might have no more than a week to live and the desire to make the most of it; or maybe she was just horny. For himself, he had been disappointed, angry, jealous, drunk, and, oh yes, horny. She was a client, of course, but he was a long way from the Ethics Committee of the New York State Bar Association, and he had never been any good at saying no to women. He reached over and lifted the strand of hair from her face, and, to his surprise, she smiled.

"I was just going to do that," she said.

"Glad to be of service," he replied.

Without opening her eyes, she reached for him and ran her hand down his body until it rested on his crotch. "Speaking of service," she said, "are you in a mood to render a little?"

"I am now," he replied, reaching over and running a finger lightly down the cleft between her cheeks.

She gave a little shudder and pulled herself on top of him.

He took her buttocks in both hands and moved them up until her pelt was in his face, then began using his tongue lightly, teasing her until she became more insistent. She came easily, as she had been doing for most of the night, then she slid down his sweaty body and returned the favor, insisting on hanging on until he was entirely spent. Then she flopped down beside him, and they panted together, laughing. Shortly they were asleep again.

They were awakened by a sharp rapping on the hull.

"Ahoy there, anyone aboard?" A female voice.

"Jesus," Stone said, "what time is it?"

"Half past nine," she replied, checking the bulkhead clock. She raised herself on an elbow. "Who is it?" she called out.

"The *New York Times*," the voice replied. "If you're Allison Manning, I'd like to talk with you."

"I really don't think the *Times* should find us like this," Stone whispered.

Allison grabbed a robe and left the cabin, while

Stone lay low. He could hear her climbing the companionway ladder, then the two voices.

"I'm afraid I overslept," Allison was saying. "Could I meet you over at the Shipwright's Arms in half an hour?"

"I'm Hilary Kramer," the woman said. "I'd really like to see your yacht."

"Maybe later in the day," Allison said. "It's a mess right now."

"All right," the woman said, sounding disappointed. "I'll meet you over there in half an hour."

Allison came back to the after cabin. "The *New York Times*! That I wasn't expecting."

"I don't know how she could have gotten here so soon," Stone said. "I wasn't expecting anybody until tomorrow, late this afternoon at the earliest. I'm certainly glad she didn't arrive at dawn."

Allison burst out laughing. "That would have made quite a story, wouldn't it?"

"I hope I can sneak over to my boat without being seen."

"You'd better start sneaking."

"I'll be there when you talk to her. Just be yourself, tell your story just as you told it at the coroner's inquest."

"I don't know any other way to tell it," Allison replied.

Stone, showered and dressed, got to the Shipwright's Arms a little before Allison. He walked over to the table where the woman was drinking coffee. "Good morning," he said, "I'm Stone Barrington, Allison Manning's attorney." He stuck out his hand.

"Hilary Kramer," she replied, shaking his hand. "Your name is familiar."

Stone shrugged. "I'm a New York lawyer; I was down here on a sailing charter when Allison sailed into the harbor. I helped her at the coroner's inquest and . . . well, ever since." He sat down. "How did you hear about all this?"

"I was vacationing on Antigua, right next door; the story moved last night on the AP wire and the paper called me late; I got a little plane over here this morning."

"Sorry to interrupt your vacation," Stone said.

"You won't interrupt it for long, believe me. I'll file something before noon, then I'll be back on my beach."

Stone looked up. "Here comes Allison," he said.

"She's cute," Kramer said. "How did you know I was here?"

"My boat is moored next to Allison's; I heard talking." He stood up. "Good morning, Allison; I think you've already met Hilary Kramer from the *Times*."

"I did," Allison said, sitting down. She waved at Thomas, who had appeared at the bar. "Can I have some coffee? You, too, Stone?"

"I've already had some," he lied, "but a second cup wouldn't hurt."

"Make it for two," Allison called.

Before the coffee arrived, Hilary Kramer was deep into her interview. She covered all the ground, most of it better than had been done at the coroner's inquest. "So what's your legal position now?" she asked finally.

"Stone can explain it better than I," Allison said, "but as I understand it, they could hang me as early as next week."

Kramer turned to Stone. "They want to hang her?"

Stone nodded gravely.

"And what do you think are their chances of doing that?"

"Off the record, I think that will depend greatly on what the press has to say about this. If enough pressure can be brought to bear in the media, her chances will improve a lot."

"Why is the government doing this, with so little incriminating evidence?" Kramer demanded.

"Still off the record, there is a body of opinion that holds that Sir Winston Sutherland, the Minister of Justice, has an ax to grind."

"What sort of ax?"

"You've got me. Why don't you ask Sir Winston?"

Thomas, who had returned with a fresh pot of coffee, piped up, "Be glad to lend you my car," he said.

"Thank you very much," she replied. "Is there a phone here? I'd like to call Sir Winston's office for an appointment."

"I think you'd have a much better chance of seeing him if you'd just show up at Government House," Thomas said.

"You might get more if he's a little off-balance," Stone chipped in.

Kramer looked around the table at all of them. "Look, this is not some sort of elaborate practical joke, is it?"

"I wish it were," Stone said. "And before you go, I think I should enlighten you a little about the system of justice as it exists on St. Marks—all off the record, of course. If you should quote me, it might react to Allison's detriment."

"Sure, off the record. Shoot."

When he had finished, her mouth was hanging open. "Is there someplace I can get a room for the night?" she asked, finally.

Thomas spoke up. "I have some rooms upstairs," he said. "We had some cancellations because of the snowstorm in New York."

"Great," she said. "Can I borrow that car now?"

"Sure."

"And where can I pick up a toothbrush?"

"There are shops all around Government House."

"I'd like to call my office, too."

"There's a phone on the bar, or in your room," Thomas replied.

Kramer produced a camera from her bag. "I'd like to get some pictures of both of you," she said, beginning to snap them. "Does Federal Express know about this island?"

"They do," Thomas said. "They'll pick up from here; delivery will likely take two days, though."

"Shit," she said. "Allison, are there any pictures of you floating around New York?"

"Paul's agent has one of the two of us together," Allison replied. "Her name is Anne Sibbald; she's at Janklow and Nesbit."

"Know them well," Kramer said, continuing to photograph. "I'll call them right now. Thomas, will you lead the way to my room?"

"Right this way," Thomas replied.

When they had gone Allison turned to Stone. "Did that go well?"

"I think it could hardly have gone better."

"She's suspicious of you and me, though; woman's intuition. We'd better be very correct around her."

"We'd better be very correct everywhere, except in bed," Stone replied. "I'd suggest we give up sex for the duration, but I don't think I could stick to that."

She smiled. "Neither could I."

"Stop smiling at me that way," he said, looking around.

The smile disappeared. "I'll be very correct," she said.

14

*S*tone had just finished his breakfast when Thomas waved at him from the bar and held up the phone. "Call for you from New York; fellow named Cantor. You want to take it here or upstairs?"

"I'll take it down here," Stone said, crossing to the bar and picking up the phone. "Bob?"

"Yeah, Stone."

"I thought you'd be on your way to the Canaries."

"I'm calling from Kennedy Airport; this morning was the first flight I could make and still do your legwork in the city."

"What did you find out?"

"Almost nothing about Allison Manning, but quite a bit about her husband."

"Shoot."

"First, Allison; she went to some New England

women's college, then worked in advertising, then she met Paul Manning, and they got married."

"That much she's told me; anything else?"

"Not yet; I didn't have the time to track down anybody who knows her."

"What about the husband, then?"

"I got luckier there. There was an interview a couple of years ago in *Publishers Weekly,* the trade magazine, right after he signed his last contract, which was for four and a half million dollars for two books. Not bad, huh?"

"Not bad at all."

"He finished the second book just before they left on the sailing trip. He had done increasingly well over the years, but three books ago he had a big bestseller, and that got him the new contract."

"Pretty rich writer, huh? And I was worried about Allison financing her defense."

"He's a big spender, at least since he signed that contract. He bought the place up in Greenwich; I called a friend of mine who's in real estate in that area, and she remembered the house. Big place—six or seven bedrooms; pool, tennis court, stables, greenhouses; on about eight acres; that's a lot of real estate in Greenwich. He paid two million eight for it, and she says it's probably worth three and a half, four million now. Then he ordered this yacht; I gather you've already seen that."

"Yeah; you find out anything about his debts?"

"He's got a two-million-dollar mortgage on the house—that's about the max you could get at that level—and he owes a million two on the boat. There's some smaller stuff, but not that small; he's got sixty grand in credit card debt and a line of credit secured by the equity in the house—three hundred thousand—and half that is used up."

"Anything about insurance?"

"His credit report shows that Chubb ran a check on him a while back, and that sounds like he's buying insurance."

"I know he had insurance; I just don't know how much."

"I reckon he has a net worth of around five, six million, if you include what's still to pay on the book contract. He's sometimes late on bill payments, but nothing serious, never more than thirty days."

"In short, he lives like a prince, but he's not all that rich."

"That pretty much sums it up."

"Any criminal record?"

"None."

"Ex-wives?"

"One. He was divorced about a month before he married Allison."

"Alimony?"

"I haven't had time to dig out the court records, but the divorce happened before he hit it big, so it's probably not too bad. They were only married a year, and it was a Florida divorce, so there's no community property law."

"What else?"

"Out of college he worked for newspapers, starting in small towns, then working his way up. His last job was on the *Miami Herald,* before he quit to write full time."

The sound of notebook pages being turned came down the line. "Graduated from Cornell with a degree in journalism; high school in Olean, New York; born and raised there. He was pretty much the all-American boy. Too young for Vietnam, so he was never in the service; won a couple of awards at the *Herald;* that's about it for now. I gotta run, Stone; it's last call for boarding."

"Get going, then; call me from Las Palmas when you've had a chance to pick up some more." He hung up the phone.

"You getting anywhere?" Thomas asked. "Sorry if I was eavesdropping."

"No problem. No, I'm not getting anywhere. That was just some background stuff on Paul Manning; nothing of any real help."

"Chester called a while ago; he's making special runs starting this afternoon—lots of requests for seats on that little plane of his."

"Sounds as though the press is heeding our call."

"Sounds like it."

"You know, Thomas, I think we might need a little security down at the marina when these people start arriving. I wouldn't like to let them too near Allison's yacht; she's going to need some privacy."

"Uh-huh," Thomas replied. "I've got two brothers on the police; they could help out and round up enough guys to stake it out around the clock, I imagine. How many you want?"

"Say two at a time, around the clock?"

"Shouldn't be a problem."

"How many brothers and sisters have you got, Thomas?"

"Six brothers and four sisters, and a whole bunch of nieces and nephews; I lose count. In those days there was less opportunity in St. Marks; it was before tourism took hold down here. Two more of my brothers left, then came back; the two on the police stayed and did all right. They're both sergeants."

"What did the sisters do?"

"They got married and had babies. Everybody's prosperous, for St. Marks."

"And you most of all, huh?"

Thomas grinned. "You could say that." The fax machine rang, and he turned to receive whatever was coming. "Hang on, this is more likely for you than for me." The machine spat out a single sheet; Thomas glanced at it and handed it to Stone.

It was typed sloppily on his own letterhead. "Dear Stone," she said, "I wanted to let you know that I'm not going to be here when you get back. Vance has to go back to L.A., and we're not nearly finished with the piece, so I'm going with him. I've no idea how long I'll be out there, but it's going to be at least a couple of weeks. I'll call you when you're back in New York. Best, Arrington."

Best. Not love, best. He didn't like the sound of that in the least, and he was suddenly very glad he'd fucked Allison Manning. He would do it again, every chance he had, for as long as he could.

He tore up the fax, threw it into the wastebasket behind the bar, and trudged up the stairs to start working again on Allison's case.

CHAPTER

15

Stone worked on his notes for the trial and tried to come up with new ideas for Allison's testimony, but he was depressed, and depression always made him sleepy. Soon he was stretched out on the bed and dead to the world.

Thomas was shaking him. "Stone, wake up."

"Huh?" He was groggy, and he felt hung over.

"You got two press people downstairs: one from *60 Minutes* and one from *The New Yorker.*"

"Jesus, we landed the big ones first, huh?"

"Looks like it."

"I'd better splash some water on my face; tell them I'll be down in a minute."

"Okay."

Stone shook himself awake, washed his face and toweled it briskly to bring back some color, then went downstairs. Two men came toward him, a tall, slim, tanned one in Bermuda shorts and a short, stocky, pasty man in a khaki bush jacket.

"I'm Jim Forrester from *The New Yorker,*" the tall one said, shaking hands.

"I'm Jake Burrows, I'm a producer on *60 Minutes,*" the bush jacket said, "and I was here first. I want to talk to you before he does." He nodded at his competitor.

"All right, all right," Stone said. "Let's all sit down and discuss this; I mean, you two guys are not exactly competitors."

"That's right," Forrester said.

"Everybody is a competitor," Burrows said.

"Come on, sit down, and let's talk." Stone herded them toward a table. "Thomas, how about some lunch menus?"

"Sure thing," Thomas said.

"I want the first interview," Burrows said; "I was here first."

"Wait a minute," Stone said. "Just listen to me, both of you. Jim, you're not exactly on deadline here, are you?"

"No, I'm not," the writer said. "I'm here to get the whole story; the soonest we could run would be a couple of weeks after the trial."

"Feel better, Jake?" Stone asked.

"A little," Burrows said grudgingly. "I've got a reporter arriving here tonight, and either I get an exclusive interview, or I'm getting out of here right now."

Stone turned to him. "Either it runs Sunday night, or there's no interview."

"I can't promise you that," Burrows said.

"Then you might as well go home, because before

the Sunday after that rolls around, my client could very well have been executed, and I'm not much interested in a postmortem feature."

"This week's show is already set," Burrows said. "There's nothing I can do about it."

"I'm sorry, Jake, there's nothing I can do for you," Stone said.

Burrows looked at him incredulously. "Listen to me, Stone, this is *60 Minutes;* do you know what that means?"

"Sure I do," Stone replied. "It means you'd be airing an interview with a dead woman. I thought your show liked saving innocent people from death row, not reporting on the execution later."

Jake Burrows looked at him intently for a moment without speaking. "I've got to make a phone call," he said finally, pushing his chair back.

"Tell them I want it in writing," Stone said.

"If I do this, will you guarantee me an exclusive?"

"I'll guarantee you an exclusive on in-depth TV, but she's going to hold a press conference, where I'll answer most of the questions, and an awful lot of photographs of her are going to be taken. The only way I can save her life is to carpet American TV wall to wall with her face, and that's what I intend to do. Anyway, all that will be great promotion for your interview."

Burrows nodded and went off to find a phone.

"You're going to have your hands full pretty soon," Jim Forrester said.

"I've already got my hands full, just with the two of you. Are you on staff at the magazine?"

Forrester shook his head. "This will be my first

piece for them. I was in San Juan doing a travel piece when they called."

"Who's your editor there?" Stone asked.

"Charles McGrath."

"He's number two there, isn't he?"

"That's right."

"What are you going to want?"

"Well, obviously, I want to see Allison again as soon as possible, then I want to cover everything that happens, including the *60 Minutes* interview and the trial. There's nothing I can do to save her life, but if what she says rings true, then I can reinforce her innocence if she survives. That could be important to her, because there is always going to be a question mark hanging over her, even if she's acquitted."

"You're right about that." Stone wrinkled his brow. "What did you mean by seeing Allison again?"

"I've met her before."

"Where?"

"In the Canaries, in Las Palmas and in Puerto Rico. I was there on assignment from *Conde Nast Traveler* when I met Paul at the yacht club in Las Palmas."

"Jesus," Stone said, "I've got a guy on a plane for Las Palmas right now, looking for somebody just like you. We have to talk." He looked up to see Jake Burrows coming toward them.

"All right," Burrows said, "let me lay it out for you: I'll give you a letter on *60 Minutes* letterhead, guaranteeing you air time this Sunday night."

"Guaranteeing me a full segment," Stone said.

"All right, all right. You give me first and exclusive access to Allison first thing tomorrow morning, and you don't hold your press conference until my reporter and I are out of here with our tape."

"Who's the reporter?"

"Chris Wheaton."

"Never heard of him. What happened to Mike Wallace and Morley Safer?"

"Chris is a she, and she's new; this will be her first story. She's already on a plane, and she's all you're going to get."

"This is a full segment, though?"

"I'll put it in writing."

"Okay, but Jim here is going to sit in." He held up a hand before Burrows could object. "He's not going to ask her any questions during your time, he's just going to observe for his *New Yorker* piece. Can't hurt to have your program's name in the magazine, can it? I bet Chris Wheaton will love it."

"Okay, it's a deal. First thing in the morning; Chris won't be in until tonight, and I want daylight, with palms and water in the background."

"How about in the cockpit of her boat?"

"Ideal."

"You go write your letter; Jim and I have to talk."

Burrows went back to the bar, opened his briefcase, extracted a sheet of stationery, and started writing.

Stone turned back to Forrester. "Tell me about your meeting the Mannings," he said.

"We had done a shoot in the yacht club, and I was having a drink at the bar when Paul sat down next to me; I recognized him, so I introduced myself."

"What was your impression of him?"

"Big guy," he spread his hands; "full beard, bear-like; as tall as me, but a good fifty, sixty pounds heavier; laughed easily. He liked it that I knew his work, and he offered to show me his boat."

"What else did you talk about while you were in the bar?"

"The outline of his cruise, where he'd been, et cetera."

"How long were you there?"

"Long enough to finish a piña colada—twenty minutes, half an hour—then we walked down to the marina, and he introduced me to Allison."

"What was your first impression of her?"

"A knockout; she was wearing a bikini, after all."

"Right. I mean, what did you think of her?"

"Bright, charming, funny. I liked her immediately, just as I did Paul."

"How much time did you spend with them?"

"It was late afternoon, and they invited me to stay aboard for dinner. Allison cooked some steaks on an outdoor grill, off the stern, and we drank a couple of bottles of good California cabernet."

"What time did you leave?"

"Must have been close to ten o'clock. I was staying in a hotel in town, and I had an early-morning flight back to New York; I wanted to get some sleep."

"Think back: What was your impression of their relationship?"

"Warm, affectionate; they shared a sense of humor. They seemed to like each other a lot."

"Were they in love?"

"Yeah, I guess they were. I remember I admired how well they got along, especially after spending several months together on a boat. That kind of intense, long-term proximity has ruined more than one relationship."

"Did you ever see them again?"

"Yeah, briefly; when I got back to my hotel there was a message from New York saying they wanted some more shots on Grand Canary, then some on the Canaries island of Puerto Rico. I stayed on in Las Palmas for another day, then flew down to Puerto Rico in the late afternoon of the day after that."

"Did you know they'd be there?"

"They might have mentioned it, but it didn't register. Next time I saw them, I was standing on a stone jetty on the south side of the island, and they motored past on the boat, heading for Antigua. I yelled to them, and they waved back and said they were sorry they missed me, then they were gone."

"What was their mood at that moment?"

"Jubilant, like they were glad to be getting back to sea. They were laughing, I remember; he said something to her that I couldn't hear, then she laughed and slapped him on the ass."

"Jim, will you testify to all this at her trial?"

The writer shrugged. "Sure, if you think it will help."

"I think it just might help; you were apparently the last person besides Allison to see Paul Manning alive."

"Glad to do it."

"One more question, Jim, just between you and me: Do you think that Allison is the sort of person who could have killed Paul?"

Forrester looked astonished. "Of course not. Well, I guess anybody could kill anybody under the right circumstances, but I would bet the farm she had nothing to do with his death. Absolutely nothing I saw in their relationship would indicate that."

"Good," Stone said, relieved to have an objective opinion that reinforced his own. "I'll ask you some form of that question under oath."

"And I'll give you the same answer."

CHAPTER

16

*T*he rest of the *60 Minutes* crew arrived at dusk, and Stone had dinner with Jake Burrows and his reporter, Chris Wheaton. They met at the bar of the Shipwright's Arms, got a drink, and found a table. Stone looked over the reporter: she was small, intense, as blond as Allison, and handsome rather than pretty. He thought she would look very good on camera.

"Allison asked to be excused from dinner," Stone told her. "She says she needs a good night's sleep."

"That's okay," Wheaton said, "I don't want to meet her until we're on camera; the interview will be fresher that way. Has Jake told you how we're going to work this?"

Stone shook his head. "We made some ground rules about the air date and the segment, but that's it; you can ask her anything you want."

"Good. I expect we'll talk for at least an hour, maybe a lot longer."

This hadn't occurred to Stone, and it meant that they would be editing the tape to show the parts they liked best, and that might not work entirely to his client's benefit. It was too late to start negotiating again, though, and he'd just have to put a good face on it. "That's fine," he said, "talk as long as you like. If she gets tired or upset, we might have to take a break."

"We'll have to change tape," Wheaton replied. "She can pee or have a cry while we're doing that." She leaned forward. "Tell me, how did you become involved in this? Did she get you down here from New York when she found out she needed a lawyer?"

Stone shook his head. "I was down here for a cruise when she sailed in alone. My girlfriend didn't make it because of the snowstorm, and I went to the inquest for lack of anything else to do. It became obvious that her questioner had some ax to grind, and at the lunch break I offered to advise her."

"Who was the questioner?"

Stone told her about Sir Winston Sutherland and his attitude toward Allison.

"I don't get it," Wheaton said; "why would this Sir Winston guy want to make trouble for this poor widow?"

Stone thought she was being disingenuous, but he didn't call her on it. "I don't get it, either," he said.

"So why isn't some local lawyer defending her?"

"A local lawyer is defending her; I'm second chair."

"Who is he? I want to talk to him."

Stone's stomach turned over. "He's not talking to

anybody but Allison and me. Maybe after the trial, we'll see."

Wheaton glanced at her producer.

"I mean that; he's got a lot of work to do between now and the trial, and I don't want him disturbed. He's an elderly man; he only has so much energy to devote to this, and I want Allison to get the benefit of all of it."

Wheaton nodded. "How much are you getting paid to defend her?"

"We haven't discussed a fee."

She smiled. "Uh-huh."

"It just hasn't come up," Stone said lamely.

"Is that how you would operate in New York?"

Stone shook his head. "Of course not, but we're not in New York. She's a fellow American in trouble in a foreign place, and I'm glad to help her if I can. Anyway, I'm not necessarily a very good buy as an attorney in St. Marks, since I don't really know the ropes of the local legal system."

"What is the local legal system like?"

"Bizarre, and I hope you'll bring that out in your piece." He told her about the preliminary hearing and what he had learned about how the court operated.

She laughed out loud. "That's the most outrageous thing I've ever heard!"

"Please make that clear on television. To tell you the truth, I think there's more than one piece in this for you. If you're here for the trial, that ought to be an eye-opener, and I'd certainly be glad to have a camera waiting outside the courtroom."

"Any chance we could get a camera inside the courtroom?"

"You can try; go see the judge. I'd be happy for him to know that the American press is taking an interest."

"Jake, you want to take care of that tomorrow?"

"Sure," Burrows replied. It was the first time he had spoken. "Look, Stone, while I, and I'm sure Chris, have some sympathy for the lady's plight, we're not here to fight your battles for you; you have to understand that."

"Sure I do, but if just doing your job happens to work to Allison's benefit, that's okay with me."

"We understand that," Wheaton said.

The menus arrived, and they ordered dinner. When the food arrived, Chris Wheaton took another tack.

"I used to work local news in New York," she said. "I remember when you were on the force."

"You mean you remember when I left the force, don't you?" Stone said, cracking a crab claw.

"That's what I mean. Your name still pops up now and then."

"Does it?"

"You haven't exactly been press-shy, have you, Stone?"

Stone laughed ruefully. "I've never sought coverage, but sometimes coverage has been thrust upon me by your colleagues in the media."

She found that funny. "Still, your occasional flash of fame must have brought you a lot of cases as a lawyer."

"I've ducked more of that kind of case than I've taken," he replied. "Most of my work has been fairly run-of-the mill."

"Didn't you get a very nice personal injury verdict a while back?"

He nodded. "Got a nice one last year; we even collected." And it had made life a bit easier for him, too, he remembered. "I'm not the sort of lawyer who gets the big cases; those usually go to the big firms, and I'm pretty much an independent."

"But you've done well, haven't you? I seem to remember something about a townhouse in Turtle Bay."

"I inherited that from a great-aunt and did most of the renovation myself. That verdict you mentioned paid off the construction loan, though. That was a relief."

"I'll bet." She was looking at him the way he had once looked at perps in interrogations.

"Chris, have you got something on your mind about me?"

"It just seems odd that you would just happen to be here when Allison Manning came sailing in. Could that be a bit more than a coincidence?"

Stone pointed toward the marina. "If you'll go down to the marina office and check their reservations log, you'll find that I booked my charter nearly three months ago, and since you're from New York, you'll know firsthand about the blizzard. If not for that I would now be south of Guadeloupe somewhere with a rum and tonic in one hand and the girl of my dreams in the other."

"And who is the girl of your dreams?"

"Her name is Arrington Carter; she's a magazine writer, a freelancer."

"I've met her," Wheaton said. "As a matter of fact, I saw her two nights ago in the company of an actual movie star."

Stone nodded. "Vance Calder. She's working on a

New Yorker profile of him that she was offered after the snowstorm hit; that's why she's not here now."

"Aren't you just a little uncomfortable knowing that your girlfriend is in New York with Vance Calder, instead of here with you?"

"Not really." He smiled. "As a matter of fact, Vance introduced us last fall." This was not quite a lie. "And she's not in New York, she's in L.A. They both went out there today."

"Ah," Wheaton said, sounding disappointed.

I hope I bent that needle, Stone thought, but it irritated him no end that she knew about Arrington and Vance. He hoped it didn't show.

There was a brief silence, then Wheaton turned to her producer.

"Jake, when we're done tomorrow, you take the tape back to New York and do the editing; you can play me the track over the phone later in the week."

"And where will you be?" Burrows asked.

"I'll be here," she said. "I'm staying for the trial, and so is the camera crew. You work it out with Don or whoever."

"Chris, don't you think you're pushing it just a bit on your first assignment?"

"I know a good story when I see one," she said. "You can explain that to them in New York. I think the network might want a feed for the evening news, too. Check on that, will you?"

"Sure."

Stone began to feel good about this. Now all Allison had to do was charm Chris Wheaton out of her socks, and that might not be easy.

CHAPTER

17

After dinner Stone said good night to the *60 Minutes* people and walked back toward the marina. He had no sooner set foot on the dock when he found himself grabbed from both sides by two shadowy figures. He made a point of not struggling.

"Is one of you Thomas Hardy's brother?" he asked the darkness.

"Both of us is," a deep voice replied.

"My name is Stone Barrington; I live on the smaller of the two yachts over there. I'm the one who asked Thomas to find some security." The pressure on his arms relaxed, but he was not let go.

"You got some ID, then?" the voice asked.

"Right-hand rear pocket," he said. "My New York driver's license." He felt some fumbling, and a flashlight came on.

"Okay, then, Mr. Barrington, we'll know you next time."

"Gentlemen . . ." Stone began.

"Henry and Arliss," the voice said.

"Henry and Arliss, I think our purposes would be better served if you stood over there under the lamp by the gate, instead of lurking in the dark. You can do the most good by being seen to be keeping people away from Mrs. Manning."

"I see your point," Henry replied. "You expecting anybody else? Anybody at all?"

"Not until early tomorrow morning, when some people, including a camera crew, will be coming down here. Please keep them at the gate until you've called me. Just rap on the hull; I'll be awake."

"Of which boat?" Henry asked.

Stone decided to pretend there was no meaning in the question. "The smaller one."

"Good night, then, Mr. Barrington."

"Good night, Henry, Arliss; see you in the morning." Stone walked down to his boat and went aboard. The lights aboard the big yacht were out. He undressed and climbed gratefully into his berth, just in time to hear a dim scrambling in the cockpit. A moment later, Allison was crawling into bed with him; she was naked.

"I take it you met Henry and Arliss," she said, snuggling up to him.

"I did, and I hope to God you didn't meet them on the way across the pontoon."

"Nope. They're standing up by the gate now; I could see them."

"Were you naked when you left your boat, or after you arrived on mine?"

"The whole time."

Stone laughed in spite of himself. "Allison, while your craving for my body may be perfectly understandable—even admirable—you have to remember that there is now on the island a camera crew for the most popular television news program in the United States of America, and we don't know yet how powerful their lenses are."

"I'm glad you understand my craving," she said.

"On Sunday night, your interview may be preceded by a shot of you, naked in the moonlight, climbing aboard your lawyer's boat. That might not exactly get the American public behind you."

She turned over and pushed her buttocks into his increasingly active crotch. "Why don't you get behind me?" She reached between her legs, found him, and guided him in.

Stone pushed into her sweet depths. "Oh, God," he breathed. "When this is over, remind me to talk to you about your interview tomorrow morning."

"Shhh," she whispered, helping him.

Stone jerked awake. Sunlight was streaming through the port above his head. He heard voices and footsteps on the dock. "Allison," he said, shaking her, "wake up."

"What is it, baby?" she asked, snuggling her warm body closer.

There was a sharp rap on the hull, and Henry Hardy's booming voice called out, "Mr. Barrington, you up?"

"*60 Minutes* is here," he whispered.

Allison's head came off the pillow. "What?"

He glanced out the port and saw legs standing next to the boat. "I'll try to get rid of them," he said. He got out of bed, tried to rub some color into his face, and brushed his hair back with his hands. He got into his swim trunks, which were lying on a seat next to the berth, went into the main cabin, climbed the ladder, and emerged, waist high, from the hatch. Jake Burrows and Chris Wheaton were standing on the dock next to the bow of his boat. "What time is it?" he asked. "Aren't you a little early?"

"It's seven-fifteen," Burrows said. "We have to set up for our eight o'clock interview."

Stone shook his head. "I haven't finished breakfast yet, and I don't know if Allison is even up." Suddenly he felt a naked body slither between his legs and up the ladder behind him. "Why don't you go back to the Shipwright's Arms, have some breakfast, and come back at eight?" He heard Allison sneaking across the cockpit behind him, then the rattle of his boarding ladder, followed by a tiny splash. He stepped off his boat, crossed the pontoon, hopped into the cockpit of the larger yacht, and yelled down the hatch. "Allison, you up yet?" He pretended to listen for a moment, then looked up at the television crew. "She's up, but nowhere near ready," he said. "Come back at eight."

The disappointed crew turned and began walking back toward the pub. As Stone stood in the cockpit, Allison climbed up the stern ladder into the cockpit and, soaking wet, slipped past him and down the companionway ladder.

"I don't know if I can be ready by eight," she said, laughing.

"You'd bloody well better be," he muttered, refusing to look at her.

"If we hurry, we could get in a quickie before they come back," she said, pulling the hair on his legs.

"Ouch! I'm getting back to my boat right now. You get yourself together." He fled the yacht and went back to his own.

At eight o'clock sharp he emerged, dressed, to find the crew standing on the dock, waiting. "Just a minute," he said, "I'll see if she's ready.

As he spoke, Allison climbed into her own cockpit, wearing a sleeveless cotton dress that showed off her tan, yet made her look like a high school senior. "Good morning!" she cried, delivering a dazzling smile. "I'm Allison; come aboard, all of you."

As the crew climbed aboard, Stone took deep breaths and tried to get his pulse rate back down to normal.

CHAPTER

18

I must be crazy, Stone thought as the interview began. *I've let this girl go on TV, before an audience of millions and at the mercy of a reporter on her first assignment who would kill for a success, which she might not define as I would, and with no preparation whatever.* He watched from the pontoon as Chris Wheaton tossed Allison a few softball questions to relax her, then tensed as the real questioning began. Jim Forrester from *The New Yorker* had shown up and was sitting quietly beyond camera range, listening and taking notes.

"Allison," Chris Wheaton said, sounding really interested, "when you and Paul left the Canary Islands and set sail for home, how much sailing experience had you, personally, had?"

"Well, I had sailed across the Atlantic and around Europe with Paul, but he had always done the sailing.

The boat was rigged for singlehanding, so he took care of that, and I just kept house—or boat, I guess."

"So how was it, after Paul's death, that you managed to sail this very large yacht all the way across the Atlantic all by yourself?"

Allison launched into an explanation of how she had learned enough celestial navigation to find her latitude and how she had managed the sails by using only the main most of the time.

Wheaton seemed fascinated by her reply and satisfied with her answer. Forrester seemed almost to be taking a transcript of the proceedings. Wheaton continued with questions about the sailing of the boat, and Allison grew visibly more relaxed. Then Wheaton changed tack, and Stone knew that the questions were not coming in the order in which they would appear in the edited version of the interview. Wheaton probed the depths of Allison's marriage to Paul Manning, taking her over and over the same ground, looking for what might appear to be a motive for murder. To Stone's surprise, Allison stood up to it beautifully, genuinely seeming to try to answer every question put to her, holding nothing back.

When a halt was called for the first change of tape, Wheaton turned to Stone. "You want a break?"

Stone looked at Allison and she shook her head imperceptibly. "No," Stone replied. "Go ahead."

Wheaton got the signal from her producer; she turned back to Allison. "Allison, how much life insurance did your husband have?"

"Honestly, I don't know," Allison replied. "Ashore, the division of our lives was pretty much the same as at sea. He handled the business, I handled the house. I

never made an investment, bought a life insurance policy, or even wrote a check, unless it was for groceries or
clothes. Paul had people who handled the business end
of his career, and they're sorting out the estate now, I
guess, and when they tell me where I stand, then I'll
know. I'm told it will be some weeks before it's all figured out. I do know from what Paul said in passing that
although he owned an expensive house and boat, they
both have large mortgages on them, so I don't know yet
what will be left when everything is settled."

"Are you going to keep the big house in Greenwich
and this beautiful yacht?"

Allison shrugged. "The house was always too big for
even the two of us, since we didn't have any kids, and I
don't know if I would want to live there alone; I just
haven't thought that far ahead. As far as the boat is concerned, what would I do with it? Anyway, the memories
are too painful; I don't think I could ever sail on her
again without Paul." She brushed away a tear.

Perfect, Stone thought.

There were two more changes of tape before the
interview ended, but Allison kept going. Apart from an
occasional sip of orange juice, she never paused. Finally,
they were done, and the crew began to pack up their
equipment. Allison chatted idly with Chris Wheaton and
Jim Forrester, answering questions about her yacht.

"It's nice to see you again, Jim," Allison said. "Paul
and I enjoyed your company in Las Palmas, and we
were sorry not to know you were in Puerto Rico until
we saw you as we were leaving port."

"I was sorry, too, Allison," the journalist replied.
"Do you think we could get together later today or early

tomorrow for a few minutes? I have some more things to ask you."

"I'm sure we can," she replied. "Let me talk to Stone about my schedule, and I'll get back to you. Where are you staying?"

"At the Shipwright's Arms."

"Good. I'll call you."

Wheaton and Burrows thanked her for her time and, with Jim Forrester, left the boat. As they were walking up the pontoon, Chris Wheaton stopped and spoke quietly to Stone. "That was some performance," she said. "I've never seen anything like it."

"I'm glad it went well," Stone replied. "You should be able to get an awfully good segment out of that."

"You bet I will," Wheaton said, then she looked back at Allison, who was standing in the cockpit, looking out over the harbor, sipping her orange juice. "She's really something," she said. "You won't have any trouble getting her off."

"I wish I could believe that," Stone said, "but from what I've seen so far, I think the odds are heavily against her. Sir Winston Sutherland wants her neck in a noose, for whatever reason, and I don't know if I'm going to be able to stop him."

Wheaton looked at him closely. "Jesus," she said with wonder, "you really think she's innocent, don't you?"

Stone looked at her in amazement. "Of course I do; after all that questioning, don't you?"

"Not for a minute," Wheaton replied. "Listen, over the years I've interviewed a couple of hundred people who were either accused of murder or who had just been convicted or acquitted; I learned to tell the guilty from the innocent, and let me tell you, not more than ten of them were innocent." She pointed her chin at Allison. "And she's not one of them."

"Show me one hole in her story," Stone said.

"There isn't one. But she's guilty just the same. Call it a woman-to-woman thing, if you like, but I look in those beautiful blue eyes and I know."

"Is that what you're going to say on *60 Minutes*?"

"Are you kidding? I'd be fired out of hand. No sir, I'm going to play it straight, let her answers speak for themselves, and ninety-nine percent of the audience is going to be outraged that this beautiful, innocent young woman could be charged with murder. That's what you want, isn't it?"

"Certainly, that's what I want."

"Well, relax, because that's what you're going to get." She paused and looked across the harbor at the boats. "Unless I can dig up something new between now and Sunday." She turned and walked up the pontoon toward the pub. Then she stopped, turned, and walked back. "One more thing," she said. "You seem like a nice guy, Stone, so let me give you some free advice: don't fall in love with her; don't even fuck her, if you haven't already. Allison Manning is a dangerous woman."

Stone was speechless. He watched her walk away.

CHAPTER

19

Stone was having lunch with Hilary Kramer from the *New York Times* at the Shipwright's Arms when Thomas Hardy waved him to the bar, pointing at the phone. Stone excused himself, got up, and went to the bar.

"It's somebody named Cantor," Thomas said, handing Stone the telephone. "By the way, Chester called from the airport, too; says he's loaded down with media folk all afternoon."

"Right," Stone said, taking the phone. "I'd like to have a press conference here Friday morning at ten, if that's okay."

"Sure."

Stone spoke into the phone. "Bob?"

"Stone? Glad I caught you; I'm coming home tomorrow."

"That was fast; were you able to cover any ground in such a short time?"

"You bet; I got into Las Palmas early, so I took a connecting flight to Puerto Rico and spent a couple of hours there, then came back to Las Palmas."

"What have you learned?"

"Nothing in Puerto Rico, except they took on fuel and water and spent one night there; more in Las Palmas, though."

"Tell me."

"They were at the yacht club marina for four or five days, doing odd jobs on the boat and provisioning with fresh fruit and vegetables at the local market. Paul had a drink at the yacht club bar late every afternoon, once or twice with Allison, but apart from the shopping, she kept pretty much to the boat. Boats go in and out of that marina constantly, so I was only able to find one boat still there with people who remembered the Mannings. Apart from their boat, which was big and beautiful, they remembered only a couple of things about them: first, their rubber dinghy was stolen, and Manning apparently had trouble finding the replacement he wanted; finally he had it flown in from Barcelona. Second, the Mannings had a terrific fight late on the night before they left Las Palmas."

"Tell me about the fight," Stone said, lowering his voice and looking around to be sure no one overheard.

"A real knockdown, drag-out domestic dispute. Crockery was thrown, names were called, tears were shed, and the whole thing happened at top volume."

"Did you get any direct quotes?"

"No, but it had something to do with sailing—with their route, or something."

Odd, Stone thought, that Allison would argue with Paul about something to do with sailing the boat. "That's all you could find out?"

"That's it. Apparently the couple did all the usual things that the yachties do when they sail in and out of Las Palmas—repairs, food, and like that."

"Funny, a guy showed up here, a journalist, who says he had dinner with them their last night in Las Palmas. Any mention of a third party there during the fight?"

"Nope, no mention. I'm afraid that's all there is here."

"About the dinghy, what was so special about the one he had flown in from Barcelona?"

"I don't know; apparently the guy was real picky about his stuff. There were other dinghies available here—Avons and Zodiacs, mostly, both good brands, one English and one French. He wanted something called a Parker Sportster, an American model, very expensive. It arrived on their last morning. Can you think of anything else I should be doing here?"

"No, I guess not; go on home."

"Soon as I'm back I'll finish up my research into Manning; there wasn't time to do much before I left."

"Do that, and get back to me soonest. It's Thursday, and the trial is on Monday; I'll need the info fast."

"Right; I'll be in touch."

Stone hung up the phone just as Jim Forrester ordered a drink at the bar. "Just the man I wanted to see," he said.

"What's up?"

"You said you had dinner with the Mannings their last night in Las Palmas, right?"

"Right."

"How late were you with them?"

"I don't know, maybe eleven o'clock."

"Did the Mannings have a fight when you were there?"

"No, not exactly; they did disagree about something, though."

"What was that?"

"It was kind of crazy, when you consider that Allison apparently didn't usually take much interest in the sailing of the boat. We were looking at their route on the chart, and she wanted to sail a direct course from Puerto Rico to Antigua. Paul pointed out to her that the trade winds blow some distance south of the Canaries, and if they wanted to take advantage of the trades, which everybody does who's crossing in those latitudes, they'd be better off sailing south or southeast from Puerto Rico until they picked up the trades, then turning west with a good breeze at their backs. She couldn't seem to grasp that, for some reason. We'd all had a good deal to drink, of course; maybe she was just spoiling for a fight. You know how married couples can be. Anyway, I was a little uncomfortable, so I said my good-byes and left. They were still arguing about it when I stepped ashore."

"Do you recall anything about Paul having a rubber dinghy flown in from Barcelona?"

"Yeah, I do; somebody had stolen his dinghy, and he wanted a new one, something special. It wasn't available in Las Palmas, so he called somebody in Barcelona and had one sent."

"A Parker Sportster?"

"Beats me."

"Did he give any reason for wanting that particular dinghy?"

"Not that I can recall. He seemed obsessive about having just the right gear on his boat, I remember that well enough; every item on it seemed to have been chosen with great care."

"Was the one that was stolen a Parker Sportster?"

"I don't know, I guess so."

"Thanks, Jim. Thomas, put Jim's drink on my tab."

Forrester grinned. "You think a *New Yorker* reporter would accept favors from a lawyer in a case he was writing about?"

"You bet I do."

"You're right," Forrester said, raising his glass to Stone, then taking a big swig. He wandered off to find a lunch table.

Stone dialed his office number in New York, and his secretary answered. "Hi, it's Stone," he said. "What's happening?"

"Not a hell of a lot," she replied. "Arrington went to L.A., but she said she faxed you about that."

"Yeah, she did."

"There's a lot of mail, mostly junk and bills; nothing that can't wait until you're back."

"Listen, I want you to do something for me."

"Shoot."

"I want you to call a couple of marine supply houses and see if you can get me some information on a rubber dinghy called Parker Sportster—a brochure or something. Apparently it's a high-end piece of equipment."

•

"Okay; you want it sent to you?"

"Yeah, FedEx it, priority."

"Anything else?"

"Not right now. Bob Cantor is coming home tomorrow; you can go ahead and reimburse his expenses and pay him for his time; he's always short of money."

"Okay."

Stone hung up and returned to his table. Allison had arrived and was deep in conversation with Hilary Kramer, who was taking copious notes. He sat down and listened to the interview, which included most of the questions Wheaton had already asked her, but in more of a chronological order.

When they had finished talking, Allison returned to the yacht with Jim Forrester, whose turn it was for an interview.

Stone picked at the remains of his lunch. "Hilary, what did you think of Allison?" he asked.

"She's a brave little thing, isn't she?" Kramer replied. "If I had been in her shoes, I don't know if I could have done what she did."

"I'd like your opinion about something that might help me with the trial."

"Sure, go ahead."

"Did you find any holes in her story? Anything that was hard to believe?"

Kramer shook her head. "Not a thing; she's a transparently honest girl; a jury is bound to see that."

"Thanks, I'm glad to have my opinion reinforced," he said. And Chris Wheaton's opinion opposed, he thought.

•

CHAPTER

20

*T*he first of the media rush began at midafternoon. Stone watched them ask Thomas where to find Allison Manning and be told of the news conference. As six o'clock approached they were still arriving, and he put back the conference until the following morning at ten, much to the annoyance of those who had arrived early. They were not relying on Chester's small airplane now, but chartering out of San Juan and St. Thomas. Stone spoke to Henry and Arliss and had the guard on the marina doubled.

Allison was nervous; she sat in the saloon of the yacht and drank a martini just mixed by Stone.

"Easy," he said. "You don't want to be hung over in the morning. We only have to do this once, and I'll be there to protect you."

"But there are so many," she said. "I had a look through the binoculars, and there must be thirty of them."

"Yeah, they got together and chartered an old DC-3 in San Juan and packed it. I hear the airplane is making another flight, due in early in the morning."

"Are you sure this is good for us?" she asked.

"It can't be bad," Stone said. "When the authorities get wind of what's happening, I hope to see a change in their attitude." At her insistence he mixed her another martini. "Tell you what, I'll cook for you tonight."

She brightened. "No kidding? I've never had a man cook for me."

"Not once?"

"You forget, I'd been with Paul forever, and he wouldn't so much as make himself a sandwich. Once, when I was sick and couldn't cook, I saw him eat beans straight out of the can rather than heat them."

"Let's see what you've got in here," Stone said, rummaging through a cabinet. He found some linguine and a couple of cans of minced clams. "Where's the olive oil?"

"Down below, under the silverware drawer," she said. "I'll find us a nice chilled white wine." She went to a cooler and produced a bottle.

Stone found some garlic, peeled and chopped it, sautéed it in some olive oil, then drained the clam juice into the skillet, seasoning with salt and pepper. "Any parsley?" he asked, adding some of the white wine.

"Only dried; up there in the spice rack."

Fifteen minutes later they were dining on linguine and white clam sauce.

"Excellent," she said.

"Typical bachelor dinner," Stone replied.

"Have you ever been married?"

"Nope."

"So you've had a lot of practice at quickie bachelor dinners?"

"Oh, I can make a few more elaborate dishes, too, if I have time to plan and shop. I don't do it all that often."

"And only early in the relationship, before seduction is assured," she said, grinning.

"You are a cynic."

She laughed. "Nailed you, huh?"

He tried not to smile. "Certainly not."

Stone washed the dishes, then stuck his head up through the hatch for a look toward the Shipwright's Arms. The bar was jammed with people, and their raucous laughter reached all the way to the marina. He noticed that two of Henry's policemen stood near the restaurant, ready to stop any journalist who so much as ventured onto the lawn between the bar and the marina.

"I think we're safe for the evening," he said, climbing back down the companionway.

She met him, tugging at his shirttail. "No safety for you," she said, unzipping his fly.

At ten sharp on Friday morning, Stone, with Allison beside him, began walking across the lawn toward the Shipwright's Arms. Somebody had nailed together a little platform and on it stood a forest of microphones, taped and lashed together, their wires snaking into the crowd of reporters like so many reptiles. There were two ranks of cameras, high and low, and the TV reporters stood by, microphones in hand, for their own comments. The print journalists stood in clutches or sat on the grass, notebooks at the ready, and photographers were everywhere. Stone had never faced anything like this, and he wasn't looking forward to it. The buzz of voices turned to a shout as he and Allison approached.

"Good morning," he shouted over the crowd, taking a sheet of paper from his shirt pocket and waiting for the noise to subside. When they were quiet, he spoke. "My name is Stone Barrington; I am one of the legal team representing Mrs. Allison Manning in the case against her, about which I am sure you have all heard. I will be making a statement, and then I will take questions for thirty minutes. Then Mrs. Manning will make a brief statement and will answer no questions."

There was a roar of outrage from the assembled media.

Stone shouted them down. "I hope you can understand that Mrs. Manning is facing a serious charge in a strange country, and that by answering questions at this stage, she might inadvertently put herself in further jeopardy. I know that none of you would wish to contribute to her difficulties." He began to read his statement, covering events from the time of Allison's arrival in St. Marks, including the coroner's inquest and her questioning by Sir Winston Sutherland. He gave them a brief primer on the workings of the St. Marks criminal justice system, and they listened, rapt and astonished. Finally, he wrapped up his statement and asked for questions, glancing at his watch. "To preserve some sort of order, I will point to a questioner and answer his or her question only. Let's do this one at a time, people." He pointed at a woman television reporter.

"Mr. Barrington, do we understand you to say that in St. Marks, the judge selects the jury, and that the defense may not even question them or object to them?"

"Both the defense and the prosecution may ask the judge to address particular questions to a prospective juror, but the judge will ask the question only if he deems it relevant to the proceedings."

The questions continued, mostly about the legal system and his plans for mounting a defense. When thirty minutes had passed, Stone pulled Allison forward. "Now, ladies and gentlemen, Mrs. Allison Manning will make a statement, and at its end, this press conference will be over. She will take no questions after that, nor will I; I hope that's clearly understood." He turned to Allison and nodded.

Allison stepped forward to the microphones and, with a shy smile, began to speak. "Good morning," she said, and after those words there was complete silence among the reporters. "My name is Allison Manning; I am the widow of Paul Manning, the writer, with whom some of you may be familiar." She recounted their voyage across the Atlantic and their time in England, Spain, the Mediterranean, and the Canaries, then she began her account of their trip back across the Atlantic.

"Ten days out of the Canaries Paul hoisted me to the top of the mast to make a repair." She smiled. "He was too large for me to hoist him." This got a laugh from the crowd. "While I was at the top of the mast I saw Paul clutch his chest and collapse in the cockpit. It took me more than two hours to get myself back down the mast." She pointed at her yacht. "You can see how tall it is. When I was able to reach him, he was dead. Some hours later I managed to bury him at sea and then began trying to sail the yacht the rest of the way across the Atlantic. Somewhat to my own surprise, I was able to manage it. Then, to my astonishment, after I had saved my own life and reached St. Marks, I found myself charged with my husband's murder. Now I must place my faith in Stone Barrington and Sir Leslie Hewitt, who could not be here today, because he is working on my defense. I thank you all for coming here and hearing my story. I hope we will meet again in happier times." She stepped back from the microphones to a hail of shouted questions.

Stone quieted the group. "As I said earlier, Mrs. Manning will answer no questions. Now you may have thirty minutes to photograph her yacht, down at the marina." He pointed to the boat, and most of the crowd sprinted across the lawn. Another clutch of reporters tried to approach Allison and were pushed back by police officers.

Stone hustled Allison upstairs to his rented room. "We'll wait them out here, then go back to the yacht," he said. He walked to the window and looked out. The reporters were swarming over the dock, prevented from boarding the yacht by the police. Then his eye was caught by another sight in the parking lot. Sir Winston Sutherland was standing next to his chauffeured car, watching the reporters, an outraged expression on his face.

Thomas was standing next to Stone. "I predict an explosion," he said, grinning broadly.

CHAPTER

21

Stone sat at the little table near the window and watched Sir Winston, who was speaking into a cellular phone. A few minutes later, a bright yellow school bus pulled into the parking lot, and the driver received some instructions from Sir Winston. Abruptly, the bus left the tarmac and started across the lawn toward the marina. When it stopped, a dozen police officers got down from the bus, one with a bullhorn.

"Ladies and gentlemen," the officer was saying, "a press conference by the Ministry of Justice will be held in ten minutes, and I have come to transport you there. Please board the bus immediately, as we are short of time."

Stone watched as the journalists crowded the entrance to the bus, ready to fight to get on, if necessary. Shortly the bus pulled away and, to Stone's surprise, took the road not toward the capital, but toward the airport. "What the hell?" he muttered.

There was a rap on the door and Thomas entered. Allison, who had been dozing on the bed, sat up on one elbow and looked at him.

"What's going on?" Stone asked.

"Half a dozen cops are going through my rented rooms, taking suitcases and clothes belonging to those reporters."

"Sir Winston wouldn't have the balls to arrest that many journalists, would he?"

"I can't see it happening," Thomas replied, "but he's taking them somewhere."

"Let's drive out to the airport," Stone said. "Allison, the coast is clear to the marina; you go back to the yacht and wait for me there." Allison nodded and put her feet over the edge of the bed, rubbing her eyes.

In Thomas's Toyota they drove quickly along the airport road and turned through the gates. In the distance they could see two DC-3s sitting on the apron; one of them already had her engines running. The group of reporters stood in a hangar listening to a young man in a business suit. There was much shouting and shaking of fists going on.

"We'd better not get too close to this," Thomas said, stopping the car. A truck loaded with luggage moved past them toward one of the DC-3s.

The reporters were now being herded onto the two airplanes by uniformed policemen; Stone noted that nobody was being beaten with the truncheons the policemen carried, but their body language told him that the cops were brooking no argument. The truck with the luggage pulled up and suitcases were thrown hurriedly into the luggage compartment of the airplanes.

"Where'd the other airplane come from?" Stone asked.

"It's a government plane, used only by high officials."

"Where do you think they're sending them?"

"I can only hope that they won't be flown out to sea, then chucked overboard," Thomas murmured. "Look, one camera crew and a couple of others are still in the hangar."

The two airplanes were taxiing now, and in a few minutes they were both taking off and heading to the northwest.

"Antigua, do you think?" Stone asked.

Thomas shook his head. "Antigua's due north; they're flying northwest. St. Thomas is my guess; that's the nearest U.S. airport; or maybe even to San Juan."

"That is the most high-handed thing I ever saw," Stone said, grinning. "Those people are going to go absolutely nuts when they get back to their respective news organizations."

"And that pleases you, I suppose."

"You bet your ass it does. If they were aroused by Allison's plight, then they're going to be mad as hell about their own treatment. The press never gets as angry as when their own freedom gets tampered with, and I'll bet half a dozen cameras got the whole thing on tape."

"You think this is going to soften up Sir Winston, then?" Thomas asked.

"When he finds out what they're saying about him in Miami and New York, it just might."

"Don't count on it. Sir Winston and our prime minister are accustomed to dealing with a more compliant press; I doubt if they give a damn about what foreigners think."

"Thomas," Stone said, "I hate to point this out, but this business is not going to be good for your business."

"I already thought of that," Thomas said glumly.

Back at the Shipwright's Arms, Federal Express had delivered two packages for Stone. One was from Bob Cantor and contained a copy of the *Publishers Weekly* profile of Paul Manning. The other package was from Alma, his secretary, and it contained two items: a brand-new black judge's robe and a brochure on the Parker Sportster inflatable dinghy. Stone sat down at a table and read the article on Paul Manning, which featured a photograph of the writer and Allison, arm in arm, in front of a large, handsome house. It was pretty standard stuff about a writer, his lifestyle, and his work, and there was nothing in particular that interested him in the piece. The boat brochure was more interesting.

He spread it out on the table and admired the many color photographs of the craft being rowed, being propelled by an outboard, and, most interesting, under sail. The Parker Sportster, it seemed, came with an aluminum mast, a mainsail, a jib, a rudder, and a centerboard. The brochure claimed it was the only inflatable dinghy so equipped. Stone thought the thing must be good for four or five knots, more if surfing with the wind aft.

Stone left the Shipwright's Arms and walked down to the marina. He stepped lightly aboard *Expansive*, tiptoed down the companionway ladder, and looked into the aft cabin. Allison was asleep on the large bed, her breathing deep and regular.

Stone climbed back into the cockpit and began quietly opening the cockpit lockers. There was the usual tangle of gear found aboard any yacht: fenders, warps, plastic buckets and deck brushes, life jackets, and in a special aft locker, an eight-man life raft. He opened another of the lockers and was greeted with the sight of an inflatable dinghy in its canvas bag; the manufacturer's name was printed boldly on the bag: AVON. Stone's heart began to beat a little faster, as much out of apprehension as discovery. There was one more locker, and he opened it expecting no new information. But there, lying packed and ready for use, was another, larger canvas bag emblazoned with another brand name: PARKER SPORTSTER. It seemed new and unused.

He closed the locker softly and sat down on a cockpit seat, feeling relieved.

22

On Saturday morning Stone fixed breakfast, then woke up Allison, who had been sleeping unusually well. "I've had a message from Leslie Hewitt," he said. "He wants us to come out and see him this morning."

"Okay," she said, rubbing her eyes. "I think a swim will wake me up." She started up the ladder.

"Hang on!" he commanded. "It's broad daylight, and there may be some press still on the island."

"Oh," she said, blinking.

"I enjoy you naked, but I don't want anyone else to," he said.

She smiled. "You're sweet. I think I'll just have a shower; join me?"

"Already had one," he replied, "and breakfast is nearly ready, so hurry."

They walked up to the Shipwright's Arms together,

to borrow Thomas's car, and the first person they saw was Hilary Kramer from the *Times*.

"What are you still doing here?" Stone asked. "Didn't you get the bum's rush with everybody else?"

"Nope. I was in the capital, buying some necessities, and when I came back, everybody was gone."

"You missed the press conference, then?"

"I didn't care anything about that. I'd already filed."

"Did anybody else survive the press purge?"

"There's a crew from CNN here who got to stay to provide pool coverage for the TV people."

"How about Chris Wheaton, from *60 Minutes*?"

"Gone with the wind, along with everybody else."

"What sort of attention did your story get at the *Times*?"

"I don't know; I modemed it in, and I'll trust their judgment, but it's a good story. Where are you off to?"

"A visit with my co-counsel."

"Can I come?"

"Sorry, this is strictly business."

Kramer shrugged. "Well, I've got nothing to do but file my story on the ouster of the international press, then it's vacation until the trial on Monday, since Sir Winston won't see me."

"Lucky you; see you later."

They got the car keys and drove out along the coast road to Sir Leslie Hewitt's cottage. They found him weeding his back garden, and Stone was relieved to see that he recognized them. "Morning, Leslie," he said.

"Good morning to you, Stone, and to you, Mrs. Manning."

"Please call me Allison," she replied with a winning smile.

"I thought we might talk about how to proceed at the trial," Stone said.

"Of course we will," Hewitt said, "but I wonder if I could ask a small favor of you before we begin?"

"Of course."

"I'd like to give you some tea, but I'm out of milk. Would you be kind enough to run down to the grocer, about two miles along the coast road, and fetch me a bottle?"

"All right, Leslie," Stone said, and Hewitt insisted on giving him money.

As he turned to leave, Hewitt offered Allison his arm. "May I show you the garden, my dear?" he asked, smiling sweetly.

"I'd be very pleased to see it," she replied, taking his arm. "See you later, Stone."

Stone drove to the grocery with ill grace, annoyed at being dispatched on such an errand when they should have been discussing how to save Allison's life. He was struck by how completely lucid Hewitt was, as compared to their last meeting; the man apparently went in and out of his haze unpredictably. Stone bought the milk and drove back to the cottage, entering through the front door. He went to the kitchen to put the milk in the refrigerator and was surprised to find a full bottle there. *Well,* he thought, *when I'm his age I'll forget the milk, too.* He walked out the back door into the garden and saw Hewitt and Allison deep in conversation on a bench at the bottom of the garden. When they saw him coming, Hewitt had a few more words to say, patted her on the knee, then rose to receive Stone.

"Come into my study, and we'll begin," Hewitt said.

Stone fell in alongside Allison. "What were you two discussing so seriously?" he asked.

"Gardening," she replied.

"Now," Hewitt said, taking his usual seat at his desk and waving Stone and Allison to a sofa. "Here's how it will go on Monday: the judge will select a jury, which should take an hour or so, then the prosecution will make an opening statement, probably a very long and passionate one, if I know Winston Sutherland, and I have since he was a lad. The jury will be very impressed. Then I will make an opening statement, which will be equally passionate, but very much shorter, for which the jury will be grateful, I assure you. That should bring us to lunchtime.

"After lunch, Winston will present his case, which will almost certainly be confined to reading passages from Mr. Manning's journal, or outline for his novel, whichever way you would like to characterize it. I would be very surprised if he called any other witnesses."

Stone interrupted. "Isn't he required to submit his evidence and witnesses to the defense?"

"Oh, no," Hewitt replied. "Nothing of the sort. Then we will call your writer acquaintance, Mr. . . . ."

"Mr. Forrester, from *The New Yorker*," Stone said.

"Yes, quite. I should think it would be best if you, Stone, questioned him. I'm sure you already have a complete grasp of what we must get from him."

"Yes," Stone said. "I want to . . ."

Hewitt held up a hand. "No need to go into that; I trust your judgment completely."

"Thank you very much," Stone said, "but shouldn't we go into this in more detail?"

•

"Completely unnecessary, I assure you," Hewitt replied with a big smile. "Then we will put Mrs. Manning on the stand, and I think you should question her as well," Hewitt said. "No need to go over that with me, but I should think that the two of you might go through it once or twice."

"You may be sure we will," Stone said. *Jesus,* he thought to himself, *is this the man's idea of preparation?*

"Then there will be cross-examination and redirect, but I urge you to keep redirect to an absolute minimum, since Lord Cornwall is impatient at such times. Then Winston will make his closing statement, which will be annoyingly like his opening one, then I will make our closing statement, which will move the jury very nearly to tears. Juries always love my closing statements. Then we will wait for the jury to make its decision."

"We have no idea, of course, how long that will take," Stone pointed out.

"Quite the contrary; I would be surprised if they took more than an hour, two at the most. The jury will, like most juries, have already made up their individual minds before the proceedings are finished. They will just need time to chat a bit to be sure they're all in agreement."

"That has not been my experience with juries," Stone said.

"Oh, I am sure that in your country there is extensive deliberation before the jury decides what it has already decided," Hewitt said, chuckling, "but in St. Marks, it is considered rude to keep anyone waiting, especially on so important a matter as Mrs. Manning's life."

"That will be very nice of them," Stone said dryly.

"Of course it will, and we will be spared the suspense."

"I hope we are spared a great deal more," Stone said.

"You may certainly hope," Hewitt said. He looked at a gold pocket watch that he produced from his Bermuda shorts. "Well, I see that time is getting on. We will meet at the court at ten o'clock on Monday morning and all do our very best." He rose and left the room without so much as a good-bye. Stone reflected that Hewitt had not offered them the promised tea, for which he had obtained the unnecessary milk.

Allison turned to Stone. "You know, sometimes I think he's not entirely all there."

Stone certainly could not disagree with her. "What did you two talk about while I was shopping for milk?"

"I told you," she said. "Gardening."

23

*S*tone was having lunch alone at the Shipwright's Arms when Thomas called him to the phone. "It's Bob Cantor," he said, moving the receiver down to the end of the bar, away from where Hilary Kramer was sitting.

"Hello, Bob," Stone said into the instrument. "You back from the Canaries?"

"I'm home again," Cantor replied, "and a little worse for the wear. The jet lag will kill you."

"I sympathize. You got something new from the Canaries?"

"Nothing at all. I have got something new from here, though."

"Shoot."

"You remember I told you I checked out Paul Manning's credit record?"

"I do, and he had a pretty good one, as I recall; paid everything on time."

"That's right, but I had that information only from a phone call from a friend at my bank. Now I have the printed report, and it shows a lot more."

"Like what?"

"Seems Mr. Manning was living right on the edge. He was pulling in a magnificent income, of course, probably something between a million and two million a year, and closer to two. But he was spending one hell of a lot of money, too."

"That's very interesting," Stone said.

"It gets more interesting. The credit report shows that he was pretty maxed out on all his credit cards and that he was borrowing heavily to make it from paycheck to paycheck."

"Writers don't get paychecks, do they? They get royalty checks."

"Okay, okay, he got paid in widely separated lumps, but they were big lumps. My point is, his credit record shows that he was borrowing heavily from three banks, usually a hundred thousand bucks at a time, then repaying it when his royalty or advance check came."

"Was he keeping up?"

"Just barely. I, ah, did a little unauthorized snooping last night."

"What do you mean?"

"I drove up to Greenwich, got into his house, and had a look through his financial records, which his secretary had neatly filed away."

"Bob, you should check with me before you do things like that."

"If I had checked with you, you wouldn't have let me do it."

"You're right about that. So what did you find out?"

"When he got a check he would pay off the three banks, and there would be only a few thousand left, not enough to get him to the next publisher's payment. Right before he set off on the transatlantic voyage, he got two checks at once from two contracts, and that squared him for a while. But he borrowed while he was away, and now the banks are lined up, waiting for the will to be probated."

"Well, I guess that's going to cut into Allison's insurance money."

"I wouldn't worry about that," Cantor came back. "Manning had twelve million bucks in life insurance."

"Twelve million bucks? Nobody has that much insurance."

"You'd be surprised how many people do. He was paying something like fifteen thousand bucks a month in premiums, which is one of the reasons, along with his lifestyle, that he was having to go to the banks to get by. And get this, he also had mortgage life insurance to cover both the house and the boat loans. When Allison pays all the outstanding bills, she's going to have at least eleven million bucks in cash, tax free, plus the house, the boat, the cars—everything—free and clear. Her biggest expense is going to be property taxes, and she won't have those long, because she's already put the Greenwich property on the market. I told you I have a buddy up there in the property business."

"Have you seen the *New York Times* piece on Allison's plight down here?"

"Yep, and you can be sure that the insurance company has seen it, too."

"That means they won't pay unless she's acquitted."

"Wrong; they've already paid. They'd have to sue her to get it back, and they'll have a very hard time doing that."

"Why?"

"Because she's already transferred nearly the whole amount to an account in the Cayman Islands. I found the receipt for the wire transfer."

"Holy shit!" Stone breathed. "Either Allison has some very sharp advice from her lawyer and accountant, or I've underestimated her by a long shot. I've never even seen her so much as make a phone call from down here."

"Well, somebody is, shall we say, acting in her best interests."

"Somebody sure is, and it isn't me."

"Bottom line is, Mrs. Manning's husband could not have kicked off at a better time for her. If Manning had lived and had continued to live as he did, I reckon he wouldn't have been able to afford the life insurance premiums much longer."

"How long had he had the insurance?"

"A little over two years, and if the company had known he was going to sail, two-handed, across the Atlantic twice, he never would have gotten it. Insurance companies frown on that sort of sporting activity."

"I guess not. This information certainly puts a whole new complexion on things, doesn't it?"

"I would say so. I mean, if you were still a cop, you'd now suspect Allison Manning of helping her husband overboard, wouldn't you?"

"That's one theory."

"The other theory which suggests itself has to do with the very special dinghy Paul Manning had air freighted to him in Las Palmas."

"Right. I got the brochure on the Parker Sportster today. It sails."

"Could it have sailed Manning back to the Canaries from where Allison says they were when he died?"

"Yes, but it wouldn't have had to; Manning could have left the yacht as soon as they were out of sight of land."

"Aha!"

"Except for one thing."

"What's that?"

"The Parker Sportster is still on the yacht."

"Could he have had another dinghy?"

"He did have, but it wasn't sailable, and anyway, that one is still on the yacht, too."

"So it looks as though Manning, when he left the yacht, was either dead or swimming."

"Looks that way."

"Could he have swum back?"

"I think we can discount that possibility; he might have been spotted near shore in the daytime and there are sharks out there; I don't think he would have tried it at night."

"Another boat might have spotted him sailing a dingy, too."

"Not if he sailed at night. That's what I would have done in his shoes, but of course, the point is moot, because the dinghy is still on the yacht."

"Well, pal, good luck with sorting this one out."

"I don't have to sort it out, thank God. All I have to do is think about getting Allison Manning acquitted. I'm not the cops."

"Good point. I'll call you if I find out anything new."

"Thanks, Bob. Take care." He hung up.

"I'm not the cops," Stone repeated to himself. "I'm her lawyer, and if she's guilty, she won't be the first guilty client I've represented." Still, he wanted her to be innocent.

24

*S*tone hung up the phone and returned to his lunch. He wasn't the cops, granted, but he was still bothered by what he was hearing about Paul Manning's affairs. He was about finished with lunch when Jim Forrester pulled up a chair.

"Mind if I join you?" the *New Yorker* reporter asked, settling his lanky frame and waving to Thomas for a drink.

"Not at all. I wondered what had happened to you; I was afraid my star witness had gotten shipped out with the other reporters."

Forrester shook his head. "Nope. I ducked into the men's room when I saw the cops, and they missed me. My luggage went, though; I've been shopping for the necessities."

"Good; can we talk about your testimony?"

"Sure."

"I don't see any need to rehearse, but I do want to be reassured that you're willing to testify that, on the occasion you met them, they were happy together, affectionate, and glad to be in each other's company."

"No problem with that."

"I think we'll skip the argument they had about their routing later in the evening; it doesn't seem germane."

"I think you're right; I've been married, so I know how those little spats can arise over nothing."

"Yeah," Stone replied, as if he knew what the reporter was talking about. It occurred to him that he and Arrington had never had that sort of spat in their time together. He hadn't heard from her since she had arrived in L.A., and he wondered how she was.

"Let's see," Stone said, "you first met Paul Manning in the bar at the yacht club in Las Palmas?"

"Well, no; I had met him earlier, much earlier."

"You didn't mention that," Stone said.

"Well, it was a long time ago. I went to Syracuse University, and Paul went to Cornell at the same time. The towns are not far apart, and we had an interfraternity basketball league. I played against Paul two or three times. I just knew him to speak to, though; at the time, I don't think we ever had a conversation that didn't involve who fouled who."

"I guess we can use that; it gives you some sort of history with Paul, however slim. What were your impressions of him in those days?"

"Pretty much the same as in Las Palmas: cheerful, outgoing, good company."

"Not the sort who might commit suicide?"

"No, absolutely not. In Las Palmas he was enthusiastic about getting back across the Atlantic; said he had an idea for a new novel based on their trip, and he was anxious to get started on it."

"That we can use," Stone said. "He apparently kept some notes in a leather-bound book; did he mention that at all?"

"He said he had made a lot of notes; he didn't say anything about a leather-bound book."

"That will be helpful, nevertheless. Sir Winston is taking Paul's notes as complaints about Allison; it's the most damning evidence he has."

"Look, I don't want to get you into some sort of ethical quandary here, but if you want me to mention the leather-bound book, I'll be glad to do it. It's not as though the other side is playing anything like what we would call fair."

"I think it's best to play this straight," Stone said. "The difference in the effect of your testimony would be small, and anytime you start deviating from the straight and narrow, you open yourself up to getting caught lying. I wouldn't want to end up with a perjury charge against you."

"Neither would I," Forrester said. "God knows what the penalty for perjury is on this island."

"Can you think of anything else during your evening with the Mannings that might help us at the trial?"

Forrester looked uncomfortable. "Can we talk off the record for a minute?"

"Sure."

"I certainly don't want to bring this up at the trial, but it's the kind of thing that I can't ignore when I come to write my piece."

"Shoot."

"You remember we talked about this dinghy that Paul had flown in from Barcelona?"

"Yes, the Parker Sportster."

"I didn't mention this before, but that dinghy can be sailed. I read something in a magazine about somebody sailing one from Norway to Iceland."

"I'm aware of the dinghy's sailing capability."

"Does that suggest anything to you?"

"What does it suggest to you?"

"That Paul Manning could have conceivably sailed the thing back to the Canaries and faked his own death, for whatever reason."

"That occurred to me, but it's not possible."

"Why not?"

"Because the Parker Sportster is still in a cockpit locker of *Expansive*. I found it there, unused."

Forrester took a deep breath and let it out. "Boy, am I glad to hear that. I didn't want to think that Allison could be mixed up in something like that, but . . ."

"I understand. While we certainly won't bring this up at the trial, I think it might be very helpful to Allison if you mentioned it in your piece. There will always be people who would think the worst, and it might help her."

"I'll certainly do that. It's the kind of detail that will make the piece more interesting. By the way, I talked with my editor, Charles McGrath, and in light of all the publicity Allison's story has gotten, they're more interested than ever in the piece."

"I'm glad for you."

"You should be glad for Allison, too; this kind of

long, detailed piece will satisfy the curiosity of a lot of people. I know it's going to be tough for her when all this is over."

"I know it is, though I haven't talked about it with her yet. I think she's got enough on her mind at the moment."

"I'm sure she has."

"Have you talked with her at length yet?"

"Twice. She's remarkably open and forthcoming; sometimes I think she doesn't really have a grasp of what she's facing."

"I know what you mean," Stone said, "and I don't see how it would help to make her more aware. She's been told all the facts and the risks, and if she chooses to be in denial, then who's to say she shouldn't be? Certainly not I. If her attitude helps her get through this, that's fine with me."

"Let me ask you something for the record, Stone, and I'd appreciate the frankest answer you can give me. Your answer won't appear until well after the trial, and I'll hold it in confidence until then."

"What would you like to know?"

"Right now, at this moment, what do you estimate her chances are of getting out of this?"

Stone sighed. "I don't really know how to answer that. There are so many variables here, most of which I have no control over, that the situation is entirely unpredictable."

"Do you think there's really a chance she could hang?"

"Yes, I do."

"No kidding, really?"

"Really."

"Jesus Christ."

"Yes."

"It just doesn't seem possible that this sort of thing could happen in this day and age. I mean, if she'd fetched up in the United States, she'd be walking around scot free, wouldn't she?"

"I believe she would. I don't think a prosecutor could get past a preliminary hearing in the United States. I'd blow him out of the water. With Paul's medical records, his note-taking habits, your testimony, and above all, with Allison's testimony, I don't think any judge would buy a murder charge for a minute. I sometimes wonder what would have happened if she'd fetched up in Antigua or Guadeloupe."

"I wonder, too."

The two men sat silently, each contemplating the worst for Allison Manning.

CHAPTER

25

Stone sat talking with Jim Forrester. As they chatted he saw a taxi pull up outside and a woman get out. She seemed middle-aged, was tall and fashionably thin, and was wearing a wrinkled silk dress and a straw sun hat. The driver got two suitcases out of the trunk, took some money from her, and drove away. Thomas Hardy saw her, too, and went out to help with her bags.

"Well," Jim Forrester said, "I'm going upstairs for a nap." He got to his feet. "I think I might be coming down with something." He ambled off toward the stairs.

Stone watched as Thomas set the woman's bags down by the bar and reached for the registration book. The woman signed it, then seemed to be asking Thomas some questions. Thomas's eyebrows suddenly went up, and he beckoned to Stone.

Stone got up and walked across the restaurant

toward the bar, getting a closer look at the woman as he walked. She was, at the very least, in her early forties, he reckoned, and she had on more makeup than suited her.

"Stone," Thomas said. "This is someone you might want to meet."

The woman turned toward him. "Are you Stone Barrington?" she asked.

"Yes, I am," Stone replied.

She held out her hand. "I'm Allison Manning," she said.

"How do you do," Stone said. Then the name sank in. "Who did you say . . ."

"I'm Paul Manning's widow," the woman said, "and I'm not very well, if the truth be told. However, I expect to be a lot better quite soon."

Thomas went upstairs with the bags, leaving Stone alone with the woman.

"I suppose you're with the press," Stone said wearily.

"I'm not with anybody," the woman replied. "I used to be with Paul Manning, but I understand he's dead. Can you confirm that?"

"Yes, I can," Stone replied. "Why don't we sit down?" he indicated his table. "You seem to have been traveling; would you like a drink?"

"Oh, God, yes," she breathed and headed toward a chair. "A very dry Gibson would be lovely."

Thomas came back down the stairs, and Stone ordered her drink. When they were settled at a table, Stone said, "I'm afraid you have me at something of a loss, Miss . . ."

"Mrs.," she said. "Mrs. Manning. And yes, I suppose you are at something of a loss. You're representing her, aren't you?"

"I'm representing Allison Manning," he said. "Why don't you tell me what's going on here?"

"What's going on, Mr. Barrington, is that I've come to claim my husband's estate."

"You're speaking of Paul Manning, the writer?"

"I am."

"And you claim to have been married to him?"

The woman opened a large purse, extracted an envelope, and handed it to Stone. "I believe this will answer your question," she said.

Stone opened the envelope and took out a single sheet of paper. It was a photocopy of a marriage certificate stating that Paul Manning and Elizabeth Allison Franklin had been married in Dade County, Florida, some fourteen years before.

"And you are Elizabeth Allison Manning?"

"Call me Libby; everyone does."

"May I see some sort of identification, please?"

She opened her bag again and handed over an American passport.

Stone examined it, and it confirmed her identity. He handed it back. "Thank you," he said. "And when were you and Paul Manning divorced?" he asked.

"Never," she replied. "Paul and I were never divorced; we were married until the day he died."

"I see," Stone said. He didn't see at all. "And what brings you to St. Marks?"

"I read of Paul's death in the papers," she replied. "I told you, I've come to claim his estate."

•

"And how do you propose to do that?" Stone asked.

She opened her bag again and produced another document. "This is a copy of Paul's will," she said, "leaving everything to me."

Stone looked it over. It was short and to the point and dated the day after the date on the marriage certificate. He handed it back to her. "Mrs. Manning," he said, "I'm afraid you've come a long way for nothing."

"Oh? How's that?"

"Paul Manning's estate is being handled in Connecticut, and there is another, more recent will leaving everything to another, more recent Mrs. Manning."

"Oh, I know all about her," the woman said. "Paul was never married to her, not really, no matter what he told anybody. I am the only woman he was ever married to."

"Can you give me a little background on all this?" Stone asked, trying not to sound plaintive, though he was feeling very plaintive indeed.

"Of course. Paul and I met when we were both working for the *Miami Herald,* some fifteen years ago. We fell in love, were married, and . . ."

"And lived happily ever after?"

She smiled sourly. "Not exactly. He ran out on me some years later."

"How many years later?"

"Four years later, four and a bit. But we never bothered to get a divorce. Paul continued to support me, though. He sent a check every month."

"And when was the last time you saw Paul?"

"When he left. After that, I dealt with his lawyer, in Miami."

●

"Do you still live in Miami, Mrs. Manning?"

"Libby; please call me Libby; everyone does."

"Libby, do you still live in Miami?"

"No, I live in Palm Beach. Well, near Palm Beach."

"And you never remarried?"

"Never."

"What sort of work do you do, Libby?"

"I write a society column for a local paper in Palm Beach. Doesn't pay very much, really, but it gets me to all the parties."

"So you live on the monthly check from Paul?"

"That's right. Only it didn't arrive this month, and when I saw the papers, I knew why. I called the lawyer in Miami, but he said he had received nothing from Paul's office this month. So I figured I'd better get down here and take charge of things."

"I see."

"You're a lawyer, right?"

"Yes, in New York."

"Well, I guess I'm going to need a lawyer. You want to handle this for me?"

"I'm afraid I'm otherwise engaged," Stone said.

"Then I'll just have to find somebody else, I guess."

"Mrs. Manning . . . ah, Libby, I'm afraid that getting a lawyer in St. Marks won't help you in dealing with Paul's estate. As I said, that is being handled in Connecticut, in Greenwich."

She stared at him blankly. "You want me to go to Connecticut?" she demanded.

"It's not a matter of what I want, and I don't want you to think that I'm giving you legal advice, which I'm not, but it seems logical that the solution to your problem, if there is a solution, is not in St. Marks." He wanted desperately for her to be anywhere else in the world but St. Marks.

"Well, shit," she said disgustedly.

"I take your point."

She stood up. "Right now," she said, "I'm going to get into a hot bath, and after I've had some dinner and a good night's sleep I think I might just get a second opinion on what you've told me."

Stone stood up. "If there's anything else I can do . . ."

"I thought the gist of what you told me was that there's nothing you can do," she said.

"That's pretty much it," he admitted, trying desperately to think of something to say to her that might make her go back to Palm Beach.

"Well, tomorrow's another day, and then I guess I'll see what I can find out about this murder trial. Who's the DA?"

"It's being handled by the, ah, local government," he replied.

"Right. I guess I can talk to them. See you around, Stone." She picked up her purse and headed for the stairs.

Stone went straight to the bar, picked up the phone, and dialed Bob Cantor's number.

"Problems?" Thomas asked, ambling over.

"You wouldn't believe me if I told you," Stone replied. He got Cantor's answering machine. "Bob," he said, "you mentioned earlier that Paul Manning had been divorced in Florida. Do whatever you have to do to find a copy of the decree and fax it to me at the earliest possible moment, please. I've got another Allison Manning on my hands." He hung up.

"Another Allison Manning," Thomas repeated, chuckling to himself.

"Thomas, please do whatever you can to keep that woman from ever hearing the name of Sir Winston Sutherland," Stone said.

Thomas laughed aloud. "Right!"

26

Stone marched over to the marina, jumped aboard *Expansive*, and went below. The saloon was empty. He went aft to the owner's cabin, and found Allison sound asleep. "Wake up," he said, patting her on the shoulder.

Allison opened her eyes slowly. "Oh, hello," she said, reaching for him.

Stone took her hands in his. "Not now, Allison; we have to talk."

"Talk? What about?"

"Come into the saloon." He handed her a robe and went ahead of her.

She came in, tossing her hair and rubbing her eyes. "What is going on?" she asked.

"Tell me about Paul's first marriage," he said.

"What?"

"Paul was married before he married you; tell me everything he told you about that."

She took a bottle of mineral water from the fridge, uncapped it, took a long swallow, and settled onto the sofa beside him. "He was married, that's all. It didn't work out."

"When did he get married?"

"When he was a lot younger, in the early eighties, I think."

"How long was he married?"

"Three or four years. What's this all about?"

"Do you know exactly when he was divorced?"

"No, not exactly."

"Have you ever seen a copy of his divorce decree?"

"No."

"Not even when you went to get your marriage license?"

"I don't think so."

"Normally, if you've been married before, you have to produce a divorce decree in order to get a license. Where were you married?"

"In New York, at the courthouse, by a judge."

"You went with Paul to get the license?"

"Yes, but I don't remember anything about a divorce decree."

"Swell."

"Stone, if you don't tell me what this is about . . ."

"The first Mrs. Manning has just checked into the Shipwright's Arms."

Allison's face fell. "Libby?"

"Yes."

"That bitch!" Allison hissed. "What the hell is she doing here?"

"She says she's come to claim Paul's estate."

"Hah! That's a laugh! She's not getting a penny."

"Allison, let me see Paul's will."

"She's not in it."

"I want to see the will. It's in Paul's briefcase, isn't it?"

"How would you know that?"

"I'm just guessing. Is it in the briefcase?"

"Yes."

"You'd better let me see it right now."

"Oh, all right." She got up, went into the aft cabin, and came back a couple of minutes later with a document. "Here," she said ill-humoredly, handing it to him.

Stone read through it quickly. There were a number of small bequests to organizations—the Author's Guild Fund and PEN—and to two clubs to which Manning had belonged, and the rest was left to Allison. No mention of his first wife.

"See?" Allison said. "I told you he left her nothing."

"Did you know he had been sending her monthly checks?"

"Yes."

"How much?"

"Three thousand dollars a month."

"Alimony?"

"I suppose."

"Was it dictated by a divorce decree?"

"I don't know; Paul called it alimony, though."

"It's not a lot of money for someone in Paul's income bracket."

"Paul didn't make any real money until after they were divorced; he was just a newspaper reporter."

"Let's see, if they were divorced ten years ago—do you know if there was any time limit on the payments?"

"No, I don't. Is this really going to be a problem?"

"Maybe; it depends on the decree, if there is one."

"What do you mean, if there is one? There must be one, somewhere."

"I've got somebody looking into that now. Do you know where they were divorced?"

"In Miami, I guess; that's where Paul lived at the time. Stone, what's the worst this could mean?"

"Well, the absolute worst, legally, would be if they were never divorced. In that case, she might have some sort of rights as the wife in either Florida or Connecticut—I'm not familiar with the domestic or estate laws in either. On the other hand, if they were legally divorced and we can get hold of the decree, it shouldn't be much of a problem. Let's say the judge gave her three thousand a month for life, or until she marries; then she'd be entitled to claim that much from the estate. Or he might have put a time limit on it. It doesn't seem likely that the payments were pegged to his income, since he was paying her only three thousand a month; they would have gone up as he became more successful. Did Paul seem to feel any great obligation to her?"

"Not really. He never complained about writing the checks, though."

"He didn't leave her any money, either."

"Right," Allison said, brightening. "How can she make any claim at all?"

"She can easily enough, if she has a court order, and that's what a decree is. But she's claiming they were never divorced, and if that's true, there wouldn't be a decree."

"Stone, this doesn't sound like the greatest problem in the world. Just tell her to call my lawyer in Greenwich, and if she doesn't like that, then tell her to go fuck herself."

Stone shook his head. "We can't do that."

"Why not?"

"Because she's here, don't you understand?"

"So what?"

"She's a completely unknown quantity. Worst case, suppose Sir Winston gets his hands on her and charms or frightens her? Suppose she turns up at your trial and testifies that Paul told her that he was afraid you were going to murder him?"

"That's ridiculous."

"I did say it's the worst case; people will do strange things when there's a lot of money at stake. The thing is, I don't want her hanging over our heads. She's a loose cannon, and she could turn out to be very dangerous."

Now Allison had grown quiet. "So what do we do?" she asked finally.

"I think we have to get her off the island as quickly as possible."

"Maybe one of Thomas's many brothers could kidnap her or something."

He looked at her sharply. "Don't even joke about that."

She held up her hands. "Sorry. So how do we get her off the island?"

"How much money have you got in your Greenwich bank account?"

"Well, I'm not sure, exactly."

"Allison, this is no time to fuck around. How much?"

"A little over a million dollars."

"In your checking account?"

"Well, it's an interest-bearing account."

"Oh, great."

"Are you suggesting I should pay her a million dollars?"

"No, but you're going to have to let me negotiate something with her."

"How much of a something?"

"Whatever it takes, if we want to get rid of her in a hurry, and we certainly do."

"Do you think we could get rid of her for half a million dollars?"

"I think a reasonable person would accept that, but I have no idea how reasonable she is."

"If she wants more than that I'll shoot her myself," Allison said.

"Goddammit, I told you not to talk like that!" he practically shouted.

"All right, all right, just deal with her. I'll trust you to handle it as you see fit."

"God, I wish I had that decree," Stone said.

"But you don't; just do the best you can."

"Give me your checkbook," Stone said.

She found her handbag, dug out the checkbook, and handed it to Stone.

He ripped out a check. "Sign it," he said.

"A blank check? Are you nuts?"

"Sign it."

Allison signed the check.

Stone ripped it out and tucked it into a pocket. "Now find two blank pieces of paper, and sign them."

She went to the chart table, found some paper, signed two sheets, and handed them over. "You see how I trust you," she said.

"I'll be back as soon as I can," he said, and left the yacht.

27

Stone strode toward the Shipwright's Arms. Dusk was falling, and the first customers were arriving for dinner. He looked around, saw no sign of the other Mrs. Manning, then went to the bar. "Give me a rum and tonic, Thomas," he said.

Thomas complied. "Seems like you got something of a mess on your hands," he said.

"Tell me about it. Will you ring Mrs. Manning's room, please?"

"She left orders not to be disturbed."

"Disturb her."

"Stone," Thomas said gently, "if you're going to handle this lady, don't you think you'd better do it gently?"

Stone took a deep breath and exhaled. "You're right," he said. "I'll wait for the lady to make her appearance for dinner." He picked up his drink. "I'm going upstairs for a few minutes; if she shows up tell her I'd like it if she'd join me for dinner."

"I'll tell her."

Stone went up to his room, switched on his computer, and began to type. When he had finished he printed out the document on the blank page over Allison's signature, slipped it into an envelope, and started to leave. Then he stopped, picked up the phone, and dialed Bob Cantor's number again, and once more got his answering machine. He swore and slammed down the phone, then composed himself and went downstairs.

Libby Manning was sitting at the bar, sipping a martini; he wondered if she were a drunk. If so, he'd better get moving. "Good evening," he said to her, managing a smile.

"Good evening," she said. "I accept your invitation to dinner."

"I'm glad," he replied. "Thomas, may we have a table?"

"Right this way," Thomas said, picking up a pair of menus.

"Something quiet," Stone whispered as he passed.

Thomas showed them to a corner table with a view of the harbor, then he brought Libby Manning another martini and Stone a rum and tonic.

She raised her glass. "Better days," she said, smiling.

"I'll drink to that," Stone said, sipping his drink. "So, Libby, tell me something about yourself. Are you a Florida girl?"

"Born and bred," she said. "Went to Dade County

High and the University of Miami, majored in journalism, went to work for the *Herald.* How about you?"

"Born and bred in New York, NYU law school, a time with the NYPD, then retirement and the practice of law."

"What kind of law?"

"Whatever comes along."

"I thought most lawyers specialized these days."

"Most do. Whatever my clients need done, I specialize in."

"And how did the lovely Allison come to hire you?"

"Well, when she sailed in alone on that boat, I was the only game in town, I guess."

"Were the papers right? Is she going to hang?"

"Not if I can help it."

"Can you help it?"

"That remains to be seen."

"The trial is next week?"

"That's right."

"And if they hang her, it'll be pretty quick, will it?"

"Libby, you are a pessimist." Or maybe an optimist, he thought to himself. "Let's order." They chatted idly until their food came, and ate mostly in silence. She was waiting for him to make the first move, he reckoned. Then, as they ate, another couple was shown to a table a few yards away. Stone looked up and gulped.

Libby leaned forward. "Who is that extraordinary-looking black fella?" she asked.

"His name is Sir Winston Sutherland," Stone replied, keeping his voice down, "and he is the worst nightmare of any white woman traveling alone in this country."

Her eyes widened. "How do you mean?"

"His greatest pleasure seems to be finding innocent American girls, charging them with capital crimes, and hanging them without much of a trial. Allison is his most recent victim."

"He's the one who's prosecuting her?"

Stone nodded. "Take my advice, Libby; avoid him at all costs, and whatever you do, don't let him find out who you are."

Libby downed the rest of her martini and started on the wine. "Why should I be afraid of him?"

"Well, another rich American widow might be a tempting target."

"Rich? Me?"

"Well, Paul was fairly rich, wasn't he? Sir Winston knows all about that."

"Jesus, Paul was only sending me ten thousand dollars a month."

"Three thousand," Stone said, sipping his wine.

"Well, I'm sure he must have provided for me in his will."

Stone took the document from his envelope and handed it to her. "I think you'd better read his will."

She dug some glasses out of her handbag and read quickly. "That shit," she said under her breath. "That utter and complete shit. I'll get a lawyer and sue his estate."

"On what grounds?" Stone asked.

"Oh, a lawyer will come up with something."

"Libby, the kind of lawyer who would take your case would bleed you dry before the court even ruled, and then you'd get nothing."

"I'd still get my alimony," she said.

"Maybe. I won't know that until I see your divorce decree. A copy is being faxed to me from Miami tomorrow morning."

She blinked rapidly, but said nothing.

"Libby, if you should sue the estate, it will upset Allison very badly, and right now, she holds the purse strings. She'll stop paying your alimony until a court rules otherwise, and that could take a long time. Are you prepared to get by on the salary from your newspaper column in Palm Beach until it all gets sorted out? It could take years."

"Oh, I'll get by all right; don't you worry," she said, smiling, but she was still blinking rapidly.

"Let me make a suggestion," Stone said.

"Go right ahead."

"Suppose Allison gave you, say, ten years of alimony, all at once. That would be three hundred and sixty thousand dollars in your bank account, right now."

"Right now?"

"The minute the check clears."

Libby stared at him for a moment, then shook her head. "No, sir; I want a million dollars."

"Allison has authorized me to offer you four hundred thousand dollars," Stone said, "and not a cent more." He took the check out of his pocket, filled in her name and the amount, and handed it to her.

Libby put on her glasses again and looked at the check. "Yeah," she said, "and as soon as I'm out of here she'll stop payment."

"No, she won't do that," Stone replied, handing her the document he had written a few minutes before.

She began reading.

"You see, it says that if she stops payment, you can sue her. And four hundred thousand dollars, wisely invested, should give you an annual income that represents a substantial raise over what you're getting now. And you'd always have that nest egg to fall back on." He took the document, filled in the amount, and handed it to her. "Allison's signature is already at the bottom, and her signature is on the check."

She looked up at him, obviously tempted.

"If you demand more, Allison will fight you, and she's the one with all the money. All you have to do is sign both copies of that document, have Thomas witness it, then go upstairs, get a good night's sleep, and take the first plane back to Miami tomorrow morning. The reservation has already been made."

Still, she hesitated.

"The money can be in your bank account within three business days, if you ask your bank to rush it."

"Suppose Allison gets hanged next week? What then?"

"The money's still yours. But if she hangs and you sue her estate, then you'll have to fight Allison's heirs, and they're going to care even less about you than she does. At least she's trying to do the right thing, even though she doesn't have to."

Libby Manning stood up and walked over to the bar, clutching the documents, with Stone right behind her. "Thomas," she said, "will you witness my signature, please?"

"Of course," Thomas said, watching her sign the documents, then signing them himself.

She handed Stone his copy and tucked her copy and the check into her handbag. "What time is the first flight out tomorrow morning?" she asked him.

"Chester flies at eight o'clock sharp. Would you like me to drive you to the airport?"

"Thank you, yes," she said. She held out her hand to Stone and shook his. "Thank you for your assistance, Mr. Barrington," she said, then she turned and marched upstairs.

Thomas looked at Stone. "I take it the matter is settled?"

"It is. Call Chester and get her on that plane, no matter who he has to throw off."

"Right."

"And kill her telephone; I don't want her talking to anybody tonight. Oh, and send her a bottle of good champagne on me; I want her to sleep well."

Thomas smiled broadly. "Right."

Stone walked toward the door. As he did, Sir Winston Sutherland smiled at him and raised a hand. Stone smiled broadly and returned his salute. Then he glanced out of the restaurant toward the marina and saw something he did not wish to see. Allison was walking fast across the lawn toward the inn, her arms pumping, and she had an angry and determined look on her face. Stone, without actually running, went to head her off.

He met her thirty yards from the inn and grabbed her arm, spinning her around. He tucked her arm in his and started steering her back toward the marina.

"Let go of me!" she erupted, struggling to free her arm.

"Shut up, Allison, and keep walking toward the boat," he said through clenched teeth.

She continued to struggle. "I'm not giving that bitch a thin dime!" she hissed. "Let go of my arm!"

"Allison, you and I cannot have a wrestling match on the lawn; Sir Winston Sutherland is up there having dinner with his wife. Don't make a scene!"

That stopped the struggle, but did nothing for Allison's temper. "I'll kill her!" she hissed.

"Shut up! That's all we need is for somebody to hear you say that. It would make very interesting testimony at your trial!" He stopped walking. "Now, I want you to go back to the yacht and calm yourself. I'll be there in a few minutes, and I'll explain everything to you."

"Oh, all right," she said and stalked off toward the marina.

Stone watched to see that she went all the way, then he walked back to the bar and ordered another drink. He wanted to be sure that Sir Winston left the restaurant without running into Libby Manning.

28

*S*tone smelled cooking as he boarded *Expansive*. He found Allison below, with lamb chops on the stove. "Smells good," he said.

"Want some?" she asked. Her fit of temper seemed to be over.

"No, thanks. I had something to eat with the former Mrs. Manning." He poured himself a glass of wine from an open bottle on the saloon table.

"So how did it go?" Allison asked, looking anxious.

"If I tell you, do you promise not to go up there and kill her?"

"I promise; I'm sorry about the way I behaved. I just got to thinking about the avaricious bitch, and it got the better of me."

"She accepted your offer."

Allison groaned. "And how much did I offer?"

"Four hundred thousand."

"Jesus. Did she sign something?"

Stone handed her the document and watched as she read it. "Don't worry, it's ironclad."

Allison threw her arms around him. "And you saved me a hundred thousand dollars!"

"That's one way of looking at it," Stone said.

"Well, I had expected to pay half a million."

"Then I saved you a hundred thousand dollars." He sat down at the table and sipped his wine. "Funny, I feel bad about it, for some reason."

"You sure you don't want a lamb chop?"

"I'm happy with my wine."

She sat down across from him and dug into her dinner. "Why would you feel bad?"

"I felt sorry for her, I guess."

"I don't; why should you?"

"Well, she's been struggling along for the ten years since her divorce on not a hell of a lot of money from Paul, plus whatever she got for writing some column for some local paper in Palm Beach, and that's not the cheapest place in the world to live. She said the column didn't pay much, but it got her to all the parties. I just have this vision of her growing old in Palm Beach with nothing."

"She's got four hundred thousand dollars," Allison said, savaging a lamb chop. "I don't call that nothing."

"You're right; I guess she's better off than she was before she came down here. I hope she doesn't blow it all on high living."

"If she does, it would serve her right, taking all that money from a poor widow."

"A very rich widow."

"Not very rich."

He felt unaccountably exasperated with her. "Come on, Allison, you're fixed for life—not like poor Libby."

"And how do you know I'm fixed for life?" she said, pausing in her attack on the chop.

"I have my sources," Stone said.

She cocked her head and looked at him with mock suspicion. "Stone Barrington, have you been checking up on me?"

"Checking up on people is a big part of my work," he said.

"And just what did you find out?"

"That you're who you say you are, and Paul was who you say he was, and you're very rich, that's all. You could easily afford the four hundred grand."

"I hope you didn't find out anything bad about me," she said, resuming her dinner.

"No, I didn't. Is there something bad about you I should know?"

"Only in my own mind, I guess."

"You been thinking bad thoughts about yourself?"

"Well, I seduced you, when I knew perfectly well that you had a girl."

"I wouldn't feel too badly about that; I knew what I was doing. I was mad at Arrington for not showing up down here and even madder at her for running off to California."

"With Vance Calder."

"Yeah, with Vance Calder. I have to admit, that didn't sit too well."

"So I just got lucky and caught you in a weak moment?"

"There wasn't all that much luck involved," Stone said ruefully. "I have a lot of weak moments."

"You mean you weren't faithful to Arrington, even before you met me?"

"Oh, yes, I was faithful to her, but not out of trying to be; we were just together all the time, and I was content, and I didn't give much thought to other women."

"Were you living together?"

"Yes."

"I sometimes wish I'd lived with somebody before Paul. Maybe I would have had a better idea of what it was like to be married." She was uncharacteristically quiet as she took her dishes to the galley.

"Is something else bothering you?" he asked.

"I guess I've been feeling a little guilty about how much fun we've been having. The sex, I mean; that's the only fun I've had lately. I mean, Paul's only been dead for a short time, and I confess, I've already been looking forward to a new kind of life." She smiled at him. "In addition to inordinately enjoying your body." She sat down beside him and held his hand.

"And I yours," he said, smiling. "And I don't think you have anything to feel guilty about. What happened at sea wasn't your fault; you did the best you could in the circumstances. You go right ahead and look forward to that new life." *If you have one,* he thought. *If I can somehow pull off an acquittal.*

"Are you going to be in this new life of mine?" she asked.

"That remains to be seen," he said. "I do have some unresolved issues to take care of."

"When they're resolved, I'd like to know about it."

"I think I can promise you that. But you're going to be a very popular lady, you know. Men are going to come out of the woodwork. They'll all want your money; you'll have to be careful."

"I will be. You want to go to bed?"

"If you don't mind, I think I'll sleep on my boat tonight."

"Going off me?" she asked, pouting.

"Not in the least." He kissed her lightly. "I'm awfully tired, though; the negotiation with Libby seems to have taken a lot out of me, and I ought to write to Arrington. She probably thinks I'm sulking."

"Okay, you do that; I'll see you in the morning."

He got up. "By the way, you should fax the Libby document to your lawyer and have him let your banker know that check is coming through. It's a very large amount, and it will make him nervous if he's not expecting it. And whatever you do, don't have second thoughts and stop payment. All hell would break loose."

"I'll write him a note and take it over to Thomas tonight," she said.

He kissed her again, and left her yacht for his own.

He wrote Arrington what was, for him, a long letter; the longest he had ever written anybody—two pages. He apologized for being incommunicative and told her about Allison's case, though he knew she would have seen the papers. Then he got romantic—unusual for him—and by the time he had signed the letter, he began worrying about faxing something so personal to her L.A. hotel; he didn't want some clerk reading it. Then he had a better idea. He would take care of it in the morning.

Some time after he had fallen asleep he stirred, hearing footsteps on the dock; Allison returning from the inn, he guessed. Then he fell asleep again and heard nothing else.

29

When Stone woke it was seven-thirty, and he jumped out of bed and into some clothes; he didn't want to miss Libby's departure, still harboring a lingering fear that she might not, after all, leave. He grabbed the letter to Arrington and ran toward the inn, zipping up his trousers. He arrived at the bar in time to see Thomas disappear around a corner, going toward the parking lot with some suitcases. "Thomas," he called, "where do you keep the Federal Express packaging?"

"Under the bar," Thomas called back. "See you later; I've got to get Mrs. Manning to the airport. We're running late."

"Just give me a minute to address . . ." But Thomas was gone. Stone grabbed a FedEx envelope and ran after him. Thomas was pulling out of the parking lot when he flagged down the car and jumped in the backseat. "Morning, Libby," he said. "I'll come to the air-port with you, if you don't mind."

"Sure, why not?" she said. She was wearing the straw hat in which she had arrived.

"Thomas, have you got a pen?"

Thomas handed one back to him.

"Libby, I'd appreciate it if, when you get to Miami, you'd drop this into the nearest Federal Express bin for me. I want it to be in California tomorrow."

"Sure, glad to," she replied.

"Nothing you can fax?" Thomas asked.

"No, I want it delivered." He sealed the letter into the envelope and handed it to Libby, who put it into her large handbag. "You're sure this is no trouble?"

"Of course not; it's like mailing a letter—they have those bins all over the airport."

"I appreciate it," Stone said.

"Do you always drive this fast?" Libby asked Thomas, fastening her seat belt.

"No, but we're running late, and I don't want Chester to leave you behind. He has to keep to a sched-ule."

"We were half an hour late arriving in St. Marks," she said. "Chester owes me. Besides, if you hadn't been delivering breakfast to somebody or other, we wouldn't be late. I was on time."

"I didn't know you offered room service, Thomas," Stone said.

"I took Jim Forrester up some food; took him his dinner last night, too, but he couldn't keep it down."

"He's sick?"

"As a dog. I tried to get him to let me call the doctor, but he said he'd be all right. He did look a little better this morning, but not much."

"He said something yesterday about not feeling well."

"At least he cleaned up after himself," Thomas said. "The maids hate it when folks get sick all over the place."

"Is there a bug going around?"

"He ate some conch from one of those street vendors in the capital yesterday. Don't you ever do that, Stone, not unless I point out the good ones."

"I promise."

They raced into the airport and across the tarmac, where Chester was waiting next to his airplane with the baggage compartment standing open. There was one other passenger, a black woman, already aboard. Thomas hustled Libby's bags into the airplane and locked the compartment, then shook hands with Libby.

"You come back when you can stay longer," he said.

Stone shook her hand, too. "You find yourself a good broker and invest that money conservatively," he said to her. Her answer was drowned out by an engine starting. He helped her into the airplane, got her seat belt fastened, and closed the rear door.

Libby held up the Federal Express envelope and gave him a thumbs up, then she stuck it back into her handbag. The airplane began to move, and Stone stepped out of its way.

Thomas turned toward the car. "Let's go," he said; "I want to get back to work."

"Hang on just a minute, will you, Thomas?" Stone

replied, watching the airplane. "I just want to be absolutely sure she's really gone."

Thomas laughed. "Glad to have her off the island, huh?"

"I can't tell you how glad." He pointed at the airplane. "Look, Chester must really be in a hurry; he's not even doing his runup check." The little twin was already rolling down the runway.

The two men stood and watched as Chester roared off the runway and got the landing gear up. The airplane turned north toward Antigua, visible in the distance across the channel separating the two islands. The early morning sun glinted on the water.

"There goes a happy woman," Stone said, waving. "Good-bye, Libby!" He turned toward the car. As he did, he noticed a change in the sound of the engines, and he looked back at the airplane. "What was that?" he asked.

Thomas looked at the airplane, now out over the water. "He's just reducing power after takeoff. It's only a few minutes' flight, and he has to start slowing down if he wants to make Antigua on the first pass." Thomas frowned. "What's that?" he asked, pointing. Smoke was trailing from the airplane's left engine.

"Looks like Chester's got a problem," Stone said. "He must have already shut down the engine."

"I see flames," Thomas said.

Stone shielded his eyes from the morning sun. "So do I," he said. The airplane began a rapid descent toward the water.

"Why doesn't he return here?" Thomas asked.

"He's trying to blow out the fire," Stone said.

"When I was training for my license, that's what I was taught to do with an engine fire, a power-on descent, to blow it out." The airplane seemed to be headed straight down into the sea, and then it leveled off. "The fire isn't out," Stone said. "He's going to ditch in the water."

"Jesus help him," Thomas said.

"If the engine doesn't blow and he can get the airplane down, they've got a good chance." He looked at the wind sock; it was standing straight out. "There's going to be a chop on the surface, though. Put her into the wind, Chester."

The airplane was flying level, just off the surface of the water now.

"Why doesn't he put her down?" Thomas asked. "He's still flying."

"He's bleeding off air speed; he'd built up a lot on the descent. He wants to touch down right at stall speed, as slowly as it will still fly. Look, he's raising the nose now; he'll be down in a second."

"I hope he's got a raft," Thomas said. "It's going to take a while to get to him."

"Surely he has; he'd have to. Here comes touch-down; don't stall the thing, Chester!"

The nose came up some more and the airplane headed toward landing. Then a wing dropped, touched the water, and the airplane cartwheeled, breaking into pieces.

"Oh, shit," Stone said, watching as the wreckage scattered over the water.

"Come on," Thomas called, running for the car. "I know a man with a boat."

Stone jumped into the car and Thomas, driving like

a madman, headed out of the airport and along the coast road. "There's a little fishing settlement along the coast, right near where Chester went down," he said.

"Thomas," Stone said, "nobody on that airplane is alive; don't kill us in the bargain."

Thomas slowed a little. "Somebody might have made it," he said.

"They might have if he'd gotten the thing down in one piece," Stone said quietly. "But when it broke up, that ended it. Anybody alive would be unconscious, and anybody unconscious would have drowned by now."

"Still," Thomas said. He threw the car into a left turn and careened down a short dirt road, screeching to a stop at a small dock. A man was already taking in the lines on a fishing boat. "Henry!" Thomas yelled, "wait for me!" He and Stone jumped onto the moving boat. "You saw the plane?" Thomas asked the skipper.

"Everybody saw the plane," Henry replied. "We're goin', but cain't be nobody alive out there. How many folks was on it?"

"Three, including Chester."

"Chester gone," Henry said. "They all gone."

Twenty minutes later they saw the first piece of wreckage—a wing tip, floating on the surface; then smaller bits of flotsam.

"Look," Thomas said, pointing to some woven straw in the water. "That's Libby's hat, I think."

"There somebody is," Henry called out, pointing and changing course. "Peter, get the boathook!" His crewman got the tool and ran forward as Henry slowed the boat. "It's Chester," Thomas said.

"He's missing an arm," Stone said quietly.

It took fifteen minutes in the swells to get a line around the body, and Stone was feeling a little queasy from the motion. He had seen enough bodies as a cop to be unruffled by the sight of Chester. The body aboard and covered, they patrolled the area for another two hours, but, except for the floating wing tip, which they brought aboard, found nothing larger than Libby's hat. A police boat joined them.

"I reckon we go in now," Henry said.

"How deep is the water out here?" Stone asked.

"Deep. We outside the hundred-fathom line." He pointed to their position on his chart.

"How much of a search will there be?" Stone asked.

"You're looking at it, I expect," Thomas replied. "I reckon the two women must still be in the fuselage, but there's no National Transportation Safety Board to go after the wreckage and the bodies, not down here in the islands. They're gone." They headed back toward the dock with their grisly cargo.

Stone thought about Libby Manning and her new-found wealth, which she would never spend.

30

*S*tone poured himself some orange juice and sat down at a table. After a moment, Hilary Kramer from the *New York Times* came downstairs.

"Morning, Stone," she said. "May I join you?"

"Please do," Stone replied.

Thomas came over with menus. "What can I get you folks?" he asked quietly.

Kramer ordered bacon and eggs. "I'm hungry this morning," she said.

"Stone, you want something?" Thomas asked.

"Just toast and coffee; I'm not very hungry."

"You're looking kind of grim, Stone," Kramer said. "Something else go wrong with your case?"

Stone shook his head. "Plane crash this morning. Thomas and I saw it."

Kramer dipped into her handbag and came up with

a notebook. At that moment, Jim Forrester joined them, looking not very well.

"Morning, Stone, Hilary," he said.

"Morning, Jim," Stone said. "You want some breakfast?"

Forrester shook his head. "Thomas was kind enough to bring me something in my room this morning."

"Oh, yes," Stone said. "He said you were ill; you're looking better."

"Guess I got it out of my system," the journalist said. "Hilary, take my advice; stay away from the street vendors in the capital, especially the ones selling conch. For a while there, I thought I was going to die."

"Apparently someone did, only this morning," Kramer said. "Stone was just about to tell me about it."

"Yeah," Stone said. "Chester's plane went down; two passengers aboard; everybody died."

"Jesus," Forrester said. "In that plane we all came over in?"

"That's the one."

"It looked in pretty good shape," Forrester said.

"Thomas and I watched them take off," Stone replied. "Chester didn't do a runup before he leapt off."

"What's a runup?" Forrester asked.

"With piston engines, you rev up to a couple of thousand rpms, then test the magnetos and the propeller and look for low oil pressure or other problems. It's the last thing you do before takeoff, and it's a very important check."

"Any idea what happened?" Kramer asked.

"Engine fire; we saw the flames. He dived to try and

blow out the fire, and when he couldn't he ditched in the water, but he stalled and cartwheeled. We saw the airplane come apart. We went out in a boat and found Chester's body, but the two women apparently went down with the fuselage."

"Who were the two women?" Kramer asked, scribbling in shorthand.

"One was a local lady; don't know her name; the other was Elizabeth Manning of Palm Beach. She stayed here last night."

"The lady in the straw hat?" Forrester asked.

"That's the one."

"Any relation to Allison Manning?" Kramer asked.

"Not really; she was Paul Manning's ex-wife."

"What was she doing here?"

"I think she had some idea of claiming part of Manning's estate," Stone said. "But that's all being handled in Connecticut, so she went home."

"Did she have some legitimate claim?" Kramer asked.

"Not that I'm aware of," Stone said. He was skating close to a line here, but he hadn't quite crossed it.

"Palm Beach, you said?"

"That's right."

"What did she do there?"

"She said she wrote a society column for one of the local papers."

"That's all you know about her?"

"That's it," Stone said.

"Is there going to be some sort of investigation of the accident?" Kramer asked.

"Beats me," Stone said, "but the airplane went

down in water deeper than a hundred fathoms, so I doubt if they could find much of it, even with a load of experts, which they don't seem to have around here."

"That's over six hundred feet," Forrester said. "No diver could go that deep; they'd need some sort of submersible, I think."

"Something the St. Marks Navy, if there is one, probably doesn't have," Kramer chipped in. "Do you know if she had any family?"

"She didn't say, but I got the impression she was unmarried. Her passport was still in the name of Manning, and they had probably been divorced for a good ten years."

"How long had Manning been married to Allison when he died?"

"Four years."

"Did the two women know each other?"

"They never met."

"You think the other Mrs. Manning just came down here in the hope of money, then?"

"Seems that way, but please don't quote me as having said so."

"Is somebody notifying next of kin?"

"I suppose the local police will handle that."

"Stone," Forrester said, "do you think she might have been some sort of help to you at Allison's trial?"

Stone shook his head. "I can't imagine how. I don't think she had seen Paul since the divorce."

"Did Sir Winston Sutherland know she was here?" Kramer asked.

Stone shrugged. "I don't think so. He was here for dinner last night; she was sitting with me, and they didn't speak."

"I take it you didn't introduce them," Kramer said dryly.

"I'm not the social director around here," Stone said with a straight face.

Kramer laughed. "Can't say I blame you."

"I suppose it will make an interesting footnote to my piece," Forrester said.

"I haven't seen you taking any notes," Kramer observed.

"I have a very good memory," Forrester said. Then he frowned, placed a hand on his belly, and stood up quickly. "Uh-oh," he said, then ran for the stairs.

"I guess he wasn't feeling as well as he thought," Kramer said.

"I guess not," Stone agreed.

"Stone, you've answered all of my questions, but why do I have the feeling there's something you haven't told me?"

"About what?"

"About this Elizabeth Manning?"

"I never saw the woman before yesterday; never heard of her, either."

"Did she demand money from Allison?"

Not until after her lawyer had made her an offer, Stone reflected. "No," he replied.

"Was she headed for Connecticut to pursue something with the estate?"

"Not to my knowledge," he said.

"If she had, would she have had a claim?"

"There's no mention of her in Paul Manning's will."

Kramer closed her notebook. "Well, I'll phone this in after breakfast."

•

They ate their food in silence, then Thomas waved some papers at Stone, and he went to the bar.

"Fax for you," Thomas said.

Stone took a stool and read through Libby Manning's divorce decree, then he laughed out loud.

"What?" Thomas asked.

"Nothing," Stone replied. "By the way, did Libby Manning make any phone calls last night?"

"Nope; no calls on her bill. Anyway, you told me to unplug her phone."

"Right." Stone was looking at Libby's divorce decree, at the instructions for alimony. "Plaintiff shall pay to the defendant the sum of three thousand dollars a month on the first day of every month," he read, "beginning immediately and continuing for a period of ten years." He checked the date on the decree. Libby Manning's alimony had run out three weeks earlier. She must have been desperate, he thought, but she had been cool enough to shake down Allison for four hundred thousand dollars, with his help.

He walked away shaking his head.

31

As Stone walked back toward the marina he could not stop thinking about Libby Manning. He was depressed, and he felt guilty, though he could not think why. Certainly a human being was dead, one he had known; but not one he had known well or had come to care about. So why couldn't he shake the feeling? He boarded *Expansive* and went below. Allison was putting something away in a cupboard.

"Libby Manning is dead," he said.

"Come again? I don't think I heard you right."

"Libby is dead. Chester crashed shortly after takeoff this morning, and Libby and a local woman were killed, along with Chester."

She stood, staring at him for a long moment. "Dead," she repeated tonelessly. "No chance she might still be alive?"

"The airplane went down in at least six hundred feet of water. Chester's body was recovered, but nobody else."

Allison sank onto a sofa, looking as if the wind had been knocked out of her. "How could this have happened?" she asked.

"There was an engine fire, but nobody knows why, and my guess is that nobody is going to know. In order to figure out what made an airplane crash, you need the airplane, or at least a lot of it, and a wing tip was all that was recovered."

"Some sort of mechanical problem, then?"

"Apparently."

"What could cause such a problem?"

"A fuel leak, maybe. I have no idea what sort of rules a pilot like Chester would operate under on this island, but my guess is he was pretty much on his own. He'd have had the manufacturer's service requirements to go by, but I doubt if there was anybody looking over his shoulder." He looked at her. "Are you feeling all right?"

"I'm fine," she said, but she didn't sound it. "I'm just shocked, I guess. Three people dead."

Stone sat down beside her. "It is pretty depressing," he agreed.

"Maybe I shouldn't be depressed," Allison said. "After all, her death saves me four hundred thousand dollars."

"Maybe," he replied.

"Maybe? Why maybe? Didn't our agreement and my check go down with her?"

"I suppose so."

"Then why maybe?"

"Strictly speaking, that money was hers, and her heirs are entitled to it."

"Heirs? Libby had heirs?"

"I've no idea, but let's say, for example, she had a sister, and she left a will leaving everything to her. She'd be entitled to the four hundred thousand. Even if Libby died intestate, that is, without a will, her next of kin would be in line for it."

"But there's nothing. The check and the agreement went with her."

"Suppose she called this putative sister last night and said, 'Guess what? I just got four hundred grand, and I'm going to give you some.' And she told her sister where and how she got it. Suppose she mailed a copy of the agreement, or the agreement itself, to the sister. Then the sister would come after you, because she'd have evidence of an agreement to pay, but no payment."

"But you don't know if there is a sister."

"No, and Libby didn't make any phone calls last night, according to Thomas, who would have a record of it if she had. She didn't mail anything this morning either, as far as I know."

"So I'm safe."

"If you want to be."

"What do you mean by that?"

"I mean, the proper thing to do would be to search out Libby's executor, if she has one, and pay him the money. Then he could distribute it to any heirs or family she may have had."

"And suppose she didn't have any heirs or family?"

"Then it would go to the state of Florida, which is where she resided."

DEAD IN THE WATER

"So you're suggesting I should give the state of Florida four hundred thousand dollars in Libby's memory? So they could, maybe, put a statue of her in front of the state capitol?"

"No, but I could have a search for heirs or family done. Then, at least, you'd know."

"I don't want to know," Allison said. "I think that in the circumstances, that's a ridiculous idea."

"If it will help, I'll add to the circumstances," he said, handing her a document. "That's Libby and Paul's divorce decree. The judge gave her ten years of alimony, and the ten years expired earlier this month."

Allison read the paragraph. "So she was bluffing?"

"Looks that way."

"She had no claim to the estate whatever, and she had the gall to come down here and extort four hundred thousand dollars out of me?"

"She didn't extort anything; she responded to an offer, an offer I made her, with your permission, because of circumstances she knew nothing about."

"So you're saying she just got lucky; that she happened to be at the right time and at the right place to come into four hundred thousand dollars of my money."

"I think that's accurate. And while you're at it, you might remember that it was I who advised you to pay her off."

"Stone, I understand why you gave me that advice and, in the circumstances, I think it was the right advice. I'm not angry with you, I promise."

"I'm glad you understand all that," Stone replied, "because I think I gave you the right advice, too."

"And now you're advising me to search out Libby's relatives and give them the money."

"I'm not really giving you advice now; I'm just pointing out to you the legal and ethical burdens of your situation."

"But if I just forget about Libby and the agreement and the check, and if I tell you, my lawyer, to forget about it, then . . ."

"Then you can keep your four hundred thousand dollars, and the ethical requirements of the attorney-client relationship would prevent me from disclosing any of this to Libby's heirs."

"Did you tell anyone else in the world about that agreement?"

"No. Thomas witnessed it, though."

"Did he read it?"

"No. If someone subpoenaed him and questioned him in court, he could testify that he witnessed a document, but he could not say what it contained."

"Then from a legal point of view, my position is airtight, isn't it?"

"I'll put it this way: if someone, a relative, an heir, a lawyer, turned up here or in Greenwich and tried to press a claim against you or the estate, he would have no grounds on which to proceed. No grounds that I'm aware of, anyway."

"So I have no legal obligation to Libby's heirs?"

"Yes, you do have such an obligation, but it is unknown to anyone outside the attorney-client relationship, and if it were known it would very probably be unenforceable, unless someone had a copy of the agreement. You also have a moral obligation, but whether or not you meet it would depend on the condition of your morals."

"So you're advising me to pay the money to her heirs, if they exist."

"As your attorney, I am required to make you aware of your obligations under the agreement that you signed."

"But you can't make me meet those obligations."

"No, I can't. Probably no one can."

"The condition of my morals," she said, thinking about that. "What about the condition of your morals?"

Stone blinked. "What?"

"You've got a woman back in New York, or in L.A., or wherever the hell she is, and you're supposed to be in love with her, but you come down to the islands and jump the first widow you lay eyes on, right?" She didn't wait for him to answer. "And you're a lawyer who's fucking his client, not that I'm complaining. Is there some canon of legal ethics that covers that?"

Stone felt his ears getting hot. "Not the first part of your contention," he said, aware that he was sounding legalistic and officious, but unable to help himself, "but as to the second part, as far as I'm concerned, there is no ethical requirement for me not to fuck you, unless my fucking you would somehow react to the detriment of your legal position."

She burst out laughing.

"I don't think that's particularly funny," he said, knowing how ridiculous he must have sounded.

"Oh, yes, it is!" she shrieked. "It's the funniest thing I ever heard in my life." She began to get herself under control again. "It's also very sweet," she said, wiping the tears from her cheeks, "and I love you for it." She moved closer to him and placed a hand on his face. "I know now, if I didn't before, that I have the most legally and ethically proper attorney in the world." She kissed him. "And you just cannot imagine how that turns me on."

She continued to kiss him, then she showed him how turned on she was.

Later, when Allison was asleep, Stone walked back to the Shipwright's Arms and called Bob Cantor.

"Hello."

"It's Stone. Thanks for the divorce decree."

"No problem."

"I'd like to dig up some more information on Elizabeth Allison Manning. It's probably going to be best to find a reliable PI in Palm Beach and let him spend a day on it."

"Okay; what, specifically, do you want to know?"

"Next of kin, other relatives."

"Has Ms. Manning clutched her chest and turned blue?"

"Worse. Plane crash, this morning."

"I see."

"Don't break the news to anybody you find; we'll let the official channels do that."

"Gotcha."

Stone hung up, walked back to the marina, undressed, and crawled into bed with Allison, who was glad to see him.

CHAPTER

32

*S*tone sat in his rented room over the Shipwright's Arms, staring at the screen of his computer, trying to write an opening statement for Allison's trial, even though he knew that Leslie Hewitt intended to open himself. He felt that he had to be ready with something if Leslie should suddenly veer off into one of his lapses. He had nearly finished a draft when there was a knock on the door.

"Stone," Thomas's voice called from the hallway.

"Come in, Thomas."

Thomas opened the door. "There're two policemen downstairs wanting you; they wouldn't tell me what it was about, but they took my guest registration forms for the past week."

Stone saved his document and shut down the computer. "Let's see what they want," he said. He followed Thomas downstairs to the open-air bar where two starched and pressed black officers waited. "I'm Stone Barrington, gentlemen," he said. "What can I do for you?"

The taller of the two nodded at an elderly Jaguar in the parking lot. "You must come with us, Mr. Barrington," he said.

"Where are we going?" Stone asked.

"In the car, please."

"Am I under arrest?"

"Get in the car," the man repeated.

Thomas spoke quietly. "Do it; I'll find out where they take you."

Stone walked toward the car without another word. The shorter officer held the rear door open for him, closed it after him, and got into the driver's seat; his tall companion sat up front, too. The car pulled out of the lot and headed inland, toward the capital.

"Where are we going?" Stone asked.

"Government House," the tall officer said. "You in a lot of trouble, man."

Stone remembered that the jail was in the basement of Government House. "What kind of trouble?"

"You see pretty quick," the man said.

The remainder of the journey passed in silence. Stone wracked his brain for some notion of what they could be arresting him for, but the only motivation he could come up with was that he was representing Allison Manning. Perhaps in St. Marks that was enough.

Eventually, the car entered the little city and drove to its center, passing the front door of Government House and going to the side, to the jail door. Stone got out of the car and, with an officer on each side of him, walked to the door. The booking desk was dead ahead. He wondered what, if anything, Thomas could do about this.

"This way," the tall officer said.

Stone turned to his left and found the officer holding open a door that led to a flight of stairs. He followed the man up two stories, with the short officer bringing up the rear. They emerged into a long, broad hallway, cooled by a row of ceiling fans and open to the air at each end, a tribute to the British desire to remain cool in hot places. The building seemed deserted. They marched to the opposite end of the hall, through a set of double doors, and into a waiting room.

"Wait here," the tall officer said, then went through another door.

Stone looked around him. It was a large room, furnished with well-worn leather furniture, and on the wall was a large portrait of the prime minister, a benevolent-looking man who, Stone guessed, had been in his mid-seventies when he had sat for the portrait. He wondered how long ago that was.

The inner door opened, and the tall officer braced just inside. "This way," he commanded.

Stone walked into a large office, and the officer stepped outside and closed the door behind him. Stone was quite alone in the room. A huge desk dominated the office; a single visitor's chair sat before the desk. In a corner were a round conference table and eight chairs, and the walls were decorated with oils and watercolors, island scenes of a high quality. From somewhere came the muffled sound of a flushing toilet, then, a moment later, a door opened and Sir Winston Sutherland emerged, rubbing his hands briskly with a towel. He was dressed in white linen trousers and a rather loud short-sleeved sport shirt. He discarded the towel and strode toward Stone.

"Ah, Mr. Barrington," he said, extending a huge hand. "How good of you to come."

Stone shook the hand. "It wasn't good of me at all," he said. "I didn't have a choice."

"Oh, I hope the two officers were not officious," Sir Winston said, sounding genuinely concerned.

"Am I under arrest?"

Sir Winston looked shocked. "Of course not, my dear fellow, of course not. This is merely a pretrial meeting between opposing counsel." He walked to a set of French doors and opened them wide, revealing a large balcony that stretched across the rear of the building. "Please come outside, and let's have some lunch."

Stone followed the big man onto the balcony and found a table set quite elegantly for two. A uniformed waiter stood at a loose parade rest to one side.

"Let me get you some refreshment," Sir Winston said, waving a hand at a bar.

"Nothing for me," Stone said.

Sir Winston snapped his fingers, bringing the waiter to stiff attention. "Mr. Barrington and I will have some champagne." He turned to Stone. "Surely I can tempt you with a glass?"

"Oh, all right," Stone said. "Just a glass."

Sir Winston indicated a chair at the table, and Stone took it. A moment later, the waiter was pouring Veuve Clicquot into two crystal flutes.

"Your health," Stone said, sipping the wine. It was perfectly chilled. He looked out at the vista, which was over the better part of the town, with green hills beyond and the sea shining in the distance. "Lovely," he said.

Sir Winston sat down opposite him. "Yes, we are fortunate on our island," he said. "God has given us great beauty on all sides."

Perhaps not on the side of town harboring the slums, Stone thought. "Oh, yes," he said. The champagne was absolutely perfect.

"Bad crash—Chester's airplane," Stone said.

"Yes, a terrible thing," Sir Winston said, not sounding too sad. "I suppose we'll have to find someone else to start a ferry service to Antigua."

"I suppose," Stone said. "Have the police found any reason for the crash?"

"They're looking into it," Sir Winston said. "I trust you are enjoying your stay with us?"

"I would be enjoying it a great deal more if my original plan of cruising could have been implemented," Stone said.

"Ah, yes, and perhaps the company of the young lady who was to have joined you."

"Quite," Stone replied, beginning to feel slightly British, or at least colonial, in the surroundings.

"I understand she was detained in New York by the unfortunate weather," Sir Winston said sympathetically.

"That is correct," Stone replied, "and then she had to go to Los Angeles on business."

"Leaving you alone to deal with Mrs. Manning's problems."

"As it turned out."

"Tell me, did you know Mrs. Manning prior to coming here?"

"No."

"Or her late husband?"

"No. I'd heard of him, though; he was quite a well-known author."

"Did she seek you out while at sea, then?"

"She didn't seek me out at all," Stone replied, sipping more champagne. "I had scheduled my cruise some weeks before the Mannings set sail from the Canaries. And I didn't know them."

"No professional connection? No mutual friends who might have referred you to Mrs. Manning?"

"None. I was just sitting on my chartered boat when she sailed in. At that time there was still some hope of my companion joining me."

"And how did you happen to appear at the coroner's inquest?"

"I had nothing else to do," Stone said. "It was the only entertainment available."

Sir Winston smiled broadly. "Entertainment, eh? I like that: a coroner's inquest as entertainment."

"Tell me, Sir Winston, how did you happen to attend the inquest? Wasn't it perhaps overkill for the minister of justice to participate in such an event?"

"We are a small island, Mr. Barrington," Sir Winston replied smoothly. "But enough of this chat," he said, taking a slip of paper from his pocket and unfolding it. "Tell me—who, exactly, is, or perhaps I should say was, Elizabeth Allison Manning?"

Stone took a long swallow of his champagne. *Oh, shit,* he thought.

33

Sir Winston stared across the table at Stone, waiting for an answer. Stone thought fast, but there was not much he could do in the way of obfuscation. Sir Winston had seen him at dinner with Libby Manning and had, no doubt, noticed the passing of documents between them. He decided to follow Mark Twain's advice: when in doubt, tell the truth.

"Elizabeth Manning was the first wife of Paul Manning," Stone said.

Sir Winston's eyebrows went up. "Ahhhh," he breathed. "Not a sister or a cousin, but an ex-wife?"

"Yes."

"Tell me, Mr. Barrington, how many ex-wives did Paul Manning have?"

"Just the one, to my knowledge."

"And what brought the first Mrs. Manning to our beautiful island?"

"Your beautiful island, I expect; and, perhaps, some curiosity about the death of Paul Manning. She'd read about it in the American papers, you see, and she wondered if she could be of any assistance."

"Ah, yes," Sir Winston said, an edge in his voice. "It seems a great many people read about Mr. Manning's death in the American papers. I have heard from a number of them, including Senators Dodd and Lieberman of Connecticut."

"Yes, I believe Mr. Manning was a very substantial contributor to the Democratic Party," he lied, "and a personal friend of the President and Mrs. Clinton." The champagne was taking effect now, and he had trouble keeping a straight face.

"Indeed?"

"Yes, I've heard that the president is an avid reader of Mr. Manning's books." He stopped himself from adding that Paul Manning was also an investor in the Whitewater real estate venture and a financial advisor to the First Lady.

Sir Winston cleared his throat loudly. "To return to the first Mrs. Manning, what business did you and she discuss during her visit?"

Stone wondered if, somehow, Libby's copy of the agreement had been found. "Sir Winston," he said, "I am sure you understand that I am bound by the confidentiality strictures of the attorney-client relationship, but I think it would not be untoward for me to tell you that Elizabeth Manning, who was not a wealthy woman, had some notion of participating in her former husband's estate. He had been paying alimony to her during the past ten years, a requirement of their divorce decree which had recently expired."

"And did she participate in Mr. Manning's estate?"

"Elizabeth Manning was disappointed to learn that she had not been mentioned in Mr. Manning's will, and, the requirement for alimony having expired, she was entitled to nothing further."

"So why were you and Mrs. Manning exchanging documents at dinner the other evening?"

"I can tell you only that the second Mrs. Manning, being of a kind nature, felt moved to improve the reduced circumstances of the first Mrs. Manning."

"Improve to what extent?"

"I'm afraid that client confidentiality prevents me from saying more."

Sir Winston stared at him for a long moment, then nodded at the waiter, who disappeared and came back with two platters of lobster salad. Sir Winston ate his lobster, sipped his champagne, and stared out to sea.

Stone ate his lunch, too, grateful for the opportunity to collect his thoughts. Clearly, Sir Winston had believed that he might turn the presence, or perhaps even the death, of Elizabeth Manning to his advantage in court. Stone was happy to disappoint him.

Sir Winston finished his lobster and sat back in his chair. "What else do you know of Elizabeth Manning?" he asked. "There is the matter of notification of next of kin, you see, and lacking her passport or other documents, we are somewhat at a loss as to how to proceed."

"I know that Elizabeth Manning made her home in Palm Beach, Florida . . ."

"But you said that she was not a wealthy woman," Sir Winston interrupted. "I should think that living in Palm Beach would be a very expensive matter. I have visited that city, you see."

Stone shrugged. "Every American city, even the wealthiest, has neighborhoods that house those who are employed by the wealthy. I do not have Mrs. Manning's address, but I am sure that she must have lived in such a neighborhood. She told me that she was employed by a small newspaper to write a column about Palm Beach society. It gave her a sort of entree to social events, but I imagine that her nose was very much pressed against the shop window of that society."

"Mmmm," Sir Winston mused.

"I should think her address would be on her hotel registration card," Stone said, "and that the nearest American consulate could be of assistance in tracing her next of kin."

"Of course," Sir Winston replied. "That is all being taken care of."

"If I can be of any further assistance in making inquiries, let me know."

"No, no; that won't be necessary."

Coffee and petit fours appeared on the table, and both men helped themselves.

"Tell me, Stone, if I may call you that?"

"Please do."

He smiled broadly. "And you may call me Winston, of course. Tell me, just what is in all this for you?"

"In all what?"

"The trial, your, ah, services to the second Mrs. Manning."

"We have not discussed a fee, Winston," Stone replied. He had no doubt of what Sir Winston meant by "services."

Sir Winston allowed himself a small smile. "But, I take it, you have accepted a retainer of sorts?"

"I'm afraid I don't know what you mean," said Stone, putting on his best poker face.

"I'm reliably informed that the second Mrs. Manning has taken you into her . . . confidence."

"I am her attorney; she would be foolish not to take me into her confidence."

Sir Winston smiled again. "While I do not wish to be indelicate, reports have reached me that you have been seen entering and leaving Mrs. Manning's very beautiful yacht at, shall we say, odd hours."

Stone tried to appear confused. "I'm sorry, I don't know what this has to do with my representing Mrs. Manning."

"Then I will be blunt," Sir Winston said, clearly out of patience, "I believe that you have been providing services to Mrs. Manning which are above and beyond those which might be construed as legal."

Stone, cornered, decided to tack. "Winston, where did you attend law school, if I might ask?"

Sir Winston pulled himself up to his considerable full height. "I read law at Oxford," he said.

"At Oxford University, in the town of the same name, in England?" Stone asked, sounding surprised.

"The very same."

"Then, with such an illustrious legal background, perhaps you could provide me with some precedent for a prosecutor—let alone a minister of justice—indulging in such conjecture with a defense attorney."

"Sir," Sir Winston said, leaning forward, "you are fucking the lady, aren't you?"

"Is that why I was brought here?" Stone demanded. "To indulge your prurient curiosity?" He stood up.

"Sir," he said, "neither my sex life nor hers is your proper concern. Rather, you should be concerned with this extremely strange prosecution of an innocent and bereaved woman for a crime which she could never have committed." He threw down his napkin and left, in the highest dudgeon he could manage.

"You listen to me, Barrington!" Sir Winston called after him, following him through the large office and the reception room into the hallway. "When this trial is over—and maybe even before—you are going to come to a reckoning with me!" His voice echoed down the long hallway.

Stone kept his eyes straight ahead, down the hall and the stairs into the street, expecting to be arrested at any moment. He flagged a cab and dove into it. Not until he was a block away did he allow himself to look back to see if he was being pursued.

CHAPTER

34

Stone directed the taxi out to the coast road and Sir Leslie Hewitt's house, then asked the driver to wait for him, hoping that Hewitt might have some explanation for the meeting he had just attended. He knocked at the open door and called out, but no one answered. He walked through the little house to the rear garden and there found Leslie Hewitt at lunch with Allison Manning. He stopped and stared at both of them; this seemed even weirder than his own lunch with Sir Winston.

"Ah, Stone," Hewitt called out, waving him over. "Come and join us, have some lunch."

Stone sat down. "Thank you, Leslie, but I've already had lunch. What's going on?" he asked Allison as much as Hewitt.

"I thought I might discuss some of the finer points of the case with my . . . excuse me, our client."

"It's very kind of you to include me in the possessive pronoun, Leslie, but may I remind you . . ." He stopped himself. "Allison, do you think I could have a few minutes alone with Leslie?"

"Of course," she said, standing up. "I was just going to the little girls' room, anyway."

"How did you get here?" he asked.

"I took a taxi."

"I've got one waiting; we'll be leaving in just a minute."

"I'm not sure I'm ready to leave," she said.

"I said, we're leaving," he said, trying to hold his temper.

She turned and, without another word, walked into the house.

"Leslie," Stone said, "what is Allison doing here?"

"I invited her to lunch," Hewitt said. "Is there something wrong with that?"

"Leslie, may I remind you that I am Allison's attorney, and you are a consultant on the case, hired to help me with the local judiciary at the trial. You are not the lead attorney, and I must ask you not to have meetings with my client from which I am excluded."

"Of course I'm the lead attorney," Hewitt said. "You vouched that to the court yourself."

"Only because local law requires a local attorney," Stone said. "I am still making the decisions in this case."

Hewitt shrugged. "As you wish," he said blandly.

"Thank you. By the way, I have just come from a command lunch with Sir Winston Sutherland."

"Oh, you must have lunched very well indeed," Hewitt said. "Winston always lays on a good spread with the taxpayers' money." He looked at Stone. "What did he want?"

"I was hoping you, with your knowledge of the locals, could tell me. We ended up shouting at each other."

"Stone, I must tell you that in St. Marks, we place the highest possible value on civility among members of the bar. You should not have shouted at Winston."

"I'm sorry, but he shouted first . . . sort of."

"Winston is not a man to be dallied with," Hewitt said.

"I didn't dally with him."

"He could be a very dangerous man to insult. I hope you did not insult him."

"I tried not to, but he really began to get up my nose."

"I sincerely hope he does not decide to retaliate," Hewitt said sadly. "It could be the end of Allison."

"Oh, Jesus, Leslie, don't tell me that," Stone moaned.

"Tell you what?" Hewitt said.

"Tell me . . ." He looked closely at the old man. His eyes had taken on that glazed look again. "Oh, never mind."

Allison came out the back door and came to the table.

"I'm afraid that was as long as I could take in the powder room," she said. "I did everything I could think of."

Stone stood up. "We have to be going," he said.

"Oh, don't go," Hewitt cried. "Please introduce me to this beautiful young woman."

Allison turned and looked closely at Hewitt. "What?"

"Leslie," Stone said, "thank you for your hospital-

•
215

ity, but we have to go now. We'll see you soon." He took the protesting Allison by the arm and steered her through the house. In the cab he leaned back and wiped his face with his handkerchief.

"What was that all about?" Allison demanded. "What did he mean, introduce me? Doesn't he know who I am anymore?"

"Allison, please be quiet until we get to the yacht," Stone said through clenched teeth, pointing at the driver. They made the rest of the trip in silence.

Back aboard *Expansive,* Allison practically stamped her foot. "Now tell me, what was that all about?"

"You first," Stone said, getting himself a beer from the fridge. "What were you doing at Leslie's house?"

"He invited me to lunch," she said, "and sent a taxi for me."

"Allison, I don't want you ever to meet alone with Leslie again."

"And why not? Isn't he representing me?"

"He is a consultant; I am representing you. Leslie is not . . . the man he once was."

"Is that why he didn't seem to recognize me?"

"Yes."

"You mean he's . . . gaga?"

"At times."

"I'm being represented by a lawyer who's gaga?"

"You're being represented by me. Leslie is simply advising me on the local judicial system."

"Well, he was talking to me as if he were my only lawyer in the world," she said. "He made me go through the whole story again, and in the greatest possible detail."

·
216

"I'm sorry that happened, but you should not have gone to see him without me."

"And speaking of you, where the hell were you?"

"Two policemen showed up this morning and dragged me to Sir Winston Sutherland's office."

"Why?"

"I'm not sure; I think he was fishing for something he could use. He asked a lot of questions about Libby."

"And what did you tell him about her?"

"The truth, but without the financial details."

"God, how could you do that?"

"Why shouldn't I answer his questions? We've nothing to lose by telling him the truth about her. Believe me, this is no time to start lying to the local authorities."

"What did he want to know?"

"Mostly, he wanted to know about next of kin. I think he's having trouble notifying someone about her death."

"Well, that's not our responsibility, is it?"

"I told him where she was from and suggested he get in touch with the nearest American consulate."

"He couldn't figure that out by himself?"

"Apparently not."

"What if he starts talking to her relatives?" she asked.

"What if he does? That doesn't matter to us, does it?" She didn't reply.

"Does it? Allison, is there something you haven't told me about Libby?"

"No, certainly not," she said.

"Because this is no time to start withholding information from your lawyer. I need to know everything there is to know."

"You do. I mean, I've told you everything I know about her."

"I certainly hope so, because I don't want to get into that courtroom tomorrow and have Sir Winston raise something I've never heard about. You do understand the necessity of my being fully prepared, don't you?"

"Of course I do," she cried. Now she was really getting upset; there were tears in her eyes.

"All right, all right, don't cry," he said. He hated it when women cried; he didn't know what to do. "Everything will be all right, as long as I know everything I need to know." He put his arms around her.

"I wouldn't lie to you," she sobbed. "Why don't you believe me?"

"I do believe you, really I do," he whispered. "It's going to be all right, don't worry." He hoped that was the truth, because he was very, very worried himself.

35

*H*aving placated Allison, Stone returned to the Shipwright's Arms to continue working on his opening statement for the trial. As he entered, Thomas beckoned.

"Bob Cantor called you," he said.

"I'll call him from my room," Stone said, then ran up the stairs, let himself in, and dialed the number.

"Cantor."

"Bob, it's Stone."

"Thanks for calling; I've got some stuff on Elizabeth Manning, but I didn't think you'd want me to fax it."

"What is it?"

"A guy I know is on the Palm Beach force, and he did a little moonlighting for me. Elizabeth Manning is, rather was, something of a gadfly in the town—a hanger-on, sponger, whatever you want to call it. She writes this column for a newspaper—an advertising sheet, really—and she practically lives on the food she gets at parties."

"Any family?"

"A mother."

"Did your man find out anything about her?"

"She's a widow in her early seventies; name is Marla Peters, a former actress, ill much of the last ten years with MS. She lives on Social Security and what she earns playing the piano in a hotel lobby at tea time for tips, plus what her daughter brought in. The two of them shared an apartment."

"Nobody else at all? A brother or sister?"

"Nobody. My guy is sure of that; he talked with the mother."

"He didn't tell her anything about the crash?"

"Nope; I didn't tell him. He told her he needed some information about some society type from her daughter, asked her to have Elizabeth call him when she got home."

Stone sat, thinking about the woman, imagining her taking requests from other old ladies for dollar tips in some faded Palm Beach hotel, scraping by on Social Security.

"Stone, you still there?"

"Yeah, Bob; I'm sorry, I was lost in thought there for a moment."

"Anything else you need?"

"No, not at the moment; I'll call you if I do."

"Sure; see you later."

Stone hung up, depressed. Before he could move, the phone rang again. "Hello?"

It was Thomas. "Stone, there's somebody named

Harley Potter on the phone; says he's a lawyer, wants to talk to you."

Now what? "Okay, put him through."

"Hello?"

"Good afternoon, Mr. Barrington; my name is Harley Potter of the law firm of Potter and Potter, of Palm Beach, Florida." The voice was elderly, courtly.

"What can I do for you, Mr. Potter?"

"I understand you are the attorney for the estate of Paul Manning."

"No, that's incorrect. I represent Mr. Manning's widow in . . . another matter. I believe the estate is being handled by a firm in Greenwich, Connecticut." He gave the man the name of the firm.

There was a long silence.

"Is there something else I can do for you?"

"I wonder, Mr. Barrington, have you, during the past few days, had occasion to meet a Mrs. Elizabeth Manning?"

"Yes, I have. She arrived in St. Marks the day before yesterday."

"Ah, good; I wonder if you could tell me where she's staying?"

"Do you represent Mrs. Manning?"

"I represent her mother, who is an old friend. Usually, when Libby travels, she keeps in close telephone contact with her mother, but nothing has been heard from her, and Mrs. Peters—that's her mother—is concerned."

"Mr. Potter, I'm afraid I have some very bad news. Mrs. Manning was killed yesterday in an airplane crash. She was on her way home to Palm Beach."

"Oh, dear God!" the man cried, more upset than

STUART WOODS

Stone would have expected an attorney to be. "Are you absolutely positive? Could there be any mistake?"

"I'm positive. In fact, I witnessed the crash. It was a light, twin-engined airplane that flies people to Antigua, where they make airline connections. There was an engine fire; the pilot tried to ditch in the water, stalled, and the airplane disintegrated. All three people aboard, Mrs. Manning among them, were killed instantly. I believe the local government has been trying to notify Mrs. Manning's next of kin, but apparently they've not yet contacted Mrs. Peters."

"No, I'm sure they haven't; I spoke with her not ten minutes ago. This is just terrible; Libby's mother is so dependent upon her."

"I suggest you get in touch with the minister of justice in St. Marks, whose name is Sir Winston Sutherland, at Government House in the capital city."

"I shall certainly do that. I will want to make arrangements to bring the body home for burial."

"I'm afraid that two of the three bodies, including Mrs. Manning's, went down with the fuselage of the airplane in deep water. I should think that it is unlikely in the extreme that it will ever be recovered."

"Oh, how terrible."

"Mr. Potter, do you know if Elizabeth Manning had any life insurance?"

"Why do you ask?"

"It occurs to me that you might need an affidavit to establish death. I can supply that, having been a witness, and there was another witness, who I'm sure would be glad to do the same."

"Oh, good. Yes, there was a small insurance policy,

222

little more than enough to cover the burial expenses. You are an attorney, you said?"

"Yes, I practice in New York."

"I suppose there will be an inquest."

"Yes, I should think so."

"I wonder if you would undertake to act for this firm in the matter of obtaining a death certificate and any other legalities which might arise. I'm afraid that Mrs. Peters could not afford to send me down there, and in any case, I would find it physically impossible to make the trip."

"I'm leaving St. Marks to return to New York the middle of next week, but until that time I would be happy to handle any details that might come up, including the death certificate."

"Let me give you my address and phone number."

Stone wrote down the information.

"You may send your bill here."

"I would be glad to render this small service as a courtesy to Mrs. Peters," Stone said.

"You are very kind, sir. Ah . . ." He paused as if unwilling to mention something. "Mr. Barrington, Libby spoke with me before she left, and I was under the very distinct impression that she expected to realize some financial benefit from the estate of her former husband. Are you aware of any such benefit? Even a modest sum would mean the world to Mrs. Peters."

Stone winced. "I am aware that there was no mention of the first Mrs. Manning in Paul Manning's will," he said, "and that the alimony required by his divorce decree had expired."

"Yes, I'm afraid that is correct," Potter said. He sighed deeply. "No bequest, eh?"

"I'm afraid not, but I will raise the subject with Mr. Manning's widow."

"Would you? I would be so very grateful. Mrs. Peters's health is not good, and I'm very much afraid that without her daughter's help she will be unable to afford to stay in her apartment, and I don't know where she would go."

"I'll speak to Mrs. Manning about it," Stone said, "and I'll be in touch with you on my return to New York next week."

"Good. I won't mention this to Mrs. Peters until I hear from you; I wouldn't want to get her hopes up, you know."

"I understand," Stone said.

"One other thing, could you learn the name of the insurance company representing the owners of the airplane? If it crashed because of a mechanical problem, Mrs. Peters might be eligible for a payment from the policy."

Stone was anxious to get off the phone before he was saddled with any other duties. "Yes, yes, I'll inquire about that."

"I'll look forward to hearing from you, then."

"Good-bye, Mr. Potter."

Stone hung up and lay back on the bed. It was worse than he could have imagined, and he didn't know whether Allison would honor her agreement. He went back to work and tried not to think of the old lady at the piano in Palm Beach.

36

*T*he inquest was held in the same village hall that had been used for the inquest into the death of Paul Manning, the coroner was the same, and the jury was indistinguishable from the first one. The only difference was the absence of Sir Winston Sutherland, who, apparently, could see no political advantage in attending.

Stone and Thomas gave their testimony, and then the mechanic employed by Chester's air taxi service was called and questioned by the coroner.

"State your name," the coroner said.

"Harvey Simpson," the mechanic replied. He was black and appeared to be in his early forties.

"Mr. Simpson, are you a fully qualified aircraft mechanic?"

"Yessir, I am. I done my training in Miami, and I

worked in Fort Lauderdale for eight years before I come home to St. Marks."

"How long had you done mechanical work on Chester Appleton's airplane?"

"For eleven years."

"The same airplane?"

"No, sir; Chester bought this one six years ago."

"Was the airplane in good condition?"

Harvey Simpson straightened in his seat. "Yessir, it certainly was. I did an annual inspection on the airplane last month; I always kept it right up to snuff."

"What about the port engine?"

"That was the newest of the two. I installed it eight months ago, and it only had five hundred and ten hours on it."

"How long is an engine good for?"

"That one was rated for two thousand hours."

"So Chester had only used a quarter of its expected life?"

"That's right, sir."

"At the time of the annual inspection, did you find anything wrong with the engine?"

Harvey Simpson opened a plastic briefcase and removed a book. "I got the engine logbook right here," he said. "There's a list of what I done to it."

"My question was, did you find anything wrong with the engine?"

Simpson consulted the logbook. "I found two exhaust brackets broken. That's a common fault; vibration weakens the metal. I replaced both brackets. The compression on all the cylinders was in the high normal range; that's a pretty good indicator of the health of the engine. All the airworthiness directives and service bulletins were up to date on it."

"We have heard testimony that the engine caught fire; can you think of anything that might have caused this to happen?"

"No, sir," the man said emphatically. "I did a fifty-hour inspection on the engine three days before the crash—that includes an oil change—and there wasn't nothing wrong with it."

"What, in your opinion, could cause an engine fire in that airplane?"

"Leaking fuel would be about the only thing, sir, but I checked all the fuel connections during the fifty-hour inspection, and they was all tight."

"Nothing else could have caused the engine fire?"

"Well, a bad exhaust leak, maybe, but there wasn't no exhaust leaks, either."

"So you have no explanation for the engine fire?"

"No, sir, I don't, and believe you me, I've done some considerable thinking on the subject. If I had the engine back and could inspect it, I might be able to tell you what caused the fire, but . . ."

"Quite," the coroner said. "Does any member of the jury have any questions for Mr. Simpson?"

A tall black man stood up. "I've got a question," he said.

"Go ahead and ask it," the coroner replied.

"Harvey, Alene Sanders, who got killed in that crash, was my wife's sister-in-law. What I want to know is, who's going to pay for killing her?"

Simpson shook his head. "I don't know, Marvin. Chester didn't have nothing but that airplane and his house."

•

"What about insurance?" the man demanded.

Simpson shook his head again. "Chester stopped paying the insurance last year. Said it was too much, it was going to break him."

The man shook his head and sat down. Stone shook his head, too. That answered Harley Potter's question.

"All right, then," said the coroner, "the jury can retire to consider their verdict. I won't recess for another fifteen minutes, because I don't think it's going to take long."

The jury retired, and everyone stood up to stretch. Stone turned to find Hilary Kramer of the *Times* and Jim Forrester of *The New Yorker* in the row behind him.

"What brings you two here?" Stone asked.

"Nothing else to do," Kramer replied. "Not until your case begins. I'll file a short piece on the crash. You happen to know anything about the Manning woman, Stone?"

"As a matter of fact, I had a call from a lawyer in Palm Beach. She left an elderly mother—no other family."

"No insurance for the mother, either," Kramer said, jotting down some notes. "Got the mother's name?"

"Marla Peters; a widow and retired actress."

"Address?"

"No idea."

"The lawyer?"

"Harley Potter of Potter and Potter." He looked at Forrester. "I don't see you taking any notes, Jim."

Forrester grinned. "I'll clip Hilary's piece; it'll all be in there. It'll be no more than a marginal reference in my piece."

•

"I guess not," Stone agreed.

"What was Elizabeth Manning doing down here?" Kramer asked.

"She wanted to know if she was mentioned in Manning's will. She wasn't."

"I heard you and she were looking over some documents in the Shipwright's Arms," she said. "What were they?"

"Paul Manning's will; she wanted to see it."

"When were they divorced?"

"Something like ten years ago, I think."

"When were they married?"

"I don't really know."

"You're a font of information, aren't you?" Kramer said suspiciously. "Is there something you don't want me to know?"

"Hilary," Stone said, "why would I keep information from you?"

She was about to reply, but the jury was returning.

The coroner waited for everyone to be seated, then spoke. "Have you gentlemen reached a verdict? If so, read it."

A man stood up. "We find that Chester Appleton, Alene Sanders, and Elizabeth Allison Manning met their deaths by misadventure," he said, then sat down.

The coroner rapped sharply on his table. "A verdict of death by misadventure having been found, these proceedings are closed."

Stone made his way forward and introduced himself to the coroner.

"Oh, yes, Mr. Barrington, I remember you from an earlier inquest."

"That's right. A law firm representing the next of kin of Mrs. Elizabeth Manning has asked me to act for them in St. Marks. They have requested a copy of the death certificate, so that Mrs. Manning's estate may be probated."

"Of course," the coroner said. "I'll give you an original." He sat down, took a pad of blank certificates from his briefcase, wrote one out, signed it, and handed it to Stone. "There you are," he said. "Nice that this inquest is so much simpler than the last, isn't it?"

"Yes, it is."

He smiled a little. "Not as interesting, though."

Stone smiled with him. "No, I guess it isn't." He shook the man's hand and left the hall. To his relief, the two journalists had disappeared.

Back at the Shipwright's Arms, a fax was waiting for him.

Dear Stone,

Just a quick note to let you know I'm not dead. My research is going well. I've been spending all my time with Vance, who has been a dear. I've been staying at his house, which is very beautiful, and I've met many friends of his. The life out here is really wonderful.

Oh, Chip McGrath at the New York Times Book Review *has asked me to review a big new book on the history of Hollywood and the studios—front page of the review, if you can believe it. It's a nice showcase for me.*

I might stay out here for a week or two

when I finish the piece. This California living gets under your skin.

Got to run. We're off to dinner.

Love,
Arrington

Stone was hurt. After all he'd said to her in his letter, she hadn't even referred to it. Then it hit him: his letter had gone down with Chester's airplane, in Libby Manning's purse. She had never received it. He swore at himself for not remembering that before now. *I'll write her tomorrow,* he thought. *First thing.*

37

*S*tone returned to *Expansive* with some trepidation. He was not looking forward to talking with Allison about this, partly because she did not need additional problems while facing a trial for murder, and partly because he did not relish a scene with her, and he had come to know that she was adept at scenes.

To his surprise, he found her packing.

"Oh, hi," she said, stuffing things into a duffel. There were two others, already full, on the aft cabin bed.

"Going somewhere?" he asked. He really wanted to know.

"Sure," she said, "next week. I didn't have anything to do, so I thought I would get some things together, and then when the trial is over I can get out of here pronto!"

"I don't blame you for wanting to get out of here," he said. "What will you do about the boat?"

"Oh, I don't know; probably take your advice and sell it in Fort Lauderdale. I don't want to think about the boat; I'm sick of it, and once I'm out of here I never want to see it again."

He could understand that, too. "We have to talk for a minute," he said.

"What about?" She kept packing.

"Could you stop that for a minute? I need your full attention."

She stopped packing and sat down on the bed. "Okay, shoot."

He sat down beside her. "I had a call from a lawyer in Palm Beach who represents Libby's mother."

Her eyes widened. "How the hell did he know to call you?"

"Libby told him where she was going, and why; also, he watches television, I guess."

"What did he have to say?"

"He was looking for Libby; her mother hadn't heard from her. He didn't know about the crash."

"Did you tell him?"

"Of course. Sir Winston hadn't been able to find a next of kin. It was the proper thing to do."

"What's this about a mother?"

He sighed. "It's bad. She's in her seventies, and she's had multiple sclerosis for years. She lives on Social Security and what little she makes playing the piano in a Palm Beach hotel, for tips."

She remained expressionless. "Go on."

"She relies on Libby for support. They share an

apartment, and the lawyer thinks the old lady will have to move, and he doesn't know where she'll go." He waited for a response.

There wasn't one. Allison continued to stare at him.

"I told you something like this might come up. Her mother is entitled to her estate."

"She has an estate?"

Oh, God, he thought; this was going to be hard. "The lawyer asked me some questions about any financial arrangements Libby might have with Paul's estate." This was true.

"So you think she might have sent him a copy of the agreement?"

"It's possible." Just. "She could have sent him the original."

"You said she didn't make any phone calls or mail anything."

"I said I didn't know that she did."

"So the lawyer might come after me for the money?"

"That's a possibility; a certainty, if he has the agreement."

"It would cost a lot of money to sue me for it, wouldn't it?"

"Maybe not; you wouldn't have much of a defense; it would be cut and dried." This was not entirely truthful, he thought, but that interpretation might legitimately be placed on the situation.

She put a hand on his knee. "Stone, I know you're worried about this, but I don't want you to be. I'll deal with this after the trial, all right? Don't worry, I'll do the right thing."

"Allison, I'm glad you feel that way, but . . ."

"But what if the trial goes wrong?"

He nodded.

"Well, then, her lawyer can make a claim on my estate, can't he?"

"Yes, I suppose so. It would just be simpler to . . ."

"Not now," she said, and she said it emphatically.

Stone nodded. "By the way, do you have a will?"

"Yes, it's with the lawyer in Greenwich."

"Do you want to make any changes to it? I could draft something for you."

She thought for a minute. "No, I don't think so; it still reflects my wishes. I gave it a lot of thought at the time."

"All right." He stood up. "I'd better get up to my room at the Shipwright's Arms; I've got some work to do." There was a folder lying on the dressing table, the folder he had given Allison containing her copy of the agreement with Libby. He took a step toward it.

"Excuse me," she said. She stepped past him, picked up the folder, and stuffed it into a duffel. "See you later."

He left the boat and started up the dock. As he did, a very modern, fast-looking motor yacht entered the harbor and made for the marina. He stood and watched her. She must have been on the order of eighty feet, and she looked as if she'd do a good fifty knots in the open sea. As he watched she moved into a berth a few yards down, and two smartly dressed crewmen hopped onto the pontoon to make her fast. She was flying a yellow customs flag, and the officer on duty stirred himself from his shack and ambled down to the marina.

Stone continued toward the Shipwright's Arms, and when he was nearly there, he stopped and looked back. The skipper of the yacht, which was called *Race,* was sitting in the cockpit, going over documents with the customs officer. A thought occurred to him; a bad thought. *No,* he said to himself, *Allison wouldn't do that.*

He picked up some Federal Express materials at the bar, stuffed the death certificate into the envelope, addressed it, and left it on the bar, then went up to his room and dialed the law offices of Potter & Potter. An elderly-sounding secretary put him through.

"This is Harley Potter."

"It's Stone Barrington, Mr. Potter."

"Ah, yes, Mr. Barrington; do you have some news for me?"

"Nothing very earthshaking, I'm afraid. The inquest was held this afternoon, and a verdict of death by misadventure was reached."

"I see."

"I obtained a death certificate from the coroner, and it will go out to you by Federal Express."

"Well, that's a relief," Potter said.

"An employee of the man who owned the airplane gave testimony that the airplane and a house were the man's only possessions, and that he had let his insurance lapse last year. I'm afraid there won't be anything to go after."

"I see. You're certain about this?"

"As certain as I can be without conducting a thorough investigation, and I'm afraid I don't have time to do that."

"That will be very bad news for Mrs. Peters," he said.

"I know it will; I'm sorry."

"Have you had an opportunity to speak with the second Mrs. Manning about . . ." He let the sentence die.

"Briefly. She won't be giving the matter any thought until her return to Greenwich next week. I expect she will want to consult her attorney there. Perhaps you'll hear something then; I'll give her your number."

"Won't you be representing her?"

"No, my work will be finished when I leave here next week."

"I see."

"I will be in touch if any further information comes my way."

"Thank you, Mr. Barrington, for your kindness," Potter said. "Good-bye."

"Good-bye, Mr. Potter," Stone replied, then hung up.

He felt sick to his stomach, but there was nothing else he could do in the circumstances. But yes, there was something he could do, he reflected. He telephoned his bank in New York, spoke to an officer he knew.

"I've got a CD maturing about now, haven't I?"

"Yes, Stone, it matured earlier this week. I sent you a notice, and your secretary called to say you were out of town. You want me to roll it over?"

"No, cash it and deposit it in my trust account."

"I'll take care of it right away."

Stone thanked the man, then hung up and called his secretary at home.

"Hi."

"Hello there."

"Anything happening?"

"Nothing I can't handle."

"Something I'd like you to do."

"Shoot."

"Tomorrow, I want you to write a check for twenty-five thousand dollars on my trust account, made payable to the estate of Elizabeth Allison Manning, and send it to a law firm in Palm Beach." He gave her the address. "Cover it with a letter saying that the money was sent at the direction of Mrs. Allison Manning."

"Pursuant to what?"

Stone thought for a minute. "Just say what I told you; nothing else."

"Okay, but we don't have a lot more than that in the trust account."

"I made a twenty-five-thousand-dollar deposit."

"That CD of yours that came due this week?"

"Right."

"We're going to need to pay some bills the first of the month."

"Woodman and Weld owes us some money; call Bill Eggers and rattle his cage. Tell him we need it right away."

"I'll do it."

"Take care, then."

"When you coming home?"

"Next week; I'll let you know when."

"You going to get that lady off?"

"Jesus, I hope so. If I don't we can kiss that twenty-five grand good-bye."

He hung up feeling both better and worse.

CHAPTER

38

Stone finished up his work feeling thirsty, and he headed down to the bar for something cold. A young man in whites and shoulder boards was having a drink, looking bored. Stone sat down a stool away and ordered a rum and tonic, then he turned to the young man.

"You the skipper of the yacht that just came in?"

"Yep," he replied, "she's called *Race*."

"There must be a reason," Stone said. "What sort of speeds will she do?"

"Sixty knots in reasonable seas; seventy in a raging calm."

"Whew! Who builds them?"

"She's a one-off, designed by a guy out of Miami who does racing boats and built at the Huisman yard in Holland."

"What brings you into St. Marks?"

"Picking up a charterer."

"Anybody I know?"

"Beats me; name of Mr. and Mrs. Chapman; they haven't shown up yet. We're supposed to be out of here by midnight. She's being refueled now."

"Where you bound for?"

"Way up the chain of islands; St. Thomas is our first call after we leave here."

"The first U.S. port, huh? That's a long passage. Can I buy you a drink?"

"Thanks, yes."

"Thomas, bring another round to . . ."

"Sam's my name," the young man said, sticking out a hand.

"I'm Stone."

"First name, or last?"

"First." Stone clinked glasses with the skipper, and they both drank. "Where's this charterer coming from?"

"Beats me. They're supposed to fly in this evening, and we leave as soon as they get here."

"A night passage, huh? They must be in a hurry."

"That's why we're refueling; the boat eats up gas at any kind of speed."

"Can you make it to St. Thomas at speed without refueling?"

"It's at the outer limits of our range, but we can do it with no headwind, and down here the trades will be on our beam. We'll be in the lee of the island chain, so it will only be rough once in a while."

"Where is the boat based?"

"Fort Lauderdale."

"I've got a client wants to sell a yacht up there pretty soon; can you recommend a good broker?"

"Sure," Sam said, taking a card from his shirt pocket. "Crockett and Smith; they handle all our charter work. They're good people."

"So if I wanted to charter *Race*, I'd get in touch with them, not you?"

"That's right; we're in constant touch. You really in the market?"

"Maybe next winter," Stone said. "How much red tape is there in that sort of charter?"

"Not much. You'd put down a fifty percent deposit, and pay the rest thirty days in advance."

"That what this guy Chapman did?"

Sam shook his head. "This one was on short notice, so he'd have to wire-transfer the money right away. The deal only got made a couple of days ago. We had just dropped off a party in Guadeloupe, so we were nearby. This charter works out really well for us, too, since it will take us back to U.S. waters. My next charter is out of San Juan, so it's perfect; we don't have to deadhead all the way and burn up a lot of the owner's fuel."

"What does she cost, by the week?"

"Fifty-five grand, dry, sixty-five all in, booze and everything."

Stone laughed. "Forget my interest in chartering; that's out of my range."

"Don't feel bad; it's out of just about everybody's range."

"Think I could get a look at her interior while you're here? I have a client or two who might be interested in chartering."

"Sure thing," Sam replied, tossing down the rest of his drink. "How about right now?"

"Great; let's go."

The two men walked out of the Shipwright's Arms and across the lawn toward the marina.

"What's her length?" Stone asked.

"Sixty-seven feet overall; draws six feet, so we can cruise the Bahamas."

"How many cabins?"

"Four; one big one for the owner, and three pretty good-sized ones. She has a little less volume than most boats her length; that's because of the speed designed into her."

They walked down the pontoon and went up the boarding ladder. Sam led the way, showing off the bridge and the navigational gear, then the saloon, complete with bar and entertainment center, featuring a big-screen television and video library. The owner's cabin was, indeed, luxurious, and the other cabins, although smaller, were equally plush.

"I'm impressed," Stone said as he descended to the pontoon again. He stuck out his hand. "Thanks for the tour, and good luck." He walked back up to the Shipwright's Arms and found Thomas.

"Thomas, I've never seen many airplanes out at the airport besides Chester's; do you get many outside aircraft in here?"

"Not many," Thomas replied. "Chester had the only license to land here any time he liked. Charter services from the other islands have to phone the airport office and get permission to land, usually twenty-four hours in advance. It's nothing but red tape, really."

"Do you think you could find out if any aircraft are expected in today or tonight?"

"I can call the guy who runs the airport," Thomas said.

"Thanks."

Thomas used the phone and came back. "Nobody coming in today or tonight," he said.

"What would happen if an airplane landed without prior permission?"

"Big fine, for sure, and they might even confiscate the airplane if they got mad enough, but no airplane from the islands would try that. All the charter services know the score. What's up, anyway?"

"The skipper of the big motor yacht that came in this afternoon says he's meeting a charter client who's flying in today."

"Well, that's going to come as a big surprise to the folks out at the airport."

"Yeah," Stone said. "See you later." He walked back down to the marina and boarded *Expansive*. "Hello, below," he called out.

"Stone, is that you?" Allison's voice called back.

"Sure is." He started down the companionway.

"I'm not feeling very well," she called out. "Would you mind coming back later this evening?"

Stone stopped halfway down the steps.

"Stone?"

"I have to talk to you right now," he said and started down again.

"Please don't!" she cried, but he was already in the saloon. There were half a dozen packed duffels piled near the steps, and Allison had a safe open behind the navigation station. "Dammit," she said, "are you deaf?"

"What time are you planning to leave?" he asked.

"I don't know what you're talking about," she replied, closing the safe and putting some papers into her late husband's briefcase.

"What time?" he asked again.

She began going through the drawers next to the chart table, apparently looking for something.

Stone walked into the aft cabin and looked around. He opened a closet door and found only a few things hanging there, along with a lot of empty hangers. He walked back into the saloon. "What time are you leaving?" he asked a third time.

She looked at him for a long time without expression. "Sometime after midnight," she said finally.

CHAPTER

39

*S*tone sat down on the sofa opposite the chart table. "You can't do it," he said. "You know the penalty if you're caught running. You'll be judged guilty without even the formality of a trial, and they'll hang you."

"They're going to hang me anyway," she said.

"Not if I have anything to say about it."

"Stone," she said. "Can't you see the way this is headed? They've stacked the deck against me in every possible way. The jury will probably be stacked against me, too. Sutherland wants my hide on his wall, and he's going to get his way."

"Allison, listen to me. We've got a shot at an acquittal, really we have."

"And if I'm not acquitted?"

"Then we turn on the pressure on the prime minister. Sutherland has already heard from both Connecticut senators and God knows who else. If they try to hang an American citizen under these circumstances, the world will fall on them. The pressure on the prime minister will be unbearable; he'll have to cave in."

"These people can do whatever the hell they want," she said. "They're in this insular little world of theirs, and nobody has ever cared about what went on here."

"Until now. Do you know that you're already very nearly world famous? Every television station on the planet has run a story about you. On American television you're right up there with Princess Di for air time."

"I'm the flavor of the week, that's all," she sighed. "And probably half the people who heard about it think I'm guilty. Anyway, there would only be forty-eight hours between a conviction and an execution. That's not enough time to build outrage and get some sort of intervention. Don't you think I've thought about this? I've hardly thought of anything else."

"But if you run and are caught, you'll appear guilty and you'll lose all that support. People will say, 'Well, she killed her husband and she got what she deserved.' Is that what you want?"

"I'm not going to get caught. That boat over there is the fastest thing afloat between here and Miami. We'll be in international waters fifteen minutes after we leave the harbor. They don't have anything that can stop us."

"Sutherland will go after you and extradite you."

"I can fight that in the American courts."

"And by the time the lawyers are finished with you, all the money will be gone. All of it, Allison, the house, the yacht, and the twelve million in insurance money will have gone right down the legal drain. Then, even if you win, you can never travel abroad. The minute you arrive in another country, Sutherland can start extradition proceedings all over again. You'd be hounded for the rest of your life."

"I'm hounded now; what's the difference? At least I'll have a life. They won't catch me, Stone; they'll have to find me first."

"So you're going to change your identity and hide out somewhere, give up who you are and worry every day about being caught. You don't want to live as a fugitive, Allison, believe me."

This seemed to have an effect. Tears welled up in her eyes, and when she reached for a tissue her hands trembled. "It's better than dying on this godforsaken island," she managed to say.

"They'll think I helped you," Stone said. "I'm an officer of the court, you know; I'm obliged to prevent you from committing another crime, and to attempt to escape is a crime."

"You'll talk your way out of it, Stone. After all, you didn't suspect anything until now."

"They won't know that. They'll know that I had a drink in the bar with the captain of that yacht and that we talked for quite a while, and that I went down and took a tour of the yacht."

"Come with me, then; we'll both get out of here."

Stone shook his head. "I'm not going to become a party to a crime for you or anybody else, and I'm certainly not going to become a fugitive." He stood up.

"Where are you going?" she asked, alarmed.

"I'm going to get as far away from you as I possibly can, although, in the circumstances, that's not very far."

"You're going to turn me in, aren't you?" she asked.

"Of course not; I'm not going to be the instrument of your death. I'm trying to save your life." He turned to leave.

She stood up and grabbed him, turned him to her, and put her arms around his waist. "Don't go," she said. "Stay here with me; I'm so frightened."

Stone disentangled himself from her arms. "I'm leaving right now. We won't be seeing each other again, Allison." He turned and started up the companionway before she could speak again.

He was furious. The stupid girl was jeopardizing them both, herself most of all, and there was not a damn thing he could do about it. At the top of the steps he looked toward the Shipwright's Arms and saw three policemen striding across the lawn toward the marina. "Oh, shit!" he moaned, and ran back down the steps.

"What is it?" Allison asked.

Stone looked around the cabin for some place to hide her luggage. They'd look in the after cabin. "Quick, fix us a drink; the cops are coming." He opened the door to the engine room and started tossing duffels down the steps.

Allison ran to the bar, got two glasses of ice, and poured some brown whiskey into both of them.

There was the sharp rap of a nightstick on the deck. "Ahoy, *Expansive*!" a deep voice called.

"Answer him!" Stone whispered, closing the engine room door and diving for the sofa.

"Hello!" Allison called back. She was halfway to the sofa with the drinks when the first policeman appeared on the stairs.

"Good afternoon," the man said. "I am Colonel Buckler of the St. Marks police." Two other officers crowded the companionway behind him.

"Good afternoon, Colonel," Allison replied smoothly. "We were just having a drink; can I get you something?"

"No, ma'am, thank you," the colonel said.

Stone stood up. "Colonel, I am Stone Barrington, Mrs. Manning's lawyer. Is there something we can do for you?" He took a drink from Allison and sat down. Allison sat next to him. "Please," he said to the policeman, "be seated."

The policeman sat down gingerly at the chart table. "I understand Mrs. Manning has made some travel plans," he said.

Stone looked at him blankly, then at Allison.

"Come again?" Allison said.

"I believe you have recently chartered a yacht," the colonel said.

Allison waved an arm about her. "Colonel, I already have a yacht; why should I want to charter another one?"

"Colonel," Stone said, "perhaps you could explain yourself?"

"Of course, Mr. Barrington," the policeman replied. "Earlier this afternoon a very fast yacht berthed here and cleared customs, stating his intention of picking up a charter passenger. And you were seen, not half an hour ago, having a drink at the bar of the Shipwright's Arms with that yacht's captain, and then going aboard her."

"That's quite true, Colonel," Stone said. "I met the man, whose name I believe is Sam, at the bar. I expressed an interest in his boat, and he was kind enough to offer me a tour. He said his charterer was a Mr. and Mrs. Chapman."

"Come, come, Mr. Barrington, you are being disingenuous," the policeman said.

"I assure you, I am not," Stone replied firmly.

"Colonel," Allison piped up, "why do you think I have anything to do with that yacht?"

"Yes, Colonel, why?" Stone asked.

"I am not a fool, Mr. Barrington," the man said.

"Of course you aren't," Stone agreed. "But what, specifically, causes you to believe that Mrs. Manning has chartered the yacht? Have you spoken with the captain?"

"Not yet," the man admitted.

"Well, when you do, I'm sure he will tell you what he told me, that someone else has chartered his yacht."

"Oh, I will speak to him, Mr. Barrington; you may be sure of that." He stood up. "In the meantime, Mrs. Manning is confined to this yacht and to the Shipwright's Arms."

Allison shrugged. "I've hardly left this yacht since I came to St. Marks, except at the insistence of Sir Winston Sutherland," she said. "I don't know why I would want to leave it now. You see, Colonel, I am quite looking forward to my trial and acquittal."

"She is not to go to the airport or anywhere else on the island or to board any other yacht," the colonel said, continuing to address Stone, "on pain of immediate arrest and close confinement."

"I quite understand, Colonel," Stone said, "and believe me, Mrs. Manning will follow your instructions to the letter."

The policeman saluted them smartly and, herding his colleagues before him, went up the companionway.

Stone followed them partway and watched as they marched off toward the *Race*.

40

Stone sat back down on the sofa and took a large swig of his drink. It turned out to be straight rum. "Jesus," he said, coughing, "I was expecting Scotch or something."

"I grabbed the first thing I saw," she said, sitting beside him. "That man frightened me very badly."

"I'm glad you still have the capacity for being frightened by something," he replied. "He was on the point of jailing you, you know."

"I believe you. What do I do now?"

"We've got to get that motor yacht out of English Harbour, that's what. How did you go about chartering it?"

"I found an ad in an old yachting magazine we had aboard, and I called them. The money was wire-transferred from my Greenwich account."

Stone looked at her in amazement. "And how the

hell did you accomplish all that? You've hardly left this yacht, and I've never seen you use a phone."

She got up, went to the chart table, opened a cupboard behind it, took out what looked like a laptop computer, and set it on the chart table.

Stone looked at the thing. "What is it?"

She opened it and displayed a telephone handset.

"A telephone?"

"A satellite telephone. The antenna is at the top of the mast."

"It works?"

"It certainly does. Would you like me to demonstrate?"

"Yes, please; call the broker and get that yacht out of here."

She plugged the unit into a jack near the chart table, switched it on, and waited. "It will seek a satellite," she said. A moment later, it beeped three times. She picked up the handset, consulted her address book, dialed a number, and pressed a button.

"Like a car phone," Stone said.

"Exactly, except it will work almost anywhere on the face of the earth." She put the phone to her ear. "Hello, Fred? It's Allison Manning; I'm sorry to bother you at home. I have some new instructions for you. Yes, the yacht arrived, and now I have to get it out of here, for the moment."

"Tell him to have them leave around nine this evening," Stone said. "No sooner."

"Please call the yacht and have them depart the harbor at nine o'clock this evening. Tell them to go back to Guadeloupe and wait for my call. It may be a few days.

What? Fred, you've already been paid. If I want the yacht to go to Guadeloupe and wait, then that's what they'll do. Right. Thank you so much." She pressed another button, breaking the connection. "There, it's done."

"And they have one of these on the other yacht?"

"Yes, or something like it."

Stone shook his head. "Technology is passing me by."

"Why nine o'clock?" she asked.

"Because you and I are going to be having dinner at the Shipwright's Arms at that time, in view of the whole world, or at least all St. Marks. We are going to appear relaxed and happy and unconcerned about the yacht's departure. Do you have a local phone directory?"

She fished one out of the chart table.

Stone looked up a number and showed it to her. "Dial that for me, will you?"

She dialed the number and handed him the handset.

"Hello, is that the St. Marks airport? Good. My name is Chapman; my wife and I are meeting a chartered yacht there, and I was told that I would have to get permission for my airplane to land at your airport; is that correct? Well, we plan to land around nine this evening, so I hope the runway is lit. What? Twenty-four hours? Why, that's outrageous! I can land at any other airport in the world on no notice at all! Well, in that case, I'll meet my yacht in Guadeloupe, and St. Marks will lose the money I would have spent there. No, no, don't apologize, I no longer wish to land at your airport. Good-bye!" He broke the connection and turned to Allison. "There, maybe that will give us some cover."

They waited until eight, then, freshly scrubbed and changed, they walked over to the Shipwright's Arms, exchanging pleasantries with the two police officers now permanently established at the dockhead of the marina, with a full view of all the yachts there. They had a drink at the bar and chatted with Thomas for a while.

"Trouble down at the marina this afternoon?" Thomas asked when he was far enough away from the other patrons.

"A bit," Stone replied. "A Colonel Buckler showed up with two other cops and accused Allison of chartering the new yacht down there in order to escape the island."

"Buckler got a call here a little later," Thomas said. "From Government House. I heard the name Chapman mentioned."

"Ah, Mr. Chapman; I'm told that he is the actual charterer of the yacht."

"I gathered from what I overheard that Mr. Chapman had tried to get permission to land his jet at the airport tonight and was turned down."

"Did you get that impression?" Stone said.

"I did. Buckler seemed confused. Buckler and his wife are at a table a few yards behind you, having dinner."

"Oh, good," Stone said.

"Why is that good?" Thomas asked.

"Because he'll get to see the yacht steam out of English Harbour, and he'll see Allison here with me. That might make him feel better."

"Good evening, Sir Winston," Thomas said suddenly. "Your table is ready."

Stone and Allison turned to see the minister of justice and his wife standing behind them.

"Good evening, Mrs. Manning," Sir Winston said. "Mr. Barrington."

"Good evening, Sir Winston," they both replied.

"Such a lovely evening," he said. "You wouldn't want to leave us on such a lovely evening, would you, Mrs. Manning?"

"Of course not," Allison said. Then she looked pointedly over his shoulder.

Sir Winston and his wife turned to follow her gaze. They saw the yacht *Race* back out of her berth and turn toward the entrance to English Harbour. She gave a couple of blasts on her horn.

"Such a beautiful yacht," Sir Winston said; then he turned to his wife. "Shall we be seated, my dear?" They followed Thomas to their table.

Stone looked at his watch; a quarter to nine. "A little early," he said, "but perfectly timed."

"Look," Allison said, "Colonel Buckler sees her, too."

"I believe he does," Stone said with satisfaction.

Thomas returned to the bar. "He asked me if you'd made any phone calls from here since this afternoon."

"I'm glad you were able to tell him the truth," Stone said.

"I try always to tell Sir Winston the truth," Thomas said, "except when I lie to him."

"I hope you haven't had to tell too many lies for us, Thomas," Allison said.

"None that I didn't enjoy telling," Thomas replied with a grin. "Would you like to sit down now?"

"Please," Allison said. "And not too near Sir Winston, if you please."

"I have a lovely table for you, one with a fine view of English Harbour."

"Perfect," she said.

They followed Thomas to their table, passing that of Colonel Buckler on their way. Allison gave him a smile, and Stone nodded pleasantly.

"Did the phone call from Chapman work?" Allison asked when they were seated.

"Maybe," Stone said. "Although Colonel Buckler has not offered to change the terms of your confinement."

"I don't mind," Allison said. "I'm as happy here as anywhere on the island."

"Just see that you don't get onto any other boats, not even mine," Stone said. "And for God's sake, don't go anywhere near the airport."

"I'll be good," Allison promised.

41

*T*hey took their time over dinner, talking like old friends and lovers. They had champagne with their fish, and, as always, the wine was an exhilarant, making them laugh easily. They emptied the place, outlasting Sir Winston and Colonel Buckler, as well as the rest of the crowd. Thomas brought them cognac at the end of the meal, and they nursed it past midnight.

There was a lull in the conversation, and Stone asked a question. "Allison, what are you going to do with yourself when this is all over?" He regretted it immediately, but to his surprise, she answered him as if she would not be on trial for her life in a short time.

"Gosh, I really haven't looked all that far ahead," she said. "I've sold the house—it's under contract now—so I guess the first thing I'll do is go back to Greenwich and start getting ready to move out."

"Where do you think you'll go?"

"Oh," she murmured, "I was thinking maybe New York. Would you be glad to see me there, conveniently located, as it were?"

He felt a little stab in the chest; after all, Arrington would soon be back from California. "Of course I'd be glad to see you," he said, after perhaps too long a pause.

"Oh, yes, there is the other woman, isn't there? What are your intentions, sir, if I may ask?"

"I don't honestly know," he replied, and it was the truth.

Allison leaned forward on her elbows. "Do you think she's fucking Vance Calder?"

Stone shrugged. "She's had the opportunity before, and she says she never did, never thought of him as anything but a friend."

"I would be," Allison said.

"Would be what?"

"Fucking Vance Calder."

"Oh. Well, if she is, then that would make life easier for me, in a way."

"Oh, Stone, you're the perfect old-fashioned man."

"How's that?"

"You'd leave Arrington for fucking Vance Calder, but you wouldn't want her to leave you for fucking me."

"What I meant was, if she left me for Vance, I wouldn't have to make a decision, she'd have made it for me. Also, I'd have some things to tell her."

"You mean about me?"

Stone nodded. He hadn't allowed himself to think about it until now, but he knew he would tell her.

"For God's sake, why?"

"I guess I'm not as old-fashioned as you think—not your idea of old-fashioned, anyway."

"Why, Stone, I believe you're an honorable man."

He felt his ears turning red, and he wondered why he was embarrassed. "If I were as honorable as you think, why would I be fucking you at all?"

She smiled. "It's not your fault," she said. "I simply made myself irresistible."

"That you did."

"Women can do that, you know—make themselves utterly irresistible."

"Some women."

"Thank you, kind sir. Do you know when I decided to seduce you? I mean, the very moment?"

"When?"

"When I was on the stand at the inquest."

"Nonsense."

She shook her head. "No, really. I was sitting there, and Sir Winston was making me absolutely furious, and I caught a glimpse of you sitting there."

"You never looked at me."

"I did. You were looking at Sir Winston. You see, after Paul's death, I was alone for another two weeks, and I had a lot of time to get used to being a widow. I had a friend once who lost her husband; she was in her forties at the time. It took her months just to accept the idea that he was actually dead. She'd walk into his study, expecting to find him sitting there reading the newspaper. It wasn't like that with me. I wasn't distracted by a funeral, or by friends and relatives coming to call or by all the details of settling the estate. I was all alone, right there, in the place where he had been for so long, and he was dead. I think that after the first week I had accepted that completely. Then I started to get horny."

Stone smiled. "I was angry with Arrington for not being here."

"And that gave you an excuse to crawl into the sack with me."

He nodded. "I guess it did."

"You are the best lover I've ever had," she said. "Not that I've had all that many, but I had the years between puberty and the time I met Paul, and I enjoyed myself. But you are the very best."

"That's high praise," he said, satisfyingly flattered.

"Do you know why?"

He shrugged.

"It's not because you're a beautiful man, though you are, and it's not because you're experienced and inventive, though God knows you are: it's because you're so considerate. I know when we're fucking that you really care that I'm enjoying it as much as you. It makes me want to please you even more."

"And you do, believe me."

"I know I do; I can tell. I think you like me best when I'm wanton, when I do the things a proper Greenwich, Connecticut matron isn't supposed to enjoy, and when I do them well."

He smiled, but said nothing.

"Take me back to the boat," she said.

"Yes, ma'am," he said.

They walked past the two policemen on guard and boarded the yacht, and as they started down the companionway, she began undressing. So did he. She led him to the after cabin and threw off the bedcover, then made him lie on his back. She began slowly, kissing him here and there, using her tongue, but staying away from his genitals until he was completely erect, which didn't take long. Then she spent several minutes bringing him to the edge and backing off, playing him as if he were a musical instrument.

Stone then found himself in a condition where he knew he could resist coming for as long as he liked but still remain rigidly erect. Finally she rolled over on her stomach, took him in her hand, and guided him home. Then, after a while, she let him slide out.

"Now here," she said, guiding him into a different place. She let him ride her for a short time, then turned on her back and reinserted him in the same place. Then, without parting from him, she rolled him onto his back and sat astride him, moving slowly up and down, making little noises. Half an hour had passed before she said to him, "Now. Come for me."

And he did.

They passed the night alternately sleeping and making love, as the mood took them.

She woke him at dawn and made him do it again, then they slept for another hour.

"Want some breakfast?" she said, yawning.

"Sure."

"Oh," she said, "all my stuff is packed. Will you bring me the smallest duffel? It's got my toothbrush in it."

"Sure." He rolled out of bed and stretched.

She kissed him on the belly. "You were perfectly wonderful last night."

"You were way beyond wonderful. I don't think I've ever had a night like that. I'm exhausted."

"You'll live." She slapped him on his naked buttocks. "Now get me that duffel."

Stone went forward to the door of the engine room, under the companionway. He opened it, walked down two steps, and looked around the small compartment, which contained the two engines and a small workshop. It was as clean and neat as the galley, he thought. On the bulkhead behind the workbench, all the ship's tools were arrayed in motion-proof brackets. He picked up a wrench and saw that each tool had been traced in black paint. He marveled at the time Paul Manning had spent ordering his ship. He turned and looked at the other equipment. There was a wet suit, hung neatly on a hanger, and a pair of diving tanks resting in custom-made stainless steel holders fixed to the bulkhead.

Then, in a sudden, sickening flash, Stone became a cop again.

He saw something that, in an earlier day, would have made his heart leap in triumph, but now made him feel sick with revulsion.

Next to the tanks, fixed to the bulkhead and outlined in black paint like all the tools, was a spear gun for underwater fishing, with brackets for the gun and three spears. One of the spears was missing, its outline empty. That would have given him pause, but it was something else that immobilized him. The spear gun was there, but it had been taken down and awkwardly replaced backward in its brackets, the opposite of its painted outline.

Stone knew in an instant that Paul Manning would never, never have replaced the gun in anything but its proper position. It had been put there by someone else, of course, but the third spear had not been returned to its place.

The third spear, he knew beyond a doubt, was still in what was left of Paul Manning's body, out there in the depths of the cold, cold ocean.

CHAPTER

42

Stone placed the small duffel on the bed in the aft cabin and looked at Allison, who was sitting on the little stool in front of the vanity, brushing her hair. She looked, he thought, like something out of a Degas oil. He was having a lot of trouble. It wouldn't be the first time, he thought, that he had represented a client whom he knew to be guilty; that was part of his job. It was the first time, however, that he had represented a guilty client with whom he had been enthusiastically making love—one he had grown very fond of—was nearly in love with. It was also the first time he had represented anyone charged with a capital crime. He was trying very hard to ignore his cop's instincts and keep her innocent in his mind.

"Allison," he said absently.

"Yes?"

"After Paul died, why didn't you use the satellite phone to call for help?"

"Two reasons," she said without hesitation. "First, I couldn't get the damned thing to work. I've never been very good at reading manuals, and I just couldn't get it to lock onto a satellite, so I gave up. After I got to port I got it to work the first time; maybe it was because the boat wasn't moving anymore, or maybe it was the crossword syndrome."

"What's the crossword syndrome?"

"You're working on the crossword, and there's a big patch of it you just can't solve. So you put the thing down for a while—maybe until the next day—and you pick it up and immediately get all the words. Maybe it's like that with following directions in a manual."

"I've had that experience," Stone agreed. "What was your second reason for not calling for help?"

"First of all, I did call for help, but on the VHF radio. I didn't know how to work the high-frequency unit—still don't—but I tried calling 'any ship' on channel sixteen, but I never got an answer. I never even saw a ship or a yacht the whole trip. Second, I would have been ashamed if somebody had come to my rescue."

"Why ashamed?"

"Well, I had a perfectly good yacht under me, and I had some idea of how to sail it, so my sense of self-reliance would have been punctured if I'd had to ask somebody else to do it for me. Anyway, in the end, I proved I could sail her." She looked at him in the mirror. "Why did you want to know about the satellite telephone?"

"I thought the police might have seen it during their search and that Sir Winston might ask the question at the trial. If he does, stick with the answer about not being able to get the phone to work, and calling for help on the VHF; don't mention that business about your sense of self-reliance. I'm not sure how it would play with the jury."

"Okay."

"Later, I'll go through your testimony with you, and we'll fine-tune it."

"You mean you're going to rehearse a witness?"

"You bet I am. Oh, I'm not going to tamper with your story; I just want to shape it in a way that will tell the jury, in a simple and straightforward way, that you're innocent."

"Okay. What are you going to do the rest of the day?"

"I have to go out and talk to Leslie Hewitt about the trial. I've made some notes that I want to give him."

"I'll be here all day," she said, "or as long as the cops are."

"You don't have some other escape plan up your sleeve, do you? Because if you do, I beg you not to try it."

"Relax, Stone; I've learned my lesson about escaping."

"I hope to God you have."

Stone borrowed Thomas's car and drove along the coast road to Leslie Hewitt's house. He turned down the dirt road to the cottage and parked out front, next to Hewitt's Morris Minor station wagon, and got out, taking a file folder with him. The front door of the house stood open, and Stone stepped inside. "Leslie!" he called. "You home?" There was no response. "Leslie!" he called again. He looked in the little study and in the kitchen, but the barrister was not in the house.

Stone walked out the back door and into the garden,

but there was still no sight of Hewitt, not even down at the beach. He walked a few steps more, looked around, then turned to go back into the house. As he turned his eye drifted to his left and there, behind a low hedge, lay the inert form of Sir Leslie Hewitt, clad only in faded Bermuda shorts. He was lying on his stomach, his head turned away from Stone; a bucket of hand gardening tools lay next to him and a trowel was near his right hand.

"Leslie!" Stone cried, turning him over on his back and brushing dirt from his face. He slapped Hewitt's face lightly and peeled back an eyelid. The pupil was contracted; thank God for that.

Suddenly Hewitt coughed, then opened his eyes. "Oh, good morning," he said, sitting up and rubbing his eyes with a fist. "I must have dozed off."

"Leslie, are you all right?" Stone asked. "You were out like a light."

"Young man, when you are my age, you will take the occasional nap, too, believe me." With Stone's help, he got to his feet. "Well now, what brings you to see me?" he asked.

Stone wasn't sure that Hewitt recognized him, and he didn't want to ask. "I brought you some material to read in preparation for the trial," he said. "Do you feel up to reading it?"

"Of course," Hewitt replied. "Come into the house, Stone."

Stone breathed a sigh of relief and followed him into the study.

Hewitt arranged himself behind his desk. "Now, what is it?" he asked, in the manner of a man who didn't have much time for whatever Stone wanted of him.

Stone placed the file folder before him. "Leslie, I know you plan to give the opening and closing statements, but I put some thoughts together on how you might proceed, and I'd appreciate it if you'd read the two statements I've prepared. There might be something there you can use."

"Of course I'll read them," Hewitt replied. "Now if you'll excuse me, I'd like to get back to my garden."

"Do you think you could find time to read them now?" Stone asked. "You might have some questions for me."

"No, no, not now," the man said. "I'll read them this afternoon after my nap; I'm more alert then. Now, I'll see you in the courtroom." He walked out of the room, leaving Stone standing there alone.

Stone followed him as far as the back door and watched as Hewitt knelt down and began digging in the earth behind the low hedge again, seemingly oblivious to Stone's presence. Finally, Stone shook his head and returned to the car. As he was about to turn toward English Harbour, he had another thought and turned left instead, toward the airport.

He drove through the gates and down the approach road, with the runway and the single hangar in full view. He pulled up in front of the hangar and got out. The mechanic who had testified at the inquest was working on an engine of the DC-3 that belonged to the St. Marks government. Stone couldn't remember his name, but he walked over to the airplane.

"Excuse me," he said to the man. "I'm Stone Barrington; I heard you testify at the inquest."

"Righto," the man said. "You're the lawyer fellow, aren't you? The one who's defending that lady?"

"That's right. I wonder if I could talk to you for a minute. What's your name again?"

"Harvey Simpson," the man said, turning away from the airplane and wiping his hands with a cloth. "What can I do for you?"

"I was just noticing that the hangar has an overhead door, like a garage," he said, pointing at the ceiling, where the door was retracted.

"That's right; there it is," Simpson said, following his gaze.

"Do you close that every night and lock up?"

Simpson shook his head. "Not unless the weather looks like it's turning bad. That door is a pain in the ass; sticks all the time. I keep meaning to do something about it, but I never seem to get around to it."

"Was the hangar door closed the night before Chester's crash?"

Simpson thought for a minute. "No, we haven't had no bad weather for a while now."

"So anybody could have come in here where Chester's airplane was?"

"That's right, I guess."

"How about your tool cabinet over there," Stone said, pointing to a large, double-doored cupboard. The doors were open, exposing an array of spanners, screwdrivers, and socket wrenches.

"I never lock it," Simpson said.

"Don't your tools get stolen?"

Simpson shook his head. "Everybody who might steal them knows that my tools are American gauge, for working on the American-built airplanes. All the cars on the island and all the other machinery are metric gauge, so my tools wouldn't be worth much to anybody."

"So somebody could have come in here the night before the crash, taken some tools out of your cabinet, and done something to an engine?"

Simpson gazed into the middle distance for a moment before answering. "Yessir, I guess somebody could have done that. But there isn't no one on this island who would want to do that to Chester."

"How about to his passengers?"

"I can't speak for the white lady, but I knew the black one well, and everybody liked her. Anyway, if somebody wanted to kill her, he wouldn't kill Chester doing it."

"Is there anybody on guard out here at night?"

Simpson shook his head. "Nope. There's a couple of people in the airport office, through there," he said, pointing at a door that led from the main part of the hangar to the offices, "but they wouldn't be out here at night. The runway lights are pilot-operated, you see. The approaching pilot just tunes in the local frequency and clicks his mike three times, and the lights come on."

"I see," Stone said.

"Mister, this is not the first time I've thought about this," Simpson said. "I been over it in my mind a few times. I thought about how it was the morning of the crash, and everything was just like I left it."

"Did Chester make it a habit of doing a runup before takeoff?"

"Well, he made it a habit sometimes, and other times he didn't," Simpson said. "If you know what I mean. Chester been flying that Cessna a long time; he didn't have much use for checklists no more."

He didn't have much use for runups, either, Stone thought. A runup might have saved his life and those of his passengers.

"Chester was a good pilot, though," Simpson said. "A natural-born pilot."

"Right," Stone said. Chester had been a cowboy; Stone had flown with him in the right seat when he had come to St. Marks, and the man was strictly a seat-of-the-pants pilot—no checklists. Stone walked over to the tool cabinet and looked at the array of tools inside; then he saw something familiar on the cabinet door. He touched it lightly. Fingerprint powder; he had seen enough of it in his time. "The police have been here?" he asked.

"Sure have; looked at everything, asked a lot of questions, took my fingerprints."

Stone nodded. "Well, Harvey, thanks for your time." He shook the man's oily hand and walked back to the car thinking, *I'll never fly an airplane off a runway without doing a runup first. Not as long as I live.*

He got into the car and headed back to English Harbour. He didn't want to think about Allison right now; he tried thinking about Arrington instead and found that he missed her. He still hadn't rewritten his letter to her; he would do it before the day was out.

43

Stone parked Thomas's car in its usual place and left the keys in it, as Thomas often did. His business with Leslie Hewitt apparently concluded for the time being, he wanted now to talk with Jim Forrester again, and he was lucky enough to find him at the bar, talking to Thomas.

"Hi, Jim; have you got a few minutes for me?"

"Sure, Stone, what's up?"

"I want to go through your testimony with you; make sure we're both on the same page."

"Great, let's get a table."

Thomas held up an envelope. "Fax for you," he said to Stone.

"Thanks, Thomas," he said, stuffing the envelope into his pocket. He'd read it when he was through with Forrester. He followed the reporter to a table, and they got comfortable. "Jim, I'll just ask you some questions, the way I will at the trial, and you answer them as you see fit. If I don't like the way you answer a question, we'll talk about rephrasing."

"Okay, shoot."

"Have you ever testified in court before?"

"No."

"They'll ask you your name for the record."

"Right."

"Now I'm on my feet in my robe and my wig, and . . ."

"Wig? You have to wear a wig?"

"I'm afraid so. You'll have to try not to laugh; it wouldn't look good for me in front of the jury."

"I'll do my best, but I'm not promising anything."

"All right, Mr. Forrester, what is your occupation?"

"I'm a magazine writer."

"And what brings you to St. Marks?"

"I intend to write an article about this trial for an American magazine."

"I see. Now, were you acquainted with Paul Manning?"

"Yes, I knew him in college."

"Tell us how you met him."

"We were on the same basketball team."

"Hang on, Jim; I thought you told me you played against him."

Forrester shook his head and raised the glass from which he was drinking. "I'm sorry, Stone; the booze must be going to my head."

"Let's start again; tell the court how you and Mr. Manning first met."

"We went to college in nearby towns—he to Cornell, I to Syracuse."

"Spell it out for them; say Cornell University and Syracuse University in New York State."

"Okay."

"Go on."

"We were both members of the same fraternity, Sigma Alpha Epsilon, and we had an interfraternity basketball league that included both universities."

"Just say club, and don't bother with the Greek; this jury isn't likely to know much about American college fraternities. In fact, just say you played in the same league."

"Right. Paul Manning and I both played on basketball teams, and we sometimes played against each other."

"And how well did you know him?"

"Fairly well, but we were not close."

"Just say fairly well, don't say you weren't close. Sir Winston may worm that out of you on cross-examination, though. Don't lie about it."

"Right. I knew him fairly well."

"How would you describe his personality?"

"He was friendly and outgoing. We got along well."

"Did there then pass a number of years when you did not meet?"

"Yes; I didn't meet him again until recently."

"Please tell the court of those circumstances."

"I was in the Canary Islands, working on a magazine piece, and I met him at the local marina."

"Not the yacht club?"

"Right, the yacht club; it has its own marina."

"Start again."

"I ran into him at the bar at the yacht club in Las Palmas, and we renewed our acquaintance."

"Had he changed much in the years since you'd seen him?"

"Well, he'd gained a lot of weight, but he was still the same friendly guy."

"Did he mention his wife while you were at the bar?"

"Yes, he said he was married to a beautiful girl that he was crazy about."

"You didn't mention that before," Stone said. "That he was crazy about her."

"Sorry; there were words to that effect."

"Good, that will help. Now, how much time did you spend with him on this occasion, at the yacht club bar?"

"We were there an hour or so, and then he invited me to dinner on his yacht."

"Did you accept?"

"Yes."

"Did you then go down to the marina and have dinner on his yacht?"

"Yes."

"Did he introduce you to Mrs. Manning?"

"Yes. She was already on the yacht, cooking dinner."

"How long did you spend with them that evening?"

"Oh, I guess four or five hours."

"And on that occasion did you form an opinion of the sort of relationship these two people had?"

"Yes."

"How would you describe that relationship?"

"They were good together; they obviously loved each other. They touched each other a lot, and always with affection."

"Good, I like that, the part about the touching; remember to say it."

"Okay."

"Would you say these people were happily married?"

"Yes, I would. Very happily."

"And how long was it before they sailed across the Atlantic?"

"I believe they sailed the next day for another island, then started across the Atlantic the day after that."

"Did you see them again?"

"Yes. I went to another island called Puerto Rico, and I happened to see them as they sailed out of the harbor into the Atlantic."

"Did they see you?"

"Yes, they waved and shouted good-bye."

"Were they in good spirits?"

"Yes, they were laughing and smiling."

"Did they still seem to be the happy couple you had met only two days before?"

"Very much so. They were holding hands."

"Great!" Stone said. "I like that as a memory to leave the jury with."

"What do you think Sir Winston will ask me on cross?"

"Oh, he may play up the fact that you didn't know them intimately. I can't think what else he might ask you. He may not cross-examine at all."

"Good. The sooner I'm off the stand, the better."

Stone stood up. "Don't worry about it, you'll do fine. I've got to go over Allison's testimony with her."

"See you later, then."

Stone walked down to the marina, greeted the two policemen on guard, and boarded *Expansive.*

"That you, Stone?" Allison called from the aft cabin.

"It's me."

She came into the saloon, wearing her usual tight shorts and shirt tied under her breasts.

She couldn't be a murderer, he thought; *she just couldn't be.*

"Are we going over my testimony?"

"Ready when you are."

"Would you like a beer?"

"Sure, why not."

She went to the fridge and got them both a cold bottle of Heineken.

Stone remembered that he had a fax in his pocket. He pulled it out, opened the envelope, and unfolded the sheet of paper. He thought it was odd that Thomas had put the fax in an envelope; he had never done that before. He read the letter.

"Stone," Allison said, concern in her voice, "what's wrong? You look awful."

He felt more numb than awful. He handed her the fax.

44

*S*tone took the fax from Allison and read it again, slowly this time, letting the words sink in, trying to make some sense of it. He might have seen this coming, he thought, but he hadn't; it was a bigger surprise than he was ready for.

Palm Springs

Dear Stone,

 I didn't want to write this letter. When I saw what was happening, I wanted to sit down with you and tell you, face to face. Circumstances prevented that, of course, and I'm sorry. This letter will have to do.
 Vance and I were married yesterday in Needles, Arizona. We flew there in Vance's air-

plane, just the two of us, and a justice of the
peace performed a simple ceremony, with his
wife and daughter as witnesses. Then we flew
here, to Palm Springs, where Vance has a house.
We'll spend our honeymoon here, and we hope
the press won't discover us.

I can't explain to you how this happened,
but it did. I had always liked Vance, and during
the time we spent together working on the New
Yorker profile, I fell in love with him.

You might wonder how I could so quickly
fall in love with another man when you and I
have been so close, living together these past
months. I wonder, too. I think I was more vulnerable to someone else than I had been willing
to admit to myself. Although it wasn't a conscious thought, I think I had come to know that
you would have the greatest difficulty making a
permanent commitment to me, and I know now
that permanence is what I wanted most. I had
meant to talk seriously with you about this
while we were on the sailing trip to St. Marks,
to see if we could work through it. I dreaded
bringing it up, hoping for a long time that you
would do so. When you didn't, I planned to
make the try.

But fate and the weather were against us,
and I have to admit to you that when I couldn't
go, I felt relieved. I think that later, if I had
thought you were pining away for me, I would
have gone, but then you became involved in the
Allison Manning business, and I knew from

*what I read in the press and saw on television
that you had your hands full.*

*I want children, and Vance does, too; that's a
big part of this. But I'm making it sound logical
and carefully planned when, really, it was entirely
spontaneous, growing day after day, until it over-
whelmed us both. The only flaw in my happiness
is that I could not resolve my relationship with
you before this happened. I certainly did not wish
to cause you pain.*

*I know you have your own very independent
life to live and over the long haul, I know that I
couldn't have fit into it without changing the things
I loved about you most—your spontaneity, your
love of your life, and your singularity as a man.*

*I hope that you and I can remain friends, and
that you can wish Vance and me well. We truly
are deliriously happy. After some time has passed,
and when we're in New York again, I'll call you,
and perhaps we can have lunch and talk about
things. Vance was very impressed with you when
you met, and he would like to know you better.*

*I hope this time hasn't been too bad for you
and that you get that poor woman off. From what
I've heard she is so obviously innocent and those
people down there are prosecuting her for their own
ends. I know you'll do your very considerable best.*

*Until I see you again, I remain your good
friend and feel nothing but affection and admiration for you.*

Arrington

Stone folded the letter and put it into his pocket.

"Are you all right?" Allison asked. "You look as though you've had the wind knocked out of you."

"I suppose I have," Stone replied. "I have to admit, I wasn't expecting this."

Allison sat down beside him and took his hand in hers. "I'm sorry you're hurt, but you really should have seen it coming. I did."

Stone looked at her, incredulous. "You did? How could you? You hardly knew anything about it."

"I knew just enough to read the signs. No girl who was really in love would have passed up a week in St. Marks with you, not even for Vance Calder. You're really not very perceptive about women, you know."

"Well, if I didn't know that, I do now," he said, sighing.

She went to the bar and mixed him a rum and tonic, then brought it back to him. "Drink that; you'll feel better in a while." She went into the aft cabin and left him alone in the saloon.

Stone sipped the drink and thought about the last few days. If his letter had reached Arrington in time, would that have mattered? Probably not, he realized. It wouldn't have healed the problems in their relationship. Presently, he did feel better. The defense mechanisms were clicking into place now, and the ego's own anesthesia was numbing the parts of him that hurt most. He took some deep breaths, and something inside him unclenched. Now, he thought, he must bring himself back to the present, because he had a lot to do.

45

*H*e sat her down across the saloon and told her to get comfortable. "Comfort is the first thing," he said. "I don't want you squirming on the stand. No, don't cross your legs, cross your ankles, and fold your hands together. Comfortable?"

"Fairly."

"Find a position early on and be still. If you have to change, do it slowly and deliberately, and remember not to cross your legs."

"I think I got that part about the legs."

"Good. Now, your attitude is going to be important. When I question you I want you to think hard and tell me exactly the way things happened. I want the jury to see that you're trying to be honest."

"All right."

"When Sir Winston's turn comes, I want you to keep exactly the same demeanor; don't use defensive body language like crossing your arms. Don't be petulant; don't show anger; above all, don't raise your voice. Take his questions very seriously, and try to answer them honestly, unless it appears that he's asking a question merely for effect, a rhetorical question, then you can look disappointed."

"Disappointed, not angry," she repeated.

"All right, are you ready?"

"Ready."

"Mrs. Manning, what was your motive for killing your husband?"

She stared at him, and her eyes grew hard.

"Sorry, I didn't tell you I was going to be Sir Winston, did I?"

"No, you didn't."

"You have to be ready for surprises. He may come right out of left field with something, but you can answer it immediately, because you're relying on the truth, not subterfuge."

She shook her shoulders and tried to relax her body. "Okay, who are you this time?"

"I'm your attorney. Mrs. Manning, did you love your husband?"

Allison looked as if she might weep. "Oh, yes, I loved him."

"Don't overdo it; this isn't a soap opera."

"Isn't it?" she asked archly.

"Mrs. Manning, what reason might you have had to kill your husband?"

"I had no reason whatever," she replied firmly.

"Now you're getting it right," he said.

"Mrs. Manning, how much life insurance did your husband have?"

She frowned and began thinking.

"Don't hesitate, tell the truth. If he asks you such a question, it's because he already knows the answer."

"Aren't you going to have some sort of structure to this questioning?"

"In court, yes; but not now. I'm deliberately throwing curves at you, because I want you to be ready for anything. Don't worry about structure right now, or even if I'm Sir Winston or me; just answer each question truthfully."

"All right, all right," she said irritably.

"If you think this is hard, wait until the trial starts. I'll tell you again, rely on the truth, because it really can set you free. If you start striking poses the jury will know it immediately. Try to think of these people as your friends, friends you wouldn't lie to, friends on whom you're depending to do right by you, friends you trust."

"Who are these people likely to be?"

"They could be this island's aristocrats, or they could be cab-drivers and shopkeepers; we won't know until they're there, facing you. Don't look at me or Sir Winston all the time when you're being questioned; look at the jury, not as a group, but as individuals. Share your answers with them, one at a time; suck them into your story, each man of them."

She nodded. "All right."

"Mrs. Manning, what is the net worth of your husband's estate?"

"I believe it will be around fifteen million dollars, but I won't know for sure until all the debts are paid."

"Good! Mrs. Manning, why would your husband have twelve million dollars in life insurance?"

"Paul had never saved much money, although he earned a lot from the sale of his books. He knew he was a candidate for a heart attack, because his doctor had told him so, and he wanted me to be secure if he should die suddenly. Buying so much insurance was sort of a way of saving, of forcing himself to save, so there would be support for me if he died."

"Good! Answer that way—fully and completely always."

"Of course," Allison replied with assurance.

"Mrs. Manning, have you ever fired a scuba diver's spear gun?"

She reacted as if struck. "Ah, I . . . no."

"That's a lie. If I can spot it, so can the jury. Answer the question."

She took a deep breath and exhaled it. "Yes, of course. Paul and I went diving whenever we were near a good reef."

"Have you ever struck anything with a harpoon fired from a gun?"

She smiled ruefully. "I'm afraid not. Paul was a good shot, but I would always miss."

"Good, get a laugh out of them. How far were you standing from Paul when you fired the spear gun at him?"

Her face collapsed into disbelief. "What?"

"Where did the spear strike him?"

"Are you crazy?"

"In the chest? In the neck? Did he fall overboard immediately, or did you have to help him?"

"Stone, goddammit!"

"Did he bleed a lot? Did sharks come when they smelled the blood?"

"Stop this!"

"Answer the questions!!!"

"I never fired a spear gun at my husband, never!" she cried, furious now. "I would never have done anything to harm him!"

"Now that's better," Stone said. "That's a good time to get angry, when he does that to you."

"You said not to get angry."

"I misled you."

"You son of a bitch."

"No, I'm the sweetest guy in the world; Sir Winston Sutherland is the son of a bitch, and he'll do anything he possibly can to get you to come apart on the stand. He already knows about the spear gun."

"How do you know that?"

"Because the police searched the yacht, remember? You think they wouldn't notice a lethal weapon hanging on a bulkhead in plain sight?"

"Oh," she said.

"What about the other weapons?"

"What other weapons?"

"What did they take from the boat? A pistol? A shotgun?"

"We didn't have any weapons on board; Paul was very anti-gun."

"What about the spear gun? That was a weapon."

"It was a tool; it was used for fishing," she said calmly.

"What didn't they find? A nine-millimeter automatic? A riot gun? What?"

"There were no weapons aboard!" she cried. "None!"

"How many knives were aboard the yacht?"

"I don't know how many . . ."

"Think! Count them in your head!"

She thought for a moment. "Maybe eight or ten, maybe a dozen."

"Enumerate them."

"Let's see, in the galley, there was a chef's knife, a bread knife, a boning knife, and two paring knives."

"How long was the chef's knife?"

"About eight inches. I could never handle the big ones."

"Is that what you used on your husband? An eight-inch chef's knife? That would do the job."

"I never harmed my husband," she said quietly.

"What other knives were aboard?"

"There were a couple of rigging knives; we kept one by the main hatch and one strapped to the mast, for deck work. Paul wore another one in a scabbard, along with a marlin spike."

"Did you take the knife from his belt and stab him with it?"

"No! I never harmed him."

"So you just gave him a shove when he was pissing overboard, huh?"

"I did not!"

"Was he wearing the scabbard with the knife and marlin spike when you rolled his body overboard?"

"No, I removed the belt first."

"So, you did roll him overboard!"

"Yes, I did; some hours after his death."

"Did you search his pockets, Mrs. Manning, for money or spare change? Was there anything you wouldn't take from him?"

She locked her eyes onto Stone's, and when she spoke she was begging him to believe her. "Please, I never, ever harmed Paul. He was dead when I buried his body at sea." Tears rolled down her cheeks.

Stone went and took her in his arms. "All right," he said. "That's my girl; that's my star witness; that's my innocent victim of perverted justice."

She looked up at him and laughed. "Gotcha, didn't I?"

Stone buried his face in his hands.

46

*S*tone strode across the lawn toward the Shipwright's Arms, thinking hard about Arrington. He thought of writing to her, maybe even calling her; then he remembered that she was at Vance Calder's Palm Springs house. He didn't have any of Calder's addresses or numbers, so there was no way to get in touch with her until she got in touch with him.

He was almost to the bar when he stopped in his tracks. A man in a seersucker suit was sitting at the bar, drinking something and talking to Thomas. He was big, over six feet, and better than two hundred fifty pounds; that was obvious even when he was seated. Stone had seen only one photograph of Paul Manning, but the man seemed to look very like him, except for the absence of a beard, and he had no idea what Manning would look like without the beard. Stone suddenly had the strange feeling that the whole business was some sort of dreadful error, that Paul Manning had simply fallen overboard near the Canaries and had swum ashore, and now he had shown up in St. Marks to save Allison's life. He approached the bar with some trepidation and sat down. "Thomas, could I have a beer?"

Thomas set a Heineken on the bar, and the big man turned and looked at him. "You must be Stone Barrington," he said.

"That's right," Stone replied.

The man stuck out a hand. "I'm Frank Stendahl."

Stone shook the hand. "How do you do?"

"Very well, thanks. Been seeing a lot about you on television the past week."

"I expect so. Where have you come from, Mr. Stendahl?"

"I'm a New Englander," he said. "The Boston area."

"And what brings you to St. Marks?"

"Vacation," the man said. "I seem to be about the only tourist around here."

"Well, first there was the blizzard in the Northeast, then we were pretty choked up with press, and then, I guess, the bad press made St. Marks an unpopular destination."

"Funny, the publicity somehow made it more attractive to me. I understand you've got a trial starting soon."

"That's right."

"I wonder if I could attend? Could you arrange it for me?"

"I'm afraid not; I'm out of my own bailiwick here, you see."

Thomas chimed in. "It's open to the public," he

said. "I expect if you were there an hour before the trial you'd get a seat."

"Thanks, Thomas," Stendahl said. "Well, Stone—if I may call you that—what's your trial strategy going to be?"

"I don't think I can discuss that," Stone replied, sipping his beer.

"Of course not; that was silly of me. The lady seems to be innocent, though; you going to get her off?"

"I'll do my best."

"Well, how will . . ."

Stone cut him off. "I said, I can't discuss it."

Stendahl held his hands up before him. "Hey, my fault; didn't mean to dig."

"That's all right."

"Well, now that I've cooled off, I think I'll get up to my room and change into something more tropical," Stendahl said. The man got down off his stool and lumbered toward the stairs.

"What's his story?" Stone asked Thomas.

Thomas shrugged. "He used a credit card with the right name on it, but . . ."

"But what?"

"There was a moment when I thought he might be a cop," Thomas said, "but after I talked with him a while, I didn't think so anymore."

"What did he want to talk about?"

"Allison, the trial, the press, anything he could find out. He was really pumping me."

"And you still don't think he could be a cop."

"A cop would have done it differently," Thomas said. "More subtly. This guy just charged straight ahead."

"You think he's just an interested tourist?"

"He doesn't feel like a tourist, either."

"What does he feel like?"

"I think he's got an agenda, but I'm damned if I know what it is. Besides, what would an American cop be doing down here?"

"I don't think I ever saw a cop wear a seersucker suit," Stone said.

"Me neither."

"What sort of luggage did he have?"

"Hartmann leather, a suitcase and a briefcase, matching."

"That doesn't sound like a cop, either; too expensive. That's a businessman's luggage."

"I would have thought so."

Stone shrugged. "Well, I guess businessmen take vacations."

"Usually with their wives; he's alone."

"Bachelor? Divorced?"

"I guess he could be."

Frank Stendahl reappeared, wearing casual clothes, exposing pasty white arms. "Think I'll walk down to the marina and have a look at the boats," he said to no one in particular.

Stone and Thomas watched him as he strolled across the lawn and came to a stop at the marina gate, confronted by the two police officers on guard there. He chatted with them for a minute or so, then turned and walked back toward the inn. Halfway, he changed his mind and walked back toward the water at an angle chosen to take him to the harbor's edge beyond the marina. A moment later, he disappeared around a point of land.

"Where will that walk take him?" Stone asked.

"To the mouth of the harbor, eventually," Thomas replied.

"I've got some work to do upstairs," Stone said. "If he comes back, see what you can find out about him, will you?"

"Sure, glad to. You think he's up to no good, Stone?"

"Right now, all I think is that he's a tourist, like he says; maybe the sort of guy who turned up at the O. J. Simpson trial. I can't think of any other reason for him to be here, can you?"

Thomas shrugged.

"See you later." Stone hopped off his barstool and headed upstairs. After what he'd been through with the press, Stendahl didn't seem to be much of a threat.

47

An hour later, Stone came back downstairs. Stendahl was back at the bar, sucking on a piña colada, and across the room, Hilary Kramer of the *Times* and Jim Forrester of *The New Yorker* were sharing a table. He walked over to them. "Mind if I join you?" he asked.

"Not at all," Hilary replied. "Sit down."

"Jim," Stone said, "did you by any chance get a good look at the man at the bar?"

Forrester looked that way. "The big guy? Nope."

"I wonder if you'd do me a favor."

"What?"

"Go over there and strike up a conversation with the guy, then come back and tell me what you think. Shouldn't be too difficult; he seems to be pretty outgoing."

Forrester shrugged. "Okay." He walked over to the

bar, ordered a drink, and in a moment was engaged in conversation with Stendahl.

"What's that all about?" Kramer asked.

"I just want to know who the guy is," Stone replied. "He seems to have come down here just to attend the trial."

"A camp follower?"

"Maybe, but whose camp?"

"Well, Jim will worm it out of him; he's endlessly curious, a typical reporter—asks hundreds of questions, answers few."

"I haven't found him to be particularly close-mouthed," Stone said. "He doesn't talk much to you, huh?"

"Maybe he's gay," Kramer said.

"Doesn't seem so, but I guess you never know for sure. Have your charms been wasted on him?"

She smiled. "Let's just say that I've told him a lot more than he's told me. I envy him one thing, though."

"What's that?"

"He's got the best memory of any reporter I've ever met. Either that, or he's just too sloppy to take notes."

"Well, he's a magazine writer, been doing travel stuff," Stone said. "He's not the died-in-the-wool *Front Page* type, like you."

"Like me?" she asked, surprised.

"You're a regular Hildy Parks," Stone said.

She laughed again, then she looked at him sharply. "Stone, while I'm in my Hildy mode, did you really just stumble into the Allison Manning mess, or is there something more to it?"

Stone raised his right hand. "Stumbled, honest."

"You were just down here all on your own?"

"Wasn't supposed to be that way."

"How was it supposed to be?"

"Want me to cry in your beer?"

"All you want; I'm a good listener."

"This isn't for publication, not even for a mention."

"It's nothing to do with the trial, then?"

"Nothing; purely personal."

"Cry away."

"My girl was supposed to meet me at the airport; we were coming together. She missed the flight because of a meeting at *The New Yorker*—she's a magazine writer, like Jim—and before she could get on the next day's flight, the blizzard happened."

"That was bad luck."

"It gets worse. The subject of her piece was Vance Calder. She went to L.A. with him for more interviews."

"Uh-oh."

"You said it."

"She's not your girl anymore?"

"Worse; she's now Mrs. Vance Calder. They were married yesterday; I got a fax."

"Hoo! Well, at least you lost her to somebody spectacular."

Stone shrugged. "I wonder if that's better than having her run off with a CPA?"

"What's her name?"

"Arrington Carter."

"Jesus; I know her." Kramer shook her head. "Well, a little, not much. She is very beautiful."

"Don't rub it in."

She started. "Does anybody know about this?"

"Just you and me."

She looked at her watch. "I wonder if I can still make tomorrow's paper."

"Oh, no you don't," Stone said.

Kramer fell back into her chair. "Oh, shit, I promised, didn't I?"

"You promised. Anyway, it's not your kind of story, is it?"

"No, but it would have been nice for the Chronicle column, which is the nearest thing the *Times* has to gossip, and nobody would have believed that I could get the beat on the story."

"Leave the Calders in peace," Stone said. "They're holed up, hoping that somebody like you won't find them until they're ready to spring the news themselves."

"Well, that's the last story I expected to get in St. Marks." She looked up. "Here comes Jim."

"Don't mention Arrington to him."

"Okay."

Forrester ambled up and sat down, tossing a business card onto the table. "Well, thanks a lot, Stone; you got me into a conversation with a life insurance salesman."

Stone looked at the card. "Frank R. Stendahl, Boston Mutual," he read.

"I barely got away with my shirt. You owe me a drink."

Stone waved at Thomas and pointed at Forrester, then made a drinking motion. "So, Jim, you think he's for real?"

"You want his whole story?"

"You bet."

"He's divorced, with two teenage kids; he lives in Lynn, Massachusetts—that's near Boston—his wife got the house and nearly everything else, and he makes the million-dollar round-table every year. I believe that, too: I told him I was getting a divorce, hoping that would keep him off the subject of insurance, and he had ten reasons ready why a born-again bachelor would need another million in coverage!"

"I owe you two drinks," Stone said.

"You owe me dinner," Forrester replied.

"Okay, okay; probably not tonight, but before we leave."

"I want to debrief you after the trial anyway; maybe we can do that over dinner."

Kramer spoke up. "Only if I can be there, too."

Forrester laughed. "It's a good thing you and I aren't direct competitors."

"Jim," Stone said. "Does Stendahl remind you of anybody?"

Forrester looked toward the bar. "Remind me of anybody?"

"Maybe of Paul Manning, a little?"

Forrester looked thoughtful. "Well, they're about the same size and build, but apart from that they don't really look alike."

"Even taking the absence of a beard into account?"

Forrester shook his head. "Very different in manner and accent, and not at all the same face, even without the beard. What, did you think he might not be dead after all?"

"It crossed my mind for a fleeting moment. My life would certainly be a lot simpler if Paul Manning walked in here and sat down at the bar."

"Well, put your mind at rest, pal; I mean, maybe Manning's out there swimming around somewhere, but that ain't him at the bar."

"And you're the only one here who knew him," Stone said, sighing.

"Allison knew him; give her a look at Stendahl and see what she has to say."

Stone shook his head. "I wouldn't put her through that."

Forrester looked sympathetic. "That would solve a lot of problems for you, wouldn't it? I mean, if Stendahl were Manning."

"It certainly would," Stone agreed.

Kramer spoke up. "It would get Allison off, but Stendahl would sure be in a lot of trouble."

"Yes, he would," Stone said. "Although I'm not sure what they might charge him with in St. Marks."

Forrester laughed. "It would be funny, wouldn't it? Stendahl/Manning stands up in court and says, 'I am the deceased; let my wife go!' I can just see Sir Winston's face."

They all had a good laugh.

48

*I*t was their last night before the trial. "Want to go to dinner at the inn?" Stone asked.

She shook her head. "I don't want to be on display. I would much rather cook dinner for you aboard."

"Why don't I cook dinner for you instead?" he asked.

"No, that would have too much of the condemned's last meal about it."

"Come on, I don't want you to worry about the trial."

"I am serene," she said, and she certainly seemed that way. "I'd just rather do something normal, like cooking. In fact, I've already thawed a chateaubriand in anticipation."

"Sounds wonderful. Can I make a Caesar salad?

"Oh, all right, but just the salad. There's some romaine lettuce in the supplies Thomas sent down."

"And I need fresh eggs, olive oil, garlic, some Dijon mustard, and a can of anchovies."

"All in the galley. I'll get the meat started and make some béarnaise sauce first. You can make me a martini."

"Pffft! You're a martini!"

She groaned.

"One martini, coming up." Stone mixed the drink, shook it, dropped an olive in, strained the crystal liquid into a large martini glass, and set it on the galley counter.

She sipped it. "Mmmm. Just right."

Stone mixed himself a rum and tonic and watched as she unwrapped the beef, the center of the tenderloin, pounded it to about an inch and a half of thickness with a meat mallet, dusted it liberally with salt and pepper, and laid it on the gas grill. Then she diced some shallots and sautéed them with some tarragon, vinegar, and white wine. While this mixture was reducing she separated half a dozen egg yolks, heated some butter, then put the yolks into the Cuisinart, turned it on, and poured hot butter into the chute. Moments later she had hollandaise, which, when mixed with the reduced shallots and tarragon, became béarnaise. She dipped a finger into the sauce and held it up for Stone to taste.

"Wow!" Stone said. "You made that look easy."

"It is easy," she replied, turning over the beef. "Now you can make your salad.

Stone rinsed the romaine leaves and left them to drain. He crushed a couple of garlic cloves and some anchovies into the wooden salad bowl, then separated two egg yolks and dropped them into the bowl as well.

Then he whipped the mixture with a whisk while adding olive oil until the consistency was perfect. He added a teaspoon of mustard and a little vinegar, some salt and pepper, and gave her a fingerful to taste.

"Absolutely perfect," she crowed, hoisting the meat onto a cutting board and slicing it deftly with a sharp knife.

Stone put the lettuce into the bowl with the dressing and tossed it until each leaf was thinly coated, then set the bowl on the saloon table alongside the beef.

Allison dug out a bottle of red wine. "You do the honors," she said, holding it out with the corkscrew for him.

"Opus One, '89," he said, reading the label. "I'm impressed."

"It's the best bottle on the boat."

"And it will need decanting. You have a seat." He poured the wine gently into a decanter, watching for the sediment to creep up the bottle's neck, stopping when it did. Then he sat down and poured them both some.

Allison raised her glass. "To the best last meal a girl ever had," she said.

Stone raised his glass. "To the last meal's arriving about seventy years from now."

She laughed. "I'll drink to that."

They ate hungrily, wolfing down the tender beef and taking the marvelous wine in large sips, then served themselves seconds of everything.

"I won't have room for dessert," Stone said.

"I'm dessert," she replied. "And you'd better have room."

They lay together in the aft cabin, kissing and

stroking each other tenderly. They both had things to forget, Stone thought—he, Arrington; she, that he might be the last man she'd ever have. There was a moon filtering through the portholes, and in its light, with her fair hair and skin, she was as white as marble. Stone bent over her and his tongue found its way through the soft, blond pubic hair into the warm sweetness beneath. He was gentle, not pressing her, and she ran her fingers through his hair, encouraging and directing him until she shuddered and came quietly.

Then she reversed their positions, taking him into her mouth, caressing him with her tongue and fingers, drawing him to his fullest—teasing, tempting, but never allowing him to climax. Finally, when he was nearly mad, she mounted him and pulled him into a sitting position. They were mouth to mouth, nipple to nipple, he deeply into her. She brought her feet behind him so that she could pull him even farther inside her.

They stayed that way for what seemed like hours, then Allison began moving more rapidly. Stone moved with her, and, locked tightly together, they came noisily, finally toppling over onto the sheets.

"If that has to be my last time," she panted, "I won't have any complaints as to how well it went. I honestly don't think sex can be any better than that."

"You won't get an argument from me," Stone panted back.

They lay in each other's arms for a while, then she surprised him by bounding out of bed. "Come with me!" she cried.

He followed her into the saloon, then up the companionway and into the cockpit, oblivious of the two startled guards on the dock. She flung herself over the lifelines and into English Harbour, with Stone right behind her, matching her stroke for stroke.

She stopped and treaded water. "Do you think they think I'm making a break for it?" she asked.

"I think they're too astonished to think," Stone replied, laughing.

They swam out into the harbor, the moon sparkling on their wake, then back to the yacht, climbing aboard again. Then they went back to bed and started over.

CHAPTER

49

*T*he drive to Government House, with Thomas at the wheel, was silent. Stone sat in the front, reading the opening statement he had written, merely for something to occupy his mind. Leslie Hewitt would probably ignore it anyway. He glanced occasionally at Allison, who sat in the backseat, gazing absently out at the St. Marks landscape, seemingly calm and self-possessed. Her hair was pulled back tightly into a bun, at Stone's request, and she wore a mostly blue, floral-printed silk dress. She looked about twenty-one, Stone thought.

They arrived in the official parking lot nearly simultaneously with Sir Leslie Hewitt's ancient Morris Minor station wagon. Everyone got out and shook hands, smiling, attempting good spirits. With Hewitt in the lead they entered the building through the police door and climbed the stairs to the second floor, passing through a short corridor to the door used by guards, lawyers, and defendants. To one side was a small robing room, and Stone and Hewitt donned their robes and wigs. Once again, Stone felt foolish.

They entered the courtroom. Stone had forgotten that Allison would have to stand in the dock, several feet behind the defense table; he would not be able to confer with her when court was in session. He felt very much out of his element. In New York he would have been at home in any courtroom and in at least partial control. Here he felt like an intruder, and he worked hard at not letting Allison know it.

Spectators were filing into the gallery, which was raised in tiers like a college lecture room or, more aptly, London's Old Bailey. The room was not paneled, simply painted, and the paint had begun to fade and peel. Stone saw Frank Stendahl, the insurance salesman, enter and take a front-row seat not far from the dock.

At the front of the room, elevated above the defense and prosecution tables, was the bench; to the judge's right was the witness box, and beyond that, the jury would sit. Stone and Sir Leslie sat down at the defense table. A moment later Sir Winston Sutherland swept into the courtroom, his robes flowing, followed by his assistant.

"Leslie," Stone asked, "did you have an opportunity to study the opening and closing statements I wrote?"

"I read them," Hewitt replied.

"There were a number of very important points, particularly in the opening statement, that I thought should be included in your opening."

"I'm aware of that, Stone," Hewitt said, arranging his robe. "Please don't concern yourself with my opening."

Stone sighed and tried to make himself comfortable in the hard wooden chair.

A moment later, the bailiff entered, stood at attention, and cried, "Hear ye, hear ye, all rise for the Lord Cornwall."

All rose, and the judge, resplendent in red robes, his black face contrasting sharply with the whiteness of his long wig, entered and sat down at the bench in a high-backed, ornate leather chair, with a gilded crown set at the top, a remnant of Her Majesty's rule. "Good morning," the judge said.

Hewitt was on his feet. "Your Lordship," he said, "a small request before we begin."

"Yes, Sir Leslie?"

"We have a long day ahead of us; I wonder if the prisoner might have a chair?"

Stone's stomach lurched at hearing Allison so described.

"Of course, Sir Leslie. The bailiff will provide a chair for the prisoner." The bailiff found a chair and set it in the dock for Allison, who thanked him sweetly, eliciting an unexpected smile.

Stone hoped that was a harbinger of things to come.

"The court will come to order," the judge said. "I will hear from the minister of justice."

Sir Winston stood, cleared his throat, and spoke. "Your Lordship, today we hear the case of the people of St. Marks against the prisoner Allison Manning, on a charge of murder. We are ready for Your Lordship to select the jury." He sat down.

"Call the first juror," the judge said.

"Call the first juror!" the bailiff cried.

A door opened at the rear of the courtroom and a man entered. He was elderly and thin and he was wearing a three-piece wool suit that fit him very well. He took the first seat in the jury box.

"State your name and occupation," the bailiff said.

"I am Charles Kimbrough," the man said. "I am a tailor by trade, and I am recently retired."

"Mr. Kimbrough," the judge said, "are you in good health and of sound mind?"

"I believe I am, Your Lordship."

"Are you acquainted with the prisoner or any members of the court?"

"I am acquainted with Sir Leslie Hewitt and yourself, Your Lordship, as I have made suits for both of you in the past."

"Anyone else?"

"I know Sir Winston, though I have never had the pleasure of his custom."

"Yes. Have you heard anything about this case?"

"Oh, yes, Your Lordship," the man said. "I have read all about it in the newspapers."

"Have you formed an opinion of the prisoner's guilt or innocence?"

"Well, Your Lordship, I think she might have done it, but then again, she might not have."

"He's okay with me," Stone murmured.

"Keep your seat, Mr. Kimbrough," the judge said. "You're the foreman of this jury."

Kimbrough sat down, and another man was brought in. He was not so finely dressed, but he was clean and neat. He was a bartender at a local hotel, and he was soon seated. He was followed by a taxi driver, an apprentice shoemaker, who could not have been more than twenty, a street vendor, and a white merchant, all of whom were briefly questioned and rapidly seated.

"We have a jury," the judge said.

"Only six?" Stone asked Hewitt.

"It is all we need," the barrister replied.

Stone was dissatisfied with only the taxi driver, who looked at Allison with something like contempt, as if he had seen her kind before, but only in his rearview mirror. But on the whole, he thought, he had tried cases before worse juries.

"The foreman is good for us," Hewitt whispered. "He is a very kind man and will not hang a woman lightly. The others will respect his opinion because he is so well dressed."

Stone hoped so.

"The bailiff will read the charges," the judge said.

The bailiff stood and read from a single sheet of paper. "The prisoner, Mrs. Allison Manning, is charged with murder, willfully taking the life of Mr. Paul Manning, her husband, on a date unknown between January first of this year and the present day, on the high seas, having departed the port of Puerto Rico, in the Canary Islands, a Spanish possession, and not yet having arrived at the port of English Harbour, in St. Marks. Be it known to all present that the crime of murder is a capital offense in St. Marks, and that if convicted, the prisoner will suffer death in the prescribed manner, which is hanging." He sat down.

Short, but not very sweet, Stone thought.

"Now," the judge said, addressing the jurors, "I will explain how we will proceed in this courtroom. The prosecuting barrister, Sir Winston, will make an opening statement of his case, then he will be followed by Sir Leslie, who will make an opening statement in defense of the prisoner. Thereafter, Sir Winston will call witnesses and question them, followed by a cross-examination by Sir Leslie. When the government has completed its case, Sir Leslie may call witnesses and question them, and Sir Winston may cross-examine them. Items may be entered in evidence by either side. When the defense has concluded its case, Sir Leslie will make a closing statement, followed by a closing statement from Sir Winston. When he has concluded I will charge the jury, and the jury will retire to the jury room to consider their verdict, which must be a majority verdict. While we are in the courtroom the bench will make all rulings on the admissibility of statements and other evidence, and the decision of the bench will be final in all matters. Is there any one of you who does not understand what will take place?"

No member of the jury moved, let alone spoke.

"In that case, we will begin with the opening statement of the people of St. Marks, who are represented by Sir Winston Sutherland. Sir Winston?"

Sir Winston rose, smoothed his robes, adjusted his wig, shot his cuffs, cleared his throat, and began to speak.

CHAPTER

50

*S*ir Winston bowed to the bench, and his voice boomed over the courtroom, stentorian and didactic. He might have been instructing the jury without waiting for the judge to do so. "Gentlemen of the jury," he began, though he was looking at the packed gallery rather than at the jurors, "we come here this day to avenge the death of a human being. Paul Manning was a gentleman in the prime of life who had made for himself a successful career, becoming famous and rich. He owned a large house; he owned an expensive yacht; he owned a life insurance policy with a death benefit of twelve million dollars. It was for this wealth that he was murdered by his wife." He gestured dramatically at Allison in the dock.

"You might not think that she looks the part of the murderess, being demure in appearance, but we will show today how she took the life of her husband, how she cruelly and heartlessly consigned him to the depths of the ocean and watched him die as his yacht sailed away from him. You will hear Paul Manning speak from the grave," he intoned, and the apprentice shoemaker's eyes became large and round. "His words recorded in his own handwriting." He held up the leather-bound diary, and the juror looked relieved.

"You will hear how she plotted his death over many months, biding her time until the moment came when he was helpless, and then she took his life." He paused and looked witheringly at Allison, as though his eyes were sufficient to punish her. Allison returned his gaze and shook her head slowly.

Good girl, Stone thought.

"When you have heard the evidence against Allison Manning," Sutherland continued, "you will reach the only verdict that the evidence will permit: you will find her guilty of willful and deliberate murder." Sir Winston bowed to the bench and sat down.

The judge turned toward the defense table. "Sir Leslie Hewitt will make the opening statement for the defense," he said.

Stone turned and looked at Hewitt. The little man appeared to be dozing. "Leslie!" Stone whispered sharply.

Hewitt's eyes popped open. "Eh?"

"Do you want me to give the opening statement?"

"Certainly not," Hewitt replied, looking around the courtroom. He rose to his feet and bowed to the bench, then, ignoring the gallery, turned his full attention to the jury. "Good morning, gentlemen," he said pleasantly. Two or three of them nodded in response. "I trust Sir

Winston has not clouded your minds," he said with a chuckle. "The defense has quite a different view of his so-called evidence, as you might imagine, and as you will come to see during the course of this trial."

He indicated Allison with a warm smile. "Here we have a young woman who, with her much-loved husband, set off on the adventure of a lifetime, sailing across the Atlantic from America to Europe, just the two of them. This is not the act of two people who do not love each other—to be confined for weeks at a time at sea with only each other for company. This was a positive act, showing that these two people were happy together. You will hear from her own lips how they enjoyed their adventure and how, on the voyage back to the Americas, her husband suddenly fell ill and died, struck with an illness about which he had been warned by his doctors, but which he had taken none of the prescribed steps to prevent. You will hear how his death endangered the life of his young wife and how with courage and fortitude she managed to sail a large yacht alone across the sea, to make landfall on our island."

Sir Leslie cleared his throat and rearranged his robes. "Finally," he said, "when this trial has been concluded, you will see how this charge of murder is spurious and should never have been brought." He gestured toward Sir Winston. "You will wonder at the motives of the prosecution in bringing it. And you will have the opportunity to set things right, to return this dear young woman to freedom and her native country, to live out her life as best she can without the sorely missed companionship of her beloved husband." With a flourish he

314

bowed to the bench, returned to the defense table, and sat down.

Not bad, Stone thought, for a periodically senile old man who had recently been asleep in the courtroom. While it may not have been all he had wished, Hewitt's opening was at least the equal of Sir Winston's, maybe even a little better. He was relieved that Sir Winston had not mentioned any witnesses or evidence in his opening statement that the defense didn't know about. The playing field was level, and that was as much as he could wish for at this point.

The judge turned to the prosecution table. "Sir Winston, call your first witness."

Sir Winston rose and spoke. "Call Mr. Frank Stendahl," he said.

Stone sat up straight. "What the hell?" he said aloud.

The judge looked at him sharply.

Stone tried to look ashamed of his outburst. He turned to look at the gallery as Stendahl left his seat and walked toward the witness box. He caught a glimpse of Hilary Kramer and Jim Forrester watching him, looking as puzzled as Stone was.

Stendahl stood in the witness box.

"Take the book," the bailiff said, offering a Bible and a card, "and read from the card."

Stendahl grasped the Bible and read, "I swear by Almighty God that the evidence I shall give in this court will be the truth."

The bailiff relieved him of the Bible and the card.

Sir Winston turned to the witness box. "State your name, address, and occupation for the record," he said.

"Frank Stendahl, 1202 Old Brook Road, Lynn, Massachusetts, U.S.A. I am the chief claims investigator for the Boston Mutual insurance company."

"Oh, Christ," Stone whispered to himself, earning a rebuking glance from Sir Leslie. He hadn't seen this coming.

"Mr. Stendahl, did your company, Boston Mutual, insure the life of Paul Manning?"

"Yes, we did."

"In what amount?"

"In the amount of twelve million dollars."

There was a stir in the jury box and raised eyebrows among the men who sat there.

"Is this, in your experience, a large sum of life insurance?"

"Indeed it is," Stendahl replied. "In fact, it is the largest policy my company has ever written on an individual life."

"And how old is your company? Was it recently formed?"

"Boston Mutual was founded in 1798."

"And in the nearly two hundred years since its founding, it has never written a policy as large as this?"

"Not on an individual life, when the individual was himself paying the premiums. We have had corporate policies that were larger, when a company was insuring the life of, say, its chief executive."

"What steps did your company take before insuring the life of a person for such a large sum?

"We did what we do for any large policy, that is, we investigate the background, the reputation, and the net worth of the applicant, and we have him examined by a doctor of our choosing. I personally conducted the background investigation of Mr. Manning."

"And what did you learn about Paul Manning during your investigations?"

"I learned that Mr. Manning was an important author with a large income; that he had an excellent credit record; and that he was known to be a person of good reputation in his community."

"And what did the medical evaluation of Mr. Manning reveal about his health?"

"May I consult notes?"

"Yes."

Stendahl took a sheet of paper from his inside pocket and read from it. "I quote from the report: 'Paul Manning is a forty-year-old writer who is in excellent health and who does not have any history of cancer, heart disease, diabetes, or any other serious illness. Neither is there any history of serious disease in either of his parents, both of whom died accidentally in their sixties, in an automobile accident."

"What was Mr. Manning's height and weight?"

He consulted his notes. "Six feet, two inches, two hundred and nineteen pounds."

"Did the examination include a test for serum blood cholesterol and triglycerides?"

"Yes, it did."

"What was the result?"

Stendahl checked his notes again. "His cholesterol count was one hundred ninety-nine, and his triglycerides were one hundred forty-seven."

"Did your company consider these to be within the normal range for a man of Mr. Manning's size?"

"Yes. We would expect the cholesterol count to be

under two hundred and twenty, and the triglycerides to be under one hundred and fifty, in order to be insurable. Mr. Manning qualified on both counts."

"Did your company's medical examiner think of Mr. Manning as a heart attack waiting to happen?"

"Certainly not. If he had thought that, we would never have insured him."

"Mr. Stendahl, has your company paid the death benefit of the insurance policy?"

"Yes, we have."

"In full?"

"Yes."

"Without investigation?"

"Oh, we investigated, all right; we'd never pay a sum that large without an investigation. We sent a man down here to talk to Mrs. Manning last week."

"And he found all was in order?"

"He did, but there was something he didn't know until later."

"What was that?"

"That Mrs. Manning was about to be tried for the murder of her husband."

"She didn't tell your investigator that?"

"No. He learned about it from the newspapers, but by that time we had already paid the money into Mrs. Manning's bank account."

"And is that money still in her account?"

"I am advised that it is not."

"Where is that money now?"

"I am advised that it was wire-transferred into an account in the Cayman Islands, so by now it could be in any bank in the world."

"I have no further questions for this witness, Your Lordship," Sir Winston said, then sat down.

The judge turned to the defense table. "You may cross-examine."

Stone stood up. "Your Lordship, may I have a recess for a few minutes in order to consult with my client?"

The judge stifled a yawn. "You may not."

Stone looked at Allison, who sent him a sympathetic glance. He was going to have to wing it with this witness.

51

Stone took some papers from a file folder and rose to address the witness. "Mr. Stendahl, how long ago did Paul Manning undergo the physical examination for his insurance policy?"

Stendahl consulted his notes. "Two years ago last week."

"And did your company's doctors see Mr. Manning after that date?"

"Not that I'm aware of."

"Had they seen him before that date?"

"Not that I'm aware of. He had no earlier policies with us."

Stone was getting into shallow water now, and he hoped he would not run aground. "Did he have any earlier policies with any other company?"

Stendahl consulted his notes. "None."

"Mr. Stendahl, when you are investigating an applicant for life insurance, is there a central record of health history you can consult?"

"Yes. If the applicant has had medical problems, we can usually find out about them."

"But if he hasn't had health problems, and if he hasn't previously applied for life insurance, there would be no record of his height, weight, or blood studies, would there?"

"No."

"Did you find any earlier medical records of Paul Manning?"

"No."

"So you don't know what occurred with regard to Mr. Manning's weight and various blood studies either before the examination or between the date of that examination and the date of his death?"

"No."

Stone breathed easier. He held up the documents for the bailiff. "May the witness read from these, Your Lordship?"

"He may."

The bailiff took the documents and handed them to Stendahl.

"Mr. Stendahl," Stone continued, "what are the documents you have just been handed?"

Stendahl flipped quickly through them. "They appear to be the results of another physical examination taken by Mr. Manning."

"On what date?"

"A year after our company's doctors examined him."

"Would you read the first paragraph, which has been highlighted?"

Stendahl found the paragraph. "'Paul Manning is a forty-year-old author who has come in for a physical examination prior to an extensive sea voyage. Mr. Manning has no complaints, but he is desirous of being examined and taking a copy of his medical records on his journey. Mr. Manning is six feet, two inches tall and weighs . . .'" Stendahl paused.

"Go on, Mr. Stendahl."

"'. . . weighs two hundred and sixty-one pounds, rather too much for a man of his frame. The results of blood tests show a serum cholesterol count of three hundred twenty-five and serum triglycerides are four hundred and ten. These are both dangerously elevated, the high end of normal being two hundred and twenty for cholesterol and one hundred and fifty for triglycerides. Because of these numbers, in conjunction with Mr. Manning's lack of regular exercise, I have advised Mr. Manning to immediately undertake a program of exercise, a diet low in cholesterol and other fats, and to bring his weight down to a maximum of two hundred pounds.'"

"Does this sound like the man your doctors examined?" Stone asked.

"No. It would appear that Mr. Manning changed his eating habits after our exam."

"Do you think it possible that Mr. Manning might have lost weight and watched his consumption of fats prior to your examination, so that he would have been insurable, then reverted to his old ways after the exam?"

Sir Winston was on his feet. "I object, Your Lordship. This calls for a conclusion on the part of the witness."

"Sustained," the judge said.

"Let me put it another way, Mr. Stendahl," Stone said. "Would you think that the man described in this later exam was, and I quote, 'a heart attack waiting to happen'?"

Sir Winston was up again.

"I withdraw the question, Your Lordship," Stone said, cutting him off. "We would like the medical examination report to be Exhibit Number One for the defense." Now he had to wade further into shallow water, violating the rule of every trial attorney: He was going to ask a question he didn't know the answer to. "Mr. Stendahl," he said, "was there a provision in Mr. Manning's insurance policy covering double indemnity?"

Stendahl hesitated a moment, then answered, "Yes, there was."

Thank God, Stone thought. "Would you explain to the court the meaning of the term 'double indemnity'?"

"It means that if the insured suffers accidental death, then the death benefit is doubled."

"So if Paul Manning had died accidentally, the death benefit would have been twenty-four million dollars?"

"That is correct."

"Now, Mr. Stendahl, I ask you to imagine the circumstances surrounding Paul Manning's death: he is alone with his wife in the middle of the Atlantic Ocean. Let us say, merely for the purposes of argument, that Mrs. Manning has decided to kill her husband. Having done so, would it not then be very profitable for her to claim that he had died as a result of an accident at sea?"

"Yes, I suppose it would."

"Profitable to the extent of an additional twelve million dollars?"

"Yes."

"But instead, she has asserted that he died as the result of a heart attack, has she not?"

Sir Winston was up. "Objection; no testimony to that effect thus far."

"Sustained," the judge said.

"Let me put it this way, Mr. Stendahl. In your experience as an insurance investigator, would a person who had decided to murder an insured do so under conditions of maximum profitability?"

"Yes."

"Not under conditions which would pay only half the available money?"

"No."

"Then, as an experienced investigator, when determining the facts of this case, would you say that Mrs. Manning is more likely or less likely to have murdered her husband?"

Stendahl sighed. "Less likely."

"One final question, Mr. Stendahl," Stone said. "As a witness in this trial, you are not entirely objective, are you?"

"I beg your pardon?"

"What I mean is, you have an ax to grind in this case, do you not?"

"I don't know what you mean." But he looked as though he knew exactly what was meant.

"Mr. Stendahl, can a person murder another, then collect on his life insurance?"

"No. A murderer is not legally entitled to benefit from his crime."

"So if Mrs. Manning should be convicted in this court, what would be the next action of you and your company?"

The ax fell on Stendahl. "Ah, we would of course endeavor to recover the money already paid."

"So, you and your company have a twelve-million-dollar ax to grind, do you not?"

"I, ah, see your point," Stendahl said softly.

"I'll take that as a yes. Thank you, Mr. Stendahl; no further questions." Stone sat down and gripped the edge of the table so that his hands would not be seen to tremble. Now the playing field was better than even; it was tilting his way.

Sir Winston had no redirect. He was not looking happy. He called his next witness. "The prosecution calls Captain Harold Beane of the St. Marks Constabulary." A well-starched officer took the stand and the oath.

Now, Stone thought, *we find out what, besides the diary, the police might have found on the* Expansive.

CHAPTER

52

*S*ir Winston shuffled some notes, then addressed his witness. "Captain Beane, in the pursuit of your duties did you have occasion to visit the yacht *Expansive* at the marina in English Harbour?"

"I did."

"For what reason?"

"I received a call from the customs officer at English Harbour saying that a death had occurred on a yacht which had just sailed into the harbour."

"What did you find when you arrived at the marina?"

"I found Mrs. Allison Manning alone on the yacht. She told me that her husband had died aboard while they were en route from the Canary Islands to St. Marks."

"Did she mention a cause of death?"

"She said he had died of natural causes; she strongly suspected a heart attack."

"Did you later have occasion to search the yacht?"

"I did, after the preliminary questioning of Mrs. Manning."

"Did you find any evidence aboard the yacht to support Mrs. Manning's contention that her husband had died of natural causes?"

"No, I did not."

"Did you find any evidence aboard the yacht to suggest that Mr. Manning might not have died of natural causes?"

"I did."

Sir Winston held up the leather-bound diary for the jury to see, then handed it to the officer. "Did you find this book?"

"I did."

"After comparing it with other documents aboard the yacht, did you find the book to be in the handwriting of Paul Manning?"

"I did. Mrs. Manning confirmed that."

"In what form is the book written?"

"In the form of a diary."

"A diary written in the hand of the murder victim?"

Stone was on his feet. "Objection; no evidence has been offered to indicate that a murder took place."

Sir Winston turned on him. "The man is dead, isn't he?"

The judge intervened. "I am sorry, Sir Winston, but Mr. Barrington is right. The objection is sustained."

Sir Winston nodded, then turned back to his witness. "A diary written in the hand of the deceased?"

"Yes."

"Captain, would you turn to page three and read the passage marked, please?"

The officer found the page. "'They had been on the boat together for months now, and she had been the perfect bitch. She had always had a temper, but now she frightened him with the intensity of her anger.'" He looked up from the book.

"Now please turn to page seven and read the marked text."

The officer found the passage. "'They argued one day as she was making lunch. She had a chef's knife in her hand, and for a moment, he thought she might use it on him. He slept badly that night, waking often, expecting to feel the blade in his back.'"

"Thank you, Captain," Sir Winston said, taking back the book. "Your Lordship, we wish the diary to be recorded as Exhibit Number One for the prosecution. Now, did you find on the yacht any weapon that might be used to commit a murder?"

"There were no firearms, except a flare gun which had never been fired," the officer replied, "but there were many knives aboard—several in the galley and two on deck in scabbards, secured to parts of the yacht."

"Was any of these knives of sufficient size and strength to be used to kill a man?"

"They were, all of them."

Sir Winston paused dramatically and looked at the jury as he asked his next question. "And did you find any other weapon?"

"Yes, I did."

Sir Winston reached into his briefcase, brought out an object, and held it up for the jury to see. Without taking his eyes from the jury, he addressed his witness. "Did you find this item?"

"I did," the officer replied.

Sir Winston handed it to the bailiff, who handed it to the witness. "And what did you determine this object to be?"

"It is a spear meant to be fired at fish by a gun operated by compressed air."

"Could this spear be fired out of the water?"

"Indeed it could."

"With sufficient force to penetrate and kill a man?"

"Yes, indeed. I believe it would be effective from a distance of as much as twenty feet."

"Is any particular strength or skill required to load and fire such a spear gun?"

"No."

"Could a woman do it?"

"A child could do it."

Sir Winston produced a spear gun from his brief-case. "Would you demonstrate the weapon for the court?"

"I would be glad to."

Sir Winston turned to the judge. "May the witness leave the box for the purpose of a demonstration, Your Lordship?"

"He may," the judge replied.

The captain stepped down from the box, and another officer entered with a sheet of plywood, leaning it against a wall. The captain loaded the spear gun, aimed it at the plywood, and fired. The spear buried itself solidly into the wood with a loud thunk. There was a stirring in the jury box as the members imagined the spear entering Paul Manning's body.

"The defense wishes the spear recorded as Exhibit

Number Two for the prosecution," Sir Winston said. "I have no further questions for the witness at this time."

"Mr. Barrington?" the judge said.

Stone rose. He wanted to address the spear first. "Thank you, Your Lordship. Captain Beane, have you had occasion to go aboard other yachts at English Harbour?"

"On many occasions," the officer replied.

"Did any of them have knives aboard?"

"Oh, yes."

"Did all of them have knives aboard?"

"I suppose so."

"Did any of them have spear guns aboard?"

"Yes, I suppose so."

"So knives and spear guns are quite common, if not universal equipment aboard yachts, are they not?"

"Yes, they are."

"Did you find any specific evidence that the spear or any of the knives aboard the yacht *Expansive* was used in the commission of a murder?"

"Well, no."

"No blood on the spear or any of the knives?"

"No."

"No blood on the decks?"

"Well, blood could have been washed off."

"Did you find any evidence that blood had been washed off anything?"

"No."

"Then what made you conclude that a murder had taken place at all?"

"Oh, the diary," the captain replied. "I found the diary very incriminating."

"Have you read the diaries of any other men besides Paul Manning?"

"One or two."

"Were they written in the third person?"

"I'm sorry?"

"Mr. Manning's diary was written to say, 'He did or she did,' not 'I did,' is that not so?"

"That is so."

"So it was written in the third person?"

"Ah, yes, I see. Yes, the third person."

"Were any of the other diaries you read written in the third person? Or were they written in the first person, where the diarist describes himself as 'I'?"

"They were written in the first person."

"In your experience as a police officer, would you say that diaries are generally written in the first person?"

"Generally, I suppose."

"Are you aware of how Mr. Manning earned his living?"

"Yes, he was a writer."

"Do you know what his specialty was as a writer?"

"No."

"We have heard evidence that he was a writer of thrillers and mystery stories. Did you know that?"

"No, I didn't."

"Have you ever before seen the notes a writer makes before he begins writing a book?"

"No."

"Can you understand how a writer might write notes and scenes that he might later incorporate into a book?"

"Yes, I suppose."

"Has it occurred to you that this so-called diary might not be a diary at all, but a collection of notes for Mr. Manning's next book?"

"Ah, no."

"Now that you have been enlightened as to a writer's working habits, don't you think it possible that the book might be Mr. Manning's preliminary notes?"

"I suppose it could be," the captain admitted.

"Is it not likely that the book is his notes?"

Sir Winston was up. "Objection; calls for a conclusion."

"Your Lordship," Stone said, "the captain has already reached a quite different conclusion, with the help of Sir Winston, based on no real evidence at all; why can he now not change his mind and possibly reach another conclusion?"

"Overruled," the judge said. "Answer the question, Captain."

The officer looked very uncomfortable. "I suppose it might be likely that the book is Mr. Manning's notes."

"Thank you, Captain," Stone said. "No further questions."

Sir Winston stood up. "Captain Beane, how long have you been a police officer?"

"For twenty-one years," the officer said, looking grateful to be back on familiar ground.

"Is it, after thorough investigation, your professional opinion that the spear gun might have been used as a murder weapon?"

"Yes, it is," the captain said, smiling broadly.

"No further questions," Sir Winston said, sitting down. "The prosecution rests."

Stone was flooded with elation. He turned to Sir Leslie Hewitt and whispered, "Is that it?"

"It appears to be," Hewitt whispered back.

"Good," Stone said, feeling relieved.

The judge produced a gold pocket watch from a fold of his robe. "We will break for lunch now," he said. "Court will reconvene in one hour."

53

Stone stood up and waved at Allison. "Want some lunch?" But a police officer was already escorting her from the dock. "Can't she have lunch with us?" he asked Leslie Hewitt.

"I'm afraid not," Hewitt replied. "Her bail was automatically revoked when the trial began. Don't worry, they'll feed her."

They walked out of the courthouse, and Hewitt led Stone to a small restaurant across the street. "Everyone from Government House has lunch here," he said.

Stone took a seat with the barrister at a small table, then remembered that he was still clad in robe and wig. He removed the wig and placed it on the table next to him.

"Put it back on," Hewitt said. "Bad form to remove it as long as you are robed."

Stone put the thing back on, and as he did he saw

Sir Winston and his assistant at the other end of the narrow room, both still robed and wigged.

"What would you like?" Hewitt asked.

Stone didn't see a menu. "Whatever you're having."

"They make a very nice seafood stew here; it's the speciality of the house."

"That will be fine."

Hewitt ordered for both of them, and the waitress brought them cold bottles of beer.

"Well, we have a decision to make," Stone said.

"What is that?" Hewitt asked.

"Whether to call Allison to the stand."

"Of course we must call her," Hewitt said.

"But why? Sir Winston has no case at all, as far as I can see. We should simply rest our case and move for an acquittal, and I think we'd get it."

"We shall certainly move for an acquittal, as a matter of form," Hewitt replied, "but it is unlikely in the extreme that we would get it."

"Even when the prosecution has offered thin evidence, and that evidence has been refuted in court?"

"I can see where you might not wish to call Allison, coming from the American legal tradition, as you do."

"She's not required to testify, is she?"

"Not legally, no; she has a right to forgo questioning by invoking her right against self-incrimination. But unlike in America, in St. Marks the jury may consider that an indication of guilt."

"Oh."

"What's more, if we didn't call Allison, Sir Winston would reopen his case and call her himself, you see."

"I see."

"In any case, Allison is her own best witness, don't you think?"

"Yes, I do think that, but it troubles me that Sir Winston has brought this case with no more evidence than he has."

"You must understand that in our legal tradition, although the presumption of innocence is given lip service, in fact even the insinuation of guilt must be answered in order to convince a jury that the accused is innocent beyond a reasonable doubt. Even the term 'reasonable doubt' has a different meaning here, as you will learn when the judge charges the jury. It more or less means that if a juror, after hearing the evidence, thinks the prisoner is probably guilty, then he votes that way. Only if he seriously doubts guilt will he vote for acquittal. I know you think all this is very quaint, but that is the way the law has developed here in the years since the British left. Of course, it has been steered that way by the likes of Sir Winston, the prime minister, who was a barrister and a judge, and Lord Cornwall. The system is very much more comfortable if it is easier to find the accused guilty instead of innocent. And, of course, they have no written constitution or Supreme Court looking over their shoulders."

"That's just wonderful," Stone said glumly. He began to feel a real longing for the vagaries of the American system of justice.

Their food came and they ate slowly, not talking much. The seafood stew was, indeed, good, Stone thought. "What do you suppose they're giving Allison for lunch?" he asked.

"Oh, the food is better there than you might imagine, since the prisoners prepare it themselves in their own little kitchen. They give the warden a grocery list, and he gets them whatever they want. Since they're not paying a cook, it's cheaper letting them cook for themselves, no matter what they're cooking."

"I haven't heard much about the prime minister," Stone said. "What is he like?"

"He is exactly my age, which is eighty-nine, if you were wondering, and in better health than I."

"How long has he been prime minister?"

"Since 1966, when the British left."

"That's rather a long time in office, isn't it?"

"The people have always liked him. He is not in the way of being oppressive, and he has never been too corrupt."

"Just a little corrupt?"

"Oh, well, you know how government officials are. They are paid very little, really. Do you think Sir Winston pays for his Savile Row suits from his meager salary?"

"I thought perhaps his beautiful wife had money."

"She does, in fact; her father held Sir Winston's job for more than twenty years."

Stone laughed aloud.

"I know you may think our country amusing, Stone, but it really does work very well, you know. Mostly we live and let live, and if some of us live better than others, well, that's the way of the world, isn't it? Sometimes I think we are able to be viable as a country because of our climate."

"Your climate?"

"It's warm year-round, you see, and hot in the summer. When people are warm in winter, they tend to think that they are not so badly off. There are fish in the sea and work in the hotels and bars, and clothing, if one is not a member of the governmental or managerial classes, is rudimentary—a length of cloth, a shawl, a bandanna, a pair of shorts will dress one well enough for most St. Marks occasions."

"This country has not been so good to you, Leslie," Stone said. "I understand that you come from some wealth."

"That is true. When I was younger I was something of a firebrand in the legal system. I would have much preferred the American definition of reasonable doubt to our own; I would have preferred better-paid and unimpeachable officials and a more frequent change of prime minister. I was not popular."

"If your prime minister is eighty-nine, then there must be a change of power in the offing."

"That is true," Hewitt said, "and Sir Winston is one of two or three who might succeed the present occupant of that office. If he wins a conviction in our case, that will probably give him a distinct advantage."

"Why?"

"Because he will be seen to have prevailed over a wealthy white American with a white American lawyer."

"Would he really have Allison put to death in order to obtain a political advantage?"

Hewitt smiled sadly. "My dear Stone, you are naive. Men have put whole peoples to death for such power. Don't believe that because we are an insignificant country, political power here is deemed to be insignificant.

Remember, if Sir Winston becomes our next prime minister, he will have, for all practical purposes, a lifetime job at the very pinnacle of our governmental and social heap, such as it is on this small island. If he went to England and worked as a barrister, he might make a living, in spite of his race, perhaps even a fine living. But here, on his home island, he can be the closest thing we have to a king."

"A big fish in a small pond?"

"In England, he would be a minnow in the sea."

"So his ambition makes him dangerous."

"Indeed it does—most immediately to Allison, but eventually to us all on this island."

"Is any of the other candidates to succeed the prime minister a better man than Sir Winston?"

"Both," Hewitt said. "One of them could be very good indeed. He has Sir Winston's intelligence without his venality or his vanity, especially that. It is his vanity as much as his ambition that makes him dangerous. If we can defeat him in court today, we will have struck a blow, perhaps a fatal one, to his political dreams. That is why I am taking part in this case. A new prime minister, whoever he is, will not reappoint Sir Winston as minister of justice. He will be back depending on his skill as a barrister and his wife's money. That would give me great satisfaction." Leslie Hewitt smiled sweetly.

CHAPTER

54

*C*ourt reconvened after lunch, and Sir Leslie Hewitt rose and addressed the bench. "Your Lordship, normally at this time the defense would move for a dismissal of the charges on the grounds of insufficient evidence. Certainly, the evidence submitted by the prosecution has been almost laughable and quite easy for us to refute. But the defense will not request a dismissal of charges, because we want the jury to hear our client, Mrs. Allison Manning, tell her own story, so that they will know from her lips that she is an innocent woman." He sat down.

The judge nodded sagely. "Mr. Barrington, please call your first witness."

Stone stood. "Your Lordship, the defense will, of course, call Mrs. Manning to testify, but before we do, we wish to call one other witness, Mr. James Forrester."

"Call James Forrester," the judge said.

The bailiff called out the name, and Jim Forrester took the witness stand and was sworn, giving a New York City address and styling himself as a journalist.

"Mr. Forrester," Stone began, "were you the last person, apart from Allison Manning, to see Paul Manning alive?"

"I think I may very well be, along with anyone else who was standing on the quay when their yacht left the Canary Islands."

"Good, now let's begin at the beginning. How long did you know Paul Manning?"

"I first met him during our university years, more than twenty years ago, when we played on opposing basketball teams."

"How well did you know him?"

"While we were not close friends, we had a very cordial relationship, and I knew him fairly well."

"How would you describe Paul Manning?"

"I always found him to be a pleasant and friendly person, very bright, and a good athlete."

"After your graduation from university, did some years pass before you saw him again?"

"Only two or three years passed before I saw him the first time," Forrester said. "I ran into him in a restaurant in Miami, Florida. He was working as a journalist for the *Miami Herald*, and I was working for a travel magazine in New York."

This was information new to Stone, and he wondered why Forrester had not brought it up before. "Did you renew your acquaintance on that occasion?"

"Yes, we had dinner together."

"And when did you next see him?"

"At a baseball game in New York City, some five or six years later. Paul was covering sports for the *Herald*, and I visited the press box with a reporter friend."

"And did you renew your acquaintance on that occasion?"

"Yes, we had dinner again after the game."

"And when was the next time you saw Paul Manning?"

"Only a few weeks ago, in Las Palmas, in the Canary Islands."

Stone felt relieved to be back on familiar ground. "And how did you come to meet him?"

"I was doing a travel story on the Canaries, and we were taking some photographs at the Las Palmas yacht club. I ran into Paul at the bar late in the afternoon."

"And did you renew your acquaintance on that occasion?"

"Yes, we talked for an hour or so, and Paul invited me to have dinner with him and his wife aboard their yacht."

"Did you detect any change in Paul Manning from your previous knowledge of him?"

"Only that he had grown much heavier and was sporting a full beard. Otherwise, he seemed the same happy person I had always known."

"Did you, in fact, dine with Mr. and Mrs. Manning aboard their yacht?"

"Yes, I did."

"How long did you spend in their company that evening?"

"I didn't return to my hotel until nearly midnight, so I suppose I must have been there five or six hours."

"What was your impression of the Mannings as a married couple?"

"They seemed very happy together; it was obviously a very successful marriage, by almost any measure."

"Did they express affection for one another?"

"Almost constantly. They frequently held hands or kissed. I was impressed that they prepared the meal together and enjoyed doing so. I've not known many husbands and wives who could share the galley of a yacht successfully."

"Did Paul Manning make mention of beginning to write a new novel?"

"Yes, he said he was making notes for a new book, and he planned to begin the writing as soon as they were home in the States. He said he planned to call it *Dead in the Water.*"

This was news to Stone, something else Forrester hadn't mentioned. He decided to mine this vein. "Did he mention that he was keeping notes in a book?"

"Yes, he showed me a leather-bound book that he had bought in a shop in Las Palmas."

"Would the bailiff kindly show Prosecution Exhibit Number One to the witness?"

The bailiff handed Forrester the book.

"Is this the book Paul Manning showed you?"

Forrester leafed through the early pages. "Yes." He held up the open book. "You see, he wrote the title, *Dead in the Water,* at the top of the first page."

"Mr. Forrester, you are a professional writer. Please look through the text of the book and tell me if what you read might correspond with the sort of notes a writer might make prior to beginning to write a book. Take your time."

Forrester read several pages while the courtroom waited. "Yes," he said finally, "this seems very much to me to be a set of notes, though an incomplete one."

"Does it appear in any way to be a diary?"

"Certainly not. It does not describe the relationship between man and wife that I saw in Las Palmas."

"After the Mannings sailed from Las Palmas, did you see them again?"

"Yes, on the island of Puerto Rico, to the south."

"Would you describe the occasion, please?"

"We were there gathering information for my article, my photographer and I, and I saw the yacht in the marina there. Paul asked me on board for a drink and told me that they were sailing almost immediately."

New information again. Stone wished that Forrester would stop elaborating on what he had said earlier. "Was Mrs. Manning present?"

"Yes, she was."

"Had anything in their relationship changed that you could observe?"

"No, they still seemed to be the same happy couple I had seen a couple of days before."

"Were you present when they left the harbor?"

"Yes, I was standing on the quay, watching them."

"Did they still seem to be a happy couple?"

"Yes, they were laughing as they sailed past the quay. They waved and called out a good-bye."

"Did anyone but Allison Manning ever see Paul Manning after that?"

"No. I believe I was the last to see him."

"You have interviewed Mrs. Manning extensively about their experiences after leaving Puerto Rico, have you not?"

"Yes, I have."

"Did you question her closely about the events that occurred on the occasion of Paul Manning's death?"

"Yes, I did."

"Did Allison Manning say anything to you about those events that you found to be inconsistent with the impression you had formed of the couple in the Canary Islands?"

"No, she did not. Everything she told me had the absolute ring of truth."

"Thank you, Mr. Forrester; no further questions."

"Sir Winston?" the judge said.

"Thank you, Your Lordship. Mr. Forrester, do you consider yourself to be an expert on marriage?"

"No, hardly."

"Are you not presently involved in a divorce from your own wife?"

"Yes, I am."

"So do you think that, on the basis of two brief meetings, you could pronounce their marriage a happy and successful one?"

"That was my impression."

"I ask you again, do you think you are qualified to judge the Mannings' marriage, one way or the other, after meeting them for only a few hours?"

"Well, I'm certainly no marriage counselor, but . . ."

"Mr. Forrester, I ask you again: are you qualified to judge the state of their marriage?"

"Well, I'm certainly no marriage counselor."

"Answer the question: are you qualified? Yes or no?"

"No," Forrester admitted.

"Did you ever see the couple again after they sailed from the Canaries?"

"No, just Mrs. Manning."

"You were not aboard the yacht with them when it sailed, were you?"

"No, I wasn't."

"So you have no personal knowledge of what occurred aboard that yacht when Paul Manning died?"

"I have Mrs. Manning's account."

"But you have no personal knowledge of these events, do you?"

"No."

"I have no further questions of this witness." Sir Winston sat down.

Stone stood. "Your Lordship, I have a brief redirect."

"Proceed."

"Mr. Forrester, you saw Mr. and Mrs. Manning together in the Canaries, didn't you?"

"Yes, I did."

"And you were the last person alive to see them together?"

"Yes, I was."

"Relying on your judgment as a journalist and as a human being, do you believe them to have been happily married?"

"I certainly do."

"Do you believe Allison Manning's account of her husband's death to be true?"

"Yes, I certainly do."

"Thank you, Mr. Forrester, I have no further questions."

"You may step down, Mr. Forrester," the judge said. "Mr. Barrington, do you wish to call any other witnesses?"

"Yes, Your Lordship. The defense calls Mrs. Allison Manning."

Stone watched Allison as she left the dock and walked to the witness box. She seemed relaxed, serene; she certainly looked beautiful. *If I can just get her through this,* he thought, *and if she stands up under cross without losing it, I can win this case.*

Allison took hold of the Bible and swore to tell the truth.

CHAPTER

55

Stone waited while Allison arranged herself in the witness chair and recited her full name and address. He began questioning her slowly about her family background and education, letting her settle down and deal with easy questions. She was following his instruction, making eye contact with the jurors as she answered. Then he began to get to the meat of the matter.

"Mrs. Manning, when and how did you first meet your husband, Paul?"

"It was a little over five years ago," she said. "I was working as an art director with an advertising agency in New York, and I was invited to dinner at the home of my boss. Paul was a guest, too."

"Did you hit it off immediately?"

"Yes, we did. Paul took me home in a taxi and asked me out for dinner that weekend."

"And did you begin to see him on a regular basis after that?"

"Yes, we began seeing each other two or three times a week, and before long, we were spending most of our time together."

"Was Paul working as a writer at that time?"

"Yes, he had given up his newspaper career and was writing his third novel when we met."

"Was he a very successful writer at that time?"

"No. He was earning a modest living at his craft, but he had not yet begun to sell books in large numbers."

"After you had been seeing each other for a time, did the subject of marriage come up?"

"The subject came up very early in our relationship," she said, "although we didn't actually set a date until we had been seeing each other for several months."

"And when did you marry?"

"A few weeks after that—about four and a half years ago."

"In what circumstances were you married."

"I gave up my tiny apartment and moved into Paul's. It wasn't much bigger; it was a three-room flat in Greenwich Village, a fourth-floor walkup."

"Would you describe it as a modest apartment?"

She smiled. "I would describe it as less than modest. We painted the place ourselves, but that didn't make the heating or the plumbing work any better."

"After you were married, did Paul's career as a writer become more successful?"

"Yes. His third novel became a bestseller, and that allowed him to get a much better contract for his next book. It also meant that his income increased sharply."

"Did your circumstances improve after that?"

"Oh, yes. We bought a house in Greenwich, Connecticut, a large, comfortable house. Greenwich is near enough to New York City that Paul could spend the day in town visiting his publisher and still be home by dinner."

"In what other ways did Paul's success change your lives?"

"Well, we both drove expensive cars, we ate out in restaurants a lot, and we entertained at dinner parties. I bought better clothes, and so did Paul."

"And did there come a time when Paul decided he wanted a yacht?"

"Yes. He had a small boat—a twenty-five-footer—when we married, and we used to sail that a lot. Then, after the success of his fourth novel, Paul ordered a larger yacht to be built at a yard in Finland."

"How long did it take to build the larger yacht?"

"About a year and a half."

"Is this the yacht which is now moored at the English Harbour marina?"

"Yes."

"Was there anything unusual about this yacht, apart from its larger size?"

"Well, it had the best equipment Paul could find, and it was designed to be sailed singlehanded."

"By singlehanded, do you mean by one person alone?"

"Yes. When we were aboard together, Paul did all the sailing, and I did all the domestic chores—cooking and so forth."

"When the new yacht was delivered, did you and Paul decide to sail it to Europe?"

"Yes; in fact, that was Paul's intention when he ordered the boat."

"Please tell us about the trip."

Allison outlined their route across the Atlantic and their stops in various ports in England, France, Spain, and in the Mediterranean, finishing her account with a description of their departure from the Canary Islands for Antigua.

"Before you left the United States, how would you describe your relationship with your husband?"

"We were extremely happy—euphoric, really. You know how newlyweds are." She said this directly to a juror, who blushed.

"And when you began your voyage across the Atlantic, did your relationship change?"

"Only in that we became closer. When you spend a lot of time with a person on a boat, you really get to know him."

"Did this constant proximity wear on your marriage?"

"On the contrary, I think it made our marriage stronger."

"You are aware that not all couples do as well at sea."

She smiled. "Oh, yes; we met a number of couples in our travels who were sick of each other. On the other hand, we met a lot more who enjoyed being alone together on a boat."

"You were nearly fifteen years younger than your husband, Mrs. Manning; did that become a problem in your marriage?"

"Never at any time. We were both very comfortable with the age difference."

"When you sailed from the Canaries for Antigua, was your marriage still a good one?"

"I would say that it was better than ever. We talked about that, and Paul felt the same way. We both felt very grateful for each other."

"Take us back, now, Mrs. Manning, to your departure from the Canaries, and tell us, with as much detail as you can, what happened in the days after that."

Allison devoted her attention entirely to the jury. She told of their start across the Atlantic and how, after ten days, it had been necessary for her to be hauled up the mast to retrieve the top swivel of the headsail reefing system. She explained this carefully to the jury, and they seemed to understand what the problem was. She told then of looking down and seeing her husband, apparently ill, and of his collapse and her fear of being stuck at the top of the mast. Tears had begun to roll down her cheeks, and she dabbed at them with a tissue. When she told how she had buried her husband at sea, she wept openly, and the judge had to call a brief halt to her testimony while she recovered herself. Stone was delighted; she hadn't cried at the coroner's inquest, but the tears flowed freely now, and a glance at the jury revealed how affected they were. Finally, she stopped crying, and the judge nodded at Stone to continue with his questions.

"Mrs. Manning, did you know how to sail the yacht after your husband's death?"

"Only in the most general sense. The deck of the boat was laid out so that Paul could easily handle it without my help. The only time I had any real job to do was handling the bow-line when we docked."

"So, alone in the middle of the Atlantic Ocean, you had to learn how to sail the boat?"

"Yes, and to navigate, as well. There was a book aboard on celestial navigation, and from that I learned to take a moon sight to establish our latitude. From then on, I just tried to keep the boat on the same latitude. I was off a little, though, when we made our landfall. I was aiming at Antigua, but I fetched up in St. Marks."

"When you say 'we,' to whom are you referring?"

"To the boat and me. I began to think of the boat as my partner in survival."

"Mrs. Manning, has everything you have told the court today been the truth, the whole truth, and nothing but the truth?"

"Yes," she said firmly. "As God is my witness it is the truth."

Stone turned to Sir Winston. "Your witness," he said, then sat down.

Sir Winston rose slowly and looked contemptuously at Allison for a good half minute before he began. "Your Lordship, I will be brief," he said. "Mrs. Manning, why did you kill your husband?"

"I . . ." she began, but Sir Winston cut her off.

"Was it for the millions he had earned?"

"I . . ."

"Was it for the *twelve million dollars* in insurance?"

"Sir Winston . . ."

She was beginning to grow angry now, and Stone had warned her against that.

"Was it because you had learned to hate him while you were confined with him aboard the yacht for protracted periods?"

"Sir Winston!" she shouted. "I did not kill my husband!"

"Oh, but you did, Mrs. Manning," he replied. "There were many times aboard the yacht when Mr. Manning was vulnerable, weren't there?"

"Vulnerable?"

"Times when a small shove would have put this large man overboard. Weren't there such times?"

"I did not push him overboard!"

"Answer me, Mrs. Manning! Were there not opportunities?"

"If that was what I wanted, I suppose so. But . . ."

"As when your husband stepped outside the lifelines to urinate, holding on to the yacht with only one hand?"

"Perhaps, but I didn't . . ."

"You could have stabbed that one hand with a knife, couldn't you?"

"No. I . . ."

"You could have *bitten* that hand, couldn't you?"

"I didn't!"

"That hand that had fed and clothed and given you every luxury!"

"I did not do that!" Tears were streaming down her face again.

"Oh, yes, you did, Mrs. Manning. This jury can look into those angry eyes and see that you did!"

"You're mad!" she screamed at him. "Completely mad!"

"But not as mad as you were with your husband. So mad that you could abandon him to his fate in the middle of a huge ocean."

"I did not!" she bawled. "As God is my witness . . ."

"Yes, you did!"

Stone was on his feet. "Your Lordship, Sir Winston is badgering the witness, not offering evidence."

The judge held up a hand to quiet him. "Sir Winston . . ." he said.

"I am finished with this witness, Your Lordship," Sir Winston said, looking at her once again with contempt. "I think the jury can see through this performance." He sat down.

Allison sat in the witness chair, sobbing.

"You may step down, Mrs. Manning," the judge said quietly.

The bailiff helped her down and back to the dock, where she continued to weep.

56

The judge looked up at the jury. "Gentlemen, we will now move to closing arguments. Sir Winston, may we have your closing?"

Sir Winston Sutherland rose and faced the jury, offering Stone and Sir Leslie Hewitt his back. "Gentlemen," Sir Winston said. "Today you have seen evil incarnate in the form of a pretty woman, not the first time the devil has used this form. You have heard how Paul Manning, a successful writer, gave his wife everything—a big house, expensive cars and clothes, a dream trip on a glorious yacht—and how she showed her gratitude by ending his life so that she could have all his money for herself.

"Think of it, gentlemen: a yacht filled with the utensils of death—knives, harpoons, and, no doubt, other weapons since disposed of at sea."

Stone was halfway to his feet, but Sir Leslie put out

a hand and stopped him. He held a finger to his lips, and Stone sank back into his chair.

"Was there a pistol aboard the yacht?" Sir Winston continued. "Was there a shotgun? Probably, but the Atlantic Ocean is a very large rubbish bin, so we shall never know. Instead, we must put ourselves aboard that yacht and see what certainly happened there—how Paul Manning was, one way or another, consigned to the sea; how he may have watched the yacht sailing away without him, leaving him alone with the sharks and other creatures that would devour the evidence of his murdered corpse.

"Allison Manning thought she could get away with it, but she had not counted on the will for justice in St. Marks, and she had not counted on you—a jury of honest men who would see through her protestations and her tears to the truth—that she coldly and maliciously and with malice aforethought murdered her husband. Not even when he suspected her motives, as his diary shows he did, could he be on guard every second of the day and night, to protect himself from his evil wife. No, his fate was sealed as soon as he sailed from the Canary Islands. At that moment, he was a dead man.

"In St. Marks we do not placidly accept the murder of human beings. We have constructed a system of justice which has no tolerance for murderers and which rids us of them with dispatch. Today, you are the instrument of that justice, and your island nation expects of you that you will swiftly reach a verdict of guilty and allow His Lordship to pronounce the sentence that follows from such guilt.

"Gentlemen," he said slowly and gravely, "do your duty!" He turned and sat down.

Stone leaned over to his co-counsel. "I hope you will speak longer than that," he said.

Sir Leslie looked at his pocket watch and shook his head. "I must be finished soon or appear to insult the jury by requiring them to attend this trial for another day. That would not rebound to our client's benefit."

The judge was staring harshly at the defense table. "Sir Leslie, will you close now?"

Hewitt stood up. "Yes, indeed, Your Lordship." He left the defense table and walked closer to the jury. "Gentlemen," he said softly but clearly, "today you have been treated to a demonstration of what happens when too much power collects in too few hands."

"Sir Leslie!" the judge barked.

"My apologies, Your Lordship," Hewitt said. "My remarks were not directed at the court but at the prosecution."

"Nevertheless . . ." the judge said, then sank back into his chair.

Hewitt turned again to the jury. "Gentlemen, my remarks were not intended to be of a personal nature but merely to comment on how the ministry of justice is operated by the whim of one man. Only in such a ministry would this case ever have been brought to trial."

"Sir Leslie," the judge said, "I will not warn you again. You do not wish to incur my wrath."

Hewitt turned and bowed solemnly to the bench, then turned back to the jury. "Gentlemen, the prosecution has not presented one whit of convincing evidence today—no evidence that a murder even took place, let alone that my client committed it. To call the prosecution's case circumstantial would be to elevate it to the realm of possibility, and the events aboard the yacht as Sir Winston has described them are not even remotely possible.

"He would ask you to believe, on the basis of no physical evidence, no witnesses, and no common sense, that this lovely woman deliberately caused her beloved husband's death—and for money. As weak as his case is, I will address the points he has attempted to make. First, the so-called diary has been convincingly shown to be notes for Mr. Manning's next novel; second, the presence of knives and harpoons aboard the yacht has been made out to be sinister, but does not each of you have a kitchen where a number of knives reside? And are you murderers because of it? Of course not. You are no more murderers than is Mrs. Manning. Sir Winston has said that Mrs. Manning must be a murderer because she had the opportunity, but each of us has opportunities to kill every day, and we do not kill. Neither did Mrs. Manning.

"The very last person to see Paul Manning alive other than Mrs. Manning, Mr. Forrester, someone who knew Mr. Manning well, has testified that he witnessed a happy marriage in the days before the couple sailed from the Canaries. Not one witness has been brought forward to testify to the contrary, because there is no such witness. If there were, Sir Winston would have found him, believe me.

"But the greatest proof of Mrs. Manning's innocence is Mrs. Manning herself. You have heard her describe her life with her husband, their delight in his success, their wonderful sailing adventure which they both enjoyed so much. You have heard her words, and every man of you can surely recognize the truth when he hears it. The prosecution has offered nothing but bluster and posturing to refute her patently truthful testimony, because the prosecution has nothing else to offer.

"Each of you, when his duty is done in this courtroom, will return to his daily life, and each of you will have to live with himself every day after that. Do you wish to spend the rest of your days in the knowledge that you convicted an honest woman on no evidence? Of course not! When you have declared this woman innocent you can walk from this courtroom with your heads held high, knowing that you have done right in the eyes of God and man, and no one can take that from you, not even Sir Winston and his ministry. Go, gentlemen, and do right!"

Sir Leslie returned to the defense table and sat down.

"Well done," Stone whispered to him.

The judge spoke up. "I will now charge the jury. Gentlemen, you have heard a case presented by the prosecution and the defense. There can be no doubt that a man is dead and that it is the province of this court and, specifically, of this jury to decide how he met his death and who is to blame for it. Sir Winston and Sir Leslie have each presented their arguments, and now you must decide, beyond a reasonable doubt, if Mrs. Manning is guilty of the murder of her husband. Your verdict must be a majority verdict. You may now retire to the jury room and consider your verdict. When you have reached it, ring for the bailiff." The judge stood and left the courtroom.

The jury filed out of their box and through a nearby door, which the bailiff closed behind him.

"That's it?" Stone asked. "That's a charge to the jury?"

"I'm afraid so," Sir Leslie answered, glancing at his pocket watch. He beckoned the bailiff over. "May our client join us here at the table while we wait?"

The bailiff nodded stiffly, then went and brought Allison and held a chair for her.

"You were wonderful, Leslie," she said, patting his arm.

Hewitt permitted himself a small smile.

"How do you read the jury, Leslie?" Stone asked.

Hewitt shrugged. "The foreman, my old tailor, is our best hope; the young boy will do whatever he thinks the others want him to; the views of the others will depend on their relationship, if any, to Sir Winston, and their vulnerability to his whim."

"After all this, that's where we are?" Stone said. "That most of the jury will act because of their vulnerability, or lack of it, to Sir Winston?"

"I'm afraid so," Hewitt said.

"Why has no one left the courtroom?" Stone asked.

Sir Leslie looked at his watch. "Because everyone knows that in living memory, no St. Marks jury has ever been late for their dinner," he said.

57

·

*S*tone looked up and saw Hilary Kramer and Jim Forrester beckoning from the gallery; he walked over and shook hands with them. "I'd be interested to have your opinion of how things went."

"I'd say you're well on your way to an acquittal," Kramer replied.

"Both you and Sir Leslie did a brilliant job," Forrester chimed in. "How can you possibly lose?"

"I'm astonished," Kramer said, "that this case could even have been brought to court with so little evidence, and I intend to say so in my coverage. This could never have come to trial in an American court."

"Unfortunately, we're not in an American court," Stone said.

"Nobody's left the courtroom," Forrester said. "Are you expecting an early verdict?"

Stone nodded. "Leslie says St. Marks juries don't like to be late for dinner. An early verdict would normally be in our favor, but in this case, I don't know what to think. Leslie says that the relationship between individual jurors and Sir Winston is going to be the deciding factor."

"Relationship?" Kramer said. "They have a relationship with him?"

"It's a small island," Stone said. "If one of them has something to fear from Sir Winston, he's unlikely to vote our way."

"That would be grounds for appeal in the States," Forrester said.

"The appeal here is to the good nature, or perhaps the whim, of the prime minister, who's eighty-nine," Stone said.

"Do you think some of the pressure brought to bear on the government will have some effect on the outcome?" Kramer asked.

Stone shook his head. "I don't know what that pressure could mean to any of the jurors. I'd hoped we wouldn't have to go to trial." He looked back to the defense table, where Hewitt and Allison were deep in conversation. "Leslie was wonderful, wasn't he?"

"He sure got in his digs at Sir Winston," Forrester agreed.

"Apparently he's spent his life digging at the government," Stone said. "Well, I'd better get back and reassure Allison. Will you both be staying for the verdict?"

"Sure we will," Kramer said.

"See you later, then." Stone walked back to the

defense table and sat down. "What have you two been talking about?" he asked.

"I've just been telling Leslie what a wonderful job both of you have done," Allison said, smiling. "After what I've heard here today, I'm very optimistic."

"So am I," Stone said, though he knew he would be uneasy until the jury came in.

"The important thing to remember," Hewitt said, "is that even if the verdict goes against us, it's not over. We still have the opportunity for appeal, and I think our position would be excellent."

"I hope it doesn't go that far," Stone said.

"So do I," Allison echoed.

They became silent, each wrapped in his own thoughts.

It was growing dark outside, and the bailiff rose from his desk and began turning on lights in the courtroom.

Sir Leslie Hewitt looked at his watch. "Almost nine o'clock," he said. "I must say, I'm encouraged; I've never known a jury to stay out this long, so they must be deliberating very diligently."

Most of the spectators had given up and gone home, but the reporters from the *Times* and *The New Yorker* still sat in the gallery, waiting.

"I'm hungry," Allison said.

"I wish we could go out to dinner," Hewitt said, "but I'm afraid the bailiff wouldn't allow it. If you want to eat now, I can see that you're fed in a cell."

"No, I'll wait," Allison sighed.

Stone was hungry, too, but he hadn't thought about it until now.

Then, from somewhere beyond the courtroom, a bell rang, something like a big brass schoolyard bell. The bailiff rose and left the room.

"They're coming in," Hewitt said. "Perhaps now we can all have dinner together." He smiled at Allison.

The bailiff returned to the courtroom and escorted Allison back to the dock. A moment later, the jury filed in.

"All rise!" the bailiff called out, and when everyone had stood, the judge entered and took his seat.

"Gentlemen, have you reached a verdict?" he asked the jury.

The retired tailor rose. "We have, Your Lordship," he said, handing a sheet of paper to the bailiff.

The bailiff took the paper to the judge, who read it without expression. "Read the verdict," he said to the bailiff.

The bailiff held up the paper and read it once to himself, then out loud. "We, a jury of freemen of St. Marks, have considered our verdict in the case of the Government of St. Marks versus Allison Ames Manning. After due deliberation, we unanimously find the prisoner guilty of murder."

The courtroom erupted in gasps and whispers; there was even a little scattered applause. Stone felt as though all the air had been sucked out of the courtroom. He turned to Allison and mouthed the words, "Don't worry."

Allison was as white as marble. She sat rigidly, expressionless, looking straight ahead of her but, apparently, not focusing on anything before her. Finally, she turned and looked desolately at Stone, who mouthed his message again. She nodded, then looked down at her lap.

"Sentence will be pronounced immediately," the judge said, nodding at the bailiff.

Sir Leslie Hewitt was on his feet, in his hand a white envelope sealed with a blob of red wax. "Your Lordship, the defense has prepared an appeal, which we request be sent to the prime minister's residence without delay, and that sentence be postponed until we have heard from the prime minister."

The bailiff took the envelope and delivered it to the judge, who glanced at it and returned it to the bailiff. "Deliver this personally as soon as court has adjourned," the judge said to him, then looked up at Hewitt. "I see no reason to reconvene court at some later time," he said. "Sentence will be pronounced immediately." He nodded to the bailiff.

The bailiff went to a small cabinet under the bench and unlocked it with an old brass key. From the cabinet he removed a fringed cushion that supported a black cloth. He walked around the bench, climbed the few steps, and presented his burden to the judge. The judge took the black cloth from the cushion and placed it atop his wig. "All rise to hear the sentence!" the bailiff called out.

Stone struggled to his feet, along with the rest of the court.

The judge looked at Allison. "The prisoner will rise," he said.

Stone looked over his shoulder at Allison, who was still seated. Her head jerked up, and slowly, she got to her feet. There was fear written across her face.

"Allison Ames Manning," the judge intoned, "you have been found guilty of the crime of murder by a properly constituted jury of St. Marks freemen. Do you have anything to say before sentence is pronounced?"

Allison looked bleakly at him. "I am innocent," she said, her voice breaking.

The judge nodded, then continued. "By the power vested in me by the people of St. Marks, I now direct that on the morrow, at the hour of sunset, you be taken from a cell in this building to the inner courtyard, where a scaffold shall have been erected, and be hanged by the neck until you are dead. May God have mercy on your soul."

Allison looked briefly at the wall above the judge; then her eyes rolled up in her head, and she collapsed backward, sending her chair skittering across the floor.

"Court is adjourned," the judge said, then left the bench.

Stone and the bailiff ran for the dock.

CHAPTER

58

Stone reached Allison simultaneously with the bailiff, and a moment later, a court aide appeared with a folding canvas stretcher and placed it on the floor beside the inert woman. Stone slapped her cheeks lightly, but she did not respond. "Please get a doctor," he said to the bailiff.

"I'm sure that won't be necessary, Mr. Barrington," the bailiff said. "Let's get her onto the stretcher."

Together, the two men lifted Allison and set her gently on the stretcher. The bailiff and the court aide each took an end and carried her from the courtroom. Stone and Sir Leslie followed them down the stairs and past the front desk of the jail into a corridor, then to the last cell before the hallway ended in a stout wooden door. By the time they had laid her on the cell's bunk, Allison was stirring. Stone put a pillow under her head and felt her neck for a pulse. It was rapid, but strong.

"What is this place?" Allison asked weakly.

"The jail," Stone replied. "You fainted; how do you feel now?"

"Weak," she said.

"I'll get her some food," Sir Leslie said, then disappeared.

"Did I dream it all?" Allison asked.

"No, but don't worry about it; your appeal has already gone to the prime minister. We should hear something tomorrow sometime."

Allison nodded. "I'm sorry I fainted," she said. "I'm usually better under pressure."

"I don't blame you," Stone said. "I still can't believe it myself. An American jury would have acquitted you in minutes."

"I'd like to sit up," she said. As she did, with Stone's help, a woman in a denim shift came into the cell, bearing a bowl of something hot.

"Here you are, dear," she said to Allison, setting the tray on her lap. "This'll do you good; I made it myself."

Allison began eating the stew. "It's good," she said. "Lots of fish in it."

From the direction of the inner courtyard, the sound of hammering came through the window high over the outside door.

"What's that?" Allison asked.

"Oh, just some work being done," he lied. "Ignore it." He knew exactly what that hammering meant.

Stone sat beside her on the bunk, and Sir Leslie returned with a chair.

"I don't want you to worry," Hewitt said. "Your appeal will be in the prime minister's hands in just a few minutes." He reached into his briefcase and retrieved two sheets of paper, handing them to Stone and Allison. "Here's a copy for you."

"I'm sure it's wonderful," Allison said, continuing to eat the stew.

"Would you like me to read it to you?"

"I'll read it later," she said.

Stone put his copy into his pocket. Apparently Hewitt had not been as sanguine as he about the outcome of the trial, since he had written the appeal in advance. He looked at his watch: half past nine. "I have some important telephoning to do," he said to Allison. "You're going to have to stay here tonight; would you like me to bring you some things?"

"Thank you," she said. "A cotton dress, some underwear, and my cosmetics case."

Stone stood up. "Thomas is outside, I'm sure; he'll drive me. I'll be back as soon as possible." He left the cell and walked down the hall to the front desk, where he found Hilary Kramer and Jim Forrester waiting.

"Is she all right?" Kramer asked.

"Yes, she just fainted; she's having some dinner now."

"I don't blame her for fainting," Kramer said. "I would have, too, under the circumstances."

Jim Forrester looked almost as pale under his tan as Allison. "When do you expect to hear about the appeal?" he asked.

"Probably not until tomorrow."

"Any way to gauge her chances?"

"None that I know of. I'm about to make some phone calls to muster as much support as possible." He looked at Forrester. "Jim, you look awful; are you feeling all right?"

"I'm okay. I guess I wasn't expecting a conviction; you don't get much of this sort of thing in the travel-writing business."

"Speaking of travel writing, do you think you could call some of your travel editors and get them to send telegrams of protest to the prime minister first thing in the morning? If he thinks hanging Allison is going to hurt his tourist trade, maybe that'll help."

"I'll call a couple of people tonight," Forrester replied.

"Good, now I've got to run back to the marina, make some calls, and get some things for Allison."

"Stone," Kramer said, "give me one good quote for my piece."

"The defense is absolutely shocked at this outrageous verdict. In the United States this case would have been dismissed out of hand, and now we face the prospect of St. Marks executing an innocent American woman who has already been devastated by the entirely natural death of her husband. If this happens, no American will ever be safe in St. Marks again. I urge every American who cares about justice to wire or fax the prime minister of St. Marks in protest."

"Great!" Kramer replied.

"Hilary, I know it's late, but this piece isn't going to do Allison any good if it runs the day after tomorrow. Is there any way you can get it into tomorrow's edition?"

"I may have to break some legs, but I'll get it done."

"Thanks; I have to go now."

Thomas was waiting at the door. "How is she?"

"Much better; she's eating, anyway. Can you run me to the marina, then let me borrow your car to get back here?"

"Of course; let's go."

As they pulled up at the marina, Stone saw the fast motor yacht that Allison had previously chartered pulling into a berth.

"What's that doing back?" Thomas asked.

"It's been in Guadeloupe waiting for a call from Allison to pick her up. Would you tell them that Mrs. Chapman has been delayed and to stick around until tomorrow? I hope she'll be here to go aboard."

"Sure." Thomas handed over his car keys, then walked off toward the big motor yacht.

Stone went aboard *Expansive* and ran down below. In a moment he had the satellite phone up and running and a call in to Bill Eggers's home.

"Hello?"

"Thank God you're there," Stone said.

"Stone! What's up? How did the trial go?"

"She was convicted."

"What?"

"I'm not kidding, Bill, and we've got less than twenty-four hours to save her life. Here's what I want you to do."

"I've got a pencil; shoot."

"Start with the State Department: call the duty officer and ask him to alert the Caribbean desk that an innocent American citizen is about to be hanged in St. Marks. Demand that they call the secretary of state and have him bring to bear every ounce of influence he can muster. No, wait—first call the chairman of the Senate

Foreign Relations Committee—it's Jesse Helms, God help us—and get him to call the secretary of state. Call Senators Dodd and Lieberman of Connecticut and get them onto him as well. Hell, tell them to call the president."

"You think they'll do that?"

"They might; we have to try. Call both Phil Woodman and Max Weld and see if you can get them to make some calls. Then call your PR people and tell them to start calling reporters at home and the wire services. We need an all-out mobilization between now and tomorrow morning. Everything should be directed to the prime minister of St. Marks; it's all in his hands now. Tell the PR people to call travel editors, too; we've got to let them know that hanging Allison will kill their tourist business. Jim Forrester is calling a couple of them."

"Who?"

"Forrester is down here doing a piece for *The New Yorker,* but he's done a lot of travel writing."

"Okay. Anything else?"

"Anything you can think of, Bill. I'm absolutely desperate, and we don't have a minute to waste. I want the prime minister to wake up tomorrow morning to the sound of his phone ringing; I want his fax machine flooded with indignant letters; I want to scare the living shit out of him."

"I'm on it." Eggers hung up the phone.

Stone switched off the satellite phone and started getting Allison's things together.

It was nearly midnight when Stone drove up to the jail door and found it locked. He rang the bell for three minutes before a sleepy, barefoot cop opened the door. "What do you want, mister?" he demanded.

"My name is Barrington; I'm Mrs. Manning's lawyer. I want to see her."

"You can't do that, man; we're shut down for the night. Anyway, she's asleep; you don't want to wake her up, do you?"

Stone shoved the duffel through the door. "Will you see that she gets these things, then?"

"Okay, I'll do that first thing in the morning."

"Thank you, and will you tell her I was here? Tell her not to worry; everything is going to be all right."

The man looked surprised. "You want me to tell her that? Everything ain't going to be all right, you know."

"Just tell her what I said, please."

"Okay, okay. Good night now." He closed the door and shot the bolt.

Stone got back into Thomas's car and drove back to the marina, worried, exhausted, and barely able to keep his eyes open.

59

*S*tone got five fitful hours of sleep aboard *Expansive*, then threw himself into a cold shower so that he would be fully alert. He made some coffee, ate a muffin, and started making lists of things to do. At 7:00 A.M. he called Bill Eggers.

"Where are we?" he asked.

"Okay, here's a rundown. I couldn't get to Senator Helms, but I did get to one of his staff; I told him the prime minister was a suspected communist."

"Good going."

"Woodman and Weld were also going to call him. I talked to the duty officer at the State Department and he put me through to the head of the Caribbean desk at home. He promised to try to get permission to send a cable in the secretary of state's name. I'll call him back after nine to see how he did. Oh, Woodman called the president last night; he was unavailable, but he did get the White House chief of staff on the line, which is almost as good. He had seen the *60 Minutes* report and promised to get some sort of protest out first thing this morning."

"That's wonderful, Bill. Anything else?"

"The PR people have been on it all night; they'll report to me at the office at nine. I'm afraid we're going to miss a lot of morning editions, but they think we'll make some of them."

"Hilary Kramer promised me she'd get us in the *Times* this morning."

"Hang on," Eggers said, "I'll see." He was gone for a moment, then returned. "She made the front page, lower right-hand corner, continued inside. It's good stuff, Stone, and she quoted you about every American sending a wire."

"Thank God we made that one."

"I'm sure we'll be all over the morning television shows, too; you want to be interviewed over the phone?"

"I'm going to be too busy; you do it."

"If they'll talk to me."

"Tell them you're Allison's attorney, too."

"Okay. I'd better get on that right now; they're already on the air." He hung up.

Stone switched on the television and, over the satellite dish, got the *Today* show. An hour later he heard Katie Couric interviewing Eggers and Eggers reading out the prime minister's fax number.

"Yes!" Stone screamed. He got into some clothes, jumped into Thomas's car, and headed for Government House. The jail door was open this time, and after searching him, they let him into Allison's cell. He held her close for a moment, then looked at her. She seemed surprisingly normal. "How are you holding up?"

"I'm nervous as a cat," she said, "but I got some sleep last night, amazingly enough."

"I was here late last night, but they wouldn't let me in."

"I got the things this morning," she said. "Thank you so much."

From the window over the heavy wooden door outside the cell came a loud noise—a creaking of hinges, a slap of wood against wood, and another sound that made chills run up Stone's spine.

"What's that?" Allison asked.

"Who knows? I want to tell you what's being done at home." He sat down on the bunk with her and filled her in on what had happened overnight. "That thing on the *Today* show is going to have half the country up in arms," he said. "And rightly so. By this time the St. Marks government has got to be up to its ass in faxes."

"Good morning," a voice said from the corridor. The door was unlocked, and Leslie Hewitt walked in with a basket. "I brought you some fresh croissants and a thermos of coffee," he said.

"Oh, thank you, Leslie," Allison replied, kissing him on the cheek. She poured herself some coffee and sipped it.

"Have you heard anything at all?" Stone asked him.

"Not exactly. I called the prime minister's residence this morning and spoke to his secretary. He sounded rather odd; I gather the prime minister has been receiving a lot of telegrams, faxes, and phone calls. He's locked himself in his study with my appeal. I hope we'll hear something this morning."

"Good, good."

They sat with Allison until a guard came and made them leave. "You can come back at four this afternoon," he said.

"Allison, is there anything I can send you?" Stone asked.

"I'm all right, I think. There are some books available here; I'll try and read."

"We'll be back at four," Leslie said. "I hope we'll have some news by then. I'll call here if I hear anything before that time."

Allison kissed and hugged them both, then they left the cell.

Outside the jail, Stone brought Hewitt up to date on what he had done, then asked, "Do you have any idea what's going to happen?"

"I hope all these calls and faxes will have an effect," Hewitt said. "I don't think the prime minister has ever experienced anything quite like this."

"Is he the sort of man who responds to pressure?"

Hewitt shrugged. "It's hard to say. He's always been a stubborn fellow, ever since he was a little boy. I just hope he doesn't dig in his heels."

"If we went to the residence, do you think he would see us?"

Hewitt shook his head. "No, that would be unheard of; we'd be damaging our own case. Do you want to come back to my place and wait?"

"I'd better go back to the marina and handle any calls that come in. Leslie, they've built a scaffold in the inner courtyard, and they've been testing it, I think."

"I know; I heard them."

"Have you ever been through anything like this with a client?"

"Once."

"What happened?"

"They hanged him."

"Oh."

"Let's meet back here at four o'clock, and if we haven't heard anything we can wait with Allison. We can't give up until . . ."

"Right," Stone said. "I'll meet you here at four."

Back at the marina, Stone called Eggers again. "Anything to report?"

"We got on the *Today* show."

"I saw it. You did good."

"I hope we stirred up something. Oh, somebody finally got to Helms; he promised to call the secretary of state."

"Has the president had anything to say?"

"Not publicly, but Woodman got a call back from the chief of staff's secretary, saying that they were putting together a cable."

"Great!"

"How's the woman holding up?"

"Like a champ. I'd be a gibbering idiot in her place."

"So would I."

"I think we're going to pull this off, Bill; I don't see how the prime minister can stand in the wind that's blowing now."

"I think you're right, Stone."

"I'll call you again later. Oh, let me give you the satellite phone number; you can dial it just like a regular phone." He dictated the number, then hung up.

Half an hour later, the calls started coming in—the wire services, reporters who recorded interviews, and, amazingly, the president's secretary, who wanted a report. She told him that a cable had already been sent by the secretary of state. He thanked her profusely.

He had some lunch at the Shipwright's Arms and took some more phone calls. Then everything went quiet. No phone calls, no press. Just a quiet afternoon with Thomas.

"How often does somebody get executed here, Thomas?" Stone asked.

"We get one every two or three years, I guess. Then they knock the scaffold apart and put it together again when another one comes up."

"I know; I heard them working on it this morning. I don't think Allison realized what the noise was; I hope she doesn't, anyway."

"You ever lose a client like this?" Thomas asked.

"Not yet."

"I hope you don't lose this one."

"Me, too."

CHAPTER

60

At four o'clock Stone met Leslie Hewitt at the jail door. "What have you heard?" he asked the barrister. "Is there any word at all?"

"Nothing," Hewitt said, shaking his head. "The prime minister's secretary won't even talk to me now. A policeman answers the phone and says that everyone is too busy to talk."

"Well, at least we've made them busy."

"I had hoped to get some sort of hint from the secretary, at the very least, but there's only silence. He didn't return my phone call."

"You look more worried than I've seen you, Leslie," Stone said.

"I confess, I am worried. I really expected some sort of word by now. We have only until sundown."

"What time is sundown?"

"Seven fifty-nine; I checked. And they always do these things on the minute."

"I've never been through anything like this," Stone said.

"Neither has Allison," Hewitt replied.

They went into the jail and found Hilary Kramer and Jim Forrester waiting at the desk, both looking tense.

"Have you heard anything from the prime minister?" Hilary asked Hewitt.

"Not yet," he replied. "But I expect to soon."

"Are you going to see Allison now?"

"Yes," Stone replied.

"Will you come out and let us know how she's doing? And ask her if she'll see me."

"Maybe a bit later. You, too, Jim?"

Forrester shook his head. "No, I don't want to see her." He turned to Kramer. "I guess I'm not much of a reporter."

Stone and Hewitt were searched, then were walked down the corridor of cells. Stone looked at the stout door at the end, with the small window a good fifteen feet above it. At least the sounds from the inner courtyard had stopped; thank God for that.

Allison was sitting on her bunk, her hair pinned up, wearing a denim prison shift that exposed her neck. Stone kissed her on the cheek. "How are you?"

"They took away my things," she said. "Even my underwear." She seemed very calm.

"You'll get them back later," Hewitt said. "Don't worry."

"Haven't you heard anything from the prime minister?" she asked.

He shook his head. "Sometimes it's like this," he

said, glancing guiltily at Stone. "We might not hear anything until the last minute."

They all sat down—Hewitt in the single chair and Stone and Allison on the bunk. She held up a copy of *David Copperfield*. "The most exciting thing they had to offer," she said. "It's good, though. I haven't read it since the eighth grade; I'd forgotten how good it is."

"I've had many calls from the press," Stone said. "The prime minister's office is under a lot of pressure."

Allison nodded, but said nothing. Nobody said anything. They sat quietly, each with his own thoughts, for more than an hour.

A jailer appeared at the cell door. "Can I get anything for anybody?" he asked.

"I'd like some water," Allison said.

"I'm sorry; you won't be able to eat or drink from now on. I thought you might like some magazines."

"No, thank you," Allison said, and the man left. "Why won't they let me eat or drink?" she asked.

"I don't know," Hewitt said, before Stone could speak. "They have their silly rules, I suppose."

Another long period of silence ensued, until Stone began to attempt small talk.

"What are you going to do when you get home?" he asked Allison.

"Get the estate wound up, I suppose. I don't really have any plans beyond that. I find it difficult to think about the future right now."

"The fast motor yacht came back and is waiting for you at the marina."

"Good. I certainly don't want to waste any time here when this is over."

He fell silent again, and so did she. Suddenly there was the scrape of a key in the cell door's lock. They had not heard anyone approach down the corridor. A tall black man in a gray suit and a priest's collar stood in the open door.

"Good afternoon, Mrs. Manning," he said gravely. "I am the Reverend John Wills; I thought you might like to speak with me. Are you a Christian?"

"I'm an Episcopalian," she replied. "Yes, do come in."

"Gentlemen," the priest said, "will you excuse us for a while?"

"Of course, Reverend," Hewitt said, then left the cell, motioning for Stone to follow him.

The two men went outside and sat on a bench against the stone wall. "I thought she should be alone with him," Hewitt said.

"Yes," said Stone. He could not think of anything else to say. The sun was lower in the sky now. Stone looked at his watch. "Leslie, it's nearly seven o'clock; could you call the prime minister's residence again?"

"Of course," Hewitt said. He got up and went back inside the jail. As he entered, Hilary Kramer and Jim Forrester came out.

"Stone," she said, "have you still heard nothing?"

"Nothing," Stone replied. "Leslie has gone to phone the prime minister."

They joined Stone on the bench. "This is driving me crazy," Forrester said.

"It's seven o'clock," Kramer said, looking at her watch. "What time is sundown?"

"Seven fifty-nine," Stone replied. "I'm told they do these things on time."

·
384

"They're not really going to hang her, Stone, surely," Forrester said, sounding distressed. "This is just some sort of torture."

"I don't know what's going to happen," Stone said. "I'm afraid to hope."

Hewitt came back outside.

"What?" Stone said.

"It's very odd," Hewitt replied. "No one is answering the phone."

"Not even an answering machine?"

"Nothing; it just rang and rang. I must have let it ring twenty-five times, then I called again and got the same result."

"Maybe they're on the way over here," Forrester said hopefully.

Nobody cared to address that possibility.

"Did they make you two leave Allison alone?" Kramer asked.

"A priest is with her," Stone replied. "We thought it best to leave them."

As if on cue, the priest came out the door. "Mr. Barrington?"

Stone looked up.

"Mrs. Manning would like to see you and Sir Leslie now."

"How did you leave her, Reverend?" Hewitt asked the man.

"I think her mind is relieved," he replied. "We had quite a good talk, although I don't think she had met with a clergyman for quite some time. She seems resigned now."

Resigned, Stone thought. He wasn't resigned. Why

the hell didn't the prime minister's office call and at least put them out of their misery?

The priest spoke again. "Are you Miss Kramer and Mr. Forrester?" he asked the two reporters.

"Yes," Kramer replied.

"She'd like to see you both for a moment; I spoke to the jailer, and he will allow it."

They all got to their feet and went inside, the priest bringing up the rear. The jailer searched Kramer and Forrester, then conducted the group down the corridor.

Forrester stopped. "I can't do this," he said. "I just can't."

"Wait for us outside," Stone said, and Forrester went back down the corridor.

Allison was sitting on the bunk, reading a Bible that the priest must have given her. She looked up, saw Kramer, and smiled.

"Thank you for coming," she said to her, shaking her hand. "I wanted to tell you how grateful I am to you, Hilary, for the reporting you did in the *Times*. It meant a great deal to me." She looked toward the door. "Where's Jim?"

Stone spoke up. "He wasn't feeling well; he asked that you excuse him."

Allison nodded.

"You will have to go now," the jailer said to Kramer.

The reporter left, leaving Stone, Hewitt, and the priest with Allison. Stone looked at his watch: seven thirty-five.

Finally, Hewitt spoke. "A phone line at the main desk will be kept free," he said, then he was quiet again.

·

"Stone," Allison said, "they asked me to fill out a form, giving next of kin and so forth. I gave them your name to handle any formalities."

"Of course," Stone said, "but that's not going to be necessary."

She smiled slightly. "It seemed like a good idea at the time." She smoothed her skirt. "I've also left some instructions with Leslie," she said. "To be opened . . ." She let the sentence trail off.

"Everything will be done, Allison," Leslie said. "I feel that I have let you down, you know."

"Don't you believe that for a moment," she said. "Both you and Stone have been perfectly wonderful. I could not have been better represented. I really mean that." She put her hand in Stone's.

There was the sound of footsteps in the front hall. Someone, more than one person, had come into the jail. Then it was quiet again. Stone willed himself not to look at his watch, but it was growing dark in the cell. Suddenly, the single bare bulb came on, making them blink.

Then, from down the hall, came the sound of men marching in step. Stone looked up to find four policemen standing outside the cell. One of them unlocked the door. At that moment, Stone heard the telephone ring. The policeman closed the door, turned his back, and leaned on it, nodding to another officer, who strode back down the hall. He was gone for half a minute, then returned. He looked at his senior officer and shook his head.

No, Stone thought, *no, this can't be. That must have been the prime minister.* He stood up. "The phone call? . . ."

The senior policeman opened the cell door. "Not

·

related to these events," he said. "Mrs. Manning, please step out into the corridor."

Stone made to follow her, but an officer stepped between them. Behind him, another officer was tying Allison's hands behind her back.

"Say your good-byes," the senior officer said to her.

She looked at Stone, panic in her face.

"Allison . . ." he began, then stopped.

"Good-bye," she said. "You have all been very kind to me." She was trembling, but she did not cry.

Then, simultaneously, a policeman opened the big door to the inner courtyard while another closed the cell door and locked it, with Stone, Hewitt, and the priest still inside.

"I want to go with her," Stone said, but the officer shook his head.

"No farther," he said.

Stone looked out the door and saw a corner of the scaffold in the gloomy light. He tried to speak, but nothing came out.

An officer stood on either side of Allison, took her arm, and marched her into the courtyard. The senior officer slammed the stout door shut behind them.

Stone turned to Leslie Hewitt. "Is there nothing we can do?"

Leslie looked at the floor and shook his head slowly. "We have done all we can."

Stone looked at the priest, who avoided his gaze. Then, sooner than Stone had expected, he heard the sound of the trap flying open, followed by a thunk, then silence. He leaned his forehead against the bars; he felt like weeping, but he could not.

The outside door opened, the senior officer and one other stepped inside, and the door closed behind them. The cell door was unlocked and the three men were waved out and marched down the corridor to the front desk.

Allison's duffel sat on the desk, and an officer waited, pen in hand, for Stone to sign for her belongings. Stone signed. "What about the body?" he asked the man.

"The body will be cremated and the ashes scattered at sea," the officer said. "It's how we do things here."

"It is so," Hewitt said.

Stone picked up the duffel and walked out of the jail into a lovely St. Marks evening. Hilary Kramer and Jim Forrester were sitting on a bench next to the outside door. Kramer jumped up. "What's happening? Did you hear from the prime minister?"

Stone shook his head. "No."

Forrester stood up, too. "For Christ's sake, Stone, tell us what's happening?

"Allison was hanged five minutes ago."

Both reporters seemed struck dumb. Kramer's mouth was working, but nothing came out. Forrester turned, leaned against the building, and vomited.

"You can quote me as saying that a monumental injustice has been done," Stone said.

61

*T*he priest shook hands with both men, then got into his car and drove away. Stone leaned against Thomas's car, which was parked next to Leslie's ancient Morris Minor. "This is completely surreal," he said.

"I know," Hewitt replied, "I feel the same way."

"Leslie, about your fee . . ."

"It has already been paid."

Stone looked at him, surprised. "By Allison?"

The barrister nodded. "She didn't want any loose ends." He took a thick envelope from his briefcase and handed it to Stone. "She asked me to give you this. She said you were to open it aboard her yacht."

Stone accepted the envelope; it felt as though it contained half a dozen sheets of paper. "All right," he said. "I guess I'll go back there now."

Hewitt held out his hand. "Stone, when you remember St. Marks I hope you will think of more than what has happened today. In ways that you cannot now know, you have helped to make sure that something like this will not happen again."

"How?" Stone asked, puzzled.

"You'll hear from me," Hewitt said. "I'll keep you posted on events here."

"I hope so," Stone said, then looked at the little man closely. "Leslie," he said, "there isn't a senile bone in your body, is there?"

Hewitt burst out laughing. "Let's just say that it helps if certain people believe there are a few such bones."

"You're a crafty man and a fine lawyer. It has been a privilege to work with you."

"Thank you, Stone. I can wholeheartedly say the same of you. I hope that in a little while you will not think badly of me."

"Never," Stone said, then embraced the barrister. Then they got into their cars and drove away.

Stone drove on automatic pilot, slowly, feeling numb and drained. He parked the car behind the Shipwright's Arms and left the keys at the bar, but Thomas was not there.

Stone arrived at the marina in time to see the fast motor yacht making her way out of the harbor, her lights reflecting on the water. The news must have reached her skipper, he thought. He boarded *Expansive,* dropping Allison's duffel on a saloon couch and switching on the light over the chart table. The rest of the saloon was in shadow, the desk light reflecting off the gleaming wood. He switched on the satellite phone and dialed Bill Eggers's home number.

"Eggers," the voice said.

"It's over," Stone said.

"Stone? What do you mean, over? Did our tactics work?"

"I'm afraid not. She was executed less than an hour ago."

"Oh, shit. I'm sorry, I know how you must feel."

"Yeah. Will you do a press release? I don't have the energy to talk to anybody."

"Sure. I'll call the PR people and get it on the wire services tonight."

"Is Allison's estate going to owe the firm any money?"

"I think we'll have a surplus to return to the executor."

"We'll talk about it when I'm back."

"When are you leaving?"

"Tomorrow morning."

"You know about Arrington and Vance Calder?"

"I got a fax from her."

"I'm sorry about that, Stone; she was a great girl."

"Still is, no doubt; just not mine."

"Let's have dinner later this week."

"Sure; I'll call you."

"Good night, then."

"Good night, Bill. Thanks for all your help." He hung up, thinking he had never been so tired. His body cried out for sleep; Allison's will would have to wait until tomorrow. He didn't think he could make it back to his own yacht, so he went into the after cabin, shucked off his clothes, and collapsed into the bed. Not until then did he allow himself to weep. He wept for Allison and for himself.

62

*S*tone dreamed that he and Allison were making love. Then, just as he was about to come, she vanished, and the bed was empty. He stirred and turned over, kicking off the covers. Cool fingers brushed the damp hair from his forehead. He opened his eyes.

"You were dreaming," Allison said.

Stone blinked rapidly. "I still am." He closed his eyes and tried to recapture the dream.

"Stone," she said, quietly but insistently.

Stone jerked as if he had received an electric shock. "Whaaat!" he yelled, sitting up and pushing away from her. He seemed to go from deep sleep to maximum adrenaline in a fraction of a second. His heart hammered against his rib cage, and he made himself look at her. She seemed perfectly normal.

"It's all right, Stone," she said. "Really it is. You're awake; I'm here; I'm alive."

Stone took a deep breath and tried to stop shaking. A moment ago, he had been making love to this woman, and now he was frightened and confused. "Tell me," he said, then took another deep breath.

"I'm sorry to have put you through this," Allison said, "but it had to be done this way. I didn't know for sure myself when they marched me into the courtyard and I saw the gallows. I thought it hadn't worked, that I was done for."

"That what hadn't worked?" Stone panted.

"Leslie's plan."

"What plan?"

"He insisted that I shouldn't tell you; he wanted absolute secrecy."

Stone was recovering from his shock now. "Allison, what the hell are you talking about?"

"We bribed the prime minister."

"You what?"

"Leslie didn't think you would let him do it; that's why we didn't tell you."

"Well, if he had suggested that, I suppose I would have been against it. I would have thought it very risky."

"He told me what we had to do that day out at his cottage, when he sent you for the milk."

"The milk he didn't need," Stone said, half to himself.

"Yes, that milk. While you were gone, Leslie told me what he had in mind."

"And what did he have in mind?"

"He said that the only thing that worked with these people was money and not even that would work with

Sir Winston Sutherland—he was already too committed to a conviction. The prime minister, though, was another matter. He was retiring, and there was always the chance that he hadn't stolen enough to make him happy, Leslie said."

"And how did Leslie go about this?"

"He said nothing to Sutherland; in fact, he said nothing to anybody. When Leslie handed the appeal to the judge, there was a cashier's check for a million dollars in the envelope, along with the appeal document."

"Jesus Christ."

"That's pretty much what I said. It seemed awfully risky, until you consider that at that moment, I had already been convicted and that the prime minister had no motivation to overturn the appeal."

"Didn't the flood of faxes and telephone calls from the States mean anything at all?"

"Merely a nuisance to the old man. He knew he wouldn't be around all that much longer, and that he wouldn't have to deal with any consequences. Sir Winston is, apparently, his hand-picked boy, and he could deal with the aftermath."

"Does Leslie know he succeeded with his bribe?"

She nodded. "When he made that last phone call to the prime minister from the jail, he was given the word, but he couldn't tell me, because you and the priest were there."

"What about Sir Winston?"

"What about him?"

"Does he know about the deal?"

"He knows nothing. That's why I have to get out of here now and why you can't say anything to anybody, either here or in the States. Does the press know about the hanging?"

Stone nodded. "Bill Eggers, in New York, had a press release sent out."

"Good; let's leave it that way."

"For how long?"

"I don't know. Until I let you know it's okay."

The rush of adrenaline was gone now, and Stone was sagging. "What happened after they took you into the courtyard?"

"They whisked me out of the building and into a car and delivered me here, to the motor yacht."

"But I saw it leaving earlier this evening."

"I was already aboard. I made them stop outside the harbor and bring me back in the tender. I had to see you and explain." She looked at him oddly. "Aren't you at all glad to see me?"

He put his arms around her and held her close. "You bet I am," he whispered.

"I'm so sorry to have put you through all this, but there just wasn't any other way."

He held her back and looked at her. "You can read your obituary in the *Times* in a couple of days, I expect."

She smiled. "Well, that will be fun. I'd just as soon be dead for a little while. I have a lot to do, and I can do it better without a lot of reporters and cameras around. Promise me you'll keep my secret until you hear from me."

"I think that comes under the heading of attorney-client confidentiality."

"Don't tell even Hilary Kramer and Jim Forrester. They'd spill the beans."

"As you wish."

She looked at her watch. "I have to get going; I've got a long way to travel."

He got out of bed and walked into the saloon with her, switching on the chart table light. "Your duffel is over there," he said, indicating the sofa.

She went and picked it up. "Thanks; a girl can't get far without her makeup."

He picked up the envelope on the chart table and began to open it, but she took it from him and put it back.

"Not now," she said. "You can do that when I'm gone. Right now, you have to kiss me good-bye." She put her arms around his waist, pressed her body against his, and kissed him for a long time.

"You sure you have to rush off?" he breathed in her ear.

"I wish I didn't, but I do. I'll make it up to you later."

"I'll hold you to that."

"Stone," she said, an uncertainty creeping into her voice, "that envelope contains my last wishes; I want you to promise me that you'll honor them in every respect, as if I really were dead."

"All right, I promise."

She kissed him again. "The days and nights I spent with you on this boat were among the happiest of my life. Remember that, too."

"How could I forget it?"

She kissed him again, grabbed the duffel, and ran up the companionway stairs.

He followed her on deck and watched her get back into the Boston Whaler, which putted slowly away from the yacht. He didn't hear the engine rev up until it was out of sight around a corner of the harbor.

Stone went back below, went to the bar, and poured himself a brandy. His heart was still beating very fast, and he was going to have to wind down a bit if he expected to get any sleep that night. He sat down at the chart table and picked up Allison's envelope, ripping it open. Inside were a letter, some papers, and a U.S. Coast Guard yacht document. He picked up the letter.

Dear Stone,

With any luck, there should be a happy ending to all this. Don't be mad at Leslie; I swore him to silence. I've paid his fee, and yours is in the envelope with this letter.

I will be very angry if you feel I'm being foolish, and I don't want to hear a word about it from you. This all feels very right to me.

The yacht, Expansive, *is ycurs now, to do with what you will. Unfortunately, Libby's dear old mother is yours, too, and you can handle that situation as you see fit.*

Whatever happens, wherever I go, I will always be grateful to you for the time we spent together and for all your hard work. I hope next year you can have a better sailing vacation.

With great affection,
Allison

Stone put down the letter and went through the other documents. There was one conveying the yacht to him as his fee for legal services, and the Coast Guard, U.S. Customs, and State of Connecticut documents were all signed, notarized, and in perfect order.

Stone took a stiff gulp of brandy. Now he would never get any sleep on this night.

CHAPTER

63

Stone managed a couple of hours' sleep, but he was up at dawn, looking over his new yacht. He went through all the cockpit lockers, making a mental inventory of the gear aboard, then he walked fore and aft, checking the way the lines led and what each was for. He thought that for such a large yacht, she would really be very simple to sail. The mainsail had been repaired, and he hauled it back to the cockpit. It took him the better part of an hour to get it bent on. Then he hauled on the line that rolled the mainsail up into the mast like a giant window shade.

Finally, he unreefed the roller-reefing genoa and hauled it down. Paul and Allison had had problems with the top swivel separating into two pieces, and he wanted to think about repairing it. To his surprise, he found that it had already been repaired, and very elegantly.

Someone, in an impressive display of seamanship, had seized it together with fine whipping wire. It looked as though it was better than new. He hauled the sail up, then reefed it around the forestay. *Expansive* seemed pretty shipshape, he thought.

"Stone!" The cry came from the lawn, and Stone looked up to see Thomas Hardy running toward him. Behind Thomas, traveling more slowly, came Leslie Hewitt, back in his accustomed shorts and T-shirt. Thomas jumped aboard and turned to give Leslie a hand up.

"What's up?" Stone asked. "You both look very excited."

"You tell him, Leslie," Thomas said.

"I've had a call from a friend at Government House. When Allison . . . when her case was resolved, the yacht, as her bail bond, reverted to her . . . estate. But my friend says that Sir Winston Sutherland has filed a petition with the Admiralty, which administers maritime affairs, claiming the yacht for the Ministry of Justice, supposedly to defray the costs of Allison's trial. It's just a naked grab of someone else's property, but he can probably bring it off."

Thomas grinned. "I hear you are a boat owner now."

"Well, for a few hours, anyway," Stone said. "Leslie, how much time have I got?"

Leslie looked at his watch. "It's just past ten. Lord, I don't know; Winston could be here with an order any minute."

"Thomas, can you put together a week's provisions for me in a hurry?"

"I'll see to it," Thomas said. He jumped down from

the deck and sprinted back toward the Shipwright's Arms.

Stone looked at Leslie Hewitt. "Well, Leslie, I hear that my co-counsel hasn't been absolutely frank with me about the way Allison's case was conducted."

"What? What do you mean? I surely . . ."

Stone held up a hand. "Don't bother; Allison came to see me last night."

Leslie looked embarrassed, but he managed a grin. "Well, perhaps I wasn't entirely candid with you, Stone, but all's well . . ."

"That ends well," Stone said. "It did end well, I suppose; you're just lucky I didn't die of a heart attack last night."

"Myself as well," Leslie said. "I was frantic when I couldn't get anyone on the phone at the prime minister's residence or in his office. I was nearly as much in the dark as you, right up until you asked about the disposition of the body, and the policeman gave you that malarkey about cremation. There's no crematorium on St. Marks, so I figured I must have brought it off after all."

"You certainly did, but you aged me ten years in the process."

"Well, I'm glad it came out all right. I got a lovely fee, the prime minister got his, ah, pension fund, and you got a very fine yacht."

"If I can hang on to it," Stone said, laughing. "I'd better get the engine started." He went aft to the cockpit, switched on the ignition, and prayed that the thing would start. The starter ground on for a good ten seconds before the engine caught and ran smoothly. He looked up and saw Thomas running across the lawn again, carrying a cardboard box and followed by an employee carrying a second one.

Stone checked the fuel gauges. Full. He hoped to God the water tanks were full, too.

Thomas and his man ran down the dock and set their boxes aboard, then Thomas ran back down the dock, untied a dinghy with an outboard, pulled it to *Expansive,* and tied it to the stern. "Come on, I'll give you a hand getting out of the harbor," he called.

Stone embraced Leslie again, then lifted him over the lifelines and set him on the dock. "Good-bye, old fellow!" he called out. "Let go our lines, will you?"

Leslie and Thomas's employee untied the lines and tossed them on board, then gave the big yacht a shove away from the dock. Stone put the engine in reverse and began backing out.

"Look up there," Thomas said, pointing with his chin, "but pretend you don't see."

Sir Winston's elderly Jaguar had pulled into the inn's parking lot, and the minister of justice was striding toward them, a piece of paper in his hand. They could hear a faint shout over the engine.

Stone shoved the gear lever to forward and spun the wheel to port; *Expansive* accelerated quickly through the smooth water of the harbor. They were about to turn past a point of land when Stone looked back and saw Sir Winston on the dock waving his piece of paper and shouting. He made a show of cupping his hand to his ear and shrugging, indicating an inability to hear, then they were around the point, and the harbor entrance lay ahead. "Thomas, you take the helm, and I'll get some sail up," he called.

Thomas tossed the mooring lines into the cockpit and took the wheel. Stone unreefed the headsail first, and when it was full and drawing, he unwound the big main from the mast. He went aft and switched off the engine, and everything grew quiet, except the fresh breeze in the rigging and the burble of water slipping past the blue hull. He stowed the mooring lines and went below, wrote Thomas a check, then came back on deck.

"I guess that's it," he said, handing Thomas the check.

"You are too generous, Stone," Thomas said, looking at it.

"You've gone to an awful lot of trouble, Thomas, and I'll never forget it. When you come to New York, stay at my house, and we'll do some serious dining and wining."

"That's an offer I can't refuse."

"Are you going to have any problems with Sir Winston?"

Thomas shook his head. "Nah; he's got nothing on me. And even if he did have, I've got enough relatives on this island to turn him out of office."

"I think Leslie has something like that in mind; why don't you talk to him about it?"

"I'll do that."

They were nearly to the mouth of the harbor now. Stone gave Thomas a big hug, then watched as he jumped into the dinghy, untied the painter, and yanked the cord on the outboard. The little engine buzzed to life, and Thomas kept pace with the yacht for another hundred yards. Then, as the smooth water of the harbor

404

met the swell of the sea outside, he gave a big wave and turned the little boat back into English Harbour.

Stone watched him go. He reflected for a moment that he had not made many friends as good as that one, then he bore away around the point and headed for the open sea, a lump in his throat. There would be time later to sort out charts and courses, but right now, he wanted to sail his boat.

That night, sailing north with the autopilot on, Stone fixed himself some supper, opened a bottle of wine, sat down in the cockpit, and began thinking about the events of the past days. There were anomalies in what he had seen and heard, and he wanted to think about them.

He slept in snatches of a few minutes, scanning the horizon often for ships and other yachts and boats. He saw little traffic. The next day, at midmorning, he fired up the satellite phone and got it working. He called his secretary and informed her of his new travel plans, then he called Bob Cantor.

"Hello, Stone; I heard the news on television this morning. I'm sorry. Is there anything I can do for you?"

"There is, Bob. I want you to take a trip up to Ithaca for a couple of days and do a little research for me."

"Sure; what do you need?"

Stone told him in some detail. Finally, he hung up the phone and sat down with his charts. He plotted a course up the leeward side of the islands, then between Hispaniola and Puerto Rico and then to the northwest, leaving the Turks and Caicos and the Bahamas to starboard, and on to Fort Lauderdale. It had not taken him long to figure out that he could not afford to own the yacht; what with dockage, repairs, and insurance, it would break him, unless he sold his house, and he wasn't about to do that.

He sailed on, thinking about what had happened to him and what to do next. He made other calls, the last of them to Sir Winston Sutherland, who was surprised to hear from him, but extremely interested in what he had to say.

By the time he had reached Fort Lauderdale, he had done all he could do. Except wait.

Two Months Later

Stone sat in his Turtle Bay garden on a lovely early spring morning, breakfasting on eggs and bacon and orange juice. When he had finished, his Greek housekeeper, Helene, took away the plates and poured him a mug of the strong coffee he loved. He looked through the *Times* idly, checking for any mention of Allison. He had heard nothing from her, and when he had called the Greenwich house, the number had been disconnected. He had thought of calling her Connecticut lawyer, but had decided just to wait for Allison's call.

Alma, his secretary, came out to the garden with the morning mail. "There's one from the broker in Fort Lauderdale," she said.

Stone opened that first and found a check for one million eight hundred thousand dollars and change. He smiled broadly.

"I take it we're not broke for a while?" Alma asked.

"We certainly are not," he said, endorsing the check and handing it to her.

Her eyes grew wide. "I had no idea it was worth so much."

"The broker reckoned it had cost close to three million to build and equip. Still, after his commission, that's a good price."

"What shall I do with it?" Alma asked.

"Write a check for, let's see"—he began scribbling numbers on his newspaper—"three hundred seventy-five thousand to that law firm in Palm Beach, for the account of Libby Manning's mother. I want that off my conscience."

"Right," said Alma.

"Then send a check for five hundred and forty thousand to the Internal Revenue Service." He groaned. "God, how proud I am to be an American and pay my taxes!"

"Right. That leaves eight hundred and eighty-five thousand."

"Send my broker a check for two hundred thousand, and tell him to call me about where to invest it."

"We're rich!" Alma squealed. "What about the rest?"

"I was thinking about buying an airplane," Stone said.

Alma's face fell. "Oh. We're not rich anymore. Well, it was fun while it lasted." She got up and trudged comically back into the house.

Stone had a thought: he could afford a car now. He got up, went into the house, and walked through the kitchen into a storeroom, then through another door. This had been a garage at one time, and there was still a folding door to the street, though he hadn't opened it for a long time. He waded through the stacked boxes and old lawn furniture to the door, which was made of heavy oak. He turned the lock, thinking, *I'll have to install an automatic garage door opener if I'm going to use this space.* He tugged at the door, which moved six inches and stopped. He tugged again, and got it open three feet. Then, with all his strength, he moved the door up all the way, until it was standing wide open. He found himself face-to-face with a tall man.

"Morning, Stone," the man said. "I was going to ring the front bell, but . . ."

"Morning," Stone said. "What brings you around to see me?"

"Oh, just a social call," Jim Forrester said. "Got a few minutes?"

"Sure." Stone dragged two lawn chairs over, made a pass at dusting them, and sat down. "Take a pew."

The two men sat, ten feet from the street. Forrester seemed a little annoyed at not being asked into the house. "How about some coffee?" he said.

"Sorry, coffee's off the menu," Stone replied. "What do you want?"

"Oh, I was just passing by."

"Were you? Say, whatever happened to your *New Yorker* piece? I haven't seen it."

"Oh, they take a long time to edit anything, you know. My editor . . ."

"That would be Charles McGrath?"

"Right."

"Chip McGrath left *The New Yorker* a couple of

years ago to become editor of the *New York Times Book Review*."

"Ah, right; I'm working with another editor now. Say, what do you hear from Allison?"

"You must think I'm a medium," Stone said, expressionless.

"I inquired about the disposition of the body at Government House. They didn't seem to know what I was talking about. I began to think that Allison might not be dead after all."

"The police told me that their policy was to cremate the body and scatter the ashes at sea," Stone said. That was certainly what they had told him. "By the way, have you been to any alumni reunions lately?"

Forrester looked at him, puzzled. "No, not for years. Why do you ask?"

"I did a little checking upstate. There was no James Forrester at Syracuse, not since the class of '38, and I think that was a little before your time."

"Must be some mistake," Forrester said.

"No, but there was a Paul Manning, at Cornell, of course."

"Yes, that's where Paul went. Why were you checking on me at Syracuse?"

"When I've been had, I like to know why and by whom."

"Had?"

"Manning did play basketball for his fraternity, as you said he did. In fact, I've got a copy of the yearbook for his senior year, and there's a very good photograph of him in it. He looks very different—thinner and no beard. Would you like to see it?"

Forrester looked at his nails. "It doesn't interest me," he said.

"I guess not," Stone agreed. "Tell me, where are you living these days?"

"I've been living here in the city, but I think I'm going to do some traveling now."

"I'm not surprised," Stone replied.

Alma walked into the garage from the house. "Oh, there you are. Bill Eggers is on the phone; he wants to know if you want to have lunch."

"Tell Bill I can't make it today, but I'll call him later," Stone said. "Oh, and call Dino and tell him to pick me up in five minutes and to bring his friends. I've got some stuff I want to give to the Salvation Army."

"Okay," Alma said, then left.

"Stone," Manning said, "I really came to see you to find out if you would represent me as my attorney."

"No, I won't."

"Why not?"

"Because you're looking for attorney-client confidentiality, aren't you?"

"In part."

"Well, you won't get it from me, pal."

"Stone, I don't understand . . ."

"Sure you do, Paul. By the way, I got a check for your yacht this morning. It brought a million eight after the broker's fee."

His face flushed. "I should have thought it was worth a good deal more."

"Oh, I know you paid more, but what with the market and all . . ."

Paul Manning looked at his nails again. "When did you figure it out?"

"Oh, I was very slow. It didn't all come together for me until I was sailing the boat from St. Marks to Fort Lauderdale. No, a little earlier, I guess, when I saw the repair you'd made to the headsail reefing swivel."

"What else do you think you've figured out?"

"The dinghy was never stolen in Las Palmas."

"Wasn't it?"

"You just made some noise about it, replaced it, then sailed the old one back to the Canaries after *Expansive* was over the horizon."

"If you say so."

"What did you do about clothes and papers? You couldn't use your own passport."

Manning looked at Stone for a long moment, then apparently decided it didn't matter anymore. "All right, I left a car on the south coast of Gran Canaria with some clothes."

"How long did it take you to lose the weight?"

"I started dieting the minute we left the States," Manning said. "Losing weight has never been easy for me, but I had some time; I lost a pound or two a week. By the time we got to Las Palmas, I was as slim as I am now."

"Careful you don't gain it back, Paul; somebody might recognize you."

"Not where I'm going."

"And where would that be?"

"You figure it out."

"It's going to be tough without the money, isn't it?"

"Damn Allison!" Manning said suddenly, and with some venom.

"Wasn't the money in the Cayman Islands account? Didn't you have access to it?"

"The money was moved to a different account the day before Allison's trial."

"I thought it might have been."

"I'd like to get my hands on her."

"I'll bet you would, but it's going to be a little difficult, isn't it?"

"She's not dead, is she?"

"Suppose she's not? I doubt if you could find her. After all, you must have given her lessons in how to obtain a real U.S. passport, how to establish new identities, and all that. All the research you did for your books, and for your own use."

"All that insurance money—tax free—the money from the sale of the house and the cars; it's all gone," Manning said bitterly.

"And even if you could find it, you've no way to get at it, have you?"

"Sir Leslie Hewitt showed me the will he drew for her, leaving everything to the Girl Scouts of America!"

Stone burst out laughing. "Paul, you've made my day, you really have."

"And she gave the goddamned boat to you," Manning said through clenched teeth.

"That's right, pal, but your heart will be warmed to know that Libby's mother got four hundred thousand of the proceeds."

"Shit!"

"So you killed Libby for nothing, didn't you?"

"What do you mean?"

"Come on, Paul; you had the skills to screw up that

•
413

airplane engine. You'd flown with Chester; you knew he never did a runup, that he'd never notice his fuel problem until he was already in the air. You killed Chester, too, and that other poor woman who was aboard."

"You can't prove that," Manning said.

"You know, right up until the moment that plane crashed, this was all just a lark, a bit of insurance fraud. But when that plane went down, you became something else entirely. You became a murderer—not just three times, but four. You stood there in that jail in St. Marks and let Allison walk out to the gallows. I'll bet she thought until she was standing over that trap door with the rope around her neck that you would step forward and save her. You could have at any time; all you had to do was to tell Sir Winston that you were Paul Manning. He couldn't prosecute her for a murder that hadn't taken place. But you didn't do that, did you? You thought all that money was safe in the Caymans account, and it would all be yours. But Allison outsmarted you."

"I can't figure out why she did it," Manning said, looking dejected.

"Because she knew you. At first she thought you'd save her, but finally she knew you'd never turn yourself in, even to save her. If you had turned yourself in, you'd have had all that money to buy your way out of the business in St. Marks, but you decided to go for broke, to keep it all for yourself, and now you're just that—broke."

"I want the money you got for my boat," Manning said. "And I want all of it."

Stone laughed aloud. "I took the boat as payment

of my fee; it was all legal and aboveboard. Why should I give it to you?"

"Because I'll kill you if you don't," Manning said calmly.

"You're not going to kill anybody, Manning." Stone stood up, drew back his hand, and brought the back of it across Manning's face, spilling him out of the lawn chair. "That's for Allison, you miserable son of a bitch. You cooked up the scam, and she went all the way with you, then you let her hang." Stone looked up and saw a car stop in his driveway. Dino Bacchetti got out. "Hi, Dino," he said.

"Stone, how you doing?"

"Just great. I want you to meet the late Paul Manning."

"How you doing, Paul?" Dino said, grinning broadly.

"Just great," Manning said, wiping away some blood from the side of his mouth.

"Dino and I used to be partners," Stone said. "He's still a cop; he runs the detective squad at the Nineteenth Precinct."

"What is this?" Manning said, alarmed.

"Dino's going to put you in jail," Stone said.

"I haven't committed any crime in the United States," Manning said.

"It's like this, Paul," Dino said. "I'm arresting you for the homicide of your wife, your ex-wife, the pilot, and the other passenger on that airplane you sabotaged."

"I didn't murder my wife or anybody else," Manning said, "and nobody can prove that I did. Anyway, I don't believe she's dead."

"Well, there are a lot of fine legal points in this case," Dino said. "I mean, in addition to the four homicides, there's the insurance fraud. It all gets very complicated, doesn't it?"

Manning smiled, showing blood on his teeth. "Yes, it does. In fact, I expect to be a free man again before the day is over. I've already retained a lawyer, and you'll never be able to hold me."

"I know this is going to come as a big disappointment, Paul," Dino said, "especially since you worked so hard to figure it all out, but I've got some really bad news for you."

"What do you mean?" Manning asked.

Dino pulled a document from his pocket. "This is for you," he said. "Consider yourself served."

"What is it?"

"It's an extradition warrant. You're going back to St. Marks for trial."

"You can't do that!" Manning said, trying to read the warrant.

"Sure I can. Of course, you'll fight extradition, but eventually you'll go back. And then you can prove to them that your wife is still alive."

Manning's jaw dropped. "How can I prove she's still alive?"

"I doubt if you can," Stone said, "but there's more bad news."

"What?"

"The St. Marks police went out to the airport after Chester crashed, and they dusted everything, and I mean everything, for fingerprints, and you know what? They found some prints on the tool cabinet in the hangar that don't match anybody else's at the airport. I had a phone conversation with Sir Winston Sutherland,

and he told me all about it. Of course, they never thought to check the fingerprints of the *New Yorker* writer, Jim Forrester. So when Dino gets you back to the precinct, he's going to fingerprint you, and then he's going to fax your fingerprints to Sir Winston, in St. Marks, and if they match the prints on the tool cabinet— and you and I both know they will—then Sir Winston is going to have a real good case against you for those three homicides. And even if they don't match, there's Allison."

"She isn't dead, is she?" Manning asked. "Come on, Stone, you know she isn't."

"I don't think Sir Winston will adopt that view, Manning. After all, he convicted her and had her hanged himself."

Manning looked as if he wanted to run, but now there were two more detectives standing in the driveway.

Stone continued. "You saw how they tried Allison, how they convicted her with hardly any evidence at all. My prediction, Manning, is that before the year is out, you're going to have your neck stretched in St. Marks."

Dino motioned the two detectives forward, and they handcuffed Paul Manning. He stared at Stone, apparently speechless.

"Good-bye, Manning," Stone said. "I'll be a witness at your trial; I'll tell the court how you admitted your identity to me and that you told me how you faked your death. Funny thing is, without our conversation today, they might not have been able to prove who you really were. So I'll see you in St. Marks." He smiled broadly. "And there won't be any attorney-client confidentiality."

The cops put Manning into their car.

"How about some dinner tonight?" Dino asked.

"Absolutely; we'll celebrate."

"Elaine's at eight-thirty?"

"That will be great," Stone replied.

Alma appeared in the garage. "Is everything all right?"

"Everything is all right," Stone said.

Late that night, Stone and Dino sat over the remains of their dinner at Elaine's.

"All in all," Stone said, "it's been a very satisfying day."

"Glad I could help," Dino said. "That guy from Boston, the insurance dick, was in my office this afternoon. He's a very happy man."

"Why?"

"Because he's going to get at least some of his money back from Allison Manning's estate."

"He'd better not count on it."

"Why not?"

"Because, unless I miss my guess, that money has disappeared into the worldwide banking system and will never be seen again. Allison moved it the day before her trial."

Dino looked at Stone sharply. "What was that stuff said about his wife not being dead?"

"I think Manning is still in denial."

"Is she dead?"

Stone was still trying to figure out how to answer Dino's question when Elaine came over to the table.

"Phone call for you, Stone," she said, pointing at one of the two pay phones on the wall nearby.

"Excuse me, Dino," Stone said. He got up and went to the phone. "Hello?" he said, sticking a finger in the other ear to blot out some of the noise.

"Stone?"

"Yeah? Who's this?"

"Stone, this is Vance Calder."

That stopped Stone in his tracks for a minute. "Hello, Vance," he was finally able to say. "How'd you find me here?"

"There was no answer at your house, and I remembered that Arrington said you were at Elaine's a lot. I took a chance."

"How is Arrington, Vance?"

"That's what I'm calling about, Stone. Arrington has disappeared."

"What do you mean, disappeared?"

"Just that; she's vanished."

"When?"

"The day before yesterday."

"Have you been to the police?"

"I can't do that; the tabloids would be all over me. I need your help, Stone."

"Vance, you'd really be a lot better off going to the police; there's nothing I can do about this."

"You can find, her, Stone; if anybody can, you can. I want you to come out here."

"Vance, really . . ."

"The Centurion Studios jet is at Atlantic Aviation at Teterboro Airport right now, waiting for you. You can be here by morning."

"Vance, I appreciate your confidence in me, but . . ."

"Stone, Arrington is pregnant."

Stone felt as if he'd been struck hard in the chest. He could count.

"Stone? Are you still there?"

"I'll be at Teterboro in an hour, Vance."

"You'll be met at the Santa Monica airport."

"Write down everything you can think of, Vance; we'll have a lot to talk about."

"I will. And thank you."

"Don't thank me yet," Stone said, then hung up. He returned to the table. "You're buying dinner, Dino," he said. "I'm off to La-La Land."

"About what?" Dino asked.

"I'll call you," Stone said.

"You didn't answer my question about Allison Manning."

"That will have to wait, I'm afraid." He kissed Elaine on the cheek, then walked out of the restaurant and started looking for a cab.

Key West
February 10, 1997

ACKNOWLEDGMENTS

I am grateful to my editor, HarperCollins vice president and associate publisher Gladys Justin Carr, and her associate editor, Elissa Altman, for their hard work, and to my literary agent, Morton Janklow, his principal associate, Anne Sibbald, and all the people at Janklow & Nesbit for their careful attention to my career over the years. I must also thank my wife, Chris, who is always the first to read a manuscript, for her keen eye and sharp tongue, which help keep my characters in line.

AUTHOR'S NOTE

STONE BARRINGTON first made his appearance in *New York Dead* and came back for *Dirt* and now *Dead in the Water*. He will next appear in *Swimming to Catalina*, which will be published by HarperCollins in the spring of 1998. I apologize to those few readers who have complained about his sexual nature, but he doesn't seem to be able to control himself.

STUART WOODS is the bestselling author of more than twenty novels, including *The Run, Worst Fears Realized, Orchid Beach,* and *Dark Harbor.* He lives in New York City.